KWANI? 2 is published by Kwani Trust

P.O. Box 75240 00200,
City Square, Nairobi.
telephone numbers:
254-20-219113
0722405577/ 0720854637
email: admin@kwani.org

email: admin@kwani.org

First Published 2004.
First Impression
ISBN 9966-98362-7
First Edition

Cover Photography by Robert Maletta
Art Direction Kairo Kiarie (Mr Mamboyote)
Design and Layout Tony Muchiri
Of Oakland Media Services

Cover Model: Collins "Kwani" Obuya

Story Graphics by Celeste, Victor Ndula, Velma Mwendwa na Jambazi Fulani.

Printed by Fotofom LTD., Occidental House, Muthithi Road, Westlands, P.O. Box 14681. Nairobi, Kenya.

Kwani Trust is a Ford Foundation Grantee.

www.kwani.org

kwani?

TABLE OF CONTENTS

THE END

www.kwani.org

Editorial

Kwani 01 was an overwhelming critical success. When Binyavanga left for England, I was left with an immense responsibility, editing 02. Soon we were swamped with submissions, writing of all sorts, Letters to the Editor that never saw their way to print, stories, poems, deeply personal documents that people gave us. Some of them handwritten in mouldy notebooks. I was petrified. There started my long journey with 02.

It has been an exhilarating, exhausting, nerve racking but more than anything else, an immeasurably rewarding experience. Kairo, secretly known as the The One, June, Amunga and the rest of the Kwani team have been living, eating Kwani with me and without them, the spirit and body of Kwani? would have stayed unrealised.

This is a larger issue, and I hope a worthy follower of the first edition. We have more poetry, more in-depth non fiction pieces, some wicked fiction, and humour with an overbite. We introduce sixteen pages of colour cartoons and a new comic strip. I would like to thank all the contributors, thank you for trusting us with your work. Not all the submissions made it to print, the sheer volume of submissions received was overwhelming, but already we are starting to sift through submissions for 03...!

STOP PRESS!!!! At the time of going to press, we learnt that one of Kwani's submissions, Parsalelo Kantai's *Comrade Lemma and the Jerusalem Boys Band*, to the Caine Prize for African Literature has been short listed. Congratulations to Parsalelo, and naturally, we are pleased silly with ourselves to have published Comrade Lemma. We tried, honest, but we surrendered to the urge to brag when we heard of two MORE East African shortlisted nominees from Uganda, Monica Arac de Nyeko for 'Strange Fruit' and Doreen Baingana for 'Hunger'. A Kwani moment, an East African triumph. If that wasn't enough to gloat about, another brilliant African writer is about to go global. Big time. Chimamanda Ngozi Adichie. And with our usual restraint, Binyavanga's muse and an old friend of Kwani, is now officially the first ever African woman to be shortlisted for the Orange Prize of Literature. She beat luminaries like Toni Morrison and Jumpa Lahiri to the list. Not bad for a 27 year old first time author….!

Thank yous:
So many many people. First our trustees, Muthoni Wanyeki, Njeri Karago, Tom Maliti, Malla Mummo and Ann Mcreath for being always helpful, always there, and endlessly patient..ahem!

For their support we would like to thank the Ford Foundation, Oakland Media, of Alliance Hotels& Resorts, the Kenya Publishers Association, Java Coffee House, Nation Media Group, The British Council, and the French Cultural Centre, The Goethe Institute, Commercial Bank of Africa, the Nation Media Group, Capitol Radio, Cafe Crème, Rob Burnet, Mundia Muchiri, Alliance Hotels & Resorts, Lynnette Kariuk[illegible] Njuguna of Java Coffee House, Mr. Michael Joseph of Safaricom. Chand Bah[illegible]

Randiki, Fatuma Hirsi Mohammed, Mumbi Kaigwa, Mwalimu Matu), Irene Wanjiru, Ralph Johnsone, Parselelo Kantai, Andia Kisia, Ali Zaidi, (Tina)Mama Kindondo, Ciru Githunguri, Patrica Amira, Lind Holt, Eva Kiiru, Olivier Lechien., George Okello Abungu, Eric Wainaina, Sheba Hirst, Abbi, Harri Kimani, Damaris Agweyu, Firoze Manji, Tony Mochama,

KWAL, Lake Nakuru Lodge, PhatMag, Fotoform, Transparency International, Judith Pyke of Booktelevision and Richler Ink. Webtouch Cybercafe.

Handy Gallery for supporting us with online sales www.handygallery.com.

Random access, Check One Entertainment, Perry Alando, Damaris Mushira, Tony Mochama, Steve Muturi, Mary Theru, Foz, Victor Ndula, Richard Mambo.

Special thanks to the whole of the Kwani? team lead by The One aka Kairo Kiarie, June Wainaina, Lilly Kavwagi, Sarah Mwihaki, Jean Wangeci, Amunga Eshuchi.

Bookshops: A million thank yous to Chand Bahal (Bookstop Yaya Centre), for taking what we were trying to do seriously, for not thrusting our books in back shelves, for being a valued friend, and for selling far more Kwani's than all the other outlets. Many thanks also to Text Book centre, Jane at Kiko Romeo, Prestige bookshop, Bookpoint. Bookcorner, Total Shops, especially Argwings Kodhek Road branch Blue Rhino, Legacy Books, Havana, Henrich Boll, Michelangelo, Le Rustique and Booksfirst, Thanks Melvin of Booksfirst Ukay Centre¡.for pushing for us.

Special thanks to Ralph Johnstone and Muthony wa Gatimu for editing sone of the stories. Thanks again.

I have surely forgotten some names, please know that I didnt do it on purpose. Thank you for being a friend of Kwani..

And finally my personal thanks to Binyavanga Wainaina for letting me share in his passion, Catherine Ngugi for ensuring that I 'pressed on', Nahas Angula for his faith in oshetu shaamu, wherever it may find itself and Oliver Lechien for everything.

Ebba Kalondo
Editor

Monday or Tuesday September, 1982 (3 Prisoners)

3 shirts.

3 pairs of trousers

3 pairs of shoes.

525/- in cash

I used to keep all the money. No one was interested in sorting out the big mess in the middle of the room. It was a while before the others caught on to the perquisites of sorting through personal effects. Now they've taken to hanging around the storeroom whenever a new batch of prisoners comes in. Not today though.

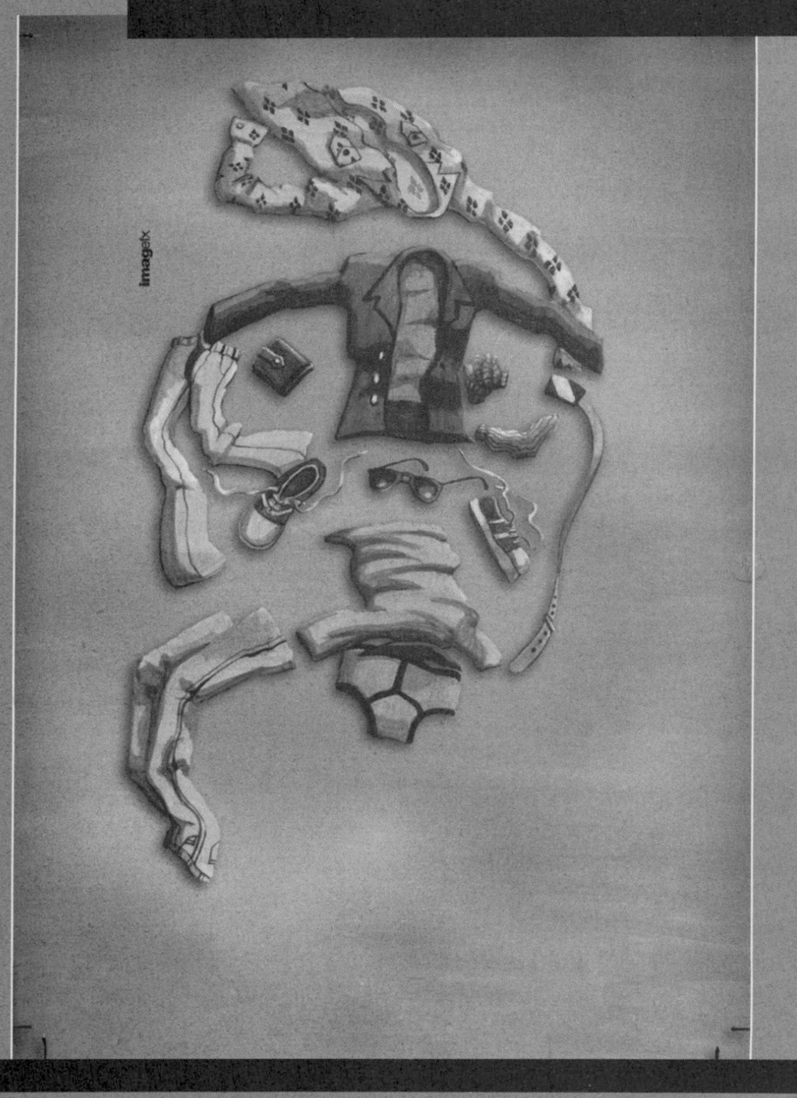

1982

by Andia Kisia

Monday or Tuesday, September, 1982 (3 Prisoners)

3 shirts.
3 pairs of trousers
3 pairs of shoes.
525/- in cash

I used to keep all the money. No one was interested in sorting out the big mess in the middle of the room. It was a while before the others caught on to the perquisites of sorting through personal effects. Now they've taken to hanging around the storeroom whenever a new batch of prisoners comes in. Not today though. Today I keep it all. I tell some of the guys I'll buy them a round if they come out with me after work. Call it guilt or generosity. They all came. Who wouldn't when someone else is buying?

We go to the canteen because Miriti insists we should. He says the only people who hang out down town are either rich or crazy. Or in the army. I'm still feeling generous so I don't push it. I tell the waitress to bring us three each at a go. She's new and pretty and obviously used to attention.

She brings the beer and says something to me in Kikuyu. When I say nothing she says something to Miriti and the others instead and laughs. But I've never had a problem ignoring women and she leaves me alone soon enough.

Four hours later, only Miriti and I are left. The other guys have gone home to their wives or their girlfriends. Miriti says they probably haven't noticed there's a curfew on. Miriti's wife knows better than to give him a hard time about his carousing. I've seen her before and the occasional black eye she tries to hide, keeping the good side of her face carefully on view. He's a big man: clean-shaven, handsome, nice muscles, bad temper and lots of chicks. Lots of girls who have to remember to keep the good side of their faces on show when he brings them out with him.

The waitress brings us the third round of three each. For such a big man, Miriti doesn't hold his liquor very well. He begins to slur. Then he unearths the usual turd of his life for public inspection. When life has become merely existence, unfolding in an interminable, level wasteland ahead of us, we grasp at relief wherever we may find it. For Miriti, it's girls. I've heard all the stories before of course, with slight amendments. Small embellishments. All of them star Miriti, intrepid protagonist and a succession of beautiful women.

He asks me about my pretty young wife. I tell him that I know about as much as anybody on that matter. No funny business until the cows come home and I don't know where they are going to come from. I tell him that I'll be sure to keep her as far away from him as I can.

He laughs and starts on another beer with a vengeance. The money's almost gone by now, but I don't care. There's plenty more where that came from.

When I've had enough of Miriti, I simply stand up and leave him there. Outside, the town wears its new bombed out look with something like shame. Devastation spills through the jaws of gaping shop fronts. Glass and miscellaneous wreckage litter the street. A few shops have brand new grilles on.

It's only 9 o'clock but the streets are deserted. Easing the curfew has made little difference. But I feel like a walk. I trust my police I.D to protect me.

I walk through the aftermath of unpleasant self-discovery. Last month we shocked ourselves, stumbled upon the realisation that it takes only a moment for people to let slip the little protocols of daily life; to embrace chaos like a friend. And close upon that, the discovery that there was little unpleasantness in it. But then, everyone wants something. The hordes of Eastlands had visited their redistributive justice on the business district, breaking into shops and carrying off whatever they could. At first only a few ventured into town, but when the first intrepid men returned home laden with gifts, the others descended in droves. Some soldiers helped themselves as well, mostly to suits and stereos. A major blasted the stubborn lock on a wholesale shop and waved in a mob. I took a television off some poor bastard on his way home.

Though the cataclysm had lasted no more than a day, the mask had slipped far enough to confirm what we had only suspected. Now we were left with a new unease of each other. The lurking suspicions, the dislikes which for years had swirled around us like fumes became solid: glass screamed, flesh met flesh, and physical theatres opened in holding cells all over the country.

September 1982 (Six prisoners)

6 shirts:
2 long sleeved
2 white, one blue, one pink (pink!),
2 short sleeved both white
1 jacket
6 pairs of trousers, one purple. Tight as hell. (Worn with the pink shirt?)

He went out on Friday night. There was a girl. There was always a girl. He felt okay about it today. Looking this good was half the problem solved. He wore his pink "get lucky" shirt and a new pair of jeans; Levi's no less that his cousin had sent him from America. His cousin lived in Wyoming. Not quite the Big Apple, but America's America right? They were so tight that at first he had serious doubts about wearing them out. A man must keep some secrets he thought. But once in them, he discovered that the secret bore quite a lot of looking into.

She was the first thing he saw when he walked into the club. He took that as a sign. She was alone. He took that as another. And she looked fine! And he looked fine. They would be good together. He bought drinks: cider for her, a large whisky soda for himself and perched himself on a stool next to her a little more carefully than was strictly cool. They both started off quiet. He sipped his whiskey soda and looked around. She looked down a lot. He grew expansive when she didn't rebuff him and even smiled once or twice. Once she laughed and he went for it, mi

the vein of a thought while she laughed out loud, throwing her head back while he drank it all in until some ham fist sent him spinning to the floor gurgling in indignation and pain. A man was standing over him, looking down at him curiously. He gurgled again, meaninglessly, and tried to get up. Then the man lifted his ham fist again.

When he came to, it was to pitch darkness and he wondered if he was awake. He heard a groan beside him and felt the pain in his face. Then he was simply afraid.

4 pairs of shoes, I pair tackies, I pair sandals

Sunglasses.

1750/- in cash: 800/- in 100/- notes, 400/- in 50/- notes, rest in change.

Tuesday, September 1982 (4 Prisoners.)

4 pairs of trousers

2 blazers

1 suit (matching)

3 pairs of shoes (closed)

1 pair of sandals

4 shirts; 2white, 1 gray, 1 blue

This was blue shirt week and being Tuesday, it was still relatively clean. Come Friday the collar and the cuffs would be grimy. Always. No matter how careful he tried to be during the week, the cuffs would always get dirty from the sliding back and forth over the counter at the bank where he worked as a teller. It just made sense to him that if they expected him to look presentable everyday, they should pay him more.

On Friday night he would take it off and put it on a hanger on the wall. He would wear it to church on Sunday then wash it himself and hang it out to dry in the little courtyard outside his room. Sometimes when he had a newspaper he would sit outside shirtless in the sun and read while he waited. When he didn't have a paper and there was none to be had off anybody, he would just sit outside and look out onto the street. He might smoke. He might pace. He might think, about nothing in particular. Sometimes he would think how stupid it was that he had to sit there in case some bastard walking by took a fancy to his clothes and helped himself to them off the line. That would leave him with just the white shirt and pissed as hell until he could afford to buy another one, which would not be for another month at least.

He thought how much he hated this place, how he hated his neighbours with their small minds and their small lives and their kerosene and cooking smells and their attempts to fashion normalcy out of this squalor. He hated how they kept leaving the detritus of their lives lying around like a trap for other people to trip over, and how often "other people" turned out to be him.

He hated how they lived their brutish lives out loud. The man had beaten his wife for years and the dull thuds and her high-pitched screams had been the background noise for his nightmares since they moved in. He remembered clearly the day she had enough, how he'd heard the tide turn in her favour and it was his yell of shock that had woken him finally from the drifting in and out of sleep that he performed every night.

He thought how much more, even than theirs, he hated his own life. How if he

had known he would end up like this, how he might have tried to run a mile from himself.

Next Monday is white shirt week. The blue shirt gets a rest. I take it off on Friday night and.....

Wednesday October 1982

Opiyo was brought in today. He's nothing like I expected. I had heard so much about him. Terrified. He knows what's going to happen. Miriti worked with him years ago. Says he used to personally certify people dead. In unnecessary detail. So he knows. Knows the ins and outs. The ups, and the downs. Now he's down.

Still, no one dared touch him. Fully clothed, crying in a corner.

Saturday September 1982 (Two prisoners)

Saturday! Stuck in here on Saturday night.

2 pairs of shoes.

2 suits, matching.

2 long sleeved shirts.

2 pairs shoes

1 pair cuff links.

One of them smells of perfume. Smells good.

5000/- in cash, fifty 100/- notes. Brand new. Smells better. Quick sleight of hand, the money goes in my pocket. All of it. The others will grumble but what can they do? Except watch me closer next time.

Lawyers both of them. Good life, good life, good life. Ended too soon. Pity. They shot them first thing in the morning.

September 1982 (1 prisoner)

Ramesh Shah of Rivatex.

Of course I recognised him. Everyone goes to Biashara Street at least once and many go into Rivatex for curtains, dresses, sheets, whatever. I went there last year, with my mother to buy three metres of lace. An old Marachi man worked there. A man in a too small suit, an old man who had learned to make himself invisible to Ramesh's eloquent glance by being perfect at his job.

"For your house?" he asked.

"For my father's coffin," said my mother.

He cut us 3 and a half metres.

Wish that old man could have seen Ramesh yesterday.

Soft hands, soft belly, soft underbelly.

And to think he had survived the coup, almost intact. The danger had been arrested as it unfurled a claw to dig him out of his house and home. They had cleaned out his shop on Sunday morning and then another mob had started to fan out through Parklands. But they were too late. It was Sunday evening and the army was taking over. When the dust settled, there were three bodies lying at his gate, all his front windows were smashed and the walls were riddled with bullets. But he and his family were safe. They would be spared the beatings and the gang rapes that others had suffered.

He tried to buy his life back did Ramesh Shah. But it wasn't his to have. Ramesh Shah of Rivatex. Rivatex now of Kiptanui Serem.

October 1982

26 shirts of a decidedly democratic stripe. Trousers too and what shoes there were. Not worth taking down. We'll burn the lot tomorrow. What a motley crew this was.

October 1982

The pair of shoes on the storeroom shelf is well worn. The heels slope noticeably and the toe on one of them has obviously come off and been glued back and not too well at that, for it had come off again at least once. There are traces of two different kinds of glue dried hard still on it. For all that, there is enough left of the stitching and the high grain of the leather to show that it had been a good and sturdy one and probably cost a lot of money.

I don't pay attention to these things, but I wondered what a man like that was doing in shoes like those.

*****

The shoes had been worn for the first time some twenty years before for an interview at Ocholla Ocholla Advocates. Had been bought in fact for that purpose. The father who had bought them, never a demonstrative man, had merely put his hand on the young man's shoulder and wished him well. They had cost him a month of his railway technician's salary from a shop on Kenyatta Avenue three months after he had first seen them.

A week before the interview, he had finally gone to buy them. He thought about sending the boy, but he wanted to surprise him, so he had gone himself. He had started to ask a question of a clerk who had walked past him and kept going then stood uneasily for a minute and tried again. Finally, he had simply pointed to the shoes and said to no one in particular, "Give me those ones. Size eight."

Another young man looked in his direction and said simply "They cost three thousand shillings." He was about to move on again when the old man had pulled out the money, in crisp 100 notes, straight from the bank. The young man called for the shoes and continued what he was doing, with a few covert, assessing glances at the customer. When the shoes had been brought out, he had beckoned him to the till, rang up the purchase, bagged them and thanked him curtly for his custom. "Come again," he said, with no anticipation of such an occasion and returned to his work.

The shoes had been worn with a badly fitting suit of a cut some five years out of fashion: three piece, navy blue, slightly faded with white pinstripes, bulging at the seams from the washing, a lighter blue shirt and a limp tie tied into a tight little knot, all of which had belonged to the older man.

Other suits had come after, after the job and the lawyer's salary, which started at five times what his father was earning: better suits, some even made to measure when he had wanted to spoil himself. The shoes though remained. They were the last thing his father had bought him.

He was wearing them and one of the nicer suits when he was brought in.

*****

"Take off your clothes. All of them," were the simple instructions given and he had began to do so, though there was no sign of an alternative set of clothing anywhere in the small, bare room.

He thought about his son and what he might be doing now and how his wife would worry when she found out. She might ask one of his partners to follow it up. Then she would go home to the horrors that her mind would make up for her. She would imagine a different story every day. A different fate at half past 9 when she got up and another one at half past ten in between mouthfuls of Weetabix.

As I watched him undress, I thought that he must be frightened, and briefly that he had every reason to be. Then I thought that his suit was just the thing, just perfect, until I saw the dark patch of wetness at the crotch. I would have to get it cleaned. Dry cleaned no doubt.

"Who told you to mess up my floor?" I asked him.

He didn't reply. He put his clothes in a pile on the floor next to the shoes and straightened. He started to move a hand to cover himself then stopped, the motion incomplete, his hand hanging before one thigh before he pulled it back to his side.

He was surprisingly well kept for a man of his position. His paunch was only in its beginnings. He had long legs and good muscles, the remnants of what must have been an active youth indeed. Whatever sport he played, he must have played well into his thirties, before no doubt taking up golf. Our eyes met and I turned away and started to pick up the clothes and shoes.

"Miriti!" I called, straightening, the clothes and shoes in hand. My clothes now, I thought. Miriti came. "Your prisoner," I said, and walked out quickly. In the logbook I wrote:

1 suit, black
1 shirt
1 pair of shoes
1 pair of spectacles
1 wallet,
then crossed them out.

*****

He shivered in the cool October air as he stood in his cell, stripped of everything except himself. He found it distasteful. He prodded at his belly, pulled at the sagging skin under his arms and sighed. He wondered how long he would be here and if they would give him back his things. His shoes especially. It was probably time he got rid of them anyway.

After those shoes, his father's job was done. It had never been said, but that's the way things went. A man did his duty by his family and then they did their duty by him.

He had done his to the tune of a new roof on the house in Yala, his brothers'

and sisters' school fees and a monthly upkeep fee. It was just the beginning of many things he would buy. For his parents, his brothers, their families, for his old school which had taken his name.

He'd gone to Yala for the "inauguration" as they'd called it, of what was going to be called "Hilary Swiga Odhiambo Primary School." It had been a sweltering hot day. Here there was only heat in all its variations. Looking round at the buildings, it surprised him again that anyone ever made it out of here into the wider world and made anything like success of it. The classrooms were wattle, or had been. Much of it had fallen off into dust. One or two had been newly redone for the occasion with mud brought in by the children, a bucketful each the week before.

The children in the green and red uniform that he had been so proud of so long ago. The headmaster was a man of about thirty, thin and full of a nervous energy, whose sunken eyes told of too much changaa liqour. His ingratiating smile and his eagerness to please freshly put on for the occasion sat uncomfortably on him. Every other day he was simply a petty tyrant, taking out on the children the frustrations of a village headmaster with little chance of escape.

The choir sang in their high-pitched children's voices songs he had sung when he was here, the unfamiliar English words had gotten more mangled over the years.

*****

I was surprised the next day to find myself asking about the prisoner. Miriti said he was still around. Still alive, but not for long.

"Why?" Miriti asked. "Do you know him?"

I shrugged and made myself some tea and sat down to read the paper.

His name was Hilary Odhiambo. There was a photograph on page two of The Nation under the caption "Missing Person." It was a good picture, a portrait like you would take in a studio. He was looking straight into the camera, smiling, a little self-conscious. Probably there was another one just like that of his wife. And probably another one of the whole family in their best clothes. Mother and father seated, children standing around them. In a corner of each would be the purple rubber stamp of Ramogi Studio.

Anyone with information of his whereabouts was requested to contact the nearest police station. I smiled a little at that. There was a number for a Mrs. Pamela Odhiambo. A "43" number. Kileleshwa.

I called that afternoon. A woman's voice answered and I hung up.

Later that day, I went to see the prisoner. I looked through the bars. He was sitting on the floor with his legs drawn up, head resting on his knees. After a minute he looked up and started. It was too late to turn away. We looked at each other for a quiet moment.

"Owadwa," he said finally. He said it calmly. It was both a plea and a statement. A recognition.

I didn't answer, just looked on for a moment longer before leaving.

Staying away proved surprisingly difficult. Two days later I went again, taking his glasses with me. I opened the door with Miriti's key and walked in. He got up when he heard the door open and stood looking at me. I held out the glasses. One of the

lenses was cracked neatly down the middle. He wiped them on his bare arm and then put them on.

"Thank you," he said. And then, "My name is Hilary Odhiambo."

"I know. It's in the paper."

He smiled. "Yes. Yes, of course."

"It doesn't make a difference," I told him. I'm not sure why I said it. I'm not sure he knew. Nothing would save him now.

The conspirators had been discovered. Pancras Oteyo Okumu, Hezekiah Ochuka. And while they remained out of reach, other targets had been found whose names were Onyango, Opiyo, Oloo, Odhiambo.

He walked over to the window and I turned to leave. "My wife." he said, then was silent. Miriti was just coming in.

"So you took it!" he exclaimed, pointing at his keys. "I've been looking for it." The man was still standing at the window, looking at us.

Miriti laughed out loud and pointed. "Your honour sir, what an ugly thing you have!" He stopped, embarrassed and looked at me. "Tell me next time you take my key," he said, and walked out quickly.

*****

The window looked out onto a Chief's camp, a collection of buildings in various degrees of decrepitude. Corrugated iron lean-tos and a clutch of old timber houses. All around were littered the debris of a base domesticity: the ravaged frame of a Velo spring bed, discoloured mattresses having had all the usage they could possibly give wrung out of them. No one threw things away lightly here.

The sound of childish laughter reached him and from somewhere further on, the tinny strains of benga from a small radio set.

The sounds of his childhood in the compound at Landhies where his father had lived and where he had spent his school holidays. There was always some one showing off their radio set, always six or seven radios turned up loud, the discordant sounds serenading the neighbours. Mostly rumba or benga. The soundtrack of life in the railway yards.

At first he had thought nothing of it. Then he had learned to dislike it. At university he had listened to the Everly Brothers and Liza Minelli and Jim Reeves. Later he had bought classical music. But now he had Franco and Tabu Ley at home along with his Vivaldi and Beethoven. He had thrown the redneck stuff out.

Once a month he indulged himself, locked himself in his study with his stereo and his records. Everyone knew to leave him alone when the door was shut and the music of beautiful, tragic Congo could be heard.

He wondered if his wife would have to leave the house if he died. Surely Peter or one of the others could sort that out? No one would expect anyone to leave a government house except for a bigger one. Or in a coffin. He had been grateful for the roof over his head, and free at that, but the place depressed him. Probably he should have bought a house of his own years ago, one he actually liked. It crossed his mind that he might never see it again.

Twenty years on it looked pretty much as it had when they had moved in, with

only the irregular modifications that four growing children will make: some indelible crayon scribblings on a wall, a broken window never fixed. His wife had touched nothing on it or around it. She didn't, couldn't see the need. What she saw was the reality of a senior civil servant's house in Kileleshwa and through the grimy windows, the mudflats and sisal of her home in Ahero getting further and further away. But then, none of the wives in the houses adjoining had done much with theirs. Obviously that is what they saw them as: houses rather than homes. Houses that they lived in while a husband worked at the coffee board or at the railways and which they would leave when he was transferred to Kisumu or Nyeri or God knows where else.

*****

"You're an idiot." I told Miriti when I walked back into the office.

"What do you want with him?" he asked me.

"That's none of your business."

"Give me back my key."

"Your keys," I corrected, tossing them across the room. "There's more than one of them."

"Teacher!" exclaimed Miriti trying to be placating. Then, "Do you know him?" then, "You know for my people..."

The police hire anyone. Primary school drop outs, secondary school dropouts and then the very grainy bottom of the pot of O'level failures. It's where you go when you haven't any other options. That's why it's full of people like Miriti. People who haven't learned to think beyond the limits of the hell holes they grew up in. People who know only people just like themselves and refuse to see the ones who aren't.

"I don't care about your people."

That shut him up for a moment. Then he said, "Don't take my key again." Adding as an afterthought, "Without asking me."

October 1982

There were 8 requiem masses scheduled for Wednesday. The rest of the week was booked solid with 11 each; one every hour. After that they took to having mass services for 10 or more dead at a time. There hadn't been a wedding in weeks. The Archbishop insisted that it was a time of mourning, a time for introspection and the dead had to be buried properly. It was the same at St. Andrews, St. Paul's, All Saints.

Half the newspaper was obituaries. More than half. Young men in their afros, old men, women. Judging from today's paper alone, there were some 500 families licking their wounds.

The Archbishop has written a letter of protest and published it in the press. It is a "protest in the strongest terms." He was collecting signatures from a hundred thousand people who objected to this "inhumane and barbarous action."

He knew where all the skeletons were he said. He had buried many of them.

The memorandum described the government's crimes in minute detail. It was reasoned. It was reasonable. It was a waste of time. Miriti said the man who shot

the archbishop cried every day for a whole week. He'd asked for leave to go to Kilifi to see the best witch doctor money could buy. If that didn't work, he'd go to Tanzania. A Tanzanian witch doctor was like a trump card. If that didn't work, nothing would. He said the archbishop had been very surprised to be shot.

*****

Mr. Odhiambo was waiting for me. He put an arm through the bars to touch me as I passed. "Please go and see my wife," he asked. "Please tell her where I am. Tell her that you have seen me and that I am," he paused thoughtfully and said finally "fine." Uttered around a wry smile.

I called the number again and again a woman's voice answered. I said I had a message for Mrs. Odhiambo. "Hold on," said the voice on the other end and then "Muuum!" was shouted out loud.

Mrs. Odhiambo gave me directions to her house.

I went the next day. He had drawn me a map but it was easy to find, half a kilometre away from the roundabout where the 48 matatu dropped me, in the old government reserve. It was a big house in a big compound covered in tall, yellowing grass. The stone walls were grimy and dusty and what had been a garden was unkempt and overrun with weeds. Plants lined the driveway at uneven intervals.

I could smell the woman from behind the front door. A big woman in a colourful African outfit. She looked like she had been crying but she said hello in a pleasant voice and even tried to smile. Then the smile froze on her face and she looked me up and down. Her hand flew to her mouth.

I hadn't realised I was wearing his suit. I had already started to think of it as my suit, really mine. I had made my peace with it, grown comfortable in it. I would have gone to see Mr. Hilary Odhiambo in it and meant nothing at all by it. The look on her face was a corrective. It was a while before she asked me to come in, in a hesitant voice as if she was thinking that she should ask me to leave and never come back.

She must be thinking the worst. Maybe even that I had done the worst and then come to throw it in her face. But there were still roadblocks everywhere and the suit got me through them with no need for the forces I.D.

She sat down on the sofa across from me and smiled against the tumult in her mind; a tight, faraway smile that said she might already be imagining the various combinations of horror that might fall from my mouth. She didn't want to ask so she said instead, "Thank you for coming," she began. " My name is Pamela Odhiambo."

"I know. I saw it in the paper."

"Yes. Yes of course." Then determinedly after an audible breath, "How is he?"

"Fine." I said. "He's fine. He's still at the police station."

"What for? What has he done?" Her voice broke.

We both knew why he was there.

"I don't know." I told her.

Her face was three shades lighter than her neck and her eyebrows plucked into such a high line that she looked always to be disapproving of something. A fat boy ambled in. His complexion was his mother's from her neck down. He said hello to

Uncle Vitalis like his mother had told him and went to call Patricia.

Mrs. Odhiambo disappeared into the kitchen to escape the silence that had grown between us. We had tried this thing and that, then given up. She left me alone with a hologram of a sorrowful Christ for company. Christ contemplating the wisdom of his passion. He stood cheek to jowl with a display plate of Buckingham Palace and another of the Houses of Parliament. There was a vase of dusty pink flowers and three framed photographs on the mantelpiece: Mr. Odhiambo, Mrs. Odhiambo and the Odhiambo family. Each with the stamp of Ramogi studio in a corner.

"Where are you from?" she asked when she came back, without adding "in Nyanza," though she certainly didn't mean "in Kiambu" or "in Garsen." I hated the way my looks gave me away so often and so quickly. The licence they gave people to make assumptions. How a man will begin to categorise me at fifty paces and have constructed certainties by the time I come up to him. I wasn't in the mood to indulge her, or her assumption that I was here to help.

The house-girl brought in the tea and poured. We drank in silence. Patricia finally came. She was tall and slim and looked at me with a frank dislike. Her handshake was a limp caress, the barest contact as if she couldn't bear to touch me. I didn't blame her. Not in her father's suit. Then she turned and glared at her mother as I stood up to leave.

"She's so difficult," Mrs. Odhiambo apologised. "You know teenagers. Patricia was my mother's name."

*****

"You're friend is asking for you," Miriti said coming in. I was surprised he had lasted the weekend and I wondered why.

I waited until my shift was over before I went to see him.

He was waiting for me again. Again he reached his arm through the bars. I walked by him without looking. He was still waiting when I came by much later. He watched me but kept his hands to himself.

"How are they?" he asked finally.

I shrugged. "They're fine." We stood in silence for some moments before I turned to go and then stopped.

"Patricia," I asked. "How old is she?"

"Eighteen." He looked away before he ground the words out.

Maybe I wasn't good enough for his daughter, but there was nothing he could do about it.

*****

His father's world was built on hard work and discipline and he made sure that his son's was as well. At first he had beaten it into him, but he learned quickly and it was very early on in his childhood that father's belt had ceased to leave its trouser loops on his account. At Mangu where his father's credo was taught as truth, he who had already internalised it, found a haven. He was deputy head boy, then head boy, football captain, chief brain. Campus was a formality, first class honours naturally.

But it was a revelation too: in the assurance of some of his peers that who they were was enough and that they had no need to do any more than that. Their lives afterwards simply served to confirm that arrogance. He went to England looking to acquire that assurance and to surpass them.

He married his wife Pamela the month he got back. She was fresh out of Ng'iya, one month in Nairobi in a secretarial course she was more than happy to abandon for him. She had taken to her new station like a pro. She developed a penchant for shopping. Preferably in London.

It was London as he had never seen it; London through the prism of money. He had it and she spent it and he felt almost indulgent watching her do it. It didn't make him feel as if he belonged, only now it didn't matter. He could have if he had really wanted to.

One day as they had gone from shop to shop, a memory had ambushed him, coming unbidden to his mind as he contemplated his wife with what he thought to be the beginnings of dislike. It was the long forgotten remembrance of a genuine affection and closeness and his one lapse in duty. Had she had an abortion?

He had left her in England and gone home to marry this woman. One of the few people in his life for whom he felt only antipathy. This realisation had erupted into an immensity that told him that it must have been there a long time.

"Stop complaining," she said. "You're always complaining."

And he had decided then that it wasn't worth fighting the only honest thing he had ever felt for her.

They went to Harrod's and lugged everything, whole boxes of it back to the Savoy. The hotel had been her idea. As had Harrod's. Clothes for the children, crockery, pots, pans, a hot water bottle, sanitary towels, shoes. Nothing for him. He began to wonder then if perhaps the dislike might be mutual, and if it was, what reason he had ever given her for it. What reason he had ever given her to be anything but grateful.

That night he had touched her for the first time in a long time. She did what she had always done, donned her righteous submission and went limp with disgust. He kept on until halfway through it and she lying transfixed under him, he found he simply didn't have the energy to prove a point. He had stopped and she had swapped righteousness for indignation.

"What's the matter?" She had asked him. She was insulted.

*****

Now when his money was supposed to be opening doors for him, freeing him to do the things he'd always wanted and to go where he would, instead it was contracting into a world that included only Karen, Muthaiga and Limuru. Clubs.

Karen Club in the morning, Muthaiga in the afternoon, Limuru if he wasn't too tired to drive. Then once a year, there was London.

And then it had tied him down to a group of people he couldn't be sure he liked and whose opinion of him he had never dared to examine. His friends. Mungai for instance.

Mungai laughed a well-oiled belly laugh in which self-satisfaction was the thick

grease that rolled smoothly along his gut. The belly was prodigious. He had not seen his feet or anything else below his chest in the years since he had made his first million, although he'd had the belly long before. Practicing. The laughter grated. His teeth were always on edge these days around these people whose company all those years of self-denial and resentment had forged into his destiny. His friends.

Mungai had never lost the presumption that comes with old money, or what passes for old money in a new country like this. And why should he? Odhiambo's own father, a man of few words and a strong sense of his own worth, had recognised it and deferred to it. There was a meekness in his voice when he spoke to Mungai, which Odhiambo had only heard him use before with men of a generation long gone. Mungai in his turn had been brusque and disinterested, had condescended to the old man for an unbearable hour before tiring of him and taking his leave. Nor had he seen the need to apologise for his rudeness. He had been forgiven so many sins he now believed himself incapable of sinning.

Mungai's own father had had the foresight to die early, leaving his son his considerable bank account and his even more valuable contacts.

Odhiambo looked at Mungai and wondered what it was that other people saw, what his father had sensed without even the benefit of seeing the Mercedes parked outside. Was it the belly? The swagger?

Mungai had been discoed after his first disastrous semester at the university. "It's the best thing that ever happened to me," is how he always began his tales of success and wealth beyond imagination.

He wielded his cheque book like a weapon. His money preceded him in every interaction and transaction. It would enter a room, pull up a chair and take a seat before he pulled into the parking lot. And it made him paranoid. He had high blood pressure and was a sure thing for the gout. At the bar, he would make the waiters bring ten bottles of beer for his inspection before picking one at random. Sometimes he made them take a sip first.

*****

"My mother's not in" Patricia had told me, the door held open as little as possible for the purpose of relaying this information and sending me on my way.

"I'll wait," I said, making to step into the house.

"Go ahead," she said, and shut the door.

I thought about going and had gone as far as the gate before I changed my mind. I walked round the back of the house. Sundowner was playing on a radio in a room I assumed was Patricia's.

"Who's that singing?" I yelled at the window. The volume went up.

The backyards of these houses always belied the front. Where the front may be overgrown, it was at least clean. The front of the house was the portal through which the family and its new cosmopolitan reality interacted. But there was no reason why an old school mate or an acquaintance made in London should ever go round back. The back was messy. Things were scattered about and random footpaths had been worn into the grass. The wall was black with soot from the jiko and a sack of charcoal leaned against it. By the fence stood what looked like a chicken coop with no

chickens in it. An industrial sized sufuria was drying upside down on a little bush outside the servants' quarters. This was the arena of the other life, the communal. The grass was too long to walk comfortably through. I went back and sat on the step.

Mrs. Odhiambo was surprised to see me. She asked me in and sent a furious Patricia to make some tea. We repeated our conversations of the previous days. He's fine. He asked about you. I think they might release him. "But when?" remained unsaid.

I complimented her on her dress.

"It's my favourite," she simpered. "I bought it in London last year. There's nothing very interesting in the shops here. Even less these days." She laughed guiltily at that.

She smoothed it down her thighs still looking pleased. "London is sooo beautiful." She said, "We go every year," then stopped.

Not this year.

The tea was warm and bitter and Patricia looked like she might have laced it with arsenic. When she had poured mine, she left the room. A door slammed in the corridor.

I stayed for supper. Mrs. Odhiambo made it herself. Patricia came into the living room and switched on the TV and proceeded to ignore me. Patricia with her Kenya High School snobbery and her mind already in Reading where she was to start her law degree this October until this new mess had made a mess of her plans. The shoulders hunched against me, the graceful curve of her back stiffened by anger, the slight flare of her hips. She squirmed on the pouffe.

Mrs. Odhiambo packed some food for her husband and some for me and gave me money for the matatu home. Enough to take a cross-country bus.

*****

There was no sign, no car parked outside, no voices in conversation. I walked into the living room as I usually did, quite at my ease now and didn't falter, even when I saw him and knew that my bluff was about to be called. He stayed seated as I walked in observing me keenly all the while. He extended his hand in response to mine, the gaze still on me.. Mrs. Odhiambo did not seem to be around. Never leave a woman to do a man's job.

I sat down in my chair and waited.

"So," said the man at last. "You're Hilary's friend."

"I know him," I said carefully.

"My name is Robert Ogola. I'm his brother."

The less said the better.

"You've become quite the regular here I hear."

I shrugged. "A messenger."

"Delivering what exactly?"

"Messages."

"How long were you going to keep this up?" He glared at me. Silence was definitely in order. "I know he's dead." He continued to look at me while I looked out

of the window. When I had made up my mind, I met and held his gaze. He was angry, but now so was I. For the last few weeks this house had been my territory. I had been needed here.

"Well?" He asked.

"He's dead," I agreed.

"When were you going to tell her?"

"I'm not sure I would have." That surprised him. The scales had shifted. We were on my territory again.

"Of course not. You were going to keep taking your handouts and delivering your messages."

"..."

"Where is he?"

"The body you mean? You want me to find it for you?"

"Can you?"

It cost him a lot to say it.

"I could."

"How much?"

*****

Mrs. Pamela Odhiambo and family regretted to announce the death of Hilary Swiga Odhiambo, son of Hezekiel Swiga and the late Dorothy Auma Swiga. Brother to Robert Ogola, Wycliffe Ouka, Doris, Paul, Lynette, Michael and Richard, father to Hilary Junior (U.K), Ezekiel (U.K), Patricia and Patrick. He would be sorely missed. Funeral arrangements would be announced later.

*****

The thing is, bodies are hard to find. I mean, particular, specific bodies are hard to find; what with the daily production of fresh corpses to add to an already impressive total. But then you can't have a funeral without one.

By the time I had my interview with his brother, Mr. Odhiambo had been dead two weeks. His family had resigned itself to a closed coffin service.

I was an hour and a half late for my next meeting with Mr. Ogola. We met in a café down town. He did not want me near the house.

I sat down and motioned for a menu.

Anger flashed from his eyes as he took a sip of his fourth cup of tea and looked out of the window.

"No luck yet." I told him. I told him I had put two men on it at the mortuary. They said they'd been looking but....."They don't seem very motivated."

"I've already given you a thousand dollars. What do you want?"

"More." I wanted more. More than I had, more than I had been allowed. More.

"How much more?"

A couple thousand. It was a reasonable amount. The going rate for the bodies of senior officials and miscellaneous "somebodies" was $5000 or more.

The city morgue, built for 100 was overflowing. There were 100 air force corpses for starters, killed on the first of August and the army men that had battled them. Then there were the looters shot in the streets and the people executed in the two months since.

The morgue was off limits to the public. Families were required to supply the attendants with a recent photograph of their dead, a photograph that was a mockery of the corruption of the flesh stacked body upon body on the mortuary floor without the benefit of ice. The mortuary attendants were doing a roaring business, but their work was beginning to get the better of them, even they who were hardened against every terrible incarnation of life and death. Perpetually drunk on the best of days, now they bristled with a morbid humour that had destroyed the carefully assembled composure of more than a few families.

Mr. Ogola paid for my coffee.

*****

They'd come for him one Friday afternoon. He'd gotten used to the cell, had started to let himself think they had forgotten him.

"Hilary Odhiambo?" a uniformed soldier had asked, reading from a list.

He got to his feet slowly and answered to his name in a low voice that cracked even on the monosyllable of affirmation.

"Come with us."

Tears sprang to his eyes and he wiped them away quickly on his arm in a mixture of anger and embarrassment.

One of the soldiers laughed. "Usijali," he said. "Sote tutaishia tu hivo." Don't worry, we all end the same way.

They led him out past my desk into a Black Maria in which sat other sharers of his fate. Some were clothed, others not, some wept. A wave of dank, foetid air drifted from the back of the truck. I wondered whether it was an old smell left over from many cursory cleanings of the cabin or newly produced by agitated bowels and fear inspired retching.

He'd walked by without looking at me.

*****

I hadn't been back to the house for three weeks now. A mournful chorus drifted into the road as I walked up. This time the compound wore its other face. By the side of the house, a young man stood sweating over a vat of ugali, heaving it over and over. Other people idled, talking and laughing. A man lay sprawled in the shade of the only tree, asleep with his mouth open. In the house, Mrs. Odhiambo was seated among a clutch of women and doing credit to her widow's weeds; no doubt the best that London could offer. It was they who had been singing. A dispirited group of men occupied another corner of the living room. All were waiting for me. Mr. Ogola gave me time enough to take it in, all of it, before rising and coming towards me. I followed him outside.

I forestalled his question by shaking my head.

"But it's been three weeks now!"

There are a lot of bodies. More money. More time.

He groaned in despair. " How much time? How much more?"

Two thousand.

"Another two thousand! Where do you expect me to get it?"

If the scene in the living room had been as much for my benefit as anything, his tears were real. He cried and held his head in his hands, he wrung them. He beat his chest. His weeping was utterly unselfconscious, a grief so raw it did not admit of restraint. He made no attempt to preserve anything of himself. It was the most pathetic thing I had ever seen.

I waited until he was done, and that took some time, before I asked again for the money.

*****

Ah! Men and their ceremonies! Men and their posing and sounding each other out and circling each other and sizing each other up. Men and proving their points. One trying to make the other pay for a sin he did not even know he had committed and that other too stupid to see what the other wanted.

I watched them through the window. I watched Bobby cry and I knew it was another "no body, more money" conversation.

I went to the morgue myself and found a man. I gave a mere fraction of what Bobby had spent.

"Find me a body," I told him, "any body. As long as it's tall with very dark skin," and collected it the next day. Nobody was going to look too closely at a body that had been lying on the mortuary floor for a month. The funeral had been planned for three weeks already so they took it home and buried it. And that was the end of Hilary and me and it suited me fine.

*****

Years later when the tide has turned again and a new world is being born, when so much of what had been simply our lives is being seen in the light of retributive justice, a young sergeant with eager eyes and a lively step will walk in and glance through the log book and give a long low whistle.

"It's all here," he will say. "All of it. Listen to this; 'Monday or Tuesday, September 1982.' I can't believe they wrote it all down."

AboutThe Author

Andia Kisia is still not fond of giving out her bio. She likes to enter and win BBC radio plays using pseudonyms. Her last incarnation, almost a year ago, was as an Igbo male person with a promising theatre career. We doni¨t know where she is and who she is currently.

WHY BUSH HAD TO VISIT AFRICA....
...I'M SORRY MR BUSH... I CAN'T SEE ANY WEAPONS OF MASS DESTRUCTION IN IRAQ....!!
©2003 JULY GADO
GADOnet.com

CARDS, AND SHARKS

When the New Breed came to power
they reshuffled all the cards, threw
Knaves of Diamonds out
and printed Knaves of Hearts,
such bleeding hearts, such big full
hearts, such kindly hearts; dealt out
the bad old Kings of Clubs, cabals
and mafias, and dealt in Kings
of Spades, of spades 'committed
to the working man and woman',
be they diggers, planters, harvesters...

A shiny, new, clean fifty two! Kikuyu,
Luo, Kamba, Luhya...: all the tribes
of Kenya represented, shuffled happily together in a deck. So multicultural, so unified, so healthy for
the nation.
Then the game began.

We soon, too soon discovered, that
the dullards' game of SNAP remains
just SNAP - for SNAP, read Nyayo;
for SNAP, read NARC; for SNAP, read
rules and systems, methods, ways and
habits left unchanged; read even faces
left unchanged; read even fifty two new
knaves; read SNAP SNAP SNAP, the game
we Kenyans have grown tired of. SNAP,
the child's game; SNAP, the cheat's game;
SNAP, the easy game for simpletons.

MAU(SE) MAU(SE) TODAY

Black Skin, White Masks - Fanon

Today, inside this sweetly chic cafe
I am a freedom fighter.
My dreadlocks dangle clumsily
in my cherry cappuccino, and I
wring them like a fat colonial's neck.
Great rows of calluses erupt along my manicure
and this fudge cake in my palm
becomes a stolen grenade I've primed.
Look, even my suit becomes rags
that thorn-trees have torn,
and my order for one more fat helping
is uttered in secret, a brotherly oath.

Some cry terrorist, traitor...
They don't understand:

I'm a dedicated freedom fighter,
finishing my lunch
before returning to the bank.

AboutThe Author

Stephen Partington is a poet. He has just realised a book of Kenyan poetry titled sms and Face to Face.

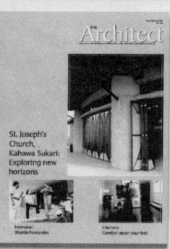

C Catherine N. Ngugi

Most of the time what I feel is that I'm looking at the society as if they were in a TV and I was outside… You know the way you watch a movie and discuss a movie? Most of the time that's how I feel – so I would criticise, sometimes embrace what I've learned – ask questions or say something and hope that the people will feel it or say something or that you'll get your message across… I guess that's our role.

Kenyan Artistic Narratives Across the Generations

by Catherine Ngugi

Most of the time what I feel is that I'm looking at the society as if they were in a TV and I was outside... You know the way you watch a movie and discuss a movie? Most of the time that's how I feel – so I would criticise, sometimes embrace what I've learned – ask questions or say something and hope that the people will feel it or say something or that you'll get your message across... I guess that's our role.

That's why they call us mad. But we're not. We are part of the society. It's just that we question everything...

Jimna Kimani, Kenyan artist, December 2003.

What is an artist?

"A person who has the luck to be able to communicate without talking."

Ghose, December, 2003.

Late last year, I attended an art exhibition at the Ramoma Gallery. Despite an ingrained antipathy to speeches, the attraction for me that night, was the guest speaker, Elimo Njau. As a child we'd had family friends who lived near his home gallery, Paa ya Paa and I have memories of a cool, dense garden, fat textured leaves, orange, yellow and bright purple flowers, a huge stone sculpture like the ones that sat in the Gardens of Safari Park Hotel when it was a humble establishment called Spread Eagle - like the one that sits near the entrance to the Nairobi National Museum - and a man with smiley eyes who let us children wander at will, through that little bit of Paradise in Ruaraka. When I arrived Elimo Njau was cautioning the artists exhibiting their work, against the dangers of imitation, urging them to define their own styles, make their own mark. The young artists from Ngecha and Banana Hill listened attentively to this pioneer of Kenyan commercial art. El Nino and fire had conspired to consume Paa Ya Paa, but Elimo Njau's eyes still twinkle despite the years, despite the loss.

I wandered through the exhibition, enjoying some of the work and trying to look intelligent in the face of the more abstract pieces, then came across what looked like a child's painting: a woman wading in a sea of water, arms outstretched, bright daubs of colour – blues, reds, browns – a wide grin on her face and a strangely proportioned bird hovering in the vicinity of her head. But the poem that accompanied this painting described a woman at peace. Peace? She looked deranged to me. I had to meet the artist.

Beatrice Njoki signs her work Bema and she assured me that the woman in the painting was indeed the same one described in the poem. But Bema, I interject, this woman has a bird flying out of her head! Bema laughed.

Look at what a woman does, she told me.

A woman cleans, she cooks, she fetches water, she is kind to the neighbours, she looks after her family…

The list went on and on. How, then, can this woman be happy – all of that is enough to drive anyone round the bend, I insisted.

Bema happily explained.

She's dead now and so she's at peace. I based her on my mother who was a preacher and she did so many, many things in her life. Now she is resting.

I was silent. And intrigued by this young woman who smiled so happily at what I thought tragic.

Some months after the Ramoma exhibition, I had the opportunity to talk with Bema again when fifteen Kenyan artists allowed me to visit them in their studios around Nairobi and talk with them about their work. I set out in search of the beginning of painting and of a path that would lead me to the present day. I found instead a group of people - black, brown, white, male, female, spiritual, agnostic - ranging in age from 29 to 60 plus – who share a passion that keeps them apart from us lesser mortals. Although they talked about continuity and identity, about being Kenyan and about their aspirations for themselves and their country, mostly, they talked about their art.

What is art?

'…art to me is entertainment for myself, is healing to my soul – it starts with me.'

Peter Elungat, Kenyan artist, 2003.

The Kenyan fine art scene is something of an enigma to many people. Some declare the very concept of a painting to hang on a wall foreign or un-African. According to this school of thought, African art is an integral part of African culture wherein music, dance, masks and even jewellery all have a specific purpose, be it religious or social – and painting is done directly onto the body or, in prehistoric times, onto a cave wall. According to this definition, it is only 'contemporary' art which includes paintings ranging from the 'naïve' (pastiches, animal paintings, etc.) to the 'modern' (abstract paintings, watercolours and oils) by Kenyans of European or Asian origin, by expatriates and by African artists whose work caught the eye of particular gallery owners or curators.

Over the past few years, however, the lines between 'traditional' and 'contemporary' – for lack of better terms – have become increasingly blurred across the arts. Theatre has moved out of the National Theatre, the Donovan Maule and The Phoenix, to Wida Hotel, Cactus and Big Wheel – out of the recognised fora and into residential areas, suburban bars and even the Carnivore Restaurant. The music scene has been enervated by a fusion of hip hop with sheng, calypso with lingala, benga with rap. Literature has taken on new life and cinema has evolved into the first Kenyan video, launched and feted in Zanzibar with promises of more to come.

These changes which once appeared so threatening to the status quo – theatre-turned-parking-lot in the case of the Donovan Maule, Kalamashaka booed for taking sheng lyrics from the estates to the suburbs – have now become the status quo, one which appears to embrace all creativity that may choose to define itself as 'Kenyan.' This new culture cuts across the socio-economic chasms, the generational abyss and the seemingly inviolable racial and ethnic borders. Kenyans are reclaiming, redefining, altering and challenging their cultural space. And Kenya's artists, who have been happily painting, framing, hanging and exhibiting their works for the past twenty years, are creating magic in this new era.

*****

Is an artist in a different league, then, from the rest of society?

'Yes. Right. Definitely, definitely. I know. They're mad people… it's that whole thing [where] you don't want to be categorised as mad [so] you just sort of become an artist so that people don't put you in, sort of saying, why is he refusing to conform.'

Is that who an artist is, someone who does not conform?

'I believe that somehow. If you start conforming you're becoming a part of an academic thing and a part of a continuity thing which – I'm trying to be as unique as I can.'

From an interview with Kamal Shah, Kenyan artist, December 2003.

IN SEARCH OF CONTINUITY, IN SEARCH OF THE PAST

Why do you paint?

For the first time, Ghose stumbles over his words. When he finally speaks, his tone is faintly incredulous.

"Why do I paint?

A pause.

'I paint because I love it… there are things one would want to say and may not be able to, may not have the audience… I'm trying to perform magic on canvas."

Peter Ngugi – Ghose – Kenyan Artist, December 2003.

Together we look at a selection of Ghose's work: animal figures which look like no animal I have ever seen and yet are immediately recognisable as themselves: beige and mauve giraffes with plump thighs tapering to stick-like ankles. It's quirky, is fun, but I still ask, why can't a giraffe just be a giraffe?

Ghose picks up one the paintings. It is his self portrait painted in 2002 for an exhibition that was to be held in Paris. It reflects his preference for 'surreal art' which he describes as "a form which aims to provoke the viewer." He points out the elongated mouth with its own individual blue canvas painted onto the backdrop, a hint of a smile in the uplifted long corner. This is the painting's starting point. The left 'eye' resembles a seed pod suspended in its place by trailing stamens, while the right 'eye' is a flower. Perhaps there is some sort of logic to this after all. A tiny brown 'matchstick' cat balances the features. Like the photos we've been looking at, this

painting too bears the rake-line markings that lend the painting depth and texture. It is a self-portrait that expresses this artist's freedom from the constraints of proportion, of realism, of day to day living. It is a joyous, cheeky painting that compliments this young man's lexical seriousness. I am entranced to recognise a world written by Ben Okri, by Marquez and Allende, transcend words; magical realism, oil on canvas, a self-portrait.

He points at a painting on the wall.

"That is Oswaggo. I don't even have to get up and look at the signature. I like work that has a clear identity: that is what I want to achieve with my work."

In his quiet, self-confident way, Ghose continues to speak, used, no doubt, to bewildered reactions to his refutation of 'realist' art. He tells me,

"Abstract art is about feeling. Elimo Njau recently spoke of a blind man who appreciated a painting, its textures and contours. Sight gives those who have it the privilege of being able to appreciate the colours and the contrasts as well as the textures and contours. When you look at an abstract painting, it's not about trying to figure it out, about trying to see a figure somewhere. The colours might convey an emotion rather than recognisable objects.

I would want everyone to be able to understand that proportionality is not relevant to art. There are no rules. When you get to break all the rules then it's easy to have your own style.

"What is realist art to you?" I ask him.

"It's art meant for the tourist market and not a forum for expression. It's purely commercialised, he continues, you know, coasts, Maasais, animals..."

"Coasts?" I ask laughing.

He laughs too, and describes a 'coast': boat on water at sunrise; palm trees on shore at sunset; picturesque dhow with improbable blue sail... all those beach scenes Kenyans have grown up seeing subliminally, in tourist shops on Nairobi and Mombasa's Biashara Streets. I want to dismiss these hackneyed images, ally myself with 'real' art, whatever that may be, but Ghose, my guide to this world of new Kenyan art is more thoughtful:

"When you visit Kenya, there are certain things you expect to see. The commercial galleries on Biashara Street have been catering to such visitors for many, many years. [They] dictate what you ought to paint – An Elephant – and they give you cash on delivery. This doesn't work well from an artistic standpoint."

I take his point, but remain intrigued by this notion of 'coasts', tourist art and market forces which dictate what an artist should paint. Is this why they paint? Is this what African art is? A commercialised venture aimed at the ravaged tourist trade? I continue my quest for Kenyan history in pictures, a history of commercial art that seems to begin in the mid 1980s, a period dominated by a gallery called Watatu – which sounds Kenyan enough – and the enigmatic persona of its Director, Ruth Schaffner.

Why do you paint?

"Because it's the best thing to do in the world. And probably, it's the only thing that I know how to do really well. It's a passion. My life would be quite empty without it. And it's not just the painting. It's looking at other people's, it's being around it, it's going to museums and it's reading about it. It consumes me."

Mary Collis, Kenyan Artist, December 2003

*****

Existing documentation suggests that in the beginning was Gallery Watatu. It was through Gallery Watatu, under the direction of Ruth Schaffner, that names like Jak Katarikawe, Sane Wadu, Wanyu Brush, Zachariah Mbutha, Rosemary Karuga, Ancent Soi and Joel Oswaggo became household names in the 1980s. These were the artists who 'made it'. I go in search of them, curious to hear the experiences of these pioneers who have been trendsetters for so many. Alongside and in their wake were others who like Mary Collis, Kamal Shah and Tabitha wa Thuku, transcended the boundaries of custom and expectation to create their particular artistic narratives. Today, there is an entire generation of new Kenyan talent, people like Richard Kimathi, Peter Elungat, Jimna Kimani, Justus Kyalo, Michael Soi, Peter Ngugi… who have something new to say and a new way of saying it. But in 'the beginning' was Gallery Watatu and then, there was no room for the naysayer.

Of the Watatu artists, I am able to speak with Jak Katarikawe, Ancent Soi, Rosemary Karuga and Zachariah Mbutha. They have surprisingly little to say about the Gallery, even less about Ruth Schaffner. They speak fluently about their early years, their dreams for the future. The effect of Watatu and of Schaffner on their lives is most discernible in their silences, in the odd unguarded comment.

A conversation, October, 2003, Nairobi:

30-something daughter: 'Mum, why don't you go to art galleries? You can afford the work.'

60-something mother: 'Why would I go to an art gallery? Those people came here and told us this is art – as though we didn't know anything. Why would I go to their galleries to see what I already know?'

Originally housed in the then New Stanley Hotel, Gallery Watatu was run by Joni Waite, Robyn Anderson and David Hart. Being artists themselves, they perhaps had a good idea of the breadth of Kenyan art in the 1980s, but as Mary Collis tells me, "Ruth completely narrowed it." She focussed her eye on Ngecha and Banana Hill, encouraging a particular style amongst the untrained artists. At that time, the Kenyan art scene was indeed divided along racial lines.

There've always been a lot of European and Asian artists in this country… The Kenya cowboys buy this wonderful art of horizons, thorn trees, Mt. Kilimanjaro and a zebra…. They're watercolours, they're oils… and there are several artists here who do that incredibly well.

'...very few people whom I know were buying African art at that stage. It was the expatriates mainly from Europe, Germans, the French... but the English, no. The Americans were beginning to buy because Ruth Schaffner had a real in into [that community because] she was an American artist herself. And she took quite a few of the artists to New York. She played a very, very important part in the development of art in this country right at the beginning.'

Ngecha-born artist Shine Tani, describes the buzz that was Watatu in the mid-80s.

'It was the major gallery and it was like the beginning, the beginning of the revolution. It was an awakening time – people were moving in to bring their products...

After me, in the 1990s, there followed so many artists... but in 1996, when the gallery owner [Ruth Schaffner] died, the numbers dropped because some of these artists were relying on the lady... To many artists it was like the art existed because of her... they drew back.'

Shine had already withdrawn from the gallery in 1994, angered by the pricing and marketing of the art and went on to be a founding member of the Banana Hill Art Studio.

At the Ngecha YMCA, I find Bema again. She is the current Chair of the Ngecha Artists Association which was promoted by Ruth Schaffner in the early 80s. Its founding members included Chain Muhandi, Sane Wadu, Eunice Wairimu, Sebastian Kiarie, Wanyu Brush, Meek Gichugu and Morris Foit. Bema was brought into this fold by Wanyu Brush, a neighbour who often passed by the salon in Ngecha where Bema worked, calling out to her that she did not look like a hairdresser to him, more like an artist. She recalls that before the Association started, there was a group of old men, talented artists, who painted in Ngecha in the early 1960s. Finding little appreciation for their work, they moved to the Rift Valley to farm.

'They are old now. Maybe their sons and daughters will continue if they grow [up] knowing about art... we don't know.'

It is beginning to seem as though the market determines not only what an artist will paint, but whether indeed, they may paint at all.

Dreams and ceremonies: Reflections of the past

I go to meet Jak Katarikawe in the apartment where he lives with his wife and a younger artist who also comes from Jak's home in Kabale, western Uganda. Jak is reclining on a canopied day bed in the back of the room and at first I do not see him in the dimly lit room, fragrant with incense. Jak rises from the shadows and welcomes me in Kiswahili. He sits behind a small table and gestures to the seat before it. I sit. On either side of me, his wife and friend also sit. The table is covered in papers – newspaper print-outs, cards, even the odd painting. The walls are covered in memorabilia: paintings, a Kibaki for President campaign poster opposite a Project Uhuru poster; newspaper cuttings alluding to exhibitions at Paa ya Paa, Gallery Watatu, the Goethe Institute, Maison Française; a framed black and photograph of an extremely attractive couple – Jak teases me – 'Would you recognise us?' His wife's dimples are just the same but around the young Jak is an air of confidence that has since been replaced by watchfulness. He does not trust me, I conclude.

I explain my purpose and there is consternation. A rapid discussion in Kikiga ensues. Mrs. Katarikawe says little. The artist on my left leans closer to me, slightly belligerent – Can he talk in Kiswahili and in English? Jak's eyes are narrowed, fixed on mine. I have no objection. The interview is slow, each question discussed at length between the three of them in English, Kiswahili and Kikiga. But I soon discover that th-e suspicion I sensed has little to do with me, much to do with past experience.

Jak Katarikawe first visited Kenya in the 1970s, when he worked as a driver to a certain Professor Cook who taught at Makerere University.

Is that the same Cook as in Cook and Rubadiri?

The question is not on my list and Jak finally laughs. It is indeed the same Cook, he assures me, whose joint text formed the bedrock of high school poetry classes in the distant era before 8-4-4. Cook and Katarikawe became friends over an incident in Nairobi when Cook's cheque book was stolen and none of his friends would lend him the couple of hundred shillings he needed to call Kampala and block his account. Jak, who had been saving part of his salary and stashing it beneath the car's spare tyre for the past year, lent his employer the money and their friendship was sealed. Jak states,

Ndiyo yeye amenitoa gizani.

To my post-colonial ear, the assertion sends alarms shivering down my spine. I had not expected to encounter this old business of being rescued by white people from our own darkness in an interview with someone of Jak Katarikawe's stature.

He continues his story, telling me how in between driving, he had time to visit galleries, to see the art on display in Kampala, in Nairobi. His childhood desires for 'paint and brush' came flooding back. He started drawing, drawing, driving and dreaming. He drew his inspiration from these dreams; from his recollections of the talk and company of his sisters, their laughter, their stories… and hid these paintings from his employer under the spare tyre in the back of the car – along with his savings. I ask him why he paints and after consideration he tells me

'I love art. And I teach. And always people want to learn.'

In the course of the next hour, Jak tells me of his life in Amin's Uganda, of teaching post-graduate music students at Makerere University the traditional music and instruments of the Bakiga, of being forced out of his university post when it was 'discovered' – a fact that Jak had never hidden – that he could not read and write. He sketches an idyllic childhood, shattered by the poverty which engulfed their home upon the death of Jak's father and is philosophical about his life, saying,

"God knows what people are going to do when he makes them. You can't be jealous of someone who never had a chance to go to school because he uses what God showed him to do and he's doing it very well. Why not be happy? You help people. Just help."

Before I leave, Jak urges me out of the open French windows and onto the narrow balcony where his current work is in progress. The cows with their long horns

are still in evidence, but their eyes have lost the cheeky lasciviousness of his older works. The colours appear flat and I feel something is missing. Later, another artist speaks of Jak's trademark pearlescence and I realise it was that that was absent, the dreamlike quality that irresistibly beckoned you in to share the artist's innermost thoughts and desires, the visions of his heart, the memories of his childhood, the vitality of his manhood.

I ask Jak what he thinks of the young artists in Kenya today and he says,

"They are very lucky. When we started, it was very difficult to sell a picture. But these days, if these young artists work very hard, they can live. Everybody is buying paintings – Africans, Muhindis , Mzungus ... now they are very lucky. Lakini sisi...

When I asked Jak about the Kenyan art scene at the height of his career, he spoke of the East African community, the travelling exhibitions which moved between Kenya, Uganda and Tanzania, the support of men like Joseph Murumbi whose personal art collection was only recently saved from expatriation by the National Archives. Like Ancent Soi whom I speak to sometime later, Jak too recalls an itinerant Congolese painter who brought to East Africa a vivid animal imagery. But not once did he or his contemporary, Ancent Soi mention Ruth Schaffner's name, nor talk about Gallery Watatu except as a passing reference.

Slightly confused by these omissions, I shut off the recorder and listen quietly as Jak sings for me in a rich baritone, accompanying himself on a small stringed instrument whose name I do not catch. His wife hums along and the younger artist joins in the chorus. Nobody has ever composed a song for me and I leave the Katarikawe home pretending that some fleck of dust is lodged in my eye.

*****

A few mornings later, we head for Buru Buru, Phase Three to talk to Jak Katarikawe's contemporary Ancent Soi who laughingly tells me of being recruited as an art teacher at Nairobi University, long before fine arts were being taught at Kenyatta University. The sign painter whom he taught alongside is now 'a very big man' – who no longer paints! He takes me upstairs to the little room that he has converted into a studio and Mrs. Soi offers cold coke which we inhale thirstily. It is an extremely hot morning.

Framed canvasses, their backs turned against the bright sun which shines through the windows behind them, cover an entire wall. The view from the windows is mostly taken up by a huge old tree, bursting with fruit and ecstatic birds which hop from branch to window ledge where the artist crumbles stale bread for them. They are spoiled for choice.

Ancent Soi has to manoeuvre a particularly large piece onto the landing before we can sit down and begin our conversation. He reveals his paintings, one by one. His attention to detail is startling – the tiniest bead on the necklace of a Maasai woman, the richness of colour and texture on the dappled hide of an animal at a water hole. These then, are his subjects, the flora and fauna and peoples of Kenya.

He talks me through his paintings recalling many happy hours spent in Maasai markets, gaining the trust of the women who sold their crafts there until eventually they would forget his presence and start telling each other the stories which women tell only to their girlfriends, laughing until they wiped their eyes and remembered to attend to a customer, faces once again haughty and immobile. Their jewellery denoted their rank in society, their age, their stature and no one woman's jewellery was the same as another's.

These are the records which Ancent Soi has inscribed. When he shows me the brush he uses for this fine work, I cannot even see its bristles. He laughs and tells me he needs his glasses to wield that brush. He tells me of a childhood spent between Ukambani and Nairobi, of ceremonies which have passed on into history and tells me this is why he paints.

'You people have never seen this. How will you know?'

*****

Zachariah Mbutha is only slightly more forthcoming about the early days. Like Rosemary Karuga, he too was a primary school teacher who went into full-time painting upon retirement. The salary from his first posting in Uasin Gishu, allowed him the occasional trip to Nairobi, where he would spend hours looking into the windows of the small commercial galleries on Biashara Street. A friend and fellow artist, Fred Oduya, introduced him to Gallery Watatu where Ruth Schaffner invited him to bring in some of his work.

Mbutha talks about his subject matter.

'Mostly, it's our culture ... I don't modernise such people because at my age - I am now 55 - I met those old people with that real culture when I was growing up. And when I think of today, those days were very good days and I think our culture was good and that's how I am inspired...'

Like Ancent Soi, Mbutha too is a diarist of sorts and although their styles are not dissimilar, to Mbutha,

'...art portrays exactly what a writer would portray. If you want to remember the history of people, if there are some people to write about it, there also must be artists to show what the people looked like, or what the events looked like.

Today, Mbutha is as interested in the future as he is in recording the past. He remembers the Kenya National Archives being set up and wishes the current government would do more still to promote art in Kenya.'

'... it is not a very sound idea if foreigners come to this country, they take all our artwork to their own countries and then we are left with nothing. So one time when we have our people in history, what shall we show them about these people? These used to be good painters – where are the works of those artists who used to be good painters? Where shall we get them? Maybe we will have to go to those countries and start borrowing the work... to bring back to our own country.'

*****

Rosemary Karuga, born in the early 1930s, is an old lady now, living in Kahawa with her husband and their grandchildren. They have no telephone, so she is not

expecting me when I arrive. It takes her a little while to get ready because high blood pressure and old age have weakened her limbs and dulled her hearing. Yet her keen sense of fun has not at all diminished with the years. Nor has the energy that takes over her frail figure once she realises the subject I have come to discuss is art. As she can barely hear me, she quickly hits on a system for the interview – write the questions down and then I'll respond to your microphone. It works and we are both pleased to have averted disappointment.

She was born in Kenya and educated firstly at St. Theresa's in Eastleigh and latterly in Uganda where she became one of the first women to attend Makerere's college of fine art. She returned to Kenya as a trained teacher and soon married. It was only when she retired from teaching in 1986, that Rosemary started making her own collages in earnest, using the materials she could afford - flour paste, tea packets, detergent boxes...

I did pictures, framed them and took them to Gallery Watatu. They liked them very much, but they couldn't buy them... at that time they saw like it was just like rubbish I was putting there.

But Elimo Njau looked for me because we had been together at Makerere. He had been looking for me for modelling, sculpting... I took those collages to him... He took them and he framed them and he exhibited them at Paa ya Paa. Njau encouraged me to do the collages.

Karuga went on to hold successful exhibitions of her work in Europe and America. Like all the artists I speak to, she is far more interested in art than in art galleries. 'An artist', she tells me, 'is somebody who is copying the greatest artist and the greatest artist is God. Copying - we are copying art from God and God is the greatest artist... Artists know beautiful things.'

What is an artist?

'I observe what other eyes do not see, the energy in terms of colour, movement, interaction...

Everything we see, it all started in the home. Everything we see outside is the result of what happens in the house, the relationships between parents and children, the relationship between husband and wife... It all comes out if you listen – the ethnic stereotyping, the religious and cultural beliefs, if you listen, you hear them, you see them enacted.'

Jacob /Ezigbo / Singh / King, Kenyan artist, December 2003

Biashara Street, rather than Gallery Watatu, proves to be the connection I have been seeking, the commercial thread which links the generations. When I mention Kamal Shah's name to Ancent Soi, his face lights up.

'Whatever people may say about muhindis in this country, that is a good man. When he was a boy, I sold his paintings. When he was a man, he sold mine.'

As a young man, Ancent Soi worked as an apprentice in a small shop in the City Market. Soi mentions the name of the proprietor and I am surprised into a rather

rude snort.

The politician?

He was not a politician then.

The proprietor encouraged Soi to paint and to scout for talent in the city's environs. A chance meeting between a rather nervous high school student who sometimes sat in his father's Biashara Street shop and Soi was the beginning of a relationship that has withstood the years.

As for Kamal Shah, he describes himself as an experiment, a Kenyan experiment.

"You can't apologise for your education. You know in my family, my father, from being a shopkeeper on Biashara Street, sent me out into the real world. Education wise, I was a real experiment because he sent me to Hospital Hill School for my primary school and then Nairobi School, whereas my brothers [went] through the community educational system – the Visa Oshawals and all of that.

...within the community amongst people of my own generation, to them I am strange and to me they are strange. I mean you know the Biashara Street community – they wouldn't be seen dead walking around dressed like this... they're laughing at me and to me it's such fun.

They only take you seriously when other people start taking you seriously."

As an artist, Kamal Shah is extremely serious and has received acclaim for his work in Kenya, Europe and Asia. But his humour is infectious.

"I would probably make more money sitting in the shop. It's not like you're that successful and selling so many pictures.... But I think they've finally managed to take me seriously – my family and everybody, in a sense, because they know now this is what I do and I'm not wasting my time...

Whether or not he paints 'African art' is in the eye of the beholder – when he exhibits in Asia, patrons see the masks which denote Africa, in Africa, patrons see the Gods which denote India. For Kamal,

... a lot of my major work ... now is more akin to music – it's like music for deaf people. Hopefully it will evoke certain feeling – not a specific one – it's quite jazzy in that sense. And I find the music analogy always works with my self. That's exactly what it is...

I'm not trying to keep up with fashion when I want to listen to young musicians today but it's nice to know what influences and what impetus and all that, what's going on behind different people. That's it."

*****

What is the role of an art gallery – or what should it be?

I actually don't know, cos I just want to continue painting. I just want to continue creating and if the gallery gives me that financial support – not give – sells my work...

Here, very few Kenyans tend to go to galleries, so you don't touch any Kenyans. Art is left to the foreigners and the rich Kenyans... to break that is very difficult because apart from how much we love our art and people say that it's a spiritual thing, we have to live. We have bills. Maybe that's where a gallery comes in.

But if our needs were met in a different way, I wouldn't see that now, a gallery plays that much of a role.

Jimna Kimani, Kenyan artist, December, 2003.

IN SEARCH OF THE PAST

I find Paa ya Paa, Biashara St., Gallery Watatu, the Goethe Institute, the French Cultural Centre, the British Council... and the artists whom they chose to recognise. In the seventies, the eighties and even the early nineties, these were the institutions which dominated the 'development' of Kenyan art, influencing what would be seen, by whom and when. From the artists themselves, I hear categorical statements like 'Africans do not buy art' – and thirty year old anecdotes about that one day, that one time, that one African person bought a piece of African art. And I hear a conversation between a mother who can no longer countenance the slightest suggestion of cultural imperialism and a daughter who learns that for that particular generation of Kenyans, the very concept of a gallery is a loaded one.

At first sight politics and art seem strange bedfellows: a politician of the nineties who ran an art gallery in the seventies; two former Kenyan Vice Presidents who step in and out of the narrative – Joseph Murumbi, whose neglected Africana Collection was so nearly lost to Kenya in April, 2003, and is at last on public display at the National Archives; the current President of Kenya is fondly recalled as a young man who in the course of his national duties, took a personal interest in some of the artists and in the work they created.

It is the issue of 'ownership' which perhaps links these unlikely companions: I recall an irascible Richard Leakey, invited by the Royal Geographical Society, (not to be confused with the National Geographical Society, purveyor of exotic people and locations), to London in 2001 to speak on global warming - opting instead to speak on wildlife. Enthusiastically introduced by an American benefactress who believed Leakey to be a native of Key-Nya, he described the context in which Kenya's game parks were created and asked, whose wildlife is it? Does it belong to the nation of Kenya or does it belong to the nations of the Wakamba, the Samburu, the Maasai, the Taita, the Agikuyu, which continue to exist within the greater nation state; or does wildlife belong to the global nation who would wish to forever see the tiger in Asia, the Kangaroo in Australia, the elephant preserved in Africa - but not the elephant-havoc wreaked on people's crops in Naro Moru... Politics define the creation of nation states, their peoples, fauna, flora– and coasts - influence the cultural heritage.

Controversy has recently surrounded the publication of Artistic Perceptions of Home by the Maison Française Nairobi and Thelathini: 30 Faces of Contemporary Art in Kenya by the Kuona Trust. Kenyan artists who did not publish these works are asking, whose art is it anyway? I find that there are as many answers to the question as there are artists in Kenya. I begin to whether I had really looked closely enough at the ceremonies and dreams, the peoples, flora and fauna so carefully represented by Katarikawe, Soi and Mbutha – or whether my eyes were blind to what they had really been suggesting. I begin to wonder how an artist like Karuga, like

Shah, could find the strength to laugh off the derision and rejection of a gallery owner who denied them the space to share their art – and continue to create anyway.

BUCKING THE TREND – ANY TREND

Do you consider yourself a Kenyan artist?

I *am an artist who was born in Kenya. Kenya is the base in which I have grown. But when I went to Europe, I was still an artist.*

Tabitha wa Thuku, Kenyan artist.

Mary Collis does not paint horizons, zebras or Maasai, although she did start out in 1980 by painting what she knew: her children, her garden, the road that leads to her home.

"When I started teaching myself about art… there was nothing written about African art, nothing at all that I could find… So I had to read what I could...

She continues the habit of reading something about art or artists every day of her life and recalls that as a young girl, she had responded to the works of abstract impressionists like Rothko,

…although I would never have even presumed to have started painting like them, it took me 20 years to feel that I could start painting abstracts."

As we step into Mary's studio, I am struck by an enormous canvas whose predominating reds and pinks are punctuated by bursts of yellow. It is a joyous picture and like the work of her exemplar, Rothko, Mary's piece appears to undulate, to breathe. The work has been commissioned by the best kind of patron – one who gives the artist carte blanche - and it reflects Mary's current experimentation with acrylics, a certain 'gaucheness, this newness to the mark, which I like.', she tells me. She shows me some original mono prints, a series of lilies created soon after the death of her father. The colours are stark, almost sombre. Despite the bright white of the petal, the dash of yellow at the lily's heart, the blue-green background reeks of despondency. It is a sad colour, reminiscent of the smell of old fishponds, overgrown with plants which have sucked the oxygen out of the water so that fish no longer swim. From them came a series of lithographs, each differing slightly from the other. Mary tells me that when hung together, the series left some patrons in tears. I am not surprised.

Later, Mary tells me about her dreams for Kenyan art –

'…that we have a Museum of Modern Art in this country and an established museum that is known the world over and respected; that we can begin to archive what's happening here, all of these things that have been ignored; that we can start saving paintings for a national collection for Kenya… '

and shares her 'predictions' on Kenya's young artists –

'The stars of the future… Michael Soi; Peterson [Kamwathi]; Peter Ngugi; Justus Kyalo – the reason he's so good is because he paints from such a true place… we might see him on the cover of Modern Painters one day; Jimna Kimani – he's way

overtaken me and you know my first thought was, you'd better pull up your straps Mary because look what's happening… absolutely in awe of him and his work these days…

As we slowly walk from the studio, evening is drawing in. The birds which have chattered and sung all through the interview are settling in the trees and their music is replaced by that of the river at the bottom of the hill. Mary confides that if she held one serious criticism of her work, it was that it was too 'pretty-pretty'. But after that trip to the soul-less cities that spawned Rothko's blocks of colour – latterly bleak and almost threatening – Mary is all for 'pretty-pretty'. She is an African artist and the life of this continent is the boon that provides her inspiration

*****

Independence and flexibility may well be Tabitha wa Thuku's defining characteristics. This acutely intelligent woman has been defying the status quo since childhood. The daughter of a carpenter, Tabitha would pinch her father's paints as a child - for which she was regularly punished by her mother: to no avail. One school holiday, Tabitha convinced her brother to help her dig up the carcass of an old cow which had died two years previously so that she could practice her watercolours of animal skulls. Her mother was horrified, as much by the overpowering stench which engulfed the family compound as by the actions of her daughter. Tabitha shrugs her shoulders and says, 'I don't think she understands up to this day.'

In 1992, Rosemary Karuga, one of Kenya's first women artists to draw public acclaim, introduced Tabitha to Gallery Watatu. It was the first time Tabitha had ever seen paintings hung on a wall and she was entranced to find a whole community of artists whose existence she had never dreamed of. At Rosemary's instigation, Tabitha took along some of her double-faced paintings.

'Ruth Schaffner asked me, are you a Picasso? I said Pi-who?'

Undeterred, Schaffner gave Tabitha acrylics, brushes and watercolours to replace the bamboo straws and local dyes Tabitha had been using. But Tabitha never used them. She had spotted sculptures crafted by artists like Morris Foit.

'I did not want to be just a woman… the women had done paintings [to show Ruth] and the men had done sculptures.

Tabitha left the gallery knowing she had to sculpt. She created her first carvings, Wa K_ih_ri (the calabash holder) and The Dwarf. They were exhibited at Watatu and at Paa ya Paa.

I ask Tabitha about the market for Kenyan art:

..the base in which [Kenyan] artists most often find themselves is not a paradise: we have never seen a country living in wealth… dirty villages… paintings from the slums… these artists did not come from a small, beautiful, rich country called the Netherlands.

I think Kenyans do not buy art because it accuses them. It shows them they are poor and they live in squalor. Noone wants to be reminded of this. Africans want not to know who they are. We show the poverty, we show the sadness – but they won't even look because they want to believe they are beautiful and smart, whereas the artists tell us we are poor – or we have made others poor.'

Somewhat wistfully, she adds,

'Artists would like things to change, to seek escape by painting a woman with a flower.'

Today, Tabitha paints abstracts, does beadwork, glasswork, weaving and some sculpting as well. I ask her if Kenya needs artists, particularly those who like her and her contemporaries, paint things that many of us do not understand. Her response is poignant:

The minute that a country refuses to accept talent – art – is the minute it refuses to accept science – creativity. Look at Michelangelo and how he dared ... our country limits its own development by hampering and ignoring talent, and leaving the artist with no way through, nothing to report on but poverty.

The minute Kenyans begin to accept abstract ideas, [Kenya] will move: even as Kenyans reject abstract art, they die of AIDS which to them is an abstract idea. We cannot continue to spoon feed people with the obvious or we will die.'

IN SEARCH OF CONTINUITY

I find that every artist I have spoken to is driven by their very sense of self to paint, to create. The ability to make a living out of their art they recognise as a boon. While valuing originality, artists across the generations display no moral outrage against those who appear to copy their style. They accept that for every successful artist are twenty or thirty others, desperately trying to get their wordless stories heard – and if some copy the style and tools of those who have succeeded, this, to those who have made it, is simply to be understood as a manifestation of a desperate thwarted creativity; and of poverty.

The effect of Gallery Watatu's implosion on the dignity and livelihood of that first generation of commercial artists is a lesson learned well by their artistic progeny. They defy geographic boundaries that will limit them to Kenya and render Watatu, the Kuona Trusts, The Godown and even the National Museum, to mere punctuation marks in their artistic narratives. The artists born in the seventies have no illusions about the reality of the digital age, the power of the global market or the ownership of their artistic rights. A cursory internet search will yield URLs on which you can buy the works of Kimani, Elungat, Kimathi or even Katarikawe and the glass maker Nani Croze. At the bottom of a page called Kenya's Virtual Arts Gallery (http://www.artkenya.net) is the terse warning, "© artKenya.net - all rights reserved. All images and artwork remain the property of the respective artist or artKenya and may not be reproduced or used without his/her written permission."

Zacharia Mbutha and his old companion Fred Oduya impressively featured alongside their contemporaries inhabit a site of gravitas, the Archive of African Artists housed in the National Museum of African Art (http://www.sil.si.edu/silpublications/africanart/AFA-VF-List-2003-08.pdf.) – in the USA! This surfer is informed that Magdelene Odundo and Joel Oswaggo are further distinguished by being amongst those named in the Library of Congress Name Authority File, "...an authoritative source of information... representing authors of more than 100 million works held

by the Library of Congress and the British Library.

The Ocharo Gallery (www.ocharo.com) in Washington DC, is the love child of American Lovelyn Ocharo and her Kenyan husband Maurice, and was born of a visit to the Kuona Trust at the Nairobi National Museum where Lovelyn stumbled across "enchanting, mostly narrative paintings and sculptures…[which] expressed the beauty, charm and contradictions of modern-day Kenya. The site bills itself, "The amazing new collection of contemporary fine art from East Africa" and draws a line in cyberspace between "tribal art" and "fine art". The Kuona Trust has it's own website, sponsored by the Ford Foundation, the Dutch funding organisation Hivos, the National Museums of Kenya and the Royal Netherlands Embassy and describes its mission thus: "to advance the skills and opportunities of artists and to make art a valued and integral part of our society."

I wonder what all these Kenyan artists would make of the web site of the African Studies Center at Boston University (http://www.bu.edu/africa/index.html) which casually displays "Pictures of people and artifacts" none of which have a name, none of which are credited to an artist, all of which are described as being '….artifacts …in possession of the African Studies Center…photographed especially for this site." I wonder what answer I would get if I asked the American Library of Congress, the British Library or even the Ocharos, whose art it is.

BORN IN THE 70S

"The second generation of artists is very, very, flexible… Kyalo, Kimathi, Mugunga, Kamwathi – between the ages of 27 and 31… I think the only person there who's older than me is Justus Kyalo. He's 32.

I'd like to see exhibition openings that are full of black people… Art is being seen as something related to expatriates, tourists… I want to see more black people. To see art being given more emphasis in schools, it's a career like any other, a career like medicine, like anything else…"

Michael Soi, Kenyan artist, December 2003.

Like many of Kenya's musicians, writers and actors, many of Kenya's rising new artists are self taught. Again, like the musicians, writers and actors, many have been trained in their craft and some of both persuasions have won national and international awards for their work. They are extremely talented, extremely thoughtful and I speak to them about what they inherited from the first generation of artists, about what inspires them and about being Kenyan – a label most of them grapple with as at once a geographical construct which has nothing to do with their art, and the place which they call home.

In Michael Soi's studio, a Spanish ballad echoes off the walls from a deceptively small stereo. The corner studio is large and well lit. Evidently it is a space for two judging from the invisible line separating two styles of painting utterly different from each other. Michael is working on an abstract piece and it is troubling him. He describes himself as 'very, very particular about what I want and at the moment, when I look at this piece, I'm not getting it so I'm actually going to work on it until I see something I like.'

Born in 1972, Michael has been painting professionally for the last ten years. I ask him how he got started.

'Well, it's got everything to do with the fact that my father is a painter too… after high school, what I thought was that I just wanted to give it a go… I don't think he was very supportive of me doing what I'm doing at the moment because… there's a lot of problems in this kind of field [and] he's got experience with it. I just decided to give it a shot and see what comes out of it. So after one or two years I found that I really, really want to do this so I went to art school.

Michael's father is Ancent Soi, one of the ten or so artists who came to epitomise Kenyan art, locally and abroad, from the late 70s to the mid 90s, the period during which Ruth Schaffner ran Gallery Watatu.

'When I was growing up my dad was having about two shows a year… We used to spend a lot of time in Gallery Watatu… I knew people like Sane Wadu and Jak before I knew their work.'

I ask Michael what he remembers of those days and their aftermath.

'… blame the systems that were in place at that particular moment for the fact that they created a lot of artists who were very, very, very, very dependant on the market. When I talk about places like Gallery Watatu, I mean at some point it was actually like the only meaningful gallery in East Africa for a long period of time… the 70s and the early 80s.

As much as I don't want to blame Ruth Schaffner for anything… she created a situation where people were very dependant on her. I really don't have a problem with that because everyone knew that Ruth was in business. This was a business to her. In the mid-eighties, if you went to Europe or America and talked about Kenyan artists, you'd be given a list of ten artists… people like my dad, Jak Katarikawe… but the problem is that they were not flexible.'

In Soi's view, while their contemporaries in Europe, America and elsewhere were doing many artistic things besides painting, Kenya's 'list of ten' was stuck in the gallery tread mill, painting to sell, selling to paint.

'When Ruth went to the grave she went with everything that she had, and many of them started struggling… It was very frustrating to see it happening. I've seen people walk into the studio nowadays... somebody from the first generation who will ask you where you sell your pieces. We're supposed to be running to them and asking them the same question. But these guys are the ones who are coming to us for help.

The minute you go into art thinking that you're going to make money, you will get very frustrated!'

For Michael, the lesson to be learned from the first generation of Kenyan artists is that of flexibility – and independence.

'I'm this kind of person who does what I want to do, not the kind of person who is influenced a lot by what others might want to see in a piece of work that I do… The first thing I want to do is to convince myself that I like the piece and then if everybody or anybody else likes it then I guess I'm happy.'

While Art School was not particularly interesting to Michael, the technical skills he acquired allowed him to experiment in new ways, and he has worked and exhibited internationally. He has often been accused of painting in a style that is not African. So we talk about 'African art' and how it is received in the rest of the world:

There's two ways to… look at it… there are British artists who do this kind of art… especially in Scotland… The difference is that there they do not call it primitive art. They call it folk art. When you come to Africa and find somebody who's doing the same kind of thing, I don't know, all of a sudden it just changes its format to be primitive art.

… It could be a piece of art in so many ways… but they think that something that is not influenced by their kind of educational background on art, it… just becomes primitive.

For Michael, art is a form of expression which transcends boundaries, any boundaries, including money.

A piece of art is not about the end product, it's about the process… the idea… The whole idea here is about appreciation and appreciation doesn't have to be financial. I mean, walk into someone's house and see a piece of yours on the wall. You feel good about it. You start feeling very, very appreciated.

Currently, the artist he most admires is the South African Art Mautloa.

One thing I really liked about his work is that he's not the sort of person who is going to sit down and produce a 'normal' kind of painting. He's going to take a canvas and do lots of things in it… put sheets of metal in it… it's very, very, chaotic. Yet at the same time it makes a lot of sense.

It actually got me thinking about doing something similar in a way…the use of charcoal, sand, acrylic and experiment of trying to balance rough and smooth… And they're together…

Nobody is going to claim that relationships end up being smooth all the way. That would be a big, fat lie.

*****

Jimna Kimani

It's close to mid-day now and the sun is hot. There aren't that many trees in Industrial Area. Jimna Kimani welcomes me into his studio and immediately offers my wilting form some sustenance. Through the glass-fronted studio, I can see into Michael Soi's studio, where he's back at work, Spanish ballads blaring once more. I'm looking at a painting of an insouciant woman sitting under an umbrella and envying her. The Rastafarian guy in the corner is unperturbed by the heat. He plays his horn to the skies and shakes his metal dreadlocks. Jimna returns bearing an ice cold Fanta. He is slightly unnerved by the microphone I am holding in his face and claims not to know what to say. At 29 years old, however, Jimna knows precisely who he is, why he does what he does, and why he does not do the things he has chosen not to do.

Jimna has painted since he was a child and his earliest pieces date back to 1985. He attended the Creative Arts Centre after high school and studied fine art and art history for two years. He has been painting professionally since 1995, full time since mid-1996.

'I guess it's where I grew up, because we had to make our own toys... you got respect for… creating good stuff…so that's how you created your authority in that small community… in Huruma.

Actually, it was my mum who encouraged me to go to an art school because I never thought of art as a career. For me it was me. How do you teach me how I'm supposed to express myself…? And she told me, you just go. If it's boring, you quit. And when I went there, it was… child's play. I found it to be fun. So I stayed.

In 2000, he ventured into a different medium, sculpture, '…because for me, painting is one language and three D is another one, so I was experimenting.'He won an award for his first sculpture, a cubistic metal sculpture which he called Warrior in the Thickets. Now, Jimna paints for maybe three months, then, he sculpts for two months, which, he says, 'makes me feel very comfortable.'

Like his contemporary Michael Soi, Jimna is bored by comparisons of his style with that of Western artists.

In my work, people just come and say, 'You paint like so and so…' One would say Monet. Others would come and say Van Gogh. Others, a bit of Picasso… Why is it a must to link me with someone? These are different individuals trying to understand what I do and if it doesn't fit in their cocoon, it becomes 'you're right' or 'you're wrong.' If it does, then, 'You're like so and so.' I'd like them just to say, 'You're Jimna.' That's it.

I ask him about art school and the place within it of African art. He reminds me that our education system does not focus on Africa, adds that he learned about African art on his own.

Maybe it's good if you do the research yourself, because your understanding will be different. I guess so. But about what has been written about Kenyan art, it's not Kenya. It's one person, because most of the books that were written in the 80s, 90s, the late 70s had something to do with Watatu, one way or another. And Watatu had their artists.

Jimna's work was rejected by Gallery Watatu in 1994. He tells me that the Gallery was promoting naïve art at the time and having been to art school, he did not conform to their mould. I have no idea what he is talking about, so he expounds:

Naïve art… doesn't have the normal format that people are used to. It's very hard to define it… If you look at artists from Ngecha, people say most of them do naïve art. That is what Watatu was promoting… People say this is Kenyan art because this is what has been documented.

In some sense, I've not tried to be African – because I don't have to try, I am. I just want to find myself. Not to find Africa. Not to find Kenya. Let me find myself first and then I'll say this is me.

People expect African art to be about masks…traditional stuff. How on earth would I paint traditional stuff when I've never experienced it? The way I would draw traditional people dancing - traditional way of life - is what any other person from another continent would do. All of it is in the books. It's not something I've lived.

I'm trying to concentrate on the here and now because that's me, doing my work. As long as I stay true to myself, there will those things that I experienced as a kid, some of our cultural ways. I have some in me. So I don't have to go and look for them. What I'm more interested in is here and now.

*****

Amongst his numerous accolades, Richard Kimathi is the winner of the prestigious Ruth Hunt Wood artist-in-residence award in Kentucky, USA – but describes 1997, the year he won the East Africa Industries art competition aimed at spotting the most promising artists in East Africa, as a breakthrough. He has been described as 'an artist to his little finger' and is an inspiration to many of his contemporaries. Over the years, Richard's style has changed in response to exposure to different art forms, different artists, and his own artistic maturity. At the moment, his style appears to be in flux as he experiments with new ideas and looks at his old ideas with a fresh eye. I ask him about the East African painters of the past two decades and he tells me,

I think most of them had to paint from a certain culture or tradition. Most of their work was… like a package of the same ideas. I think as an artist [today] I can paint anything, I feel like I can do anything and nothing has to dictate [to] me… it comes from inside me. That's the difference.

Richard expounds on what he means:

'For instance, in Tanzania, there's Tinga Tinga and there's Makonde. That's like a tradition whereby when you become an artist, you feel like you have to do that if you're in that society - over and over and over… Of course it's good, but… you're not free… It's like a culture… you inherit it and you have to do it.

At the end of the day, when you look at all of it collectively, there's no difference except maybe the signature… I think what I'm talking about is creativity.

I quiz him about the high prices artists charge for their work, putting their pieces beyond the reach of most people and he assures me that

If you like a certain artist, there are so many ways you can get their work. It doesn't mean you have to pay that fifty thousand or whatever it is… we make prints of our work, we make cards of our works. Sometimes we even make really small pieces…

I ask him why he paints and Richard is almost incredulous.

Why do I paint? A laugh.

I think I need to. I need to. It's just a feeling... that - I think that's the best thing I can do… for myself… I can just paint, nothing else, I don't know. Maybe. Yeah.

It's just a feeling that you have to express yourself, what you feel sometime…you know… otherwise… that's the best way people can understand – I mean myself, personally… Yeah. Yeah.

In conclusion Richard says,

The most important thing about being an artist is being more creative. Everybody can be better... as long as you have the talent and you can think and you can create.

Jacob Njoroge (Ezigbo / Singh / King), who won the Kentucky fellowship the year after Kimathi describes his first visit to America as an eye-opener that left him yearning for Kenya. I ask him if he would like to go back and the artist becomes thoughtful.

No. The social life has been thrown out of a window of a fast moving train. Here, I feel at home.

Only two things would take me back: education and the possibility of marketing my art.

Jacob draws his inspiration from Mathare, where he was born and lives. As a skinny kid with a turban, he used his skill to survive in school by charging a small fee to lampoon fellow students and teachers on the classroom blackboards.

'It meant there was something to eat at lunchtime for me and my siblings.'

Jacob talks me through his 1999 self portrait, a curious abstract piece in which a turbaned figure is set against a sombre background. The figure bears a blue turban and a pair of horns. It is surrounded by growing stalks of malevolent looking greenery. I ask Jacob why the figure has horns and he tells me that for many in Kenya, his Mukorino turban is '...a sign of backwardness... they say, huyu ni ng'ombe tu! They believe we are an ignorant community that does not believe in hospitals or in education.'

An arrow points outwards from the blue turban.

'If you want to hunt a gazelle, you use an arrow, a transfer of energy from self to target which results in a meal. It also begs a question and only if and when you ask it will you know who is Jacob and who is a Mukorino.

When I ask Jacob about the weeds, the artist reminds me that Jesus once warned his disciples against uprooting the oats which grew in a field of wheat in case the wheat was accidentally uprooted in the process. These oats, which the disciples equated with weeds, are a symbol to Jacob of his own artistic life.

'I am still growing, despite...'

*****

Peter Elungat has visitors when I arrive in his studio. His paintings are huge. Their subjects are women, statuesque women with long hair, and sepia toned skin. I am transported back to the National Museum in Addis: Raphael meets the Coptic Church. The women play mandolins or flutes, ephemeral creatures floating through life. Just two or three of these huge pictures fill one of the studio's longer walls. Elungat's world is a place of serenity and of beauty, classical music playing gently in the background. When he finishes with his visitors, I am gushing. He asks me what I like about them and I have no words to describe the peace that the colours make me feel, the elation which wells up in response to these magnificent women. 'The feminine side of me.' is how Peter describes his paintings.

Born in the border town of Malaba in 1978, Peter has been painting full time since he stumbled on Kuona Trust on a trip to Nairobi to visit to his aunt, in 1997. I ask him about the women in his pictures and he tells me they are his 'maximum power of love.' He talks to me about the strong influence exerted on his artistic development by his mother, his sisters, their songs, their company and describes one his favourite pieces, Pot of My love.

Although I've sold it, I have a photograph of it at home, I think. That painting - that was a masterpiece.

Before I married, I had a girlfriend and we couldn't get married ... Then, I got another girlfriend who is this one, Elizabeth. I loved her and we got married. But one interesting thing is that these people still love each other, they are still friends. They are all my friends. The first one had a pot full of love...Oh I love that painting!

(!!! exclamations of joy!!!)

She gave that pot to Elizabeth, the pot of love. And they still held each other. Now Elizabeth was in front, while this other one was behind. Elizabeth has the brighter face because she is so happy to posses this pot. The pot was so full of love that it was over pouring...Oh. That was the painting. It was sweet!

Those are amongst the most powerful paintings that I've done. The other is called Spear of Love. This lady had a spear and she is so strong and fit, physically – twisting in the air, throwing her spear, aiming at that scroll. The scroll has written on it the words of love.

(More exclamations.)

Oh! I've sold them all!

Elungat admits that he prices his work according to his attachment to the pieces rather than more conventional methods. He is inspired by the Renaissance period – artists like Rembrandt and Caravaggio, and by the work of Katarikawe, Kyalo, and Mukabi. I ask him about Kenyan art and he responds,

I'll say what people say about Kenyan art. Kenyan art is Maasai paintings. Many people think if you go to an exhibition in Kenya, it's Maasai or something close to Maasai.

But Kenyan art is an individual art... I don't call myself an old time artist or an African artist. I paint what I love.

When I ask him why he paints, Elungat's rich baritone drops almost to a whisper.

'I can't do without painting, 'cos...

He clears his throat, recollects his manhood.

'One, I can't do without painting and two, it's for my living. I've got to get money for a living. But even if there was money supplied for my living... I just can't stay without painting. I'm not myself without painting.

Without paint? No!

MY JOURNEY along the trajectory of Kenyan painting spanned three generations, seasons of anomy and aeons of magic on canvas. As a child, I remember losing myself in a tale of a magical boat ride to some hidden forest kingdom. When I close my eyes today, I can still see the enchanted fruits – pears, apples, plums like so many garnets, rubies and sapphires - which grew from silver and copper hued trees, and turned to dust if picked without the proper authority; hear the sound of the water splashing gently against the wooden hull, taste again the allure of expectation, feel the certainty that around the next bend and around every bend thereafter, would be more to see, more to learn, more to experience. Fifteen Kenyan artists allowed me into their world and for that brief moment in time, I inhabited their parallel universe, recaptured the beguiling excitement of an infinite enchanted journey.

It is suddenly clear to me why our government wants Kenya's matatus painted regulation white. With a yellow stripe. Not much chance of sending any messages with that. I mourn the demise of the abundant creativity that made every matatu different from the next, brought a reluctant smile to our contorted traffic-jammed faces even as we furiously composed fittingly elegant epitaphs and shook baleful fists at errant matatu drivers, grimaced at irritatingly suave touts - now destined to a khaki uniformed life. With a yellow stripe.

But back to the journey. When I began, I had no idea where I was going, so I looked for signposts like 'artistic generational divide' and 'leagues of controversy', and 'conformity v anarchy.' - which brings me back to the matatus, our own homegrown symbol of arrested anarchy. The artists I spoke with were not the village madman but nor did they conform to society's way of seeing. They live in our neighbourhoods, walk beside us, but confronted with a pothole on the road, rather than walk around it, they stop to examine it. They see things differently and not surprisingly, are sometimes narrators of our lives, social commentators who, as Ghose said, have "the luck to be able to communicate without talking." At other times, they are diarists, recording the moment before it becomes history, before it turns to dust. Sometimes they tell us things we do not understand, abstract ideas that we may wish to resist.

The same forces which act upon us act upon them – the constant choice between integrity and pragmatism, the challenges of 'earning an honest living' v the lucre of Mamon. A choice which so often involves some bargain with the conscience, a certain compromise that like bitter medicine lingers a while at the back of the throat even as we say it's for the best. We have all been there. And so galleries too have their place in the grand scheme of things. To some, they may appear an insidious form of cultural imperialism; a store house in which others extract from us what they perceive to be good – as though perhaps, like the 'discovered' rivers and mountains of Africa, we who live alongside them had failed to notice their existence, requiring to have them pointed out to us by those who had pens and paper to record their vision - and into the gallery of 'I saw it first!' – it goes. To others, galleries, much like

a job, appear a necessary evil, a means of paying the rent. But there is more to the gallery story than that.

Art has infinitude of expression and to be with the artists is at once peaceful and stirring. Peaceful because to be with a person who loves what they do, the doing of it, the speaking about it, is a kind of benevolence. Yet stirring because the artist values creativity above all and so is always questioning, always pushing towards the next frontier and the next and the next; a tenacity that makes for bold statements, demands a clarity of vision that would belie the fiction of an Emperor's robes. And so a gallery, above all, should be a treasure trove, the place where we keep our best things. The vision of the late Murumbi was just such a place in which the things which express the culture we value, things of cultural value, are displayed for posterity. Those who come after will know, regardless of what is written about us by intrepid explorers, curious anthropologists and myopic historians all speaking from their particular culture – not ours – that we have always been here, we have always recorded our own narratives, we have always questioned the world in which we find ourselves. We continue to do so now. We always will.

Kenya's artists 'know beautiful things'. They make 'music for deaf people'. Are we ready now, to take cognizance of their vision, ownership of ours?

AboutThe Author

Catherine Ngugi is a writer, art lover, and academic. She is based at the University of Cape Town.

NYOF NYOF

Nyof Nyof

by Jambazi Fulani

Ati the makanga of the fifty-eight mathree was mbolox so Koi fuatad nyayo and placed herself in the admirable eyes of Waf (short for Wafula). Waf was the dere of Western Bull the mathree known for its bullish horn that attracted the choosiest of the bunch in Buru. She had dissed Maish because he was not focused; he happened to be bila chums and needed also to improve on perso. Lately it was rumoured he was courting some ka high school projo which made Koi feel old and intimidated. Koi was a typical Boma girl trying to organize her perso and recently employed as a marketer for Safaricom. In as much as she had at some point endeared herself to Maish and had said yes to him her discovery made her take a better option and as far as she was concerned Waf may not have been well connected but at least she was willing to enjoy for his availability.

Unbeknownst to her Waf was not what she envisaged trust deres. There was this afti when she happened to be marketing near Mesora and for some reason after calling the office established it was not necessary to go back. So she went like to look for some lunch. She remembered the kajoint where the deres normally buy their nyam chom and headed there just in case she could capitalise or perchance Waf would be there.

The joint wasn't really parked but the nyam chom was calling yaani the aroma was beckoning her to some lunch. Njoro happened to be the one running the joint on this day. He gave her that knowing look and asked her

"Kama kawaida?"

" Lakini usijaze" she replied she juad that if she kulad so much it would take some time before she shed of the kathreatening pot.

"hizi ndizo masaa za Waf mulikuwa nakadate nini?" Njoro asked

" Zii ni kuchance tu" she responded knowingly. The kiosk was another of those information agencies. Vibe must have gone round that something was cutting between her and Waf.

She thought she heard Western Bull mathree honk and brake. Then she heard the familiar voice Waf's

" Soja si unipigie roundi utapata ka nishaa beng kidogo?"

"Sawa Waf" Soja seemed to oblige

Then she thought she heard some kagiggle and Waf's voice seemingly inducing some concern like he was vibing some kagirl. She just tuliad and in came Waf. He was with some kasupu holding her compromisingly and as he entered he shouted,......"Vipi Njoro nijazie kama kawaida na unitreatie haka ka KAR.

Njoro tried to contain himself and pretended he was wiping the table then he whispered to Waf

" We ushaabambwa si uchecki one o'clock".

He turned in shock in time to see Koi leaving. Tongue tied and slightly embarrassed he stayed on guilty as charged.

Meanwhile Koi realised that she had been taken for a ride and begun to understand that he was a man of the industry and things had just gone Nyof Nyof. It was seemingly a pretty mbof storo.

AboutThe Author

Jambazi Fulani - is a scribbler, a possible storyteller one who juad long time that writing is a process he can't brag about. Yaani haringi! He makes use of his time thinking of what to write about ... (He is thinking).

Stupid Japanese tourist. During breakfast, on the open-air patio that faced the plains of Lake Nakuru National Park, he saw the gang of baboons, saw the two large males, fulfilling with every grunt and chest bang every human cliché about male brutality. Here is an aspect of reality as consensus: the man has spent his entire life watching nature documentaries. He said this to Matano, with much excitement, over and over again, on the van to Nakuru last week. How can he remind his adrenalin that these beasts can kill, when he knows them only as television actors?

sHIPS IN HiGH tRANSIT

Stupid Japanese tourist. During breakfast, on the open-air patio that faced the plains of Lake Nakuru National Park, he saw the gang of baboons, saw the two large males, fulfilling with every grunt and chest bang every human cliché about male brutality. Here is an aspect of reality as consensus: the man has spent his entire life watching nature documentaries. He said this to Matano, with much excitement, over and over again, on the van to Nakuru last week. How can he remind his adrenalin that these beasts can kill, when he knows them only as television actors?

So, he hid a crust of bread and, when everybody was done with breakfast, threw it at the group of baboons outside, and aimed his camera at them. The larger male came for the bread, and then attacked the man, leaving with a chunk of his finger, and decapitating the green crocodile on his shirt. The baboon was shot that afternoon. A second green crocodile replaced the first.

That was last month.

Then there is Matano's boss/business partner, Armitage Shanks, of the Ceramic Toilet Shanks, or maybe the Water Closet Shanks, or the Flush Unit Shanks. Or maybe a Faux Shanks: it is possible he borrowed the name. Matano had never asked. He knew that Shanks carried a sort of hushed-whisper weight in Karen and Nyali and Laikipia, together with names like Kuki and Blixen. Matano also knew that somewhere in The Commonwealth, some civil servant shat regularly in an Armitage Shanks toilet.

Shanks lives in Kenya, running a small tour firm, hardly heroic for a man whose family managed to ship heavy ceramic water closets around the world. But he hit on a winning idea.

Some dizzy photographer woman, Diana Tilten-Hamilton, had been telling him about the astrological history of the Blue-Breasted Boog Boog tribe, told him about her theory that they were the true ancient Egyptians, showed him her collection of photographs, just days before they were shipped to the publisher of coffee table books: photos packed with pictures of semi-naked Boog Boog astrologers, gazing at the night sky, pointing at the stars, loincloths lifted to reveal lean, scooped out buttocks, copper coloured.

He found his great idea.

Heirlooms.

So he hired ten of the best woodcarvers from the Mombasa Akamba Cooperative, hid them out in a small farm in Laikipia, and started a cottage industry. Masai heirlooms. The spin:

Thousand of years ago, in the great Maa Empire, Maa-saa-i-a, a great carver lived. It was said he could carve the spirit of a moran warrior from olivewood. At night he occupied the spirit of the bull. During the day, he spins winds that carve totem spirits out of stray olivewood.

When the Maa-saa-ia Empire fell apart, after a great war with the Phoenicians over trade in frankincense and myrrh, the remaining Maa scattered to the winds. Some left for the South, and formed the great Zulu Nation; others remained in East Africa, impoverished but noble. Others fought with Prester John, and others became gladiators in Rome.

The great Carver, Um-Shambalaa, vanished one night in the Ngong Hills, betrayed by evil spirits who had overwhelmed the ancestors. He waits for the Maa to rise again.

Until last year, nobody knew the secret of Maa-saa-i-a, until Armitage Shanks went to live amongst the (rare) Highland Samburu. He killed his first lion at 17, with his bare hands (witnessed by his circumcision brother, Ole Lenana), and saved the highland Samburu with his MTV song, Feed the Maa (sang with his former rock band, the Faecal Matyrs). Shanks was asked by the Shamanic Elder of the Greater Maa to be an elder. His name was changed. He is now called Ole um-Shambalaa – 'the Brother Not Born Among Us'. The elders pleaded with Ole um-Shambalaa to help them recover their lost glory. They gave him all 300 of their ancient olivewood heirlooms to auction. To raise money to make the Maa rise again…

This was how Matano came to manage WylDe AFreaKa tours. Shanks was now a noble savage, and could not be bothered with tax forms…

Or Airport Welcoming Procedures:

Dancing girls in grass skirts singing: "A wimbowe-a wimbo we."

Dancing men singing: "A wimbowe-a wimbo we."

Giant warrior with lion whiskers and shiny black makeup walks on all fours towards clapping German tourists, flexing his muscles and growling: "A Wimbo We, a Wimbo We."

In the jungle…

Actually, Shanks lost interest in WylDe AFreaKa right from the start. Apart from an annual six-month trip to wherever Eurotrash were camping out, to 'market' (where he avoided all the Scandinavian Snowplough Drivers and Belgian Paper Clip Packers and Swiss Cheese Hole Pokers who were his real clientele, and spent time in Provence and Tuscany and the South of France), he generally worked on other projects. First, there was the constructed wetland toilets (it is hard for a Shanks to keep off the subject), then the Fecal Matryrs, who got to number eight in the charts on the Isle of Man and toured Vladivostok ('Feed the Maaa-aaa-aah, let them know it's Easter Time…'); then the Nuba Tattoo Bar he started in London, opened by a cousin of Leni Reifenstal. The tattoo bar had naked Nuba refugees operating the tills, before the SPLA threatened to bomb him (Shanks claimed in a BBC interview). Then there was the spectacular failure, Foreign Correspondent, the Nairobi coffee shop that failed because people complained that they kept losing their appetites in a place decorated with grainy black-and-white pictures of whichever Africans happened to be starving at the time. In between all these ventures, Shanks was learning tantric sex, polishing off a bottle of Stoli every night, and keeping away from Mr. Kamau Delivery, his coke dealer, whom he perpetually owed money. Lately, though, he has been more scarce than usual. Sombre. Matano knows this is a phase, a new project, which always means a short season where more money will not be available. He paid out salaries three days early, before Shanks could get to the account.

The van leans forward to the ramp, as Matano prepares to board the ferry. He looks at the rear-view mirror. The couple he has just picked up at the airport stop gesticulating excitedly; their faces freeze for a second, they look at each other, the man's eyes catch Matano's. Jean Paul turns away guiltily, and says to his wife/lover/colleague:

"Isn't this great? What a tub? Wonder when they built it – must be before the war."

"Is it safe, do you think?"

Matano smiles to himself. He looks out at the ferry, and allows himself to see it through their eyes.

Stomach plummets: fear, thrill. Trippy. So real. Smell of old oil, sweat and spices. So exotic.

Colour: women in their robes, eyes covered, rimmed with Kohl; other women dark and dressed in skirts and blouses looking drab; other women sort of in-between cultures, a chiffon blouse, and a wraparound sarong with bright yellow, green and blue designs. Many people are barefoot. An old Arab man, with an emaciated face and a hooked nose, in a white robe, sitting on a platform above, one deformed toe-nail sweeping up like an Ali Baba shoe. A foot like varnished old wood, full of cracks. He is stripping some stems and chewing the flesh inside. There is a bulge on

one cheek, and he spits and spits and spits all the way to the mainland. Brownish spit lands on some rusty metal, pools and trickles, slips off the side onto some rope that lies coiled on the floor.

The tourists' eyes are transfixed: somewhere between horror and excitement. How real! Must send a piece to Granta.

Same scene through Matano's eyes:

Abdullahi is chewing miraa again, a son of Old Town society; banished son of one of the Coast's oldest Swahili families, who abandoned the trucking business for the excitement of sex, drugs and Europop (had a band that did Abba covers in hotels, in Swahili, dressed in kanzus: Waterloo, niliamua kukupenda milele…). Now he is too old to appeal to the German blondes looking for excitement in a hooked nose, and cruel desert eyes. To the Euro-wielding market, there are no savage (yet tender) Arab sheiks in Mills and Boon romance books anymore; Arabs are now gun-toting losers, or compilers of mezze platters, or servers of humus, or soft-palmed mummy's boys in European private schools. There are no Abba fans under 60, now that everyone listens to Eminem and Tupak. Now Abdullahi has become a back-drop, hardly visible in the decay and mouldy walls of Old Town, where he has gone back to live…

Matano's cell phone rings, jerks him out of his daze.

" Ndugu!"

It is Abdullahi, and he turns to look at him. Abdullahi smiles, the edges of his mouth crusted with curd from the khat. He lifts his hand in an ironic salute. Matano smiles.

"Ah," says Abdullahi. "Your eyes are lost in the middle of white thighs again, bro. You're lost, bwana."

"It's work, bwana, work. Si you know how it is when the mzungu is on his missions?"

"So, did you think about the idea? I have everything ready. The guy can come into Shank's house tonight."

"Ah, brother, when are you going to see that I am never going to play that game?"

"Sawa. Don't say I didn't warn you when you see my Porche, and my house in Nyali, and my collection of Plump Giriama sweetmeats. You swim too much in their waters, brother. I swam, too, and look what happened. Get your insurance now, bro. They will spit you out. Dooo do… brother! This deal is sweeeet, and the marines are arriving tonight, bwana."

Abdullahi sends a projectile of brown spit out into the sea, and laughs.

Matano shakes his head, laughing to himself.

Poor Abdullahi. Ethnic hip-hop rules the beaches: black abdominal muscles and anger. The darkest boys work the beaches, in three European languages, flaunting thick, charcoal coloured lips, cheekbones that stand like a mountain denuded of all except peaks, dreadlocks and gleaming, sweaty muscles.

Abdullahi makes a living on the ferry, selling grass and khat, chewing the whole day, till his eyes look watery. These days he isn't fussy about how he disposes of his saliva. They used to hunt white women together. Once in while, Abdullahi comes to Matano with some wild idea – first it was the porn video plan, then the credit card scam, always something proposed by his new Nigerian friends.

Abdullahi forgot the cardinal rule: this is a game, for money, not to seek an edge. Never let the edge control you. The players from the other team may be frivolous; they may be able to afford to leave the anchor of Earth, to explore places where parachutes are needed. This is why they are in Mombasa. The Nigerians would discard him as soon as he became useless, like everybody else.

Matano once got a thrill out of helping Abdullahi, giving him money, directing some Scandinavian women to him, the occasional man. Being Giriama, Matano resents the Swahili, especially those from families like Abdullahi's, who held vast lands on the minland, and treated Giriama squatters like slaves. But Abdullahi was a victim of his own cultural success. How are you able to pole-vault your way to the top of the global village if you come from 3,000 years of Muslim refinement? You are held prisoner by your own historical success, by the weight of nostalgia, by the very National Monumenting of Old Town, freezing the narrow streets and turning a once evolving place into a pedestal upon which the past rests.

Matano, the young boy in a mission school, from a Giriama squatter family has not got this sort of baggage (the our civilisation has better buildings, more conquests than yours baggage). Every way directs him upwards.

He hates the ferry. As a child, on his way to school, sitting on his father's bike, he would get a thrill whenever they climbed aboard. These days, he hates it: hates the deference people show him, their eyes veiling, showing him nothing. They know he carries walking, breathing dollars in the back seat. Once, a schoolboy, barefoot like he used to be, sat on one of the railings the whole way and stared at him – stared at him without blinking. He could taste the kid's hunger for what he was. Sometimes he sees shame in people eyes, people carrying cardboard briefcases and shiny nylon suits, shoes worn to nothing. They look at him and look away; he makes their attempt to look modern humiliating.

Then there is the accent business. Speaking with the white people with so many people watching, he always feels self-conscious about the way he adjusts his syllables, whistles words through his nose, and speaks in steady, modulated stills. He knows that, though their faces are uncertain here, on this floating thing carrying people to work for people who despise them, he will be the source of mirth back in the narrow muddy streets of the suburbs, where his people live. They will whistle his fake mzungu accent through their noses, and laugh.

In a town like Mombasa, his tour-guide uniform is power. He has two options to deal with people. One: to imagine this gap does not exist, and be embarrassed by the affection people will return. Behind his back they will say: such a nice man, so generous, so good. It shames him, to meet wide smiles on the ferry every day, to receive a sort of worship for simply being himself. The other way is to stone-face. Away from his home and his neighbours, to reveal nothing: to greet with absence, to assist impersonally, to remain aloof. This is what is expected. This is what he does most of the time, in public places, where everybody has to translate themselves to an agenda that is set far away, with rules that favour the fluent.

Of course, he can be different at home, in Bamburi Village, where people find themselves again, after a day working for some Kikuyu tycoon or Gujarati businessman or Swahili gem dealer or German dhow operator. Here, people shed uncertainty like a skin; his cynicism causes mirth. He is awkward and clumsy in his ways; his fluency falters. His peers, uneducated and poor, are cannier than him in ways that matter more here: drumming, finding the best palm-wine at any time of night, sourcing the freshest fish, playing bao, or draughts with bottle-tops, or simply filling the voided nights with talk, following the sound of drums when the Imam is asleep and paying homage to ancestors that refuse to disappear after a thousand years of Muslim influence.

What talk!

Populated with characters that defy time, Portuguese sailors and randy German women and witches resident in black cats, and penises that are able to tap tap a clitoris to frenzy, and a padlocked Mombasa City Council telephone tweaked to call Germany, and tell your SugarOhHoneyHoneyMummy, oh baby I come from the totem of the Nine Villages. Warriors (growl) no women can resist us, how can I leave you baby, so weak and frail and pale you are, my muscles will crush you, my cock will tear you open, we cannot be together, you cannot handle me in bed (sorrowfully), I am a savage who understands only blood and strength, will you save me with your tenderness? Send me money to keep my totem alive, if my totem dies, my sexpower dies baby, did you send the invitation letter to immigrations, I am hard baby, so hard I will dance and dance all night, and fuck the air until I come in the ground and make my ancestors strong. My magic is real, baby. Have you heard about the Tingisha dance, baby, taught by my grandmother, it teaches my hips to grind around and around to please you one day. Will you manage me? A whole night, baby? I worry you may be sore.

You must be entertained. Material is mined from everywhere, to entertain millions of residents in whitewashed houses and coconut thatch roofs, who will sit under coconut trees, under baobab trees, under Coca Cola umbrellas in corrugated iron bars. Every crusted sperm is gathered into this narrative by chambermaids, every betrayed promise, every rude madam whose husband is screwing prostitutes at Mamba Village; every leather breast, curing on the beach, every sexcapade of every dark village boy who spends his day fuck-seeking, and holding his breath to keep away the smell of suntan lotion and sunscreen and roll-on deodorant and stale flesh stuck for 12 months of the year in some air-conditioned industrial plant.

The village is 12 huts living in a vanishing idyll. From the top of the murram road, where Bamburi Cement Factory is situated, there is a different territory: the future. Beyond the cement factory, an enormous constructed ecology in a park, incredible to all, but not yet larger than the sum of its parts: it still needs a team of experts to tweak its rhythms. There are also enormous ice-cream cake hotels, crammed rooms in thousands of five shilling video halls, showing ONE MAN, ONE MAN, who can demolish an entire thatched village in NAAM, with a mastery over machinery full of clips and attachments and ammo and abdominals. Even the movements are mastered and brought home, the military fatigue muscle tops bought in second-hand markets, the bandana, the macho strut, the lean back, missile launcher carved from wood, lean back and spray; the sound of the gun spitting out of your mouth.

" Mi ni Rambo, bwana."

" Eddy Maafi."

Video parlours rule. With Chinese subtitles.

The couple at the back of the van are still talking. He is lean and wiry and tanned and blonde and has a sort of intense, compassionate Swedish face, a Nordic Nature-lover. He has the upright American accent continental Europeans like to adopt. He is wearing glasses. She is definitely an American and looks like she presents something on TV, something hard-hitting, like Sixty Minutes. She has a face so crisp it seems to have been cut and planed and sanded by a carpenter, and her hair is glossy and short and black. She is also wearing glasses. They are the producers of some American TV programme… Shanks told him to give them the fat Sultan treatment, which he defines as,

' Grapes, recliners over a sunset, hard but honest barbarian boys, or voluptuous barbarian girls and anusol suppositories always in the glove compartment.'

"The place is a bit cheesy, but the food's great, and anyway we'll be roughing it in Somalia for a while. Jan said he hasn't found anywhere with running water yet. We mustn't forget to buy booze – Mogadishu is dry, apparently."

"Shit. How many bottles can we take in?"

"Oh, no restrictions – there's no customs and they never bother foreigners."

"Do you think we'll get to meet Shanks? He sounded great on the phone..."

"He'll come across great on camera. He does actually look Maasai, you know, lean and intense sort of..."

"The red shawl won't work though. It's too strong for white skin."

"It's amazing, isn't it, how real he is? I could tell, over the telephone, he has heart...."

"Do you think he's a fraud?"

"A sexy fraud if he is one. He hangs out with Peter Beard at his ranch in Nairobi. I saw it in Vogue. He drinks with Kapuscinsky."

There was a brief and reverential silence as they digested this miracle.

"Should we call him Shanks, or Um-Shambalaa?"

They both giggle.

When they met Matano at the airport, they said they were thinking about doing a film here, although wildlife wasn't their thing. They say they like Human Interest Stories – but this is all sooo gorgeous. So empowering. We must meet Um-Shambalaa, isn't he positively Shamanic?

There is something about them that Matano dislikes. A closed-in completeness he has noticed in many liberals. So sure they are right, they have the moral force. So ignorant of their power, how their angst-ridden treatments and exposes are always such clear pictures of the badness of other men, bold, ugly colours on their silent white background. Neutral. They never see this, that they have turned themselves into the World's ceteris paribus, the invisible objectivity.

He puts on a tape. Tina Turner: Burn, baby burn...

"Looking for something real," they keep saying.

Twenty years he has been in this job, ever since he took it on as a young philosophy graduate, dreaming of earning enough to do a Masters and teach somewhere where people fly on the wings of ideas. But it proved impossible: he was

seduced by the tips, by the endless ways that dollars found their way into his pockets, and out again.

He has seen them all. He has driven Feminist Female Genital Mutilation crusaders, cow-eyed Nature freaks, Cutting Edge Correspondents, Root-Seeking African Americans, Peace Corps workers and hordes of NGO-folk: foreigners who speak African languages, and wear hemp or khaki. Dadaab chic.

Not one of them has ever been able to see him for what is presented before them. He is, to them, a symbol of something. One or two have even made it to his house, and eaten everything before them politely – then turned and started to probe: so is this a cultural thing or what? What do you think about Democracy? And Homosexual rights? And Equal Rights?

Trying to Understand Your Culture, as if your culture is a thing hidden beneath your skin, and what you are, what you present, is not authentic. Often he has felt such a force from them to separate and break him apart – to move away the ordinary things that make him human – and then they zero in on the exotic, the things that make him separate from them. Then they are free to like him: he is no longer a threat. They can say, "Oh I envy you having such a strong culture," or, "We in the West, we aren't grounded like you... such good energy... This is so real."

Da-ra-ra-ra.

Ai!

All those years, the one person who saw through him was a fat Texan accountant in a Stetson hat, who came to Kenya because he had sworn to stop hunting and start takin' pictures. After the game drive they had a beer together and the guy laughed at him and said, " I reckon me and you we're like the same, huh? Me, I'm jus' this accountant, with a Dooplex in Hooston and two ex-wives and three brats and I don' say boo to no one. I come to Africa, an' I'm Ernest Hemingway – huh? I wouldn't be seen dead in a JR hat back home. Now you, what kinda guy are you behind all that hoss-sheet?"

The van lurches out the ferry, and drives into Likoni. What is a town in Kenya these days? Not buildings: a town like this is nothing but 10,000 moving shops, people milling around the streets, carrying all they can sell on their person. The ingredients of your supper will make their way to your car window, to your bicycle, to your arms, if you are on foot. If you need it, it will materialise in front of you: your suit and tie for the interview tomorrow; your second-hand designer swimsuit; your bra; your nail-clippers; your cocaine; your Dubai clock radio; your heroin; your Bible; your pre-fried pili pili prawns; your pirated gospel music cassette; your stand-up comedy video; your little piece of Taiwan; your Big Apple, complete with snow

falling, and streets so pure that Guilani himself must have installed them in the glass bubble.

The hawker's new sensation is videotapes. Reality TV Nigerian-style has hit the streets of Mombasa. Every fortnight, a new tape is released countrywide. Secret cameras are set up, for days sometimes, in different places. The first video showed a well-known councillor visiting a brothel; the next one showed clerks in the Ministry of Lands sharing their spoils after a busy day at the deed market (title for the highest bidder, cashier resident in a dark staircase). Matano hasn't watched any of them yet. He hasn't had the time this tourist season.

The Swedish Nature-lover, Jean Paul, looks out at produce knocking on the van window. His face seals shut, and he takes a book out of his bag. Jambalaya, the Water Hungry Sprite. Matano has read about it in a New Yorker magazine that one of his clients left behind. A book written by a voodoo priestess (and former talk show host) who lives in Louisiana, which had the critics in raptures. The Next Big Thing. The movie will star Angelina Jolie.

Matano's Blind spot:

Extract of a conversation that Matano had with one of his annual Swedish lovers, Brida, who adores Marquez:

"What is it with you white people and magic realism?"

Brida runs her nails down his chest, and turns the page in her book.

"Don't you find it a bit too convenient? Too guilt-free? So you can mine the Ashrams of India, or the Manyattas of Upper Matasia, or Dreamland Down Under, with a didgeridoo playing in the background, without having to bump into memories of imperialism, mad doctors measuring the Bantu threshold of Pain, Mau Mau concentration camps, expatriates milking donors for funding for annual trips to the coast to test, personally, how pristine the beaches aren't anymore..."

"Don't be so oppressed, darlink! I'm Swedish! Can we talk about this in the morning? I promise to be very guilty. I'll be a German aid worker, or maybe an English settler's daughter. And you can be the angry African. I will let your tear off my clothes and..."

"Why should it bother you? You come every December, get your multicultural orgasm, and leave me behind churning out magic realism for all those fools. Don't you see there is no difference between your interest in Marquez, and those thick red-faced plumbers who beg for stories about cats that turn into jinnis, flesh-eating ghost dogs that patrol the streets at night, the flesh-eating Zimba reincarnated. I mean, every fucking curio dealer in Mombasa sells that bullshit: 'It is my totem,

ma'am, the magic of my family. I am to be selling this antique for food for family. She is for to bring many children, many love. She is buried with herbs of love for ancestors to bring money. She was gift for great grandmother, who was stolen by the ghosts of Shimo La Tewa...'"

Brida laughs, and puts her book down for a moment.

"It is life, eh? Much better way to make money than saying: 'Oh, I be sell here because I be poor, my land she taken by coloniser/multinational beach-buying corporation/German Dog Catcher investing his pension/ex-backpacker who works for aid agency..."

Brida runs her fingers across his forehead, clearing the frown.

"Don't spoil my book, darlink. I'm in a good part. In the morning we talk, no?"

"Why should I make it easy for you? Why don't your read your own magic realism? At least you are able to see it in context. You nice, liberal, overeducated Europneans will look down on trolls and green-eyed witches and pixies, though these represent your pre-Christian realities, but you will have literary orgasms when presented with a Jamaican spirit-child, or a talking water closet in Zululand."

"You think too much, Matanuuu. I shall roll you a joint, eh? Maybe we fuck, and then you can present your paper at the Pan African Literature conference, while I finish my book in peace."

Matano laughs.

Jean Paul turns to the Sixty Minute woman, and says, "God her prose sings. Such a hallucinogenic quality to it."

She looks dismissive. "I prefer Allende."

She leans forward towards Matano, and slows her drawl down, presenting her words in baby-bite sized syllables:

"So, which Kenyan writers do you recommend, Matanuuu?"

"Karen Blixen," he says, his face deadpan. "And Kuki Gallman..."

Ngugi is only recommended to those who come to Kenya to self-flagellate; those who would embrace your cause with more enthusiasm than you could, because their cause and their self-esteem are one creature. They also tend to tip well, especially after reading Petals of Blood.

When he is alone. When he is alone he reads Dambudzo Marechera, who understood the chaos, understood how no narrative gets this continent, who ends one: "And the mirror reveals me, a naked and vulnerable fact."

He remembers the name of the Sixty Minute woman: Prescott Sinclair.

There is nowhere Prescott has been where the sea smells so strong, and she opens the in-flight magazine one more time just to look at the piles of tiger prawns being grilled on the beach, and the fruit cut into fancy shapes.

She is irritated at Jean Paul again. She likes to work with him outside America; he makes a good and harmless chaperone. But she finds his matter-of-factness annoying. He motors through everywhere and everything at the same pace, disinterested in difference. He reads the right books, is perfectly accommodating to her moods, is never macho, bossy or self-serving. He is apologetic about his fastidiousness. She has tried, many times, to goad him to reveal himself, to crack. She is starting to think the person he presents is all he is.

Brynt, her boss: the work maniac, sex maniac, and ulcer-ridden, seeker-of-mother-figure (who must come) wrapped in pert breasts, fat free. He is exactly the man she has constructed herself not to have to want. She cannot resist him. He wears her out, demanding she leaves her skin behind with every new job, becomes somebody else, able to do what she never would. In bed, she must be the tigress, the woman able to walk away purring while he lies in bed, decimated. Sex for him is release: he carries electricity with him everywhere, but can't convert it into a memorable experience. She has in her mind, whenever she thinks of him, the image of a loose electric cable, writhing around aimlessly on concrete, throwing sparks everywhere. She can't leave him alone – his electricity continues to promise but always fails to deliver, and often it feels as if it is her fault: she isn't being for him what he needs to convert his electricity into light.

She broke up with him a month ago. Has avoided his calls. Taken her work home. Volunteered for jobs abroad. Jean Paul must know, but hasn't every said a word. Why is he such a coward?

The driver who has been quiet since she tried to make conversation with him turns to them, smiles and says, "Welcome to Diani! We are now turning into Makuti Beach Resort. Karibu!"

Does the person define their face, or does one's face define their person? Matano often wonders why it is that people so often become what their faces promises. Shifty-eyed people will defy Satre, become subject to a fate designed carelessly. How many billions of sperm inhabit gay bars, and spill on dark streets in Mombasa? How does it happen that the shifty-eyed one finds its way to an egg?

Trust can have wide eyes, deep-set; mistrust is shifty, eyes too close together. Or is it? Among the Swahili on the coast, it is rude to look at someone directly in the eye; one must always be hospitable, hide one's true feelings for the sake of lubricated relationships, communal harmony. Smarmy, an English person may call this, especially when it is accompanied by the smell of coconut oil and incense.

Armitage Shanks, by the born-with-a-face-personality-theory, is a martyr. Eyes that hold you: sea-green, with mobile flecks that keep your eyes on them whenever he says anything. Spiritual eyes: installed deeper in the sockets than usual, little wings on the edges of the eyelids lift them to humour, and lines of character. He would be a spiritual leader, a man whose peers would come to seek quiet advice from. If he were a Muslim, he would be interrogated at every airport in the West.

What sorts of mechanics define these tiny things that mean so much to us? What is done to the surface of the eye, to make light gleam on it in such a liquid manner? Are there muscles that are shorter than most people's, attaching the eye to the face, sinking the eyeball deeper into the face? What child was born, a million years ago, with the eyes of an old and humorous man? What words were whispered around the village? About this child's wisdom, his power to invoke ancestors, so women threw themselves into his bed as soon as his penis woke up and said Hello to the world?

Ole um-Shambalaa's face is lean, ascetic, lined and dark, nearly as dark as Abdullahi's. The hair is blonde, closely cropped. Ole um-Shambalaa is not supposed to be frivolous. Any more.

He leans forward to open the door of the van, and smiles. Prescott and Jean Paul make their way out, both flustered by the heat and by the fact that they are not sure what rules he plays by. Will he bow down to greet them? Or kiss their noses? Would shaking hands seem terribly imperialist? Shanks does not guide them; he stands there, still, in a way only Eastern religious people in films or certain animals can be: muscles held tense, smiling with enough benevolence to awaken the belly. Wings of warmth will flutter in the stomachs of these two guests.

A millisecond before Prescott blurts out her learned Maasai greeting, he reaches both his hands to her, and takes her hand. He does the same with Jean Paul, looking shyly at the ground, as if humbled by their spiritual energy.

He turns, without greeting Matano, and heads for the lobby, tight lean buttocks clenching as he walks. Prescott is shocked at her thoughts. It seems sacrilegious to think of sex with this man; but she wonders, despite herself, whether he practices tantra or some exotic Maasai form of spiritual Orgasmism. Oh shit, don't they practice FGM?

Matano makes his way to the staff quarters. He always has a room at the hotel, but he uses this only for what Shanks calls Vagina Dialogues.

The staff houses are all one-roomed: cheap concrete and corrugated iron structures, arranged in an unbroken square. Matano finds his colleagues seated on three-legged stools in the inner courtyard, playing bao.

"Dooo... do. Matano mwenyewe amefika. Umepotea ndugu." "You've been scarce, brother."

Outside this courtyard, Otieno is known as Ole Lenana. Every day, shining like a bronze statue, dressed in a red loincloth, with red shoulder-length hair braids, he heads off to the beaches to get his picture taken by tourists, a pretend Maasai. He used to be a clerk at Mombasa County Council. He receives a small pension from Frau Hoss, a 50-year-old German lady who comes to Mombasa for two weeks every year, to paint her wrinkles tan, and to sleep with a darker tan.

Otieno swears by vunja kitanda: Break The Bed. A combination of herbs he insists gives him stamina, even with old, gunny bag breasts. Matano has something to tell him, about Frau Hoss.

Matano says his Hellos, then goes into Otieno's room. Inside it is partitioned with various kangas. The bedroom is a curtain stretched across the side of the bed; the living room a money plant in a cowboy cooking fat tin, three cramped chairs, covered in crocheted doilies and a small black-and-white TV. There are photo albums on the coffee table. In a trunk under the table are Matano's books, most given to him by tourists, maybe half of them in German. He picks out one that he received a week ago. He has been waiting since to see Otieno, to show him Frau Hoss's book.

He strips, puts on his black swimming trunks, wraps his waist in a blue kikoi. He joins the rest, sits on a stool, legs left higher than his shoulders, kikoi curled into his groin for modesty. He can smell coconut milk and spices. Women are cooking at the other end of the courtyard, chatting away, as they peel, crush, grind and plait each other's hair.

"So, did you see Um-Shambalaaaa?"

The group of four burst out singing: "Um-Shambalaa, let's go dancing. Ole um-Shambalaa, disco dancing..."

Matano laughs. "He has lasted till lunch without coke? He is serious about this maa-neno?"

Otieno turns to Matano. "He is paying me, bwana, to be Ole Kaputo, the Maa chief's son."

"Nooo! Ai! This deal must be of much money! That is why he was afraid to talk to me. There'll be bumper harvests this time. I think these ones are television people. From America."

There is silence as the rest digest the implications of this. America. The bao game proceeds, and conversation weaves languidly around them.

Matano passes the book around. Kamande, the chef, takes one look at the cover and hoots with laughter. Otieno is on the cover, body silvery, courtesy of Photodraw, kneeling naked facing the mud wall of a manyatta. Everything in the shot is variations of this silvery black, his red Maasai shawl, the only colour, spread on the ground. Two old white hands run along his buttocks, their owner invisible. It must be near sunset: his shadow is long and watery, a long wobbly silhouette of cock reaches out to touch his red shuka.

Otieno looks bewildered, then grabs the book. His eyes frown, confused: who is this person? Recognition. Gasp. The books changes hands, all round the circle, and everybody falls over themselves laughing. The women come to investigate. Fatuma, Kamande's wife looks at it, looks at Otieno, looks back at the book.

"Ai! Why didn't you tell me you had a beer bottle in your pants? I will find somebody for you if you learn to use it properly! Not on these white men – what can they show you?"

The women laugh, and carry the book away to pore over it.

Otieno turns to Matano: "Where did you get it?"

"A tourist left it in the van last week. Frau Hoss said she taught you – tantric love."

"I will sue!"

"Don't be stupid," says Matano. "Write your own book. Let's write it, bwana! The publishers will eat it up! African sex is hot in Germany... you will make a killing! Call it My Body Defiled. Then make sure you sit without your shirt on on the cover looking sad and oppressed. "

They laugh.

x

Prescott sits with Jean Paul at the Pool Bar next to the beach, watching the sunset, having a drink and waiting for Shanks.

There is no barrier from here to India. There are scores of short muscular boys silhouetted against the dusk, covered in and surrounded by curios, doing headstands and high jumps and high-fives and gathering together every few minutes to confer. Sometimes they look at Prescott; one winks, another bounces his eyebrows up and down. Then she is relieved as they spot a tourist, gather up their wares, and go to harass someone else. There is music playing at the bar: some sort of World Music for Europop fans. "Jambo, jambo bwana, habari gani, mzuri sana..."

From a well-known guidebook: "The Kenyan's smile is the friendliest in the world. He will tell you Jambo, and serve you dawa cocktails."

The beach boys cannot come to the hotel, but Prescott has been told that they will be all over her in six international languages if she crosses the line of the coconut trees.

One of the boys walks towards her, managing to bounce off the balls of his feet with every stride, even in the sand. He has a brief chat with the security guard and walks up to their table. She looks at his lean face, eyes like a startled giraffe, with thick stiff strands of eyelash.

"Jambo!"

"Jambo. I'm afraid I'm not buying anything today. No money."

Jean Paul is shut away, among characters that talk like blackened fish, and look like bayous, and make love like jambalaya. Somebody with a banjo is searching for the lost gris gris bag.

Beach Boy frowns, and slaps at his chest, puffed up. "Us, you know, BEACH BUOYS, it is only money! We want to sell you Bootiful Hand-U-craft of the Finest T-u-raditional Africa. Eh! A man like me, how it feels to run and chase white mzungu every day: buy this, buy this? I dig to get cool job, any cool job: garden, office, or bouncer in Mamba Village Disco, even Navy Offisaa. I have diploma, Marine Engineering, but Kenya? Ai! So now t'fuzz, the pow-lice, they chase homebwuoys. And the hotel, they chase homebwuoys. But this beach – this is our hood. Dig? So you want special elephant-hair bracelet? Is Phat! Very Phat!"

He isn't smiling. He is looking out to sea, tapping his foot on the ground like a glass vase of testosterone, just waiting to be shattered. In Philadelphia, she would have been terrified of him. She would walk past, her tongue cotton wool, a non-racial smile tearing her reluctant face open. Now she wants to pinch his cheeks and watch him squirm as his friends look on.

"I want a necklace, a Maasai necklace. Can you get me one?"

He looks at her with seamless cool, and raises one eyebrow, then frowns. 'Tsk tsk,' he seems to say, 'that is a hard one.' The silence lasts a while, then he looks at her and says, "For you, Mama, because you so bootiful. I will try." And he bounces back to his mates, one arm swinging with rhythm around his back like a rap artist walking to his Jeep.

She laughs.

Jean Paul says, "God, look at that sunset..."

Prescott says, "It's never as good as the postcards, is it? Fuck, poets have a lot to account for. They've killed the idea of sunsets, made meadows boring, and completely exterminated starry nights. Sometimes I think they're just as bad as Polluting Industrial Conglomerates Run by Men."

Jean Paul smiles patiently and looks across at her, compassion in his eyes. She wants to slap him. Brynt hasn't phoned. Though she isn't taking his calls, it's important that he calls, so she can get the satisfaction of not taking his calls.

Shanks appears from the glass doors on the other side of the pool. He has tucked in his red Maasai cloth into his shorts; his torso is bare, and his arms are draped over an ivory walking-stick that lies on the back of his neck. His silhouette is framed by the last vague rays of the sun, the postcard silhouette of the Maasai man who National Geographic Television will introduce, deep voiced, as "an ancient noble, thriving in a vast, wild universe, the colour of shadow."

He squats on his haunches next to them, and glides his eyes around them both. Smiles.

"Peace."

Prescott smiles vaguely. Jean Paul has cracked already: his mouth is wide open.

"You have eaten?"

They nod.

"Come..."

They follow him. His walk is not graceful, like Prescott expected. Rather, it is springy: he bounces to one side on one leg, then does the same on the other. It is a distantly familiar movement, something from The World Of Survival or Discovery. Some walk some ethnic peoples do somewhere in the world, and they are noble.

They leave the residents' area of the hotel, and cross through a gate; before them, sitting under a huge baobab tree, is a huge whitewashed mud-and-wattle hut, with a beach-facing patio constructed of rugged acacia branches, stained pine coloured. There is an enormous apple green couch shaped like a toilet, with large sewn lettering that reads 'Armitage Shanks'.

Shanks points to it. "My great-grandfather had a great sense of humour. He furnished his drawing rooms with seats that looked like toilets."

They sit on the cushions on the floor. Shanks crosses his legs as he stands, and lowers himself straight down into a cross-legged sitting position.

A very tall man walks out of the hut, carrying a tray. He is introduced as Ole Lenana. It is Otieno.

"My circumcision brother."

Shanks and Ole Lenana chat away in a strange language. Ole Lenana joins them, unplugs the beaded tobacco pouch hanging from his neck, and starts to roll a cigarette.

"Did you know..." His voice startles them, suddenly the voice of Shanks, not um-Shambalaa. "In the 16th and 17th centuries, before commercial fertiliser was invented, manure was transported by ship, dry bundles of manure. Once at sea, it started to get heavy, started to ferment, and methane would build up below deck. Any spark could blow up a ship – many ships were lost that way. Eventually, people began stamping the bundles 'Ships in High Transit' so the sailors would know to treat the cargo with respect. This is where the term 'shit' comes from. Ships in High Transit. Many of those around these days..."

Prescott is wondering whether this is how the Shanks family sanitises their history. Fecal anecdotes that have acquired the dignity of a bygone age, presented in a dry, ironical tone.

"The Maasai build their houses out of shit. This is a house built from the shit of cattle, mixed with dung and wattle, and whitewashed with lime. You know, forget the bullshit in the brochure. That was for Vogue. I can see you two are not from the fluff press. I don't really believe this Maa-saaia mythology stuff because it makes no sense to me. I make myself believe it because I need to. Maybe, being a Shanks, it is the shit that attracted me. Maybe it was to do something that would give me a name and a life different from something branded in toilets around the world. Maybe I was tired of being a name that flushes itself clean with money every new generation. Maybe I like the idea of having the power to save an entire nation. Or maybe it was just for the money. All I can tell you is that I want to help save these people, that these heirlooms you will see tomorrow are the most exquisite creations I have ever seen. The world must see them."

Prescott says, "But don't you think there's something wrong with that? Isn't it like taking ownership of something that isn't ours?"

She is thinking, 'Houses of bullshit, my God, what an image...'

Shanks says, "I earned my membership, like any Maa. They trust me. I am one of them," he was Um_Shambalaa again, and stood and he and Ole Lenana gripped

forehwands and looked deep into each other's eyes, and Ole lenana fell to his knees, and mutted something guttural, emotional and grateful.

The cigarette is being passed around: Jean Paul, Prescott, um-Shmabalaa. Dope. She looks up, starled by a shadow. It is the tour guide, Matano, his torso bare, muscles gleaming. He is drinking beer.

"The sisters are here to sing."

They walk in, women shrouded in red cloaks, singing. Voices, mined from a gurgly place deep down in the throat, oddly like percussion instruments. This is a society that lives laterally, Prescott thinks, not seeking to climb up octaves, find a crescendo, no peaks and troughs: ecstacy sought from repetition, as the music grabs hold of all atmosphere, the women begin to bleat, doing a jump every few moments, a jump that thumps a beat to the music, and lifts their piles of necklaces up and down. Up and down. Ole um-Shambalaa stands up, Ole Lenana joins him. They head out to the garden, and start to jump with every bleat. Prescott has an image in her mind of the stomach as a musical instrument, bagpipes squeezed to produce the most visceral sounds the body can. She finds herself jerking her neck forward and backward, to the beat. The tide must have risen, for the waves seem to be crashing on the beach with more fervour than she can remember. Damn him, damn Brynt. She will not cry.

The women have gathered around Jean Paul's cushion. There is an expression of mild panic on his face, which he can't shut out. They grab his arms, stand him up. He starts to jog himself up and down, a tight smile on his face, his eyes wild, looking for a way to bolt.

None of the women singing know a word of what they are singing. Not three hours ago, they were chattering away in Kiswahili, while cooking supper. After dark, they don beads and kangas and practice in the servant's courtyard, heaving and gurgling and making all kinds of pretend Maa sounds. This is why the hotel allows them to stay in the quarters with their husbands.

Matano is watching Prescott. She is just about to allow herself to be reckless. He slowly makes his way towards her, stands behind her chair, allowing his presence to occupy her space.

At the airport he caught her standing alone, looking bewildered about this new place. Those eyes, her skin so white, made him shiver. He has in his mind the constant idea that white women are naked, people with skin peeled like baby rabbits, squirming with pain and pleasure in the heat. It is always profoundly disturbing to him that they are rarely like this in reality, so forward and insistent, interrupting his seduction with demands. THERE! THERE! Grabbing his face, holding on to it, making his tongue work until they are satisfied. Many of them have no faith in his abil-

ities, feel they need to manage all his activities.

Was it Anais Nin who wrote the erotic story of a wild giant beast of a man, an artist, and a brash and demanding woman came on to him, and he rejected her, and she chased and chased him, learning to be demure. One day, long after she had submitted and become who he wanted, he jumped on her and they molested the bed for the whole night.

Jean Paul has succumbed. It started with the women laughing at him, as they watched his body awkwardly trying to find a way into the rhythm. He burst out laughing at himself, and his movements became immediately more frenzied. Now he howls, and jerks faster, a string puppet out of control.

An hour later, Prescott sits with Matano at the edge of the camp. Ole um-Shambalaa is sitting cross-legged in the garden, absolutely still. Matano wraps his hand around her waist, and is singing a Maasai song in her ear, ever so softy. Behind him, the women's self-help group are still singing. Their eyes have become glazed: they look like they could go on forever.

She can't seem to stop shaking. It must be the dope. And the music.

She jerks out of his embrace and says, "I'm sorry, I'm just wiped out. I've got to go and lie down."

He shrugs and turns her to him and smiles, looking at her, looking at her. Then his large hand reaches and pushes her hair behind her ear, his wrist leaving a smear of sweat on her cheek. She is singed by it, and immediately afraid.

She can't sleep. Her heart is thudding in her chest and when she lies on her back, an enormous weight seems to force her down, pushing her into her bed, and she has to struggle to breathe. It must be the dope. She stands. It is quiet outside; they've all gone to sleep. She stumbles out of the tent, her legs numb, stinging like pins and needles. The feeling spreads over her body and she goes to the bathroom and looks at her face in the mirror. It looks the same, a bit wild, but not much different. She sees the Maasai necklace hanging out of her toilet bag and takes it and puts it around her neck. She looks in the mirror: on her it looks tacky. The strong colours suck up her face.

There is a message from Brynt on her cellphone. 'Did you find Shanks? Call me.'

What reigns you back in, she wonders, what makes you want to be what you were again? After this mindbending magic? How can Chicago compete with this primal music, with bodies rubbing themselves against thick moist air?

Maybe truth is always a consensus. Maybe it doesn't matter what kind of proof backs up your submission; maybe your submission has no power without being subscribed to by a critical mass of people? What is the truth here?.

Back home: there is fear so farinside fear you don't feel it. Mortgages, a lifeline that cannot escape upward mobility: you have to be sealed shut from those who live laterally to thrive. If you cannot maintain openess to this, you can always control it. Packaging. Sell it, as a pill, a television programme, a nightclub, a bonding retreat, a book, jambalaya prose. Control it. Make the magic real. Allow it only to occupy a certain time. This is the human way – the rest is animal. But tonight, it will be real, it is real, Brynt is a faraway myth. It will be different in the morning. But now, she heads back to um-Shambalaa's.

Matano finds himself thinking about Abdullahi's proposal. A week ago, Abdullahi took him to meet the Nigerians, who intimidated him, strutting like nothing could govern them, buy them. Noticing his scepticism about the deal, one of them laughed at him.

"You Kenyans! You let these Oyibos fock you around, man. Eh! Can't you see your advantage, man? You know them, they know shit about you. So here you are, still a boy, still running around running a business for a white guy. So stoopid! I saw him in the inflight magazine when I was coming from Lagos with new stock. Ha! Um-Shambalaa!"

The group of Nigerians broke into the Kool and the Gang song on cue: "Let's go dancing. Um-Shambalaa, disco dancing..."

"So do you dance for um-Shambalaa? For dollars? We're offering you real money, man. Four hours, you let our guy in, and you have enough money to fuck off and buy a whole disco, where you can dance for German women the whole night, brother."

Matano wonders for a moment why this deal is worth so much, then remembers the numbers. The thousands who gather under baobabs to listen to stories of the strange hotel tribes. The closed loop system the Nigerians ahave devised to reduce piracy. All the videos are realsed to the Video parlours on the same day. At the same time. FM stations who have taken to advertising in the videos. Politicians who pay to feature in the urinal breaks. NGO's who pay to send Wear Condom messages between sex scenes.

Matano looks at the group on the grass now. Jean-Paul is slow dancing with (Ole Lenana) Otieno, who will argue in one of the afternoon sessions in the courtyard that the best way to get his revenge is to fuck them.

"There is nothing more satisfying than making a white man your pussy!"

The rest will laugh and call him 'Shoga'.

They will all make sure Fatima does not hear them speak. They value their lives. Kamande will look back nervously to see that she is otherwise engaged.

For what, Matano thinks: 50 dollars? Maybe a watch? Why should Jean Paul give a shit how he is judged in the laugh sessions under baobab trees? Who, in his circle of peers, in his magic-made-real characters, will care?

He calls Abdullahi, and says, "Send them in, bro. Bring in the guy, the back door is open."

He sees Prescott walking towards him. He will perform on the sofa of um-Shambalaa's house. The drinks are laid out, the dope. Servants wander in and out and are soon invisible in the revelry.

Morning is another part of the lottery. The sun will rise. Somebody will receive a call, Chicago will roar back into her life, down a telephone line. She will wash Matano's smell off her, sit on the toilet and cry, still stuck to chasing the spewing electric cable. Jean Paul will see a pile of tacky plasic beads on the floor, red-hair dye on his pillow, will smell stale nakedness on his sheets. That Lenana is no other reality in the morning. He wants money, is listening to Kiss FM, has spashed himself with Jean Paul's cologne, before examining the shadow of his penis with some satisfaction. He must spend the next few weeks practicing his German. He will be on German TV soon, if all goes according to plan. Jean Paul is itching for him to leave, for the chambermaid to come in and clean last night away. He will sit on the beach and escape to the Bayous. Tonight, he will only see um-Shamabala's reality through a camera, for their programe 'A World of Cultures.'

Fatima and her troop of women share the spoils in the morning. Ole um-Shambalaa paid them an extra bonus, just to make sure there was no mischief. Fatima cannot stand um-Shambalaa, and is not afraid to hide it: he cannot do without her. She is the most plausible gurgler and Kamande, is the best chef this side f the Island, and because he has the same name as Blixen's badly spelled 'Kamanti', is worth more in drinks-before-dinner anecdotes. Fatima managed to get 30 dollars from Jean Paul, by threatening to take his shirt off while they danced last night. About 3 dollars of this money will be offically declared to husbands; the rest will go to their communal slush fund. Things will appear in the household, conveniences explained away. School fees is mysteriously paid.

"Ai! Don't you remember? It was a gift from mama so-and-so, after I helped her cooking when her relatives went away."

The nest egg is growing. Every three months, each get a lump sum. Khadija is planning to leave her husband soon. She works as a chambermaid, and will return, after the morning shift, with a collection of forensic stories: red hair-dye on a pillow, how Otieno smells just like Jean Paul's bathroom, and Matano, when will he leave those white women? It is definitely time they found him a wife...

Abdullahi is thirsty. The ferry smells of old oil. Last night, after the operation in um-Shambalaa's house, he took an old lover to bed and performed like never before, surrounded by Abba, incense and cocaine. Today, he will buy himself a car.

The practiced will thrive in the morning: both made their transitions before dawn. Matano left um-Shambalaa's room, after carefully pulling strands of her hair from his short dreadlocks. He made his way back to the courtyard, lay out on his kikoi watching dawn and counting the stars, the way he used to with his mother as she cooked in another courtyard, not five miles away. He reads Dambudzo.

Ole um-Shambalaa is in his small plane. He woke up at four in the morning. He sat on the art-deco Shanks toilet and expelled. Sunrise will find him in Laikipia, talking to the elders, tracking an elephant, chatting to the young morans, learning new tricks. He will visit his factory, explain to the greediest of the elders how they can benefit from it, dish out wads of cash, enough to buy a goat or two. He will call his new enterprise a Conservancy. The Maa Conservancy. He will return at dusk, when his colour is hidden by shadow, ready to play for Prescott's cameras. Tonight, he will show them the heirlooms.

Abdullahi brings Matano the tape and his cut in the afternoon. Two hundred thousand shillings.Not enough to buy the disco, but just fine thank you. They sit in the TV room of the hotel, with some of the staff, and laugh and laugh and laugh at the lateral gurgles and drunken sex talk. For the next few months, this will be the main feature in every video hall at the coast. Sold to them, one time, and in a closed loop to limit piracy (as if anybody would risk pirating the Nigerians), for 5,000 shillings per tape. Ten bob entry, sex, imitation Maasai women, and "Um-Shambalaa, let's go dancing."

Fock the copyright, we're Nigerian.

Someone is shouting loudly in the lobby, drunk. The first marines are checking in: ship landed today, exercises for Iraq. Matano smiles to himself, and catches Abdullahi's eyes. Which one of the will call the Nigerians?

"Hey Bud, did you see them honkin' hooters hanging at the pool-bar?"

"I wanna beach-view room, you stoopid fuck. Fucking Third World country. Fucking Ay-rabs everywhere."

AboutThe Author

Binyavanga Wainaina is a writer, and is the founding editor of Kwani? In 2002, he won the Caine Prize for African Writing. It was the first time in the prize's history that the judge's vote was unanimous. Binyavanga is currently studying a Masters degree for Creative Writing at the University of Norwich, UK.

MiMicry

by Dipesh Pabari

...you know, the whole business of living- why is it a problem? Is it not essentially because we think from a particular point of view, from a fixed point of view? We are always thinking from a centre towards the periphery but the periphery is the centre for most of us and so anything we touch is superficial.
(Krishnamurti, The First and Last Freedom)

It is a love song to our mongrel selves.
(Salman Rushdie, Imaginary Homelands).

A scene from an Indian home in Birmingham, UK:

Dinnertime. Seated around the table is three generations of a Gujurati immigrant family. Grandfather, father and son. Mother continues to keep the chapattis coming while the males eat. Daughter is in the lounge eating pizza and watching TV with two Anglo-Saxon friends. Son sulks at the table because mother won't let him have any pizza until he has eaten his curry and chapatti. TV is on here as well: Zee TV, and eyes are fixed to the Indian soap. A few words are exchanged in Gujurati between grandfather and son. Mother tells son to eat up in Gujurati. He responds in Birmingham English. Grandfather understands English but makes no attempt to use the language unless he absolutely must. He has been here twenty years, after raising seven children in Kenya. He didn't speak English then. There was no need to, even though he would have depended on the English farmer for trade, but they had Swahili. Swahili is a trade a language after all. And Swahili belonged to neither the white farmer nor the duka-wallah. This was on neutral grounds: the duka-wallah (shop keeper) a migrant settler himself in East Africa, and the white farmer. Both were here for the same reasons and had their different means of obtaining it. As long as the Indian posed no threat to the authority of the white man, he could stay as long as he wanted, make as much money, just so long as he remembered he was still subordinate to his fellow immigrant, so long as he remembered which toilet to use. So why would the Indian bother to learn his superior's language?

For the black man, it was a different story altogether. Right from childhood, you were to be educated in a manner that would make sure you understood your primitive heritage. Language was a key strategy of colonial power, mastery of which can be seen as a form of mimicry. Not only was formal education in the colonies conducted in English for all subjects, proficiency in the language was regarded as the most important aspect for success in education. Ngugi Wa'Thiongo, a Kenyan novelist and postcolonial critic recollects his years in school where to pursue further education, he had to have top grades in English. He remembers a classmate who passed all subjects with distinctions but failed English. He failed the entire exam and went

on to become a turn boy on a bus for his livelihood. Ngugi, on the other hand, was an average student in all subjects but excelled in English and was rewarded with an opportunity to attend Makerere University in Kampala, which at the time, was the only Institute of Higher Education in East Africa.

Vernacular language was targeted as a strategy for subordination:

> One of the most humiliating experiences was to be caught speaking Gikuyu in the vicinity of the school. The culprit was given three to five strokes...or was made to carry a metal plate around the neck with inscriptions such as I AM STUPID or I AM A DONKEY...And how did the teachers catch the culprits? A button was initially given to one pupil who was supposed to hand it over to whoever was caught speaking his mother tongue. Whoever had the button at the end of the day would bring out all the culprits of the day. Thus, children were turned into witchhunters and in the process were being taught the lucrative value of being a traitor to one's own immediate community.

(Ngugi, 438).

And what of the outcome? For many theorists and critics from the postcolonial world, the most effective form of domination was the subordination of identity, the displacement of the constituting factors of one's self-definition, and in its place, installed by a blend of acquiescing and cajoling 'spoon-feeding' of the colonizers identity. Thus, the colonized's ostensible future success depended on how much s/he mastered being anglicised. Almost the same but not quite.

In August 1981, the Zimbabwe Herald reported the opening of the Kamuzu Academy in Malawi by President Banda. This was to be a grammar school for the cream of the educational elite which will, "...produce boys and girls who will be sent to universities like Harvard...Oxford...and be able to compete on equal terms with others elsewhere. The President has instructed that Latin should occupy a central place in the curriculum..." (Cited: Ngugi, 444). Furthermore, teaching staff will only be recruited from Britain, as the required standards certainly could not be entrusted to the natives whose own mother tongue accent will certainly be detrimental to the polished fluency required. Almost the same but not white.

For Homi K. Bhabha, the most, "...effective literary strategy of colonial power and knowledge" is the trope, mimicry, which, in relation to colonialism is defined as, "…the desire for a reformed, recognizable Other, as a subject of difference that is almost the same but not quite. Which is to say that the discourse of mimicry is constructed around an 'ambivalence', in order to be effective, mimicry must continually produce its slippage, its excess, its difference" (Bhabha, 86).

As apparent from the case studies related, the concerns here are situated within the context of settler colonies of the English empire. There is no intention to essentialise on the strategies and outcomes of colonisation nor to suggest the subjects of postcolonialism are applicable to all forms of domination prior to, and during self-governance. The concept of colonial mimicry, which is to be the general focus of

this paper, shall be examined in relation to Bhabha's propositions: for him mimicry is applicable to strategic domination of the 'colonial world'; and its effects, which he seems to suggest have taken their toll globally. My purpose in the essay is to examine the English language as a form of colonial mimicry. By reviewing how postcolonial critics and writers who use English see it, I hope the effects of colonial mimicry will be revealed as surpassing any concious use for strategic domination and present itself not at the center, but rather playing around, crossing paradigms and occassionaly showing itself through the little cracks in the proscribed structure

The Indian house dinner time scenario was described in order to take into serious consideration for whom the politics and notion of cultural colonialism through the use of the English language is problematic. This family described are immediate relations to the author. As far as economical success, they have been extremely successful by any standards. For an Indian family who have never lived in India, they seem relatively at ease with being Indian. The boy's fluency in his mothertongue is not up to standards, and his reluctance to eat mother's food, I imagine, is something any child aged thirteen or there abouts has antipathy towards particularly when he knows there is pizza lurking At An Outlet Near You. His bond to his grandfather is particularly interesting, for, despite the slight communication restrictions between them, and despite the old man's Indianess in every aspect, and adamant refusal to be anglicised in any aspect, the boy still insists in sleeping in his grandfather's room, even when his friends are over. English has become his language as much as pizza has become the symbol of universal cuisine.

Following on from Ngugi narrative, much the same could be said of the African peasantry under the colonial regime. More than an indifference towards the language of the master,

> They saw no necessary contradiction between belonging to their immediate nationality, to their multinational state alon the Berlin-drawn boundaries, and to Africa as a whole. These people happily spoke Wolof, Hausa, Yoruba, Ibo, Arabic, Amharic,...without this fact tearing the multinational states apart. No, the peasantry had no complexes about their languages and the cultures they carried! In fact when the peasantry and the working class were compelled by necessity or history to adopt the language of the master, they Africanised it...so totally as to have created new African languages, like Krio in Sierra Leone or Pidgin in Nigeria, that owed their identities to the syntax and rythems of African languages.
>
> (Ngugi, 448).

"Mimicry conceals no presence or identity behind its mask" (88). For Bhabha, the idea of mimesis holds profound revelations about the effects of colonisation on its subject. In place of what is seemingly palimpsestic, which Ngugi's story of his school days may reveal, of a 'presence Africaine' (ibid.), is far more complex. The lack, or absence of an 'original' identity and in its place is the irony of, "The desire to emerge as 'authentic' through mimicry – through a process of writing and repetition – is the final irony of partial representation" (ibid). This is the ambivalence of mimicry, a 'partial presence' which is both 'incomplete' and 'virtual'. For Ngugi, no where

better is this to be seen than in the world of the petty-bourgeois (bear with the rather long quotations but the idea trying to be revealed in this essay is as much in the discourse of the postcolonial writer as it is in the inescapable deferral of meaning within the texts):

> Because of its indeterminate economic position between the many contending classes, the petty-bourgeois develops a vacillating psychological make-up. Like a chameleon it takes on the colour if the main class with which it is in the closest touch and sympathy. It can be swept to activity by the masses at a time of revolutionary tide; or be driven to silence, fear, cynicism, withdrawal into self-contemplation, existensial anguish, or to collaboration with the powers-that-be at times of reactionary tides. In Africa this class has always oscillated between the imperialist bourgeoisie and its comprador neo-colonial ruling elements on the one hand, and the peasantry working class (the masses) on the other. This very lack of identity in its social and psychological make-up as a class was reflected in the very literature it produced...In literature as in politics it spoke as if its own identity was that of society as a whole.

(Ngugi, 447).

For Ngugi, they are guilty of high treason. For when African writers use English to represent the culture of its people, including that of the peasantry with such ease as if the very subject of the narrative was constituted within the English world, then some from of neo-colonialism is in act; the colonized has been transformed into a 'recognizable Other'. This lack of identity described by Ngugi, or the mask with no identity behind it put forth by Bhabha, is the embodiment of repetition bound within language where meaning through deferral becomes transformed. For Ngugi, it is relatively clear cut: the adaptation and use of the English language is the submission to perrenial enslavement. The African writer, the postcolonial critic, the cultural theorist in writing against colonialism using the medium of the dominant, in this case English, are creating a false discourse which defeats its own objective.

The virtues of mimicry, however, do not end there. For Bhabha, this minor trope really only begins to unravel itself completely, within (in Lacanian terms), the unconcious. There is a disruption of authority, a rupture in the discourse of the dominant that was completely unforseen by the colonizer where by appropriating the Other as almost the same but not quite, the subject which the dominant depends upon for his own positionality no longer becomes recognizable: "The menace of mimicry is its double vision which in disclosing the ambivalence of colonial discourse also disrupts its authority. And it is a double vision that is a result of what I've described as the partial representation/recognition of the colonial objects" (Bhabha, 88).

This will hopefully tie in but for now let us turn to the other perspective of English as the medium for postcolonial writers. Salman Rushdie, like Ngugi, is a writer in exile ironically settled in the sanctity of the present colonial powers of a type; the UK and the USA respectively. Although, hitherto, the concentration has been on east Africa in order to avoid essentializing on postcolonial experiences, it

is necessary in some ways to shift paradigms which are commensurable as a means to reveal a multiplicity of contradictions within the mimetic nature of the English language as part of one's postcolonial identity:

> How are subjects formed 'in-between', or in excess of, the 'parts' of difference (usually intoned as race/ class/ gender, etc.)? How do strategies of representation or empowerment come to be formulated in the competing claims of communities where, despite shared histories of deprivation and discrimination, the exchange of values, meanings and priorities may not always be collaborative and dialogical, but may be profoundly antagonistic, conflictual and even incommensurable?
> (Bhabha, 2).

In more than one way does Rushdie stand in direct opposition to Ngugi. The latter, is re/presented as a self-exiled Marxist, a hero to his people, and a man with a very strong message who uses literature as a political postcolonial tool to liberate the Third World from all the forces of domination. Rushdie, on the other hand, could not be a better example of the postmodern. His novels, like himself transcend the globe, literally defying gravity. Although he takes postcolonialism and neo-colonialism very seriously, Rushdie does not tie himself down to one side but positions himself as the culmination of something that is much older than the 'Age of Empire'. Quite simply put: interrelations.

In 'Babelian terms' (to make use of a wonderfully coined term by Bart-Moore Gilbert), Rushdie is a case example of the 'final irony of representation,' whereby the, 'truest eye may now belong to the migrant's double vision' (ibid. 5). What is being attempted is a discourse of the postcolonial identity, or absence of identity, through explaining how mimicry functions here. To do so, I will try and take it through step by step in juxtaposition with Rushdie, as he presents himself (the novelist, the postcolonialist, the migrant, the exile); how is represented (the great novelist, the postmodernist, the postcolonialist, the neo-colonialist, the traitor); and how his work presences itself (disjunct, liminal, interstial, hereandthere).

The immediate reaction from within the postcolonial paradigm, categorizes Rushdie as the 'complicit type' of postcolonialist. His embracement of the English language as more than just a part if his identity, but also, as a means of freeing the colonized puts him in direct opposition to Ngugi. In his own words, "To conquer English may be to complete the process of making ourselves free" (182). We shall come back to Rushdie's self-representation of himself in a moment, but for now, turn to his apparent 'complicit' disposedition which is also analogous to Bhabha's 'first stage' of colonial mimicry.

In this milieu, the emergence of mimicry is rather saddening, for the novelist is transformed and represented ironically as one of his own interdictory characters, by, his so-called 'own' people. Saladin, (from Midnight's Children), the 'chamcha' becomes Rushdie, the 'chamcha' who, in Rushdie's own definition (and here is the real irony!) is someone who, '...sucks up to powerful people, yes-man, a sychophant! 'The Empire', would not have lasted a week without such collaborators among the colonized people" (cited: Mishra & Hodge). One barely has to mention the author's name and immediately he is the great author of Satanic Verses, is already

considered a classic of 'English Literature' of our era, or he is the traitor of Islam...need I say more, except in both cases such opinions can only come from populist minds who have likely not read beyond the tabloid commentary never mind the novel, or in the latter stereotype, can be excused for the book was not even translated into an accessible language so they will just have to agree with Ayatollah Khomeini dead and gone and keep their guns raised until further notice.

Bhabha is similarly often criticized for his style of writing being only accessible to academic intellectuals and his own 'liminal space' denouncing him for his complicity with neo-colonial strategies through his use of 'western theory' and jargon. He also comes under attack for his choice of subject, which supposedly only refers to a minority (i.e. the hybrid productions of colonialism), and takes no account of the, 'material conditions', nor the 'exiled working class' of the colonial world (Graves, 1). Choice of jargon aside, such criticism as that of neglecting the majority of the colonial-world, the 'real' subordinates, really holds little validity. Rather, Bhabha's accountability of the rest must be envisaged through another contingency. For it is the antagonism towards Rushdie for example, that Bhabha's hybrid ties in with the disposition of the mass migrant population from the Third World and settlement in the First World; and/or also the idolization and selective accommodation by the west. These are constituents of the majority. Bhabha clearly states, this type of positionality within the 'Location of Culture': "The Western metropole must confront its postcolonial history, told by its influx of post-war migrants and refugees, as an indigenous or native narrative internal to its national identity" (Bhabha, 6).

Within a carriage on the tube where the only recognizable Anglo-Saxon something comes from the English announcements, from the predominant Muslim suburbs in London, from the duka-wallah invasion in Wembley; to the incenstual open markets in Camden Town, to the Italian chef in the Hare Krishna Restaurant on Soho Street; to the cocktail party in 'White' Northwood with talk of that pretty Indian, God of Small Things: the 'International collaborations', the 'critical comparitivism', and the 'aesthetic judgements', are, "...no longer found in homogenous structures but in the perspective of minorities" (ibid.). English may indeed be the medium; but whose English is it really? Or as Mr. 'Whiskey' Sisodra profoundly enunciates: "The trouble with the Engenglish is that their hiss hiss history happenend overseas, so they dodo don't know what it means" (cited: Bhabha, 6).

INTERLUDE

Metonymy: "an attribute or a cause or effect that signifies the thing". The definition proposed is taken from Roman Jakobson's essay, The Metaphoric and Metonymic Poles primarily part of a highly technical investigation on aphasia. According to Jakobson, "The development of discourse may take place along two different semantic lines; one topic may lead to another either through their similarity [metaphorically] or through their contiguity [metonymically]" (...).

This is a vital moment where hopefully, the lack of structure in this essay becomes understandable (at least for the author, if not for the reader which for now

will just have to do), in relation to all this badabing badaboom herethereeverwhere 'postpostism' stuff, if I may call it so. So let us pursue on step by step, and…take one step back.

Hence, what is on offer is no claim to truth, but only the real McCoy, which needs to be metaphorically named so, in order to revert to Jakobson. Previously, in the good old 'pre-postism' days, things looked so much more understandable and one reason it seems so, is because Jakobson and his Structuralist comrade proffered that all these complicated structures that make up this thing called life, could be understood in binary structures. Claude-Levi Strauss, particularly, stands guilty for professing a universal 'theory of culture' in, 'this and that' terms (i.e. binaries). Thus, nothing could escape explanation, because it could all be understood in terms of sharing underlying essences, no matter how far-fetched or abstract the connection. Even when immaculate exceptions were admitted, like honey, the rather mundane recognition denied any novelty or pleasure in its unique composition. For Structuralists, there was an identity, a presence behind everything: a structure.

This model just seems to defeat the point though, as in many ways Ngugi's extreme adversity towards English does. For it is the creations, the productions, the presentations, the petitions; and the recreations, the reproductions, the representations and the repetitions which we have to turn our focus to. These are the joys; these are the unique moments that life has to offer. Yes, we all have identities, and yes, we all suffer from identity crises, but what of it? It is what it stands in its moment of existence, what is without, not what is within, so that when Bhabha states: "Mimicry conceals no presence or identity behind its mask", it is not so much as literally a void, a vacuum, that I think is what is meant, but rather, a presence that belongs neither here nor there, or to be frustratingly tautological, both here and there.

This is the menace that everyone is upset with because we just can't seem to be able to tie it down for long enough. So, often enough, for those who accept the slippery dynamism in reconstructing the model, will put forth a model with, "…meaning which advances metonymy over metaphor, hybridity over purity, syncretism over difference, pluralism over essentialism or pantextualism, and disglossia over monoglossia" (Mishra & Hodge, 286), all of which ought to be given precedence over their antonymous other but often enough, it all gets siphoned, and the 'pure' stuff left over is packed into the barrel of a gun, and shot right back at where you shat, and splattered in your face, so that now I know you must be different because you stink of shit!

Hence, back to the 'Babelian Performance' whereby, for those who must take sides, then, "The menace of mimicry is its double vision which in disclosing the ambivalence of colonial discourse also disrupts its authority. And it is a double vision that is a result of what I've described as the partial representation/recognition of the colonial objects" (Bhabha, 88). But, why, one should ask, is there all this obsession with colonialism? Could we not say much the same for literature, or anthropology, or history, or navigation for that matter? For it is by bumping into one another (which unfortunately, in the event, we seem to become more obsessed with who's right and who's wrong, and who is going to take charge), it is through interaction and

who's wrong, and who is going to take charge), it is through interaction and exchange (usually on unequal terms), that the Portuguese were able to build a boat (and I use this example metonymically) strong enough to sail around the globe. It is the combination of the Arab lateen sail and the skills of the Portuguese that led to such possibilities as with all great works of humanity. Literature, which for Bhabha following Goethe (yet another example of creative invention, not innovation that comes though interaction), is manifested through 'cultural conflict', through war, dispute and domination, so that nations, for Goethe, "...could not return to their settled and independent life again without noticing they had learned many foreign ideas and ways, which they had unconsciously adopted, and come to feel here and there previously unrecognized spiritual and intellectual needs" (cited: Bhabha, 11). Unfortunately, once again, we are more obsessed with ourselves, so instead of what should be recognized and constituted as 'World Literature', becomes a "way in which cultures recognize themselves through the projection of 'Others'" (ibid. 12); a desired interdictor yet disavowed transformation takes place that creates a metonymy of presence, one that is almost the same but not quite.

In other words: the first point is to dominate; claim. So what is yours becomes mine: call this the material condition of colonialism. The next step is to maintain that domination so as to exploit and pillage as much as possible. To do so, brute force may initially be necessary but it is also physically diminishing for both sides. Moreover, brute force usually results in a response that is also brutally forceful, so really, it defeats the point. So, create a subject that is passive, submissive and subservient (I am aware of how simplified and how superficial such discourse is but it also serves a purpose in reflecting on the reference to Structuralism, particularly Strauss who comes across almost as self-flagellating having extensively observed and recorded every minute detail in his ethnographies and then essentialized it all in terms such as 'hot' and 'cold' societies!) i.e. civilize the barbarian. One's notion of civil can only come from what one considers to be civilized, i.e. Myself. And if they really are beyond redemption, well lets choose one and give him and give him a taste of what it feels like to be in control; but, not the way they went about controlling; but, what it feels like to have authority from our seat.

So, 'chamchas' were cajoled, chiefs chartered and Christianity chanted and, "Mimicry is, thus the sign of a double articulation; a complex strategy of reform, regulation and discipline, which 'appropriates' the Other as it visualizes power" (Bhabha, 86). Missions were encouraged and education was to be granted (to the selected few, recollecting Ngugi's account). And thus, Africa began to be civilized, the sub-continent to be tamed, and a feeling of homeliness, belonging, began to creep into some. The nostalgic cries lamented by Karen Blixen for her dog and servant, Daniel Dafoe unable no longer to tell where home is and Conrad, achieved the hardest of all: to stabilize the unstable and fix the image of that interdictory desire that everyone needs, to recreate the necessity for adventure; a transcendental signified value of Africa as the Heart of Darkness. Or would it be more appropriate to now call it the Hindrance of Development?

But the story does not end there; it only comes to a halt because we have a word limit to abide by. Hence, in many ways there may not be a difference between char-

acters such as Ngugi and Achebe, or Conrad and Rushdie, except one minor but important diff_rance, which reveals itself through one's positionality on either side of the fence, but even that is becoming more and more hazy all the time. As Rushdie puts it:

It may be that writers in my position, exiles or emigrants or expatriates, are haunted by some sense of loss, some urge to reclaim, to look back, even at the risk of being mutated into pillars of salt. But if we do look back, we must also do so in the knowledge –which gives rise to profound uncertainties –that out physical alienation from India almost inevitably means that we will not be capable of reclaiming precisely the thing that was lost; that we will in short, create fictions, not actual cities or villages, but invisible ones, imaginary homelands, Indias of the mind".

(Rushdie, 10)

References

1. **H.K. Bhabha, The Location of Culture, (Routledge, 1994).**
2. **J. Derrida, 'Structure, Sign and Play in the Discourse of Human Sciences', in D. Lodge ed. Modern Criticism and Theory- A Reader (Longman, 1988).**
3. **R. Jakobson, 'The Metaphoric and Metonymic Poles', in D. Lodge ed. Modern Criticism and Theory- A Reader (Longman, 1988).**
4. **B.M. Gilbert, Postcolonial Theory: Contexts, Practices, Politics, (Verso Publications, 1997).**
5. **B. Graves, "The Commitment to Theory" (http://landow.stg.brown.edu/post/poldiscourse/bhabha/bhabha3.html) 1998.**
6. **Krishnamurti, The First and Last Freedom (Harper & Row, 1975).**
7. **V. Mishra & B. Hodge, 'What is Post (-) Colonialism in, P. Williams & L. Chrisman eds. Colonial Discourse and Post-Colonial Theory- A Reader (Harvester Wheatsheaf, 1993).**
8. **Ngugi Wa'Thiongo, 'The Language of African Literature' in, P. Williams & L. Chrisman eds. Colonial Discourse and Post-Colonial Theory- A Reader (Harvester Wheatsheaf, 1993).**
9. **S. Rushdie, Imaginary Homelands (Granta Books, 1991).**

AboutThe Author

Dipesh Pabari is an anthropologist in the broadest sense of the word. He swings from research to teaching to make a living. Between the two professions, he has managed to publish poetry, short stories , produce plays, work in the film industry and conduct ethnographic research. He hopes one day to settle and develop his passion for writing.

Flight From Fate

By Evans Kinyua

We all know how we Kenyans cover up things: we show faces designed to imply who we think we should be, rather than who we are. Evans Kinyua has a sterling CV, one that would give him access to the highest Kengeles and Tamambo circles if he wanted it.

Now, in order to be a successful member of the Nairobi middle classes, you delete your shags. You may speak charmingly about your coffee farm in Meru (We had a farm…); quaintly about Nguwraiows. You become the person Lenana told you to be.

In the process you become a one dimensional person with a trophy wife and pretentious children. You quote Time Magazine and Newsweek, and think that Uhuru Kenyatta (because he has the right accent) is right for Kenya. You think people are poor because they are lazy. You are unable to cope up with any original thoughts ideas or solutions because you are too busy holding back the skeletons in your cupboard. Wannabes are the most unoriginal people in the world.

On the surface, Flight From Fate is a lyrically written memoir about Kinyua's life. But it is clear, from the beginning that Kinyua is out to dispense with the gentle mythologies we carry about life in Kenya. It is a testament to the kind of violence meted out in Kenya in the name of climbing-up-the-ladder-of-progress.

Kinyua is brutally honest about his background. His father, a hard-line Christian does not allow the children to play. They work, from dawn till dusk, backbreaking labour working on their fields. Not because they are poor: these are coffee boom days, and his mother is a schoolteacher. They work because he sees his wife and children as free labour His patriarchy is sanctioned by GOD and THE CHURCH. Any diversions from the Mzee's rigid schedules meant beatings of the sort usually associated with Administration policemen. Kinyua rebels by eating soil. He eats so much he spends months in and out of hospitals, with all kinds of ailments and worms.

Kinyua excels in primary school and goes to Lenana; and we are briefly relieved of the tension, thinking…ahhhhh! Salvation! Apana. Lenana is more of the same. To qualify, to become a Lenana Laibon, Kinyua needs his cultural limbs broken and reset; and the school is full of people who are only to happy to beat his accent out of him; to beat his manners out of him; or just to beat him to practice the general art of beating, which seems to need much practice.

Kinyua's mother dies, possibly partly out of sheer exhaustion; his elder brothers leave him and rarely visits; and his younger brothers are treated like animals by his father. Eventually Kinyua makes his way into the job market, encounters the sort of usual mzungu and muhindi discriminations that many in Nairobi from the corporate sector are familiar with.

After reading his beautifully written and unflinching memoir, it is hard to disagree. Read it, buy it. It is about all of us.

Reviewed by Binyavanga Wainaina, April 2004

THE UNBEARABLE HEAVINESS OF COMFORT

By Rasna Warah

I was late, as usual.

I could see Wendy, pacing up and down her verandah, mumbling, "That Maya let me down again."

But I couldn't this time. Not after all that happened. I had to put on my dinner party face and just go.

I was reluctant because I knew the kind of guests Wendy invited -- UN-types (loud cars, loads of money), her Karengata crowd (the gin-and-tonic types whose grandparents all had farms in Naivasha or Laikipia). Alice and I were invariably the only two "coloured" people invited, and Alice never went to these dos, so I ended being the ambassador for an entire race – two races, actually. It was a heavy assignment, especially for someone like me, who did not feel like I belonged anywhere, not quite exile, not quite refugee, just something in between.

But what to wear? Punjabi salwar kameez with Rajasthani earings? No, too ethnic. Jeans and a Tinga Tinga T-shirt? Might do with the NGO crowd, but not with this one. Embroidered Nigerian robe with Ashanti earings? Too pseudo-ethnic. (Besides I can never figure out how to tie the turban.) Fusion? Yes. OK, so it's going to be Afghan shirt (embroidered by Afghan women during the Taliban regime, nice conversation piece), African Heritage porcupine earings (never cease to fascinate the UN crowd, except the ones working for UNEP, who inadvertently ask if porcupine is an endangered species), black trousers and Masai beaded sandals. Perfect.

I could smell the sweat on my armpits, but it was too late to shower. Besides, I wasn't on a date. I'd just have to splash on the Opium and stay outdoors as much as possible. Lipstick, mascara. I'm done.

Driving to Wendy's fills me with morbid fear. She lived on those lonely lanes in Karen, surrounded by acres of virgin land, untilled, untamed. At last count she had at least 78 species of indigenous trees and plants in her so-called garden. And I had to get there through the dreaded Ngong Road, a haven for carjackers, corrupt police officers and drunk matatu drivers. I said a quiet prayer as I got into my battered Toyota.

I could feel the Nairobi night chill and wished I'd carried a shawl. It was mid-June, the beginning of the cold season, when Nairobi and the highlands become foggy and dull. But tonight the sky was unusually clear. A full moon was visible right above the gentle, breast-like slopes of the Ngong Hills. My heart skipped a beat. Full moon nights, in my experience, were best spent at home. The last time I had gone out on a full moon I had bumped into Sunil and his twenty-something America-returned girlfriend and public relations manager, Dipti. It was bad enough seeing my ex-husband happy with another woman, but Alice had gone and made it worse.

"Not even divorced six months and out grazing already, huh?" she'd quipped in her usual acidic tone of voice, the one she uses when she's mad, which is ninety-nine per cent of the time. Sunil and Dipti made a quick exit and I haven't seen them since.

It wasn't that I hadn't got over my divorce. I wanted it more than Sunil did. It was just that when the papers finally came through, an odd melancholy took me over, as if an old friend had just died. Sometimes it felt as if someone had stolen a piece of my brain, the part where memories are stored, and left just tiny bits behind, so that all my memories appeared like incomplete jigsaw puzzles. When did we stop loving each other? I couldn't recall. I couldn't even remember the exact moment we decided to get married. And why didn't we have children? Amnesia.

I couldn't blame Dipti for falling for Sunil either, because he was the kind of man who made women want to take care of him. He was handsome, in an Indian film star kind of way. Sad, tragic eyes, nice build and a permanent 5 o'clock shadow. Problem was, like the film stars, he also wanted women to adore him. Which is probably why he recruited Dipti as his public relations manager. Dipti didn't talk, she exclaimed. She never used everyday adjectives, such as "good" or "bad". Things were either "fabulous" or "disgusting. She didn't just love Sunil, she worshipped him.

There were four cars in the parking lot when I arrived. Always a good indicator of the type of people who might be there, in Nairobi anyway. Let's see, a Pajero with diplomatic licence plate, two Landrovers, a Volkswagon beetle with one light missing. Oh, so Alice did make it after all.

I entered the house through the kitchen door in the back. "Ah our Indian friend," said a voice from behind the refrigerator. It was Tom, in his signature knee-length shorts and T-shirt.

"Kenyan actually," I replied.

"Yeah, but once an Indian, always an Indian, right?" he chuckled, mocking me with a put-on Peter Sellers Indian accent.

"I don't know Tom. My ancestors came from Lahore, which I believe is now in Pakistan. So I don't know what that makes me."

"Oh let's not quibble. Come in and have a drink. What will it be? Vodka?"

"Yes, please, and don't forget the slice of lemon."

I made my way to the verandah. A scent of jasmine hung in the air.

Alice saw me first. "Maya!," she exclaimed. "We were missing you."

Her enthusiasm was infectious. I suddenly felt better. She looked radiant, her black skin illuminated against the white and blue dress she was wearing. She was one of those women who stood out in a crowd, not because she was exceptionally beautiful, but because she dared to display her face and body as if they were pieces of art. To emphasise her long slender neck and chiselled cheekbones, she had shaved off her hair. Her perfectly-shaped bald head, which she highlighted with large cow bone earings and a Turkana beaded necklace, was often construed as a political statement. I knew that the main reason she had decided to do away with her hair was because she didn't have the patience for hair-straightening perms and weaves.

"Meet Owino, my artist friend," she said, as a tall, rather youngish looking man approached us.

"Where do you pick up these guys Alice," I muttered. "In art galleries?"

"Oh don't be so cynical. He's brilliant. Won a scholarship to the States last year, didn't you Owino?"

Owino was now standing close enough so I could smell the beer that he had probably been drinking since that afternoon."

"Oh, so you're Maya," he said, and swaggered off to get another drink.

From the corner of my eye, I could see Giselle, speaking animatedly to a youngish looking blonde guy. It suddenly struck me that if Wendy had had a daughter, she might have looked exactly like Giselle – tight bony body, small breasts, dark wavy hair, angular face and green eyes. I had only met Giselle once before, in the first few weeks of her arrival in Kenya, when she was staying in Wendy's guest house in the garden -- the same guest house that became a lover's den when Wendy was out at the neighbourhood association meetings. Then, Wendy had described Giselle as "a lovely young French woman who's rented the guest house while she looks for a job." I wondered what she would call her now. La pute?

Tom was standing next to the bar, facing a man whose face I could not see. Wendy hadn't told him what she knew. I wondered if she would ever tell him. Like many women, she probably thought confronting an adulterous spouse made the adultery more real, less manageable. "I'll talk to him in my own time," she'd said.

"I'm not ready yet."

"Alice, where's Wendy?" I asked.

"In the bathroom. Said she had to change or something."

I hadn't told Alice about my conversation with Wendy. You never knew when she might blurt out confidential information. She often thought nothing of it, but I had seen many relationships shattered by her seemingly casual approach to secrets.

"Don't you want to know about Owino?," she asked, with a slightly wounded look on her face.

"Alice, we've been through this before. And I know why you're here. Probably because the booze ran out in your place and he couldn't afford to take you out. Am I right? Otherwise you'd never come to a mzungu party."

"Oh come on Maya, Wendy may be a mzungu but she is my friend. I had to come."

I thought of the last time Alice had come to one of Wendy's dinners and a chill went through my spine. Not only had she insulted everyone, but she went home with the guy she had insulted the most – a young Dutch aid worker, who for some reason resigned from his job soon after. Last I heard, he was happily married in Amsterdam and was expecting his first child.

"Okay, but just behave, alright?"

There were people at the main door and Tom had gone to let them in. I couldn't believe my eyes. It was Sunil, with a glowing Dipti in his arm. I couldn't imagine why Wendy would do this to me.

"Hello Maya," said Sunil, stretching his right hand towards me. Did he really expect a handshake?

"Hello Dipti" I said, ignoring the hand.

"How nice to see you," she said, faking a smile. She had a new haircut, cropped close to her head. I could see she had put on weight – or was that a pregnancy under her loose kurta?

"I didn't know you'd be here," he said. "Tom invited us this afternoon when we bumped into him at Kengele's."

I could see now why I had never taken to Tom. He had a mean streak, which

he disguised as humour. He thought he could get away with being rude just by hiding behind the laughter, which invariable followed a malicious remark or inconsiderate behaviour.

Just then Wendy appeared, regal in a purple silk skirt and spaghetti straps top, hair up, and a tinge of pink lipstick. At 42, Wendy still had the figure of a girl. The only tell-tale signs of age were the deep wrinkles around her mouth and a slightly receding hairline, which made her long face look even longer. They made an odd couple, Tom and her. If she was Princess Anne, he was Andy Capp. In the seven years I had known the couple, I had never seen Tom without shorts, or without a Tusker beer in his hand. Luckily, he had nice legs, muscular with tufts of blonde hair peeking out of deeply tanned skin, so the shorts were bearable.

"Thank god you're here," she said, as she reached out to hug me. "I needed someone in my patch tonight." I took her aside into the living room so we could talk.

I noticed that Alice was making leopard-like advances towards Sunil and Dipti, who quickly retreated to the far corner of the verandah to escape.

"How could Tom do this?" I was almost in tears.

"I'm so sorry Maya. He only told me about it this afternoon, and I didn't want to alarm you. Dinner's almost ready. We can talk later, okay?" she said as she rushed off to the kitchen.

"Okay."

From the corner of my eye, I could see that Sunil and Dipti were talking quietly to each other, ignoring everyone else.

I decided then to face my demons. I would walk to the verandah and have a perfectly civilised conversation with my ex and his girlfriend.

"How have you been?" Sunil looked genuinely concerned, as I approached them.

"Oh very busy. You know the new restaurant in the Mall, well, they're expanding and want me to do the interiors. Life's been good."

"I'm glad. I just thought I should be the first to tell you. Dipti and I are getting married. Next month."

No, Sunil, I thought to myself, I really didn't want to know that piece of information.

"Congratulations. Hope you know how to cook parathas and saag Dipti. Sunil's a real Punjabi. Can't do without home cooking dripping in ghee."

I surprised myself. How did I get so civil?

"Oh don't worry, I've been taking lessons from his mother. Of course, he still misses your biryani." She seemed almost apologetic. I knew that look. I knew where it came from. Sunil relished pitting women against each other. But it still surprised me that he would use my biryani against Dipti. I mean, how low can one get?

"Anyway, we just popped in for a quick drink," said Sunil. "We'll be on our way. Have to go to another function in town."

"Dinner's ready," Wendy shouted from the kitchen, just as they were leaving. "Sunil, Dipti, you can't leave without eating."

"No, we're invited for dinner somewhere else. But we'll pop in again, soon." Wendy left the kitchen to let them out. And they were gone.

The faceless man whom I had seen talking to Tom was now standing besides me. "Hi, I'm Oscar," he said in a deep German accent.

"I don't think we've been introduced," I said. "I'm Maya?"

"I know," he said, with a slight flirtatious smile. "I heard your friend over there shout your name out when you walked in."

"Oh Alice, she really must learn to whisper."

The young blonde guy approached us.

"Hi. I'm Kevin, I work for the UN," he said in a slightly contaminated British accent.

"Oh, you must be the guy with the big Pajero out front," quipped Alice.

"Actually I just bought it last week. Quite cheap, really. Twelve thousand dollars, from a friend who was leaving."

"You mean you had twelve thousand dollars saved up? Aren't you lucky." Alice had started again. I knew this was not going anywhere pretty.

"Which agency?," I asked, trying to change the topic.

"WFP, I work in the information section."

"So I take it you've just arrived in Kenya," I quickly asked, hoping to keep Alice out of the conversation.

"Yeah, two-months old and loving every minute of it."

I knew this was Alice's cue to begin her diatribe. "And what part do you love the most, the servants or the weather?", she asked in a slightly put-on upper class British accent.

"Give him a break, Alice," Wendy interjected. "Kevin's the son of old friends of Tom. They lived in Kenya years ago. Kevin was born here, but they left for England when he was ten. He's delighted to be back, aren't you Kevin?"

"Yes, actually I've been dreaming about it for years."

I was glad Wendy had intervened, although I could see that it was only a temporary setback for Alice. No-one could stop her when she started, and someone always left in tears. In journalistic circles she was known as "Acid Alice", and with good reason. Her weekly column was called "Below the Belt".

"Yes, that's what that Italian woman in Laikipia, what's her name, did, and then wrote a book about how she dreamt of Africa, and then came, and then never left, even after Africa ended up killing all the men in her life, including her son."

"Well, that's Africa for you," I said, "trying to ease the tension. "Sort of like Hotel California."

"Hotel what?" Wendy asked.

"You know, the Eagles song, the one from which you can check out any time but you can never leave? Many people come to Africa and for some reason can't leave. My ancestors, for instance. And you."

"Who are the Eagles?" asked Wendy, and for the first time, I felt ashamed of calling her my friend. Truth is, she really didn't know. It was as if she had left all the remnants of Western popular culture behind in England. In this – and only this -- she reminded me of those expatriates you meet at Gypsy or Florida 2000, the type who decide to give up all trappings of Western civilisation – television, toasters, heaters and even daily newspapers, just because they're in Africa. So they don't get to know what's happening in the world, or in Nairobi, the whole time they are here, and then look clueless at parties when someone talks about Goldenberg or the matatu strike in the city. Of course, Wendy never gave up Western home comforts – she had a top of the range TV and toaster – but she did seem somehow stuck in a time warp when it came to music.

Alice was humming the tune from the Eagles song -- "Mirrors on the ceiling, they drink champagne on ice, we are all just prisoners here, of our own device. And in the master's chambers, they've gathered for the feast, they stab it with their stealing eyes, but they just can't kill the beast." She was looking directly at Tom.

I wondered if she knew. Alice had a sixth sense that made most people nervous, including me, because her intuition often became the weapon with which she took small stabs at people, committed little murders. It wasn't as if she was deliberately cruel; just tactless, and quite often justifiably so. But I knew that behind that harsh exterior lay a vulnerable woman who "at three o'clock in the morning of her soul," as she put it, could cry herself a river, and often did.

She was also incredibly loyal. That is why, even though Wendy's white Kenyan suburban lifestyle represented everything that Alice despised, Alice never picked on her. In this case, the friendship was more important than the political statement. Besides, in Alice's eyes, Wendy couldn't help who she was – she was born into it, and her people had somehow paid the price for staying. They may have continued having gin-and-tonics on the verandah at sunset, but their demeanor, their attitude reeked of guilt, which was good enough for Alice.

I often wondered what she really felt about Kenyan Asians. In school, when some of the other girls once derogatively called me a muhindi, Alice gave them a long lecture on race relations in Kenya. "I don't see you saying nasty things about mzungus," she'd said. "And they're the ones who raped this country. Why pick on just the muhindis? They wouldn't even be here if it wasn't for the mzungus." That was the last time anyone picked on me in school. I guess it was also the moment that sealed our friendship.

It wasn't as if Alice didn't harbour stereotypes of her own. I had often heard her derogatively refer to expatriates as "backpackers". "Look at them," she'd say, "they're here because being white is enough to get you them best tables at restaurant, the best jobs and the most beautiful women." She particularly hated the aid workers, UN staff and others in the so-called "development business", supposedly here to develop the country, but who were only interested in their own career development. "Frauds", she called them, "who were living a life they could only dream of having back home." She hated them for being here, but she hated Kenyans more for tolerating them. "Who's saving who?" she would ask. "Are they saving us or are we saving them from the dull life of boredom and loneliness that they are escaping from in Europe?" In Alice's eyes, the development business only attracted three types of people – missionaries, mercenaries or misfits, and all three types were represented in equal numbers in Kenya.

"I do see Alice's point," whispered Oscar, leaning towards me. "I myself am quite surprised at the level of arrogance and ignorance among the UN crowd here in Nairobi."

"And what are you doing here, a German in Kenya?", I asked. "You don't look like a tourist."

"Actually, I'm an engineer, working with a German-funded NGO."

"Oh, and that makes you a better person?"

"No, just different. And what do you do for a living?"

"I'm an interior designer, well, sort of. You could say I help people choose fabric and furniture."

"Really? Any people I know?"

"Well my last big job was the Hotel Royale. You know it? But otherwise, it's mostly restaurants and private homes. But I'm not very popular. Most of my clients think I'm too under-stated and have poor taste, literally. Can't figure out why I pick calico over velvet, or why the Turkish rug is preferable to wall-to-wall carpeting, particularly in Africa."

He laughed. I noticed a gap between his top front teeth. If he was a woman, he'd be considered extremely sexy among some tribes in Kenya. Come to think of it, he was sexy. Big blue eyes, the colour of the sea in Watamu, and a slightly crooked nose. Dark hair in need of a haircut, falling over one side of his forehead.

"Please come and eat," announced Wendy. We all made our way to the dining area.

Dinners at Wendy's were always a proper affair. Her dining table was stately with enough room to host a football team, or accommodate unexpected guests such as Owino -- unlike my dinners, where most guests ended up eating while standing or sitting on the floor. There were always wine glasses and silver cutlery and a snow white table cloth and napkins wrapped in pretty silver rings. I almost half-expected an elderly Kamande (Karen Blixen's cook) to emerge from the kitchen with a bowl of soup, asking, "More memsahib?"

This was the Wendy that I didn't know. The one with perfectly trained house-help and linen from Laura Ashley. Complete stranger to the Wendy who knocked on my door two weeks ago, bruised and wounded, eyes swollen, spirit broken.

Mercifully, dinner went without any incident. I noticed that Wendy had not said a word to Giselle. Tom and Owino, both equally drunk, were having a typically Kenyan dinner conversation – arguing about whether President Moi was good or bad for the country. I found it best to keep out of such conversations because no-one won in the end. If you supported Moi, you were a bastard, or ill-informed; if you didn't, you were no better than a wimp or an accomplice to a crime – you saw it happen and had done nothing to prevent it.

We moved over to the verandah for coffee. I realised I had not exchanged a single word with Giselle. I walked up and introduced myself.

"I think I've heard about you. Aren't you the one who designed this house?" she asked, in a slightly Americanised French accent.

"Actually we've met briefly, when you were still living in the guest house. Remember, about six months ago? Anyway, this house was a joint effort between me and Wendy. Wendy and I have been friends since. I guess you could say the house brought us together. Do you like it?"

"Well it's different from most houses I've been to since I came. None of that glitzy fake chandeliers and stuff. I like the African-ness of the place. A mix of Zanzibar and Morocco. Very nice."

"Thank you. Tom wanted the safari look, but it's so overdone and somehow doesn't provide the comfort needed in a home. So how do you know Wendy and…Tom?" I asked, hoping she wouldn't notice the irony in my voice.

"Oh Tom and I met in the Mara. He was the water engineer, and I was the French tourist whose hotel room had a plumbing problem."

"I didn't know Tom was also a plumber." Now the sarcasm was obvious. I had to change the topic.

"When do you leave?"

"Actually, I'm not leaving. I'm working with the UN now. What do they call it, ah yes, a consultancy, for six months, to organise a conference. A friend who works there offered it to me."

"Wish I was so lucky. I was in Paris last year, and Yves Saint Laurent didn't even want to see me."

She laughed. This made me nervous. It meant she could laugh at herself, which meant she was human and smart, and therefore, in my book, likeable. Not a good sign. Any woman who initiated a fling with a married man cannot be likeable. So what was I to say to Wendy, who had specifically instructed me to make an assessment of Giselle? Intelligent girl with a sense of humour, or scheming witch with no sense of morality?

"There is another reason why I'm here," she said. "I'm in love."

"Really?" I said, putting on the best poker-face I could summon. "And who is the lucky man? Kevin?"

"No, actually, it's someone else. It's a bit complicated. I'd rather not talk about it right now. He's just the best thing that's happened to me in a long time."

I decided then that I would not tell Wendy this bit of information. Sometimes, it's the little details that can kill you, not the big truths. For instance, it's enough to know that someone has died, not how they died, what their last words were, how they gasped for their last breath, or what they smelled like when the air around them grew still and the soul departed. I know, because even now, ten years after Papaji died, the image that has stayed with me is of him lying in bed, eyes open, as if staring at the ceiling. It took us at least 45 minutes to realise he was dead. If only I had not seen him like that, it might have made his passing away easier to take.

I walked over to the others, who had gathered in a circle around the fireplace, probably the only fireplace in the world that was built into a verandah. Tom's idea of course. No point being in Africa if you can't be outdoors, and no point freezing while you're out there. That's why Tom always wore a heavy pair of knee-length socks with his shorts. Made perfect sense. The best of both worlds.

Tom wasn't alone. Each and every one of us in the room was straddling many worlds, but didn't know which world defined us, made us who we are. Yet, these worlds, which brought us together, also threatened to tear us apart.

I often wondered why Wendy, the quintessential English rose, had married the Tom, the Kenyan cowboy who hadn't ever set foot in England except when he went there for the first time to wed Wendy. Why Wendy endured the chaos and confusion of Nairobi when she could have the unending predictability and order of England. Or why Alice agonised so much about race, yet spent much most of her time with people who were neither African nor black. I also wondered why I had ended up with this motley crowd of friends when nothing in my background had prepared me for it. Maybe it was because we secretly suspected that we didn't belong to each other that we tried so hard to stay together. Sort of like a bad but enduring marriage.

I could see that Wendy was slightly drunk, and was stroking Kevin's back in a half-flirting, half-motherly way. Giselle was in the garden/forest smoking a cigarette. Tom and Owino were still discussing the KANU government, Owino gesturing wildly, his voice almost quivering. Obviously an opposition supporter. Alice was going through Tom's CD collection, apparently looking to change the music.

"Can we stop listening to this Out of Africa shit?" she shouted. "Don't you have any Miriam Makeba or Gidi Gidi Maji Maji?" No-one responded, so she proceeded to turn the drawer of CD's upside down, in the end settling for Salif Keita.

"I can't stand pretentious nostalgia in music," she said, walking towards me. "If I hear the theme music from Out of Africa once more I'm going to throw up."

"Music is music Alice," I said. "Not everything is political, you know? Just take it for what it is, good music."

"Everything is political, Maya", she answered. "Everything."

"I agree," said Oscar as he sidled up next to me. "Nothing in life is without a political dimension."

Oscar was now standing so close to me that I could smell his after-shave, a musky scent. The vodka must have got to me because I suddenly became aware of his maleness, an unmistakable quality that only men who know they are desirable carry around. I suddenly felt a need to touch him.

I looked up to see if he had noticed. His deep blue eyes were looking directly at mine. I felt a shudder in the pit of my stomach. There was an intensity there that I had not seen in a long time. It was as if he could see right through me.

"Would you mind if I said something?" I asked. I knew the vodka was acting up, but it didn't seem to matter at this point. Oscar was an expatriate and I would probably never see him again.

"Sure."

"You have beautiful eyes."

"So do you." His face was impassive, but I detected a slight smile.

"No, I mean really beautiful, like they could drown an ocean."

My hands were now almost touching his. I made a quick scan of the room. The change of music had clearly changed the mood and tempo of the party and everyone was now dancing. This was not like me. Flirting so obviously. What was wrong with me?

His hands were now in mine.

"Come on," he said. "Over there, in the garden."

I hoped no-one would notice us walking towards the gigantic jacaranda in her forest/garden. I'm not sure who kissed who first. Our lips just fell on each others. His were soft and sweet. His tongue was gently exploring my mouth, my tongue responding in kind. The deep yet tender thrust of his tongue into my eager mouth made me want to cry. I couldn't remember the last time I had been kissed like this. Sunil fumbled with my mouth, as he fumbled with everything else. Most of the time, I didn't feel anything. I guess he didn't either or we'd still be together. It was like getting off at the wrong station, and waiting for the next train, so you could go to where you really want to be. We were both waiting at the wrong station, but pretending that we had arrived at our destination.

His lips were now on my neck, making their way to my breasts. At that moment, it didn't matter that we were under a jacaranda tree in a friend's garden, or that I didn't even know his last name or his phone number. All that mattered was that my body craved his.

"We have to stop Oscar," I whispered, hoping he'd say no.

"I guess you're right. Sorry."

"No, don't be sorry. That was wonderful. In fact, it was more than wonderful. Come on, let's go."

I could see Wendy waving from the verandah. We had obviously not been good at camouflage. She and Alice were in the corner, whispering. I could just imagine what they were saying.

Alice came up to me first. "So, did you get any?"

"Any what?"

"Oh come on stop pretending. Your lipstick is all smudged."

Wendy was glaring at me.

"How could you, Maya?" whispered Wendy. "He's married, with a wife and child living in Munich. You know what I've been through and you go and do the same to another woman!" Luckily, Oscar had quickly made his way to the bathroom, so was not within earshot.

"Calm down Wendy. It was only a kiss. Nothing else happened. But if you must know, I don't regret it. I only kissed the man, I didn't propose. It's okay if he's married. Really. We'll probably never see each other again." I knew I was lying. No-one gets kissed like that and then never tries to see the kisser again.

"Just be careful. I don't want you to get hurt."

"I'm almost 40, Wendy, not 16. I can handle this, okay?"

"Come with me to the kitchen. I think I need a brandy."

Wendy's loyal maid, whose name I had never figured out, was washing the dishes. In all the years I had been to Wendy's house, "the maid" had been a constant feature, ever-smiling, never saying a word. Always discretely disappearing when guests arrived.

"You can do this in the morning," Wendy gestured to the maid. "Thank you and goodnight."

"The maid" left quietly through the back door.

"I have an uncontrollable urge to confront Giselle," Wendy whispered, pouring herself a large shot of Remi Martin.

"Why? Remember what I told you when you came to my house two Sundays ago? Don't blame the other woman. And don't cling and plead. If he wants to go, let him go. But being a man, he'll probably never leave you for another woman. Men don't usually take such risks. It's too scary. Women are natural risk-takers because they know they can survive. So, the decision is really yours. You can either live with it and hope he gets over it, or leave him before this thing consumes you."

"Where do I go? Back to England? I have no job, no skills. And what about Michael?"

Michael was Tom and Wendy's 12 year-old son, who was safely tucked away in a British boarding school.

"To be honest, I really don't think you're ready for a separation Wendy. Not yet. Giselle is a young, naïve French woman, who thinks she discovered Kenya through Tom and is confusing her love for the country with her love for Tom. She'll get over it soon enough, and Tom will get over her. The problem is not Giselle. The real issue is, do you want to continue with your marriage. Is it worth it? But that's a question only you can answer, not me."

I surprised myself with this little piece on insight. Where did it come from, I wondered. But then, it wasn't difficult to figure out. I had seen enough young white women arrive in Africa, falling madly in love and then leaving as suddenly as they had arrived, but with their hearts broken and their dreams shattered. Alice called them "the women who love Africa more than they love themselves".

Alice had spent a lifetime studying these women. For her, Kenya was a favourite destination for these women because it was only in Kenya that they could choose which world they wanted to belong to. "If they wanted," she wrote in one of her weekly columns, "they could pretend they were in Karen Blixen's Africa -- wild and unpredictable, but one that could be tamed and domesticated, if they had the patience. Or they could go completely native, like those crazy Swedes who marry Masai men and live in manyattas, and then one day, pack their bags and leave to write a book entitled 'My Life with the Masai', hoping some Hollywood moghul will buy the rights to make it into a film. If they had the means, they could also pretend they were not really in the country, like those UN expatriates who only hang out in the posh Village Market and live in Muthaiga, throwing dinners only for each other, and only interacting with those locals who they hire as nannies or gardeners."

In Alice's book, Giselle probably fell into the first category of expatriates. Tom was a challenge, as was Kenya, and if she could have him, she could have the country too. Sort of like what Wendy herself did fourteen years ago. The difference was that Wendy quickly learned that the "idea" of Africa was more appealing than the place itself. She knew, like the rest of us, that one encounter with a reckless matatu driver or a corrupt police officer was enough to kill all the romantic feelings you might harbour about the place. If that didn't do it, then daily living will. Like getting a telephone line two years after you applied for it, or not having water in your tap when mudslides clog up the one dam supplying water to the whole city, or the constant fear of getting robbed every time you get into your car.

Wendy did not respond. She knew, as I did, that she didn't want a solution. She just wanted to be heard. And I was one of the few people she could talk to you. I guess it was because in her eyes I was already a damaged, flawed person, so I was in no position to judge her. Even though she never once said it, I know that she felt "safe" with me because I was both divorced and childless. This meant I could never claim to be successful in either marriage or motherhood, two roles she cherished more than any other.

"Maybe you should move back to England for a while," I said. "You may even enjoy it."

"I can't. I don't know how to any more."

"Oh come on, how difficult is it to operate a washing machine? And even I got to learn the names of all the underground stations within a week," I said, slightly irritated. "Besides, Tom makes enough money to support you. Just go!"

My anger caught me by surprise. I guess I envied her for having the choice of leaving. I was stuck here, not because I loved Nairobi, but just because I had nowhere else to go, not even my ancestral land. The truth is, I hated Nairobi. I hated the fakeness of my life, my pretentious clients, and their even-more pretentious homes. It all seemed so surreal, considering we lived in the slum capital of Africa. We measured our lives with the level of comforts we could enjoy. We envied each other over things like who had the best gardener, the best cook, the best furniture.

What I hated most of all was being an Indian in Africa, or what they called "an Asian". I mean, what the hell were my ancestors thinking? Was life in Lahore so unbearable that they took the first opportunity to get out, even if the place they were going to was one few had ventured into before? And when they got here, to build the railway, or whatever else the colonial government wanted them to do, didn't they worry about being eaten alive by mosquitoes or lions or dying from malaria or dysentry? Didn't they miss the food, the music and the culture they left behind? I mean, why did they stay after their contract expired and not leave like the others? On the other hand, maybe being in Africa at that time was a blessing. What might

have been their fate if they were still there during the partition? Would they have died, like millions of others, while trying to cross the border into India?

"Go where?" It was Alice. Funny how she always dropped into conversations just when something life-altering was being said.

She noticed that her presence had made us both uncomfortable. "I had to get away from Owino. It's funny how a few drinks can make even the most gorgeous man look unbearably ugly."

"Anyway, I have something important to tell you. I need your advice."

I couldn't imagine Alice wanting anyone's advice. She was always so sure of herself, or appeared to be, I couldn't imagine what it might be.

"I've got a job in Washington. Africawatch, Communication Officer. Pays 30,000 dollars plus benefits. I can't say no, can I? I mean what do I earn here, not even a quarter of that amount, and I don't even get entertainment allowance."

"Looks like you've already made up your mind. When do you leave?" I couldn't imagine Alice in the U.S., with all those stoic faces on the train, wearing a winter jacket for eight months of the year, unable to stand out in a crowd, except for her colour, anonymous, alone – and cold.

"In two weeks. I have to book the ticket tomorrow. But I'm scared. What if I can't stand it?"

"Well, it will be an experience. If it's unbearable, you can always come back."

"I don't know. Somehow, I feel as if I am betraying my country. I can't leave like everyone else. I feel like a sellout, like I didn't give it a chance, and ran to the first country that accepted a black African woman with half a brain."

"Let's celebrate." Wendy had poured three stiff brandies into her "special" crystal glasses, the ones she only takes out for royalty. "Tonight, we will celebrate freedom."

"What freedom?" I asked.

"Come on, let's go. I have an announcement to make."

There was an awkward silence in the living room. Owino was fast asleep on the sofa. Tom and Giselle were in the verandah, silently staring at the night sky. Kevin was going through Wendy's Africana book collection. Oscar was sitting quietly in the corner, looking slightly nervous.

"Ladies and gentlemen, I have an announcement to make," said Wendy. She had obviously had too much to drink.

"Tom, you might want to bring Giselle in here." Oh no, I thought, she's gone bonkers.

"Tom, I am leaving you and going back to England. Thank you for marrying me, and giving me an opportunity to enjoy this wonderful country. But I'm afraid I have to let you go."

Oscar and Kevin were fumbling with their car keys, ready to leave.

"On no, you don't." Wendy moved to push them back into their chairs. Owino was still asleep.

"Oscar, I am so glad you met Maya. She is a lovely person, but slightly inhibited. She hasn't had sex in over five years. I hope you will do the honours. And Kevin, please don't think you're doing Africans a favour by being here. If anything, they're doing you a favour by allowing you to live here in luxury while they wallow in poverty."

Alice had a glint of triumph in her eyes, obviously pleased that her political brain-washing of Wendy had worked.

"Oh, and I do have another announcement to make. Alice is going to Washington D.C.. We will miss her, but America needs her more. Who else, but Alice, can tell Americans what the world really thinks of them. Now she can do it in their own country instead of blasting them here through her column. "

"Wendy, I think it's time for you to go to bed. Thanks everyone for coming. And sorry about this." Tom had now stood up and was gesturing to Giselle to leave.

"No Tom. I really want you to be happy, even if it is with one of our guests here tonight. It's only fair."

Alice moved closer to Tom, her eyes sparkling with anger – or was it hate?

"Tom, we all know what you've been doing behind Wendy's back. Admit it and move on."

"You witch!" Tom's tanned face had turned a beetroot red. "You have no right to interfere in my marriage. And you're a fine one to talk. Is there anyone you haven't slept with in Nairobi?"

Alice's hand rose to hit Tom in the face. The sharp sound of the slap stirred the night air. Tom stood still, stunned, then turned to Giselle and said, "Come on, we're leaving."

Kevin was already half-way through the door as they left. Oscar walked up to me and placed a piece of paper in my hand. It had a mobile phone number scribbled on it. Within a few minutes they were all gone, leaving the three of us and a sleeping Owino alone in the house.

"What a performance. Bravo." It was the only thing I could think of saying at that moment.

Wendy was now crying uncontrollably.

"I love you, you know. You're my best friends. But I think it is time for me to leave. I want to be nearer to Michael, and I need to re-connect with my family. I'll file for divorce in England. It'll be much easier. Tom's basically a decent man, and will provide child support. And I need a skill. Maybe I'll take some courses and get a job."

My heart swelled up. I could feel the tears starting up in my eyes. What would I do without the two women who had made my life bearable?

"What are we doing?" I was now sobbing. "Wendy, who loves Kenya and can't stand England, is going back there. Alice whose made a career of hating all things Western is now going to live in America. And I, who hates Nairobi, am stuck here. Where's the justice in all this?"

"Maya, you'll only be an e-mail away" said Wendy. "And before I forget, I also want to tell you that I am sorry for being so judgemental about that incident in the garden. Oscar's very sweet and I know for a fact that his wife has no plans to join him here. In fact, they might as well be separated. She hasn't visited him once, and nor has he been back to see her."

I didn't know what I could do with this piece of information. Should it matter? If it didn't, why did I suddenly feel elated?

"Can I say something?" Alice's normally hardened eyes looked suddenly soft and vulnerable. "Maya, when I think of what I will miss most about Kenya, I can't help thinking of you. I mean where else will I find a friend who puts up with me and who hasn't once failed to buy the Sunday newspaper just so she can read my column?"

"No, Alice, Wendy, you must go. Go before it's too late, before you're too tired, or too old, or too jaded. I guess the real reason why I am so upset is that I wish that I too had an announcement to make tonight, like I was getting married again, or was pregnant or had found nirvana or something. I mean, look at me, I have a boring, predictable life. I live in a flat alone and my family barely speaks to me because I committed the sins of getting divorced and remaining childless. Maybe I should just shoot myself."

"You're not going to shoot yourself. You're going to move on, like of the rest of us."

We stood up and walked to the verandah, holding hands like nursery school children. A million stars looked down at us. In the distance I could hear crickets singing their night song. The menacing night suddenly seemed comforting.

The tranquillity of the moment was broken by a short, sharp snore coming from the living room. We couldn't help but laugh. Owino was now in full-foetal position, his hands hugging his knees, as if they would fall off if he didn't.

Suddenly the phone rang. Wendy ran to pick it up.

"When? Where?" She sounded hysterical. "Tom? And Giselle?" There was a long pause. "I'm coming."

"We have to leave," she said. Her face looked ashen, like she'd seen a ghost. "That was Oscar calling from Nairobi Hospital. Tom and Giselle have been in an accident. Tom's critical. Giselle…"

"What about Giselle?" I asked.

It felt like hours before she responded.

"She's….. dead."

"I'll drive" I offered. "We'll leave Owino here. Come on, let's go."
I was surprised at the matter-of-fact way I was handling the situation. Because of my fear of driving, I was usually the last person to offer to drive anyone anywhere.

Alice was very quiet as we got into the car. I didn't want to know what she might be thinking, but I could sense it was not something she wanted to share. Wendy, on the other hand, looked unusually calm and serene.

As I switched on the ignition, I realised the radio was on. It was the midnight hour on Capital FM, and they were playing Hotel California. "The last thing I remember/I was running for the door/I had to find the passage back/To the place I was before/Relax said the night man/We are programmed to receive/You can check out anytime you like/But you can never leave. Welcome to the Hotel California."

"I guess I can't leave now, can I?" Wendy was looking at me, her eyes pleading, as if they wanted my permission.

"No, not yet anyway. One thing at a time. We'll get through this – together." I wished then I had said something more substantial but my mind had gone blank.

All I could think about at that moment was how cold it had suddenly become, and cursed myself for not carrying a shawl.

I switched off the radio as the car swerved out of the driveway. As we approached the Karen roundabout, I noticed that a lonely grey cloud had covered the moon.

THE END

****

AboutThe Author

Rasna Warah is a freelance journalist based in Nairobi. She is the author of Triple Heritage: A Journey to Self-discovery (1998), a book that explores the social, economic and political history of Asians in Kenya. From 1994-2002, she worked at the United Nations Human Settlements Programme (UN-Habitat) as editor of Habitat Debate, a quarterly periodical focusing on shelter and urban issues. She is also a keen photographer and has held exhibitions in Nairobi, Fukuoka and Amsterdam. She is currently in the process of completing her Masters degree in Communication for Development at Malmo University in Sweden. This is her first attempt at fiction.

Mukoma Ngugi

A Poem for Arthur Notje

My name is Mukoma Wa Ngugi, a Kenyan poet currently working on an MA in African Languages and Literature at the University of Wisconsin. I hold an MA in Creative Writing from Boston University and a BA in Political Science and English from Albright College. My writing has appeared in Brick Magazine, Smartish Pace, Student Under Ground, and Teeth in the Wind amongst others. My poetry has been featured in the following anthologies: One Hundred Days, Barque Press and New Black Writing, John Wiley and Sons. A political manuscript on Africa, Conversing With Africa, is scheduled for publication in August by Kimaathi Publishing House. I can be reached at mukoma@hotmail.com

Mukoma Ngugi

A Poem for Arthur Notje

Your forehead jutting outwards swelling with the wretchedness
of inheritance, watching your trail of black dust, ashes
of a cremated past swirl and twirl, a dance with voiceless ghosts
that see through the film of your eyes. Your eyes frozen deep
in the monotony of the past holding a black and white
photograph of a still born baby's wail.

Your nails thrust deep into the palm of your right hand until
it explodes like a grenade reading blood will flood the River
Nile, your reflection lies face down in Thames River, I see
a corpse in an Ocean sized fitting room. Consult neither
the Yoruba gods nor oracles, what you need is an internal shift
of perception, find beauty sufficient enough to thaw feeling.

Once you found beauty and said a true word, one true word spills
its truth at seams, swells beehives until the honey trickles
down to oasis. You said, lift up the cup gently to your scorched
lips and drink lest you spill. The warm sun light seductively
filters through the BaoBab branches onto my hungry skin, oval slits
of light swaying with the wind that moves the palm shaped leaves.

Is there a true word so terrible to face? That creates such
anguish? Only in its absence, the vagueness of an articulated
absence that churns ghosts, births easy theories of dualism and
memory of a childhood that dreamt what it cannot now fulfill leaving a

solitary poet staring into the abyss with nothing in front or behind,
the sole saxophonist in the middle of Oxford Square playing long

after the mourners have left. It once was beautiful. Wearing your martyr's
cap, you sat too long defenseless, the lone aeolian harp battling a screaming
wind that has upon itself the role of redeeming the world. Thames River
cannot not mummify as winter is not here. City lights flicker industrialization
onto the river's glass, your face distorted by the city's disco lights, two dark
eyes peering into the display of orgy that dances before them.

Everyday the world ends with our eyes glued on the next shipment
of happiness. Nightmares of land mines, sequestered Palestinians
and Zulus who no longer believe in either the pointed tip of Shaka's
assegai nor in the poet's pen. Let it hurtle along at the pace of my mind,
Bao-Bab fiend sprout a branch, trip a thought, middle of inferno,
take a plunge into the fire next time of a mind through which the world

whistles tunes of its madness. Shoot a straight arrow into the sky, create
wavy parallels, dance opposites in its wake, I see your face actualizing
the possibility of life, the fact of death. The Police records show your
fingerprints on a beer bottle, a witness who watching the orgy of depression
asked you to dance, "I have to leave, I am almost late, but thanks", he said.
"Another time then?" she asked. "Maybe, but not here". She watched your
black coat that hid your back till it was swallowed by the dancing bodies,
one slice of darkness and the you spilled onto Wordsworth Street.

* * *

Letter to My Nephew

for Ken Saro-Wiwa

The sun is locked in evening, half shadow
half light, hills spread like hunchbacks over
plains, branches bowing to birth of night.
It's an almost endless walk until the earth

opens up to a basin of water. You gasp
even the thin hairs on your forearm breathe,
flowers wild, two graves of man and wife
lying in perfect symmetry, overrun by wild

strawberries. Gently you part the reeds,
water claims the heat from the earth, you
soak your feet, then lie down hands planted
into the moist earth. You glow. Late at night

when you leave, you will fill your pockets
with wet clay. But many years from now,
you will try to find a perfect peace in many
different landscapes, drill water out of memory

to heal wounded limbs of the earth. You
will watch as machines turn your pond
inside out, spit the two graves inside out
in search of sleek wealth. Many years

later, after much blood has been lost and your
pond drained of all life you will wonder, shortly
before you become the earth's martyr, what
is this thing that kills not just life but even death?

AboutThe Author

Mukoma Ngugi is a Kenyan poet currently working on an MA in African Languages and Literature at the University of Wisconsin. He holds an MA in Creative Writing from Boston University and a BA in Political Science and English from Albright College. His writing has appeared in Brick Magazine, Smartish Pace, Student Under Ground, and Teeth in the Wind amongst others. His poetry has been featured in the following anthologies: One Hundred Days, Barque Press and New Black Writing, John Wiley and Sons. A political manuscript on Africa, Conversing With Africa, was published by Kimaathi Publishing House.

It was stifling in the crowded bus as more sweaty people to continued get on board. The driver stepped on the gas pedal to rev the engine, which roared back as if angered by its operator. He looked bored and a bit sullen as he eyed the boarding passenger. Some passengers were lucky to obtain seats in the laden bus. They then looked hard outside the windows, unwilling to make eye contact with fellow travellers who might demand their seat as custom would demand. I was not among the lucky ones, I had to stand and brace myself for a long uncomfortable ride that was to follow in the well-laden bus. More people got on the bus and each meekly dropped a 100-peso coin in the fare box.

In The Heat of the Moment

by J.B. Chege

It was stifling in the crowded bus as more sweaty people to continued get on board. The driver stepped on the gas pedal to rev the engine, which roared back as if angered by its operator. He looked bored and a bit sullen as he eyed the boarding passengers. Some passengers were lucky to obtain seats in the laden bus. They then looked hard outside the windows, unwilling to make eye contact with fellow travellers who might demand their seat as custom would demand. I was not among the lucky ones. I had to stand and brace myself for a long uncomfortable ride that was to follow in the laden bus. More people got on the bus and each meekly dropped a 100-peso coin in the fare box.

As the driver gave a final warning rev, a short powerfully built man shuffled hurriedly into the bus. He was pitch black, sweat shone on his brow where a thin film of brown country dust could be seen against his dark skin. A hush swept through the bus; those in the front who saw him enter passed their feelings to those in the back who had not seen the man, and a peculiar silence filled the bus. Suddenly, the driver lost his lethargy.

"It will be 100 pesos", he snapped loudly, his voice filled with officialdom. The Black man stiffened, powerful muscles under his flimsy shirt tightened. He was still breathing hard from the dash to catch the bus. His eyes shifted from the driver to the passengers sitting or standing near the driver.

The driver spoke again impatiently: "You heard me sir, the trip will cost you 100 pesos" and, he added "If you have the money make it quick, others are waiting to get on". Then he stared ahead.

The dark stranger did not respond but he stared at the driver. A dry tongue passed over his lips, he seemed about to say something. Then his eyes shifted from the driver to the passengers who were watching with expectancy. The bus was ready to go, but it was not moving. The silence was louder than the steady harsh roar of the idling bus engine.

The dark man shifted the bag he carried in his left hand and tried to say something. The driver cut him short, and yelled: "Are you paying or not ? If you're not, get out and let us move!"

A bulging vein began to throb on the left side of the black man's neck. A woman standing next to him wedged herself away towards the back of the bus.

"Why do you yell at me ?", said the man finally in a quiet voice, his accent clearly of rural, southern Mexico. He had a husky voice, not rough, controlled, an adult speaking to a troublesome child. "Do you think I have no money ? Or do you suppose I don't know the fare?" He paused, then added in a humorless chuckle, "What if I don't pay, what are you going to do?"

The driver was lost for an answer. He looked surprised at his own angry outburst. Perhaps it was the heat, or this dreary job, or just the stranger's darker than usual skin color...

He looked up at the dark man: steady eyes, black pupils stark against white, a low, sloping forehead and a jaw that said much of the character of its owner. There was a new expression on his face. It could have been fear. He revved the engine angrily, threw the poor bus into gear and started off with such force that everyone fell backwards.

The dark passenger did not stumble. As soon as the bus recovered from the abrupt movement, he reached into his pocket and deliberately pulled out two fifty peso coins which he dropped into the slot of the fare box. A wide path opened for him as he moved into the mass of passengers, towards where I stood near a window.

*****

I had been watching the drama with much interest and thinking to himself: "Bravo!, Tell it to him brother, tell him!"

I had never witnessed such a spectacle before, and I was fascinated. From the corner of my eye, I saw the dark man coming down the aisle toward where I stood, holding onto the top rail to keep his balance. He stopped near me and took a position as someone edged away nervously. He seemed to throw glances at me in a way that made me certain that we would break into a conversation.

I was keen to speak with him, as was usual when I came across a Black person in Mexico City. There were so few of us in the vast city. It was even better when the person was Mexican. With an unmistakable Coastal accent, he turned to me suddenly and enquired.

"Is the Periferico very far?"

"No señor, its only a bit further on. I'll let you know when they get there".

"Gracias".

The next question came with the same breath. "Where are you from?"

"Africa", I answered with an encouraging way.

"Africa?" the dark stranger echoed with wonder, "all that way!"

"Yes, señor, from a country called Kenya". There was no sign of recognition. Africa was enough to know.

I observed his face closely as we talked, standing as we did in the crowded bus, our faces inches apart. He had the down-to-earth manner of a countryman, looking me straight in the face and talking loudly in a way characteristic of Guerrerro people where many Black Mexicans are from. It is a rough and ready demeanour with an abrasiveness that Mexicans from the City or Native Mexicans regard as rude or aggressive. Ordinary Mexicans are used to deference, nuance and undetectable sarcasm.

The man's skin and physical features were African but his hair was silky:Native Mexican, Indigena, with rough dark curls all over his head. He had a low forehead and small shifty eyes that could shine with intensity when he spoke. Small ears were laid back like a cat. Apart from his height, and stocky build, he could have easily passed for a Somali. He spoke with energy, crooking his right arm on the rail to leave his hands free to gesticulate. He looked up at me with honest curiosity and a tilted, wistful look. After a reasonable pause during which he seemed to be collecting his thoughts, he spoke abruptly in a very loud voice.

"Over there , its all negritos, no?"

I could feel ears prick up in the cowed bus. No one else spoke.

"Quite right, señor. Most people are like me-", then I caught myself just in time from adding "and you". It was too soon. From the little I had learned so far about race and color in Mexico, I knew I had to be careful, for 'Black' - negro in Spanish - could offend even the darkest of peoples when used as a term of address, even though it could be used by others elsewhere with no apparent insult.

"So from there - Africa- are negritos like you - totally - with chino, chino hair like that!", he exclaimed with wonder, emphasizing the word chino- "curly"- with quick movements of his short, chipped hands. He went on quickly before I could respond.

"You know that that guy, Joe Frazier - they have so many like me in my pueblo!"

Here he puffed up his face and barrel chest although he already looked like a pugilist. Many passengers near them were pretending hard not to listen to the animated talk, but the man did not seem to notice or care.

"There are are many negritos - and very pretty girls!" he said, making a luscious figure in the air with his hands, smiling wickedly. He suddenly turned serious and as abruptly changed the topic.

"They say the whole of that race of people came from over there in Africa, not true?".

"Yes", I answered, "The ancestors of all those Black people came from Africa".

"And its true too that they came shackled as slaves?", he put his wrists together to underline "shackled". I agreed with him, becoming very impressed. Conversations like these with an Afromexican were rare in public or private.

"Are there many many negritos like you?"

"Sure", I replied, "there are very many of us, not only in your pueblo, but also in the United States, in Cuba, in Veracruz..", he picked up: "...and in Honduras, Nicaragua, Belize, not true?".

I was amazed by this Afromexican who knew something about Africans. As the bus approached the busy Periferico - Ring Road -- a highway that skirts the whole of Mexico City, I remembered with regret that I had to inform the man that we had arrived at his destination. The man waved away this information with a vague "I know" and I gladly realized that his initial request had only been a way of starting a conversation. The bus pulled to a stop and there was a pause in their conversation as people got on and off. As it started again, the man returned to the conversation with a strange remark.

"You know", he said thoughtfully, "those negritos are really funny".

"What do you mean?" I asked.

"I mean they are so damned lazy! They do nothing if they are comfortable for the moment. They don't like to work".

"But..! Don't they work in their pueblos just like everyone else?", I wondered with surprise

"Exactly! They just stay there and don't come here to the city to make money. They just stay there". He said, dismissing them with great disdain.

"Now , wait a moment..!" I said, seeing that the Afromexican was using pronouns to refer to Black people in a way that did not include himself in their reference: was he not part of them? I was still new to the Mexican use of language with its subtle exclusions of self in sensitive matters such as that of race. Was he using a language of double consciousness? Was this a double-edged sword of pride and prejudice? Was this man not too intelligent to see these contradictions?

"Maybe they don't like the city and prefer to stay in the pueblo". I said.

"No, no! They are just lazy. The negrito is very lazy", he added with a grimace. I was shocked by the turn of the talk. Màny in the bus stopped pretending not to listen to this conversation which carried easily in the campesino's intimidating voice.

"It is not true señor. That is a lie. An untruthful myth - una historia falsa! A lie". I answered hotly, and, as the man paused to chew on that, I continued hastily, feeling the juices of a rich argument flowing in both of us. I decided to change tactics radically and dangerously. "Look at me, am I not Black?", I said.

Warily, the man mumbled back: "Yes?"

"Okay, I am Black and African ...but I am not lazy or stupid...I am a University student!"

It was the only thing that came to my mind and I felt foolish, like a lame student before his teacher. I added feebly. "Are those negritos not as good as the others in school?" The man pounced on the word "school" lighting up with the smell of victory I had thought was mine.

"Ha! Let me tell you", he said shaking a stub of a finger in my face. "You see those inditos, they are much more intelligent than the negritos. They do better in school. I'll tell you this: I have a brother who has negritos - just like you! He took his little daughter to school but when he talked with the teacher she tells him "There is no hope', that she learns nothing while all the others do. She just sits there and doesn't learn a thing", he ended in triumph.

I felt frantic. My destination was not far away and soon I'd have to leave, trapped by the man's logic which I knew was wrong without knowing how to start to correct it.

"It is not true!" I cried, "those are lies told to us. The child is not dumb, maybe she's not taught well, or she has other problems, but Black children are not dumb! They are all equally able...". I sounded hollow even to myself. Frustrated, I felt exactly what I was: a young student so harangued by my emotions I couldnt seem tio express. Nevertheless, the intense man was quiet as if my words had touched him somewhere, as if he'd heard me say what he already thought, or wanted to hear. As I got ready to get off at the next stop, the man from Guerrero fired a last shot, never ceasing to amaze me.

"Hey, what about that guy - Martin Luther King - he was an African, wasn't he?"

"No...yes, I mean, he was an American African... African American...he was a leader who fought for exactly what we talked about - to end the lies against Black people and for their equality with other races...!" The driver revved his engine. I had no more chance to continue what seemed to have caught the man's attention. It was with uneasy relief that I shook his rock hard hand and quickly got off the bus. Once outside, I looked back into the bus hoping to wave adios to my nameless friend, but he could not see me. He was seated next to a window with index finger pointing at the temple of his bullet head, seemingly lost in deep thought. I walked quickly towards the university library.

AboutThe Author

Chege wa Githiora is a writer and academic. He works at the School Of Oriental and African Studies in London.

NAIROBI

RELOADED

Nai Reloaded

By Jambazi Fulani

Nish juad Malo was going to pick her up at Kengeles of ABC, I mean that is where he said he would be after Pavements. She picked up her Siemens again to call but nasikitika mteja hawe ..., It wasnt even over 'Shit!' She cussed and nearly crushed the poor thing in Raju, the bartenders face.

" Hey you are just being patient you are knowing him he is being very bijjy" she looked at Raju as if to say the guy did not know how she would have unlash a koso-vo there. So she moved away and went to the ladies.

Meanwhile Mose alikuwa amepanda five eight, ameelekea tao kukutana na Steph hapo Kenya Cinema. Kulikuwa na hi movie ya sijui, How to Lose a Guy in Ten Days. Hizo stori zilikuwa zimemkwaza sana unajua tu Steph vile ukuwa marshy marshy yaani ubabi mob. Hi haikuwa movie poa lakini ilibidii tu aoblige. Sa ashaingia ndae, Njoro naye ka kawaida ndio alikuwa makanga basi Mose akajua atapanda sare. LL Cool J na Jay Lo washapandisia ile song yao eti Jay Lo anashinda akisema pride haiezi kumfanya arudie hilo lidude, naye LL anamshow pride alikuwa nayo lakini sasa hana ene. Hiyo song ilibaki imekwaza Mose sana sijui kwa nini?

Nish came back na bado Malo had not come neither had he called. She itishad two Pilis and washaad some five five five mozo from AFCO. She mused over her kanywaji, and her kamozo. Kanwaji, kamozo kanywaji, kamozo then a sigh. Kanywaji kamozo kanywaji kamozo then a sigh. She turned to watch Dstv but ilikuwa boring. Kanywaji, kamozo, kanywaji, kamozo and then the last sigh picked up her kabag chucked some kagee and paid. Raju was about to say something but the daggers he was given froze him. She started walking out.

Mose alibaki ameshuka hapo rounda ya bomblast, asha bounce na lebo za Sean Jean akang'arie manzi. Akafika Kenya Cinema. Waacha angoje, ilikuwa one, one thirty, two, two fifteen movie nayo ikaanza waacha ajam. Akajaribu kupiga simu ikaiingia, the mobile subscriber cannot be ... Haiya! akapanda Dodi's kumanga ndiyo apige mpango. Ashaadishi ikafika alipe hiyo bill, kuweka mkono kwa mfuko hana ene, wallet inakaa ililapwa, ashaingiza baridi. Waacha ajaribu kuexplainia waiter, kukatokea na vuguvugu alibaki ameharakishwa na kubebwa bebwa juu, hizo vita zikafika huko nje, ilikuwa saa mbaya movie ilikuwa imeiisha, watu wanatoka na huku Mose anaharakishwa na mawaiter. Nani akatokea Steph na Njoro wakibehave as if wamenokiana vinoma sana. Mose huku akijitengeneza, tengeneza asha wakolola na kumezea tuu. Hana feri hana manzi. Song ya Jay Lo na LL ikamrudia na akaunderstand hata hiyo movie ilifaa iitwe How to Lose a Guy in One Day.

As Nish walked out guess who comes Pato the couzo, she asked for a lift and while at Waiyaki Way she asked Pato if she can pass just for a short while at Pavements he said its sawas so she went in. First she thought she was dreaming but she moved closer Malo had not seen her. She songead and got close sat down pole pole behind him and you guessed right ordered for some Pilis and washaad her AFCO, five five fives then Kamozo, kanyawaji, kamozo, kanywaji, then a sigh. She did it again kamozo, kanywaji, kamozo ,kanywaji, meanwhile eavesdropping on Malo's vibe waiting just for the right moment and scheming on how to deal with this muhanyaji. For Nish and Moze they had learnt the hard way about the Nairobi Matrix - this was Nai Reloaded

AboutThe Author

Jambazi Fulani - is a scribbler, a possible storyteller one who juad long time that writing is a process he can't brag about. Yaani haringi! He makes use of his time thinking of what to write about ... (He is thinking).

My Uncle died many times before he really died. Ever a poet and a lifist, he lived each day like it were to be his last, bursting into song for any reason, dispensing kisses, poems, songs and hugs to his nieces and nephews while collecting friends and acquaintances like shillings from his pocket wherever he went.

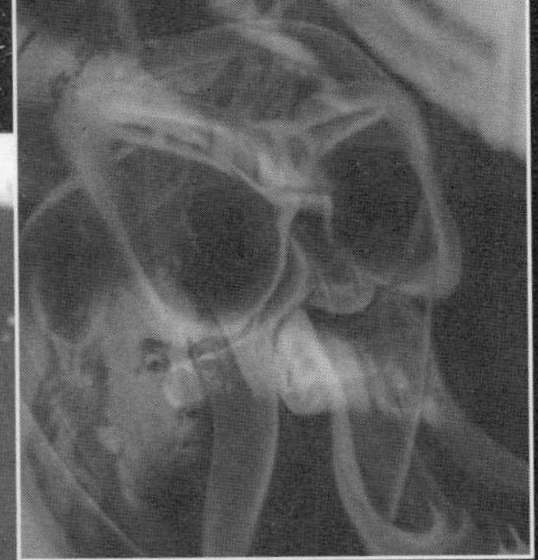

The Wake

by Judy Kibinge

My Uncle died many times before he really died. Ever a poet and a lifist, he lived each day like it were to be his last, bursting into song for any reason, dispensing kisses, poems, songs and hugs to his nieces and nephews while collecting friends and acquaintances like shillings from his pocket wherever he went.

In his quest to live, he came across to many of those who knew him as reckless and careless - everything he was not. Who could blame them? Once, he had somersaulted over the edge of a cliff blind drunk and strapped to the roof of his upside down car, fumbling for the seat belt he heard a woman's voice spin down to him as he spiraled down, "oh my, what a terrible death that one has had". Another time he had been flattened in his vehicle, sandwiched like a slab of ham slapped between two slices of super loaf between the roof and the floorboard. So numerous were his accidents that his insurance company, tolerant for so many years refused to insure him. As though deciding that death by accident was desirable but improbable, he proceeded to drink himself to death with an admirable persistence. Finally his body had begun to show the cracks. First to go were his teeth, loosened by innumerable knocks and then his innards, poisoned by the gallons of spirits they absorbed and expelled through the years.

One day, on a hospital bed, he whispered goodbye to the world.

Every night, the world of people he had accumulated in his 72 years on earth spilled into his house, some to meet his children and wife for the first time, others to bring back some of the cheer he had flung their way for so long, returning it back its rightful owners living cold in a house without his laughter and song. We cousins would sit in his son's room, all brothers and sisters again, and while the night away with stories and spirits masqueraded as soft drinks, all squeezed upon on the narrow spring bed like we were all 16 years old again. And every night would summon forth a few new faces from my uncle's colorful and generous life.

It was there in that very room, on the fifth night - just 3 days off from his funeral - that I met KK. He had ridden into the compound in the modern European equivalent of a white horse, a blindingly white Mercedes one of two existing in the country, both owned by him. His arrival had therefore created quite an undercurrent of emotion, with young women scrambling in their bags for lipstick and the youngest cousins bursting through into the bedroom where we older cousins sat, like pageboys bursting into a palace court to announce the arrival of a king.

"Man," announced little Mwangi breathlessly "A guys' arrived in the coolest white Merc!"

"A Mercedes? What registration?"

What model?

Who is it?"

He entered, or perhaps I should say he made an entrance. He looked like a paper cut out, all dressed in white, astoundingly unsullied for a city as dusty as this. It was hard to tell his age – he could have been thirty even or forty something. His bald head gleamed as though shined along with his shoes and his eyes twinkled as they darted about the room. At once, a few people sprung off the bed I was sat on. He glided over, settling down right next to me.

"My name is KK", he said his pupils sliding to the left of his face, towards me. That's what they call me". His eyes slid away again and he reached into his jacket magically extracting a bottle of 10-year-old whiskey. The spirit of the wake assumed a different flavor and voices rose, joviality was awakened at the prospect of a night filled with pleasant surprises to be sprung from the same general direction. Suzie sprung up and kissed him on the lips. I noticed she closed her eyes while his drooped a little- like a lazy cat, lips puckering; amused to have another pair so suddenly aquainted with his.

"My darling!" he declared smoothly pushing her back with one hand while unreliquishing her wrist with the other. He looked at Suzie up and down, pleased by what he saw. Her hips were thrust forward, above her jeans, belly button and hip joints on view, famine made fashionable. A glassy stud glittered from her belly button.

KK spun her around, and she pirouetted like a ballerina. They could have been in a black and white television musical - Fred Astaire twirling Ginger Rogers – not in a 6 by 4 foot jam-packed, smoky bed room in Nairobi. Releasing her hand, he excused himself to go pay his respects in the main house where my bereaved aunt and the older relatives sat deep in mourning over tall glassses of spirits tainted orange, yellow, golden and brown by mixers.

The room felt cold and empty for a moment. But the moment passed as a hand cupped fingers found my ear.

"Careful" hissed my cousin, Jones. " Willy's here". He looked furtively towards Willy, a tall, handsome man with a dimple in his chin and the a rich, deep, voice. "Mmmmh…" I murmured appreciatively. Willy was cute - had Jones noticed me looking at him?

"You know Willy has a problem with his fingers," continued Jones.

There were worse disabilities I could think of in a man. I shrugged. causing Jones to stand up with an exaggerated casualness to fetch my bag from the corner of the room, where it lay by.

"Willy has sticky fingers," he whispered laying it beside me.

"He's a lawyer",said a voice.

Suzie sat heavily down by me, to me sucking furiously at a cigarette, staring around hungrily. She may have been my cousin but she frightened me. She looked like she wanted to bite someone on the neck and suck blood. Suzie had the low-down on everyone – who was sleeping with who, which family had money and which were just pretending, who's uncle had raped who as a child, who was seeing

a psychiatrist and who was into drugs big time. She kept track simply because she was fascinated by other people's pain.

"Willy?"

"No, silly. KK"

"Oh, flash pants. What's with the outfit?"

"Remember the accident that took place on the old Naivasha Road where 23 civil servants from the Criminal Investigation Department died in a road accident? He was their lawyer".

I remembered the case all too clearly. The truck ha d been overloaded that Thursday morning, headed back to the Nairobi, returning from a seminar, presumably on how to beat civillians up and not leave marks on them. The families of the dead offivers had clubbed together and successfully sued the Kenyan Government for negligence. They received a huge settlement, thanks to their lawyer who had fought their case well. But of the $2 million dollars awarded, of which he was the custodian, each family had gotten no more than a few hundred dollars.

"He's a nice guy. He's really funny," she continued.

"I'm sure the bereaved families will agree"

"No, really, he is. He's very generous".

"Wouldn't you be with almost two million dollars of someone else's money? How on earth did he get away with it? The newspapers were on his case for months!"

"So? This is Kenya. The case just -" she snapped her fingers – "disappeared." Her eyes closed as she sucked hard on the last bit of her cigarette and flinched a little as the butt burnt her fingers. I could see the filter was wet and slippery, which is why no one ever asked Suzie for a drag of her cigarette.

I looked round and wondered who else I would find something unpleasant about. This congregation of mourners were a "thirty-something-we-wanna-be-kids-again" crowd, dangerous company because they were such fun and their Peter Pan mentality contagious. They drank in dark corners as though still afraid their parents would catch them out and cracked the kind of infantile jokes that had you doubling over with laughter. They had known each other all their lives, lived in the same hood forever and refused to be serious about anything. They were perfect company for sad and mournful times such as this, because all they talked of was sunshine, hangovers and foolish happy things, though each, I knew, carried smouldering embers of private pain somewhere deep and inaccessible.

Willy left to make a phone call and the floor was now officially open to Willy stories. It started with a single word from Harold, a chubby baby faced cutie with a baseball cap pulled down low.

"Willie", said Harold shaking his head and smiling, and the room erupted with the anxious laughter of a group who had all been thinking the same thing.

"Remember that time at my house?" Said a thin, small girl with untidy hair extensions that should have been re-done a month ago. Clearly everyone did, they roared.

"Hey, Ciru, that was my wallet, it's not funny" said Evie, another girl in a purple velvet jumpsuit one size too small. More laughter.

"Who told you to drink so much and black out on that chair with Willie about?"

"But I didn't know he was like that". She said. More laughter. Evie threw a pillow at no one in particular and half the room ducked as it flew across the room knocking a bottle of flat beer over.

The door opened hitting Harold who was sat on the floor in front of it. There stood KK, dramatically surveying the room with a smile, neither happy nor sad, but benevolent, like a grand old man watching his grandchildren play.

"What say you I buy you all a drink up the road? At my local? C'mon, one in memory of the old man". He spoke grandly, waving a hand about. Such generosity could not go unsampled.

"All of us?" I asked.

""Why not?" he rolled.

"But it's Tuesday. It's almost seven thirty", I said thinking of work the next day and remembering that the Peter Paner's never had any money.

"Don't be so old" said Suzie. "It's early. You'll be home by ten. And besides, you pay taxes don't you?"

"So?"

She leaned over and tugged my ear towards her mouth, her nails hurting me: "Look at an evening on KK's account as a tax rebate"

Her logic was undeniably appealing. But really, I ought to get home before I forgot myself and joined the Peter-Paner's forever. I pictured my desk in the office gathering cobwebs a year from now as I skipped and giggled years away on an endless Tax Rebate Party spree.

And out of nowhere came my brilliantly stupid idea.

"Listen up, everybody" I said to the tipsy cluster. "Why don't we go to my place? A wake… A cousin's wake. I have some drinks at home too and I'll roast up some sausages".

"When? Saturday?" someone asked.

"No! Now!"

Objections flowed: "But Kikuyu's don't have wakes".

"So what? So what?" I was getting passionate about this. The room looked back at me, suspecting trickery. "No, really! I don't live far away and most of you keep asking me why I never had a house warming! Jones has been meaning to come over for months, haven't you Jones? Why not? We really shouldn't be in a bar at a time like this. We should be together, in a home. My home – why not? Uncle would understand".

But KK was king and clearly the decision would be his. The crowd would go wherever he was buying. He surveyed me for a long time, and laughed aloud alarmingly unexpectedly, rough laugh. ""We'll stop and get drinks," he said. "On me. And then we'll follow you to your place."

I didn't know what did it, the sausages or the booze, but already jackets were being put on, bags picked up. The room was on the move, like a swarm of fruit flies, thirsty for something sweeter. I joined the spill out into the cold night.

Glancing in my rear view mirror at the convoy of cars behind me, I squirmed. We had stopped at a noisy bar by the flyover and KK had bought two bottles of

vodka, a case of beer and soft drinks. I tried to temper the quantities but he had silenced me with a wave of a wallet stuffed with a wad of notes.

"God, I'm so stupid" I said to Suzie who was riding in my car clouding it up with smoke.

"Relax," she said. "It's a good idea. Uncle would have liked it, all of us together for a drink at your house because of him. Thinking of him. Talking about him. How he died. How his stomach and his chest hurt him so hard. How he suffered. How the drink that we will be gathering to enjoy killed him. God, he liked vodka, didn't he? And he smoked too much too, didn't he?" She coughed a chesty cough. "That can't have helped so much either".

I began to feel a little queasy.

"Susan?'

"Hmmm?"

"Tell me more about KK".

"He's rich`'

"What else?"

"Don't ever make him mad".

"How would I do that?"

"Oh anything sets him off. And when he's really angry he starts to shake his head, slowly at first, then faster and then he shouts out: 'no, no, no, no!"

My eyes left the road to momentarily check Suzie - who was prone to exaggeration - out.

"Oh no, no, no? That's it? That's all he does?"

"No, that's the beginning. It's like the opening. When you hear him say that haki, duck, just duck, coz he's flipped"

"Oooh, I'm so scared. Come on Suzie, give me the juice, the real story".

"Like?"

I don't know. Like, like... what he did with all that money".

"How would I know?" she retorted.

"You guys seem to be quite good friends".

"But why would he tell me?"

"Because you seem like good friends".

"KK's doesn't have friends"

"So what are you?"

"A jweeze buddy. A sloshing partner. A one-for-the-road mate. No more. If you want to know dangerous shit like that, ask him yourself".

"Alright then, I'll ask him"

She looked at me. Abruptly. Hard. "Don't. I was kidding. Please don't ask him. He has a really bad temper. And you don't want to see him loose it".

"Like how? By saying, 'no, no, no?'"

"Yes, yes, yes".

It was midnight and my little flat was rocking. A deceptively cold and gray exterior opened up to a small but funky space, my caged balcony overlooking the angry splashes of the muddy river below. On a quiet night, I loved to sit on the little bal-

cony, amidst the brooms and mops and old boxes filled with string and old newspapers and magazines, and listen to the river frogs singing hoarse songs of love to each other. Inside, moody red walls alternated with sunny yellow ones, painted by myself on a succession of tipsy nights. On some walls, colors ran into each other producing an inconsistent orangey - red mix, which by the grace of God appeared daring as opposed to drunken. There are Indian rugs, floor cushions, huge plants everywhere. A square ebony table seats eight and it's lined with chairs with improbably high backs. On the walls are big acrylic paintings I've done over the years. But only one sofa. You would imagine the colors would make everyone's stomachs turn, but the effect is quite the opposite. The flat sends most visitors into some bohemian frenzy and this was never truer than on the night the Peter Pan Crew and KK dropped by for a wake.

I was sitting on the floor, cross-legged talking to a now untidy looking KK. His eyes were blood shot and he kept saying, "this is a crazy looking flat... red, red, red. Red, red, red."

"And yellow" Harold kept interjecting. But all KK could see was the red, red, red. He and I were getting very pally, so pally .

"KK, tell me something".

""Anything my dear".

"What happened to all that money?"

He was silent for a beat, his tiny eyes narrowed. Then he laughed, that big, rough, loud laugh. He reached out at me and for a split second I was afraid he would strangle me. I noticed Suzie stop conversation and look from my face to his, panic clearly written on her face. His short arm wrapped itself round my neck in a humid embrace, the kind drunk men give each other at four a.m. in the morning. His jacket was off, he was sitting on it. Underneath, short sleeves, and fragrant but damp armpits. It was only 11.30p.m. in my book, too early for love too late for bed, But that didn't stop him.

He said, egging me on: "No ones ever asked me that before".

"Well I'm asking", I said bravely. In front us was an almost empty bottle of vodka and we had been matching each other drinking pace double to double for the past 3 hours. I felt good, real good and brave, so brave.

"I hid it." He said.

"Hid it? How do you hide two million dollars?"

"Well," he replied, leaning back, a nostalgic look in his eye," It's not that hard, if you know the right people. I had to pay off a big amount to some highly placed... individuals. To keep the wolves off my back. To help me get the money out of the country.

"Out of the country?"

He turned his head slightly and once again, his eyes sidled to the side of his face, snakelike, regarding me for a long, long time. What did he want? To kiss me? To kill me? He smiled. I noticed a crack on the corner of one of his front teeth. A little crack. His tongue dipped out and explored it, as though surprised and curious about it.

"Some to Botswana. Such a big, under populated country. So tired of people coming in to take diamond money, so shocked and grateful to people bringing it in. Zimbabwe. A little in Switzerland. A friend of mine - " at this point he named a well connected, highly corrupt minister – "He gave me some advice which I follow: never trust those Swiss people. They worship money. They'll hide it for you but just because it means more to them than it does to you!" He finished with a big laugh opening his eyes wide to emphasize TO YOU!

"And the rest I divided".

"How?"

"Some, I spent of course. My cars. The house. My girlfriend. My wife. That one, I don't know what she did with it."

He strangled the air in front of him.

"She left with it, I haven't seen her since. But after all that was done, I had over half a million dollars left. It's distributed in various accounts. I have a very good accountant".

"But it's… stolen…"

He smiled, benevolently. "So?"

"So… that makes you a …" out of the corner I saw Suzie waving her arms about tightly, crossing a finger across her neck, presumably trying to tell me that if I pursued this line of questioning, I was dead. I continued:

"…a thief",

KK squinted at me then let out a long and hard laugh. His face cracked into a smile of brotherhood, as he rammed my face into the depths of his arm pit which, incidentally, reeked of now, not cologne but sweaty balms, fruity, feminine, flirtatious; at odds with the shiny bald head, slightly cracked tooth and oppressive head locks : "I like this woman! Come on! Another vodka!"

Suzie exhaled and slumped back, I think surprised to see me unscarred. I rubbed my bruised throat and smiled. This KK guy was a pussycat.

You do not have to be a concert pianist a football star or even an hard working desk-bound official to recognize the deafening sound of silent applause ringing in your ears. Silent applause, the delicious moment when you look round a room and every ones eyes say, "I don't know how you did that but I wish I had been the one." I bowed without bowing, smiled without smiling rising to empty the overflowing ashtrays in front of me accepting unspoken praise for my dare-devilish line of questioning. I stumbled a little, interrupting the encore – jarring the feeling of daring accomplishment. The stumble reminded me: I was drunk. Really was drunk. Willy sat alone sucking on a beer. I wondered what he was thinking. Then, all at once, I felt I knew what he was thinking. Yes I did. He wanted comfort. I knew things about people, knew when to ask them stuff others wouldn't and when to back off. I felt pain and anguish in his eyes. I was the conqueror, the dare devil questioner. Yes, I would massage his pain away.

"Willy how's your mother?"

"Why? D'you know her?"

"Well, no…"

He turned away. "Good, cos I can't stand the bitch".

My silver Zippo lighter lay uncomfortably close to his lovely long fingers. I put it in my pocket.

Willy, noticing, said in a sad, gentle voice, "Oh."

Still splayed on the floor in front of the rapidly diminishing vodka sat KK. He reached for the bottle and threw the last drops of it into his glass. "Why don't we get some more? We're almost dry".

I sat down beside him. "There's still half a case of beer and the other vodka's not done…" I said remembering it was a Tuesday and I still had a chance of getting to work the next day.

"Nonsense", said KK sticking his hand into the inside of his jacket and pulling out his wallet. It had just a few notes in it. His brow creased. He flung his jacket open. And felt about the inside pockets. He turned them inside out, emptying empty chewing gum wrappers, a fistful of coins and a few loose condoms onto my carpet and then, he sprung up, like a cat, and scowling, hands shoveling deep inside his trouser pockets. And back into his jacket pocket again. More scowling. Into his shirt pocket. Fingers running along his waistband, an army of ten, searching. His breathing was ragged, his eyes narrow, pig like, mean. From my angle, sitting on the floor looking up at his boiling face and red eyes against my red red wall he looked like the devil himself.

"God dam it! KK roared. "Gudam - it - mother - say - who – shit-man-up –it-all-now nita kugonga, bloody fool!" He roared.

Suzie leapt up like a cat and held his face in her hands, looking afraid. He flung them off him as though they were burning her. The room hushed. And then, shaking his head vehemently he said the magic words:

"No, no, no, no, no!"

"No!" said Suzie raising her hands to her face as though preparing to have blows rained down upon her.

The next thing I knew, he was standing up and kicking at my carpet. I got the feeling he would have rather it be somebody's head. "My money, dammit! My money! Who took my money? Eighteen thousand shillings! Who took it, bastards?" His whole gentleman of leisure façade fell away, like sheepskin off a wolf.

Jones stood up, not very coherent but quite brave. "Listen hear, KK, you spent a lot of money tonight. Are you sure – "?"Dammit! Are you calling me a liar? Whose the Godamm thief?"

He lunged at Jones his hands outstretched and cupped, ready to fit themselves tightly round a neck. Jones stepped deftly aside: it wasn't going to be his. KK stumbled and fell into the girl in a purple jumpsuit who had been kissing Dave, a guy I found hard to talk to because he had such bad breath. KK staggered to his feet, using the girl in purple as a launch pad. His head swung about. The Peter Pan Club shrunk back. I noticed Harold asleep in the corner; head slumped onto his chest, dribbling a string of saliva onto his shirt, blissfully unaware that we were all about to die. He smiled in his sleep, and drew an imaginary woman closer.

Then all at once KK's eyes fell upon Willy who was sat where I had left him, at the dining room table. He was pretending to be a plant. KK pointed at him, his finger trembling, for once, words failing him.

Suzie was now sat on the floor, arms crossed, hugging her bony shoulders as she rocked back and forwards, weeping silently. I heard her saying over and over again, "no, no, no".

"I know all about you". He said to Willy. "All about you. It was you, wasn't it? When did you do it, you mongrel? In the car? Where's my money? Give me my money!"

"I don't have your money. Why would I have your money?" mumbled Billy so quietly you had to lean forwards to hear him.

The thin girl with untidy braids turned around and spoke to Evie, the girl who at the start of the evening was being teased about the day Billie stole her bag. "See", whispered the untidy hair girl, rather unkindly. "Told you every body knows about Billie".

"Shut up", said Evie.

There was a blur, like when a dog spots a cat in a crowded house and makes a dash for it and you know what's happening but you can't really see it at all because the dog and the cat are everywhere in the room at once. KK made a lunge for Billie. Billie dived under the table and somehow emerged on the other side of the room. KK looked around for a weapon but found only a wooden fruit-bowl. He picked up a rather soft orange and flung it across the room hitting Harold squarely in the middle of his forehead causing him to wake with a start. Somehow, Billie made it across the room and leapfrogged over my single chair to the tiny verandah, to the glass door, slid it open, raced through and then shut. KK raced clumsily over, and rattled the glass door.

"Open this fucking door before I break it".

"Oh no you don't" I said.

He turned slowly to face me. "Oh no I don't?" to me. And then to himself; "Oh no you don't?' Quietly he turned, walked to the front door, pausing to look long and hard at Willy who stood shivering outside, a thin pane of glass separating his life from his death. He then walked through the door and shut it gently behind him.

"Jesus. What was that?" I said.

Suzie was still weeping on the floor, rocking and hugging herself. "It's not over, lock the door, lock the door! "

""For Gods sake Suzie, he's gone, calm down. He's gone. Billie, come back in, he's gone".

Willy was shaking his head and I could see by the way his mouth was moving he was saying, "no way. No damn way".

"You know", said Jones, I don't think he even had that money by the time we got here. He spent most of it buying all this stuff in the bar and I saw him give a huge wad of it to that hooker – you know the one who works at the bar".

Suzie looked around at everyone as they relaxed, unwinding like springs, one moment coiled and tense now wobbly, easy. "Lock the door, lock the door, lock the door!" she was screaming now, upsetting everyone. Evie and the thin girl held each other, and Harold sat up and stared about him bewildered like a man who had fallen asleep at a party and awoken to find himself on the moon. Which, incidentally, he had.

"Lock it, lock it lock it!" screamed Suzie like a demented woman.

I began to talk to her the way schoolteachers talk to very young, slow learners. "Now Suzie, I'm just going to open the door and have a look and you will see that there is nobody out there. He's a bad man, a very bad man but he's gone home now, Suzie, I promise you."

I moved towards the door and opened it. I could hear Suzie screaming behind the door. The cold air hit me I felt jolted awake.

I heard a determined crunch of gravel, and looked up. Illuminated by the moon, no longer red and devilish, strode KK, down the hill, his white suit almost silver, like an evil prince of the light towards me. I saw a glint of metal like a silver bird dancing a half arch around him. I squinted. It was an axe its cold blade slicing through the air. I looked up the hill, and saw he had parked his white Mercedes across the gate, blocking an escape route for anyone imagining they might drive off in a hurry.

He had an odd look on his face, like he wasn't really there. I called his name but he didn't answer. He just kept striding down the hill towards me. Spinning round I turned and ran towards the flat and hammered on the door, my hands shaking. "Open the godamn door!"

Inside I slammed the door shut, slid the bolt on, and twisted the key in the lock, The Peter Paner's looked at me confused, wondering. The room was silent apart from a voice that could have been mine saying "oh shit, oh shit oh shit" over and over again.

""What? Said Jones, staring at me from across the room. "For god sakes, what? Say something".

"Oh shit oh shit oh shit oh shit".

There was a crash and a splintering sound and everyone jumped into a ball of arms and legs as a steel blade crashed its way through 5 inches of door, into the red and yellow flat and closer to Willy.

Out of the corner of my eye, I saw Suzie reach into her left boot and pull out a wad of money. She threw it at the door, crying, and I scrambled over to the door on my hands and knees and shoved all eighteen thousand shillings of it under the crack as woodchips rained down on me.

The hammering stopped. For eternity none of us dared breath. Then it was over.

No body finished their drinks. Nobody thanked me for a great party. Quietly, like people leaving a wake, everyone picked up their things and left, without a word.

AboutThe Author

Judy Kibinge is a film director, writer and painter. She has directed two films: A Dangerous Affair and The Aftermath.

It was a long time ago. I was seven years old, and the bad weather had stormed the sea-sons out of order. Our light December rains seemed diluted, coming down in angry spurts like diarrhoea. That evening the city sat in a low flood, and night approached us with watery foot-steps. The cold descended on us from the mountains, which evening had already hidden from our view. Occasionally wind swelled up our brown waterproof walls like a football. Above us, lightning burnt the sky into ashes, tracing its flashes in blood. Mama got up sluggishly and pulled her hands away from my elder sister's trunk box.

An Ex-mas Feast

by Uwem Akpan

-One-

It was a long time ago. I was seven years old, and the bad weather had stormed the sea-sons out of order. Our light December rains seemed diluted, coming down in angry spurts like diarrhoea. That evening the city sat in a low flood, and night approached us with watery foot-steps. The cold descended on us from the mountains, which evening had already hidden from our view. Occasionally wind swelled up our brown waterproof walls like a football. Above us, lightning burnt the sky into ashes, tracing its flashes in blood. Mama got up sluggishly and pulled her hands away from my elder sister's trunk box. Then she panicked and began to reach here and there with her hands. Without standing up, she groped from wall to wall, frisking my two-year old twin brother and sister and Baba, who were all sleeping, entangling one another like puppies. She was looking for Baby. I made to tell her where it was, but then she remembered and relaxed. Mama was still slightly drunk and had been sleeping since the previous night.

She stood up with a speed that made me want to stop her: the roof was too low for her full height. She hit her head against the woodwork, almost breaking a rafter of cork. One of the stones that weighted our roof fell down outside. Her white T-shirt, which she got two months back when she delivered Baby, had wet twin milk stains on the front.

Now she put her hands under her shuka and retied the strings of her money purse around her waist. Sleep and alcohol had swung it out of place. She dug through our family carton, scooping out clothes, shoes, useless documents which Baba had picked from people's pockets, and a framed picture of our late grandfather. Grandpa was loved by our fellow street people, and when he died, they raised enough funds to get his body to our village for burial. There was enough money left to pay my school fees for a year and sponsor Baba's thirtieth birthday party. Mama dug on, and the contents of the carton piled up on Baba and the twins, Atieno and Otieno. Then she unearthed the tin of New Suntan Shoe Glue. The glue was our Ex-mas gift from children of a street family that lived nearby.

Mama smiled at the glue and winked at me, pushing her tongue through the holes of three fallen teeth. Grandpa had beaten them out of her. She snapped the tin's top expertly, and the place swelled with the smell of a shoemaker's stall. I watched her decant the glue into my plastic "feeding bottle," the glue glowed warm and yellow from the dull security light from the back of the store where our home leaned. Though she was still drunk, her hands were so steady that her large tinsel Ex-mas bangles, a gift from a church Ex-mas party, did not sway. When she had poured enough, she cut the flow of the glue by tilting the tin up, inch-by-inch, while slowly moving it away from the plastic. The last stream of the gum entering the bot-

tle weakened and braided itself, twisting flashes of light around before tapering in midair like an icicle. She covered the plastic with her palm, to retain the glue's power.

She turned to Baba, shoving his body with her foot. "Vegetables are for eating, not marrying. Wake up, bwana, you never work for days!" Her voice flew out of our home and disappeared into the short Nairobi alleys. He turned and groaned. His feet were poking outside the house, under the waterproof wall. Baba was dressed in wet tennis shoes. His toes had broken free of the shoes. Mama hit him again, and he began to wriggle his legs as if he was walking in his sleep.

Our three-legged dog growled outside. Mama snapped her fingers, and the dog limped to her, her ripe belly swaying like heavy washing in the wind. Two months before, Mama, who was good at spotting dog pregnancies, had baited her with tenderness and food until she became ours. She wagged her tail and licked Atieno's face. Mama probed her stomach with crooked fingers, like a midwife. "Oh, Simba, childbirth is chasing you!" she whispered into her ears. She pushed the dog outside. Simba went and lay down, covering Baba's feet with her warmth, and slept facing our bag of utensils and food, which was leaning on the wall of the store. Baba liked to push it in to wedge our door from inside once everybody had found a space for the night. Occasionally, she barked to keep the other dogs from tampering with our mobile kitchen.

"And you Jigana, did you do well last night?" Mama asked me.

"Sawa sawa. I made a bit," I said. I passed her a handful of coins and notes, which I had made standing with Baby at the bus-stop. She pushed the money under her shuka. The zip of the purse farted crisply.

"Aiie! Son, you never see Ex-mas like this year!" her face widened in a grin. "Kwanza we shall pay school fees zako za next year. No more randa-meandering around without any missions. No more chomaring your brain with glue boy! You going back to school . . . did the rain beat you and baby?"

" Uh uh. Rain caught me here," I said.

" Na baby? Who is carrying her?"

"Naema."

"Eh!.. Na Maisha? Where is she to do her time with the child?"

"Mama, hataki. Ame jam..she is very angry!"

" Gmm! Fala! That girl is beat-beating my head. Wiki tatu! Three weeks she is not talk-ing to me. What dudus are eating her brain? ?" She was shouting. Sometimes the words came out like a yawn because the hole in her teeth was very wide. " Eh! Now that she shakes-shakes her body to moneymen she thinks she has passed me? Nogojaa tu! She will see."

She gave up for the moment, reached forward and seized the glue from me. She took quick, hard sniffs from it, as if her concentrated efforts would answer her question. "Again – why did she kataa to stay with the baby,?" she asked when she paused to catch her breath.

"She says its child abuse."

"Child abuse! Who told her ati-she is our social worker?"

"Me I don't know Mama. She just went with those ma-men."

"With the mukora who took her last night? That thug?"

"No, not them."

Mama spat on the side " Puu! That man is useless. He does not ever pay the Ex-mas rate — and he can let even his monkey fuck her! Jigana, talk with that girl. We need the money for shule boy – uniform and all the doidos you need. She must stop buying those ma-fuuny clothes. Ah! Ati-Gucci, ati- Deesaynah! Clothes smelling of dead white people. Whose stomach does Deesaynah feed?"

As she said this, she was pounding angrily on the trunk, which took up a fifth of our living space. Maisha always opened it in private, its secret contents surrounding us with a persistent perfume. The trunk was a big obstruction. It was the only furniture with solid and definite shape. It was not flexible to our street rhythms. The trunk brought us both suspense and consolation, and these grew each time the owner came back with new things. Sometimes, when my sister did not come back for a long time, our anxiety turned the trunk into an immov-able assurance of her return.

" Malaya! She doesn't come and I break the box tonight!" Mama hissed, spitting on the combination lock.

She handed over the bottle to me. Since it was potent kabire I did not sniff it straight, but put my two lips around the mouth of the bottle and smoked slowly like an oversized joint of bhang (Indian hemp). Initially, it felt as if I had no saliva in my mouth, and then it began to numb my tongue. The heat climbed steadily into my throat, my nostrils tickled like an aborted sneeze. I cooled off a bit and blew off the vapour. Then I sucked at it again and swallowed. My eyes became watery. When I looked up, mama had poured herself the kabire, and was sniffing it. She and Baba hardly took kabire. "Kabire is for children only!" Grandpa used to admonish them each time he caught them eyeing our glue.

Baba had managed to get three cups of rice and zebra tripe, which a tourist hotel had donated. We had that for dinner on Christmas eve.

"Happee happee! Hapee Ex-mas!" Mama toasted me after a while, still looking away.

"Na we Mama!" You too Mama.

" Now where are they all...okay, we wait for them before we start to eat Ex-mas. Hapee..happee. happee Ex-mas!

She sniffed the bottle and her eyes receded, her face pinched like the face of a sick cow. " Ahhhhhh... Auwww! Mambo yote. Mambo yote!" She giggled, but her voice was guttural because she spoke into the plastic. "And they banned this sweet thing! Say asante to the neighbours boy, son. Where did they find it?"

Her eyes fixed on the bottle. It looked as if she was counting the molecules of the col-ourless fumes. Sometimes she held the bottle with two hands, her fingers playing among them-selves or tapping the plastic. Her face was cool. The drunken look had disappeared. She smoked and sniffed, sometimes releasing her lips from the bottle with a kissing sound. As the night thickened, her face began swell, and she kept pouting and biting her lips to check the numbness. They turned red, like Maisha's did when she had lipstick on. The glue kept cooking the lips until they died

to the bites, and puffed up. Each time we heard people approaching the house, she panicked and hid the bottle, using her tongue to moisten her lips with a film of saliva.

*****

" Mum? So, what can we give the neighbours for Ex-Mas? "

"Petrol," she answered, my question jerking her back from the world of kabire fantasy. "Ehh! Halflita ya petrol." She sucked hard on the bottle and pinched her nostrils with her fin-gers, blew out and wobbled her cheeks, then swallowed hard. When she looked up again our eyes met, and I lowered mine. "Okay, next year, we get better things," she said as she exhaled. ". . . God will give us a person to ingia an Indian shop for us to buy kabire next year. I don't want police business this year…"

"Maisha's men can help us!" I quickly told her. I did not want to tell her how much my friends laughed at me. Any self-respecting streetkid should always have his own stock of kabire. No boy of my age should bring money to his parents. It was humiliating.

" Uh Uh. Apana boy. NO wasting money." She belched.

There were two drunks stumbling towards our house. Mama hid her bottle. They stood outside and announced that they had come to wish us a Merry Ex-mas. Mama dismissed them, " He is not here!". She quickly covered the trunk in rags. Baba had owed them for four years, and they came every time they smelled money and Baba had to take off for a few days. When Baby was born, we pawned three quarters of its clothing, donated by an NGO, to defray the debts. A week before Ex-mas, the couple had raided us, confiscating Baba's working clothes in the name of debt servicing.

" Ahh! Mama – ni X-mas – forget the money." Said one, "Happeee Happeee Ex-Mas!" they all chorused and burst out laughing. Mama laughed out loud and invited them in. They staggered to our door, swaying like masquerades on stilts. They were coming from a street-people party. The husband wore his trousers upside down, belted across the forehead, the legs, flailing behind him, tied into knots. The wife had only her jacket and rain boots on. " Happee Happeee..." They sang. Mama wedged herself between them and the house to ensure they did not pull it down.

Baba whispered to us from within, ready to slip away " Ha! Si they told me the same thing last year? Hebu you watch and see tomorrow they come looking for me".

They staggered away. The stuffed trousers bounced along behind them. Mama came back inside, pulled out the bottle again, took one sniff, became uncomfortable under my stare and gave up. She fished out two little Uchumi Supermarket waterproof bags from the carton and straightened. She wore them over her canvas shoes, tying their handles around her ankles in little bows. When she walked out into the flood, her winged galoshes scooped the water like a duck's feet. She tried to untie our bag of utensils and food, her eyes searching for a dry spot to set up our stove, to warm some food for Simba. After a while she gave up and came back, for the

rain came down hard. She bent down and removed a board—which served as our door—from the roof and put it against the wall.

"Jigana, So how much did that man your sister went with say he was paying..eh? Did you hear?" she asked me suddenly.

"There were three of them, plus driver na monkey."

" Ai! And where are they? She should be here now. He bwana! Does she want to learn with a knife in her back?"

"Mama, you should have seen the motorca! And there were white men, they even shook my hand!"

"Motoca? They had a motoca"

"Imachine! A motorcar to pick my daughter?"

I licked my finger and clicked two fingers to the sky, " Haki..mama…To God, I saw a car.."

She stretched forward and held my two arms, smiling, "Hapana! You mean my daughter is big like that? "

Otieno woke up with a start. He stood groggily. Then consumed by a pained urgency, he climbed over Mama's legs, levered himself over me with his hand on my head and landed in the flood in a crouch. He began to lower thin spools of shit into the water, whiffs of heat un-wrapping into the night. The stink disturbed Simba, making her yelp in her sleep. Mama went outside and held onto Simba so she would not eat the faeces. She stuck her hands into the curves of the animal and came up each time with a tick or two, which she passed to me to burst on the wobbling door-frame. With Simba restrained, another dog swooped in, and Mama watched her new pregnancy carefully, nodding and smiling. She had given us puppies when we first arrived there. " Those puppies will bring us good money. I think she is a European type dog!" Mama explained to her. The dog ate the shit so fast that soon Otieno was defecating straight into her mouth and had to hold up his private parts away from the snapping jaws.

-Two-

After Musioka had cleaned him up with a long tongue, Otieno returned to the house and sat on Mama's legs. He brought out her breast and sucked noisily. With one hand, he grabbed the toy Maisha had bought for them, rattling its maracas on Mama's head. She reached into the carton and brought out our family Bible. The front cover had peeled off leaving a dirty page full of our relatives' names, dead and living. She read them out. Grandpa had insisted that all names of our family be included, to remember the instability of street life. Mama liked to read from our history every Ex-mas. She started with her father, who was killed by cattle rustlers, before she ran to this city and started living with Baba. She called out Baba's mother, who came when the villages were completely razed—because some politicians wanted to redraw tribal boundaries. She disappeared one day forever into the city with her walking stick. Mama invoked the names of our cousins in our village, who used to send us letters through our church, asking our parents to send them school fees. She called out her brother, who was shot by the police in a case of mistaken identity. They gave his corpse to a medical school because we could not pay the

bill. She invoked our landlord in Kibera who evicted us violently without seizing anything when we could not pay the rent. After spending a year there, we learnt that survival was more difficult in the slums than on the streets. She called her second cousin, who had never written us since she fell in love with a Honolulu tourist and eloped with him to avoid female circumcision in the village. She called Baba's sister, who rebelled against the city and returned to the villages. There she discovered that the same politicians from both tribes had grabbed the land and turned it into jointly owned hectares of fenced coffee and tea farms. She came back to the city.

The sky rumbled. Within an hour, a short thick rain had pelted our house and disap-peared. "Bwana, I hope Naema put clothes on baby before she left." Mama said to me, the middle of her sentence wobbling because Otieno had bitten her.

"She wekad the Baby in waterproof paperbags. Then sweater."

"Uh? It was not hot?"

"We put Baby legs in cold w

" Hmph!" she said.Dissatisfie

Otieno, having satisfied hims
and took over the other breast
Soon they fell back to sleep. She
weak voice vibrated because his

"No food," Mama told him.

" ....."

"We must finish to call the n

"Tsk! You'll be calling mine

" Here is food! New Suntan
plastic bottle from me. "It can kill your stomach till next week." She laughed

"Kabire is children's milk!"

"Si you go to the buses and work?"

"All the children are here?"

"Baby and Naema still out. Last shift....and Maisha"

"Ah—there is hope! They will bring Ex-mas to eat!"

"Ex-mas is school fees. Why waste this good kabire!"

"Okay. Tomorrow," he said.

"It will be dead tomorrow."

Mama gave up and started to grope in the carton-box again. She unearthed a dirty can-dle, pocked by grains of sand. She got off the trunk, lit the candle, and cemented it to the trunk with its wax. Taking the Bible, she began to thank God for the gift of Baby after two miscarriages. With a thankful smile, she praised God for blessing Maisha with white clients at Ex-mas. Then she called out " funny eyes" the name we had given to the young Japanese volunteer who unfailingly dropped shillings in our begging plate. Funney EyesShe was very fond of Masaai tyre sandals and ekarawa necklaces, which held her neck like a wire trap, and never replied to our greetings or let our eyes meet hers. Then she asked God to bless Simba with many puppies.

" I am sure her husband was also a European, Lord."

It started to drizzle again, and my sister came in with Baby. It was asleep, damp in the waterproof underwear. She handed over the money to Mama, who banked it away in her purse. She also gave Mama a packet of pasteurized Milk. It was half full and she explained she had to buy it to stop Baby from crying. Mama nodded. The milk pack was soggy and looked like it was about to disintegrate. Mama took it carefully from Naema, in two hands like one receiving a certificate. She put it on our roof, in the direct gaze of our security light. When Naema brought out a half-eaten turkey drumstick. Before Mama could grab her ears, Naema quickly explained that she did not buy it. Her boyfriend had given it to her. He was a big shot in the street gang that controlled our area.

"Maisha is moving out tomorrow," Naema said to Mama.

Mama's face froze. Numb and swollen.

No matter how rootless and cheap street life was, sometimes you could be broken by departures. Unlike most, our family had stayed together.

Actually for two weeks before that night, Maisha had been behaving like a cat going feral: she came home less frequently, stayed only to change clothes and give me some money to pass on to my parents. She was doing well. Recently, she had taken the Atieno and Otieno to the barber's, and Baby for a check-up in Kenyatta National Hospital.

Everything was silent for a moment; even the usual street sounds seemed to cower under mama's silence. Baba started awake, as if a loud noise had hit him.

" Is that Maisha?"

" No – Maisha is working!" Mama said gleefully, her mood returning only to score a point against Baba. "My Maisha commands tourists motorcas!"

"What? What tourists?" Baba asked, sitting up immediately, rubbing sleep and fatigue off his eyes with the bases of his palms.

"White people!" Mama sighed.

"Uh? They must pay ma-dollar or euros! You hear me, woman?"

"Yes."

"And no Honolulu business! What kind of motoca were they driving?"

"Jaguar." I answered, "With driver."

" Did you thank the men for us?"

"No," I said

"Aiiee! Where are your manners?"

" Number plate? Did you ask where they were going?"

"No, Baba."

"So if they take her to Honolulu what do I do?"

"Maybe, we should send you to a street gang—or send you back to the slums…Eh…boy, have you not learned to grab opportunities!"

The week before, in his anger, Papa had stood up straight and his head had gone right through the roof. Mama patted his shoulders, and offered him some kabire. He brushed her aside and went outside to cool off, cursing himself for drinking too much and sleeping through Ex-mas Day and missing the chance to meet the tourists. Then he started singing "A Jaguar is a Jaguar is a Jaguar!" to the night, leaping from

stone to stone, tracing the loosely cobbled walkway that studded the water like heads of stalking crocodiles in a river.

In the sky, some of the shadowed tall city buildings were branded by lights left on by forgetful employees, and a few shopping centres wore bright Ex-mas glitter; with flashing lights ascended and descended, like angels on Jacob's dream ladder. The long city buses, Baba's hunting grounds, had stopped for the night.

In some of the shop verandas, gangs of street kids massed together in sound sleep, some still clutching their kabire bottles. Some gangs slept in graded symmetry and arranged patterns, like a Ex-mas decoration. Some groups slept in freestyle, like my family. Some had a huge waterproof above their pile to protect them from the elements.

Prostitutes fluttered about under streetlights, dressed like winged termites. As the streets become emptier, cars drove faster through the floods, kicking up walls of water, which collapsed on our house all night.

When Baba came inside, he plucked his half-used miraa stick from the rafter and started chewing. He fixed his eyes on the trunk. A mysterious smile dribbled out of the corners of his mouth. Eventually, the long stick of miraa subsided into a formless sponge in his mouth. His spitting was sharp, and arched across the room and out of the door.

Suddenly, his face brightened up. "Hakuna Matata!" He blew off the candle and swept everything into the carton. Then he dipped into the carton and came up with a roll of wire, and started lashing the wheels of the trunk to the props of our house, whistling and drumming on the trunk. Mama tried to discourage him from tying down the trunk.

" Bwanaaa….stop it! She will leave if she finds you manga-mangaring with her things!"

"Woman, leave this thing to me!" he rebuked Mama. "Didn't you insist to circumcise my cousin before marrying Mr. Todd of Honolulu. This way she will not leave with those Honolulus."

"You can talk! Did you come to my fathers house for me…pllllssssp!You can talk! "

"All me am saying is mpaka we treat these tourists well . . . Come, I want chemusha some food for Atieno and Otieno?" Baba suddenly changed the subject, scratching his belly. Atieno was shivering, as her hand had reached out of the house. Baba reached out and yanked it back in. He stuck the girl's head through the biggest hole in the middle of our blanket. That was a family way to ensure that the one who most needed it maintained their place in the centre of the blanket. Baba grabbed the legs of Otieno and pushed them through two holes on the fringe of the blanket. "Children of Jaguar" he whispered into their ears. " Ex-mas ya Jaguar!!" He tried to tuck them properly into the blanket, turning them this way and that, without success. He continued to thread their limbs and heads into the holes in the cloth without thinking. Then he became impatient, and rolled them up towards each other like a badly wrapped meat roll. Their heads were facing opposite directions, their feet in each other's face, their knees folded and tucked into each other's body—a blanket womb.

Mama reminded him to wedge the door, but he refused. He wanted us to wait for Mai-sha. He winked at me as if I was the co-sentry of our fortune, and dared not sleep. I sat there, sniffing kabire until I became drunk. My head swelled, and our roof-work relaxed and shook, then melted into the sky.

I was floating, my bones were inflammable. My thoughts went out like electric currents into the night, its counter currents running into each other, and in a flash of sparks, I was hanging on the door of the city bus, heading to school, my uniform hidden in my bags. Num-bers and letters of the alphabet jumped at me, scurrying across the page as if they had some-thing to say. The flares came faster and faster, blackboards burnt brighter and brighter. I raced down our lopsided, bald play-ground with an orange of a rugby ball, jumping the gullies and breaking tackles.

I was already the oldest kid in my class.

Mama touched my shoulders. She relieved me of Baby and stripped him of the plastic rompers. With a rag, she wiped Baby clean and put him in a nappy for the night. She began to pick things again out of the carton, then shook it and pressed down the remains. With a cushion, wrested from my sleeping sister, she padded the top of the carton into a cot. After placing the Baby in it, she straightened up the four covers of the carton. On these paper bedposts, she folded and hung our NGO-donated mosquito net. Then she pushed away the limbs hanging around it, and wrapped her frame around the carton. She slept

-Three-

I woke Baba up when Maisha came back just before dawn. The rain had stopped, but clouds kept the night dark. The city had gorged itself on the floods and now its skin swelled and burst in places. The makeshift tables and stalls of street markets, littered the landscape, torn and broken, as if there had been a bar fight. Garbage had spread all over the road: dried fish, stationery, trinkets, wilted green vegetables, plastic plates, wood carvings, second-hand underwear. Some furniture survived, chained to the pillars in the verandas, or bunched up and left in the paid care of street gangs. Outside the ill-lit streets lay still, without the usual press of peo-ple, sounding hollow and amplifying the smallest of sounds. Long after it had gone out of sight, you heard the police car negotiating potholes and the officers harass-ing and extorting Ex-mas kitu ndogo from the few people who could not afford to go to their upcountry villages for the holidays.

My sister had returned in an old Renault 16 taxi. She was slouched in the back. There were huge waterproof bags on the passenger's seat. Kneeling and applying pliers to open the back door, the driver let her out of the car. Baba's sighs were as loud as the morning muezzin. My sister stepped out then leaned on the car, exhaust-ed. She gestured at Baba to go away. He ignored her.

"So where is our Jaguar?" Baba asked the taxi driver, peering in the rotten car as if it could change at any moment.

"What Jaguar?" the driver asked, monitoring Maisha's movement.

"The nini Jaguar . . . Where is she coming from?" Baba charged him. The driver silently pointed to his passenger.

Maisha's neon blouse burnt through the dim light. She bent before the only functioning headlamp of the taxi to count out the fare. Baba paced up and down. Her trousers were so tight that they had crinkled on her thighs and pockets as she struggled to get to the notes without breaking her long nails. Yesterday, her hair was gold, wavy and crisp from a fresh perm and crew cut. Now, it stood in places, and lay flat in others, you could see patches of her scalp, bruised and raw from the chemicals. It was hard to distinguish peeling face powder from damaged skin.

The driver could not easily roll up the window, he reached out to guard the bags beside him. His collateral.

"Me I can't answer you that question," he told Baba.

Baba brought out a six-inch nail, and went for the worn tires. " What dawa have you given my daughter! She always comes home strong!"

The driver came down immediately, his pleas laden with fright. "Mzee, my name is Ka-rume. Paul Kinyanjui wa Karume. . . Me I be an upright Kenyan! I fear God. Me I don't know what jaguar. . ."

"And you want steal my daughter's bags?"

"No. Please, take the bags. Please!" the man begged, still trying to restrain Baba from bursting his tires.

"Aiie Baba! You shame me, Baba! Shut up!" Maisha said weakly, pushing the money towards the driver.

My sister apologized and paid the driver. Baba who was strolling, his nose full of the good smells in the bags, suddenly broke into a run, to untie and dust the trunk. He woke up everybody in the process.

The driver got into his car, and was about to put the money into his breast pocket when he started frisking himself. Soon it was as if he had soldier ants in his clothes. He zipped his pockets, then unzipped them quickly, afraid that the thief was still lurking. He removed his coat, then his shirt, and searched them. He recounted his itinerary to the skies with eyes closed, his index finger wagging at invisible stars. He bent down and started searching his socks, and then he was on all fours, scouring the wet ground. He dabbed at the sweat or tears coming down his face.

Maisha charged forward and attacked Papa's pockets. She screeched at him until he re-turned the fat wad of notes. The driver thanked her curtly, brushing his clothes shaking hands to clean himself. As soon as he reconnected the ignition wires to start the car, he creaked off, his horn blaring, his headlamp pointing up and to the left, an unblinking eye watching our every move.

***

She walked into the house, holding her high heel shoes over her shoulders. Mama had made room for her and the bags, and sprayed our home with insecticide to discourage mosqui-toes. The bodies inside started coughing. As Maisha came in, she stood aside like a maid, wringing her hands and looking down. Then she made space for herself, opened the perfumed trunk, and took out a blanket and slept, leaving us with the sweet smell of her life in places we could only dream about. With our sort of walls, it was not long before the insecticide wore off and the mosquitoes were back in business.

My parents and I stayed outside and sat out the night. Fog brought the dew down, thickening the darkness, and turning the security light into distant halos. Maisha twisted and turned on the floor, cursed the limbs of her siblings and swatted at mosquitoes.

She as twelve and none of us knew how to relate with her any more. Sometimes Mama went out of her way to provoke her, "Malaya! Whore! You don't even have breasts!" she would tell her. Maisha would ignore her

She shared her thoughts with Naema more than with all of us combined, mostly talking about the dos and don'ts of a street girl. She let her try on her high-heels and heavy heels, showed her how to doll up her face or how to use toothpaste and brush. She told her to run away from any man who beat her, no matter the temptation. She told Naema that it was better to starve to death than go out with any man without condom.

When she was at work, she ignored Naema. I could chat her up on the pavements no matter what rags I was wearing. We knew how to pretend for everybody that we were just strangers, a streetkid and prostitute talking.

Her tortured sleep got to us. Her arrivals always reminded us that life could be better than what we were getting. We were dying to know about her Jaguar adventures. When my sister moaned one more time and clapped twice to kill mosquitoes in the dark, Mama could not stand it anymore. She rushed inside, took off the folded mosquito netting from the flaps of the carton, and tied it to the roof so that my sister was inside. She sprayed the place again before bringing out the baby to breastfeed. Baba wanted to sniff kabire badly, but was too afraid to wake up Maisha. He reached and grabbed my bottle, but the kabire was dead. The coughing got worse. Since there was no wind, he picked up the door and used it as a big fan to whip the air into the house.

In the morning, it was Atieno and Otieno who came out first. They looked tired, and were sniffling from the insecticide. They stood before us, spraying the morning with yellow urine, sneezing and whimpering.

The streets began to fill up. The street kids were up and scattered into the day like feed-ing chickens. Some moved about groggily, dizzy from kabire, and still sniffing and smoking. One of them recounted his dreams to others at the top of his voice, gesticulating maniacally. One man was screaming, pointing at two kids. The public was not interested. His pocket was ripped to the zip, leaving a square hole in front of his trousers. He pulled out his shirt to hide his nakedness, hurried away, a sheepish smile straining his face. There was no sun, only a slow ripening of the sky.

The twins started to wail and attack Mama's breasts. Baba spanked them hard. They sat there with pent-up tears they were afraid to shed. It was Naema who broke the spell. She came out of the house bearing the bags of food. She placed them on the ground and tore into them, filling the morning with hope. Baba bit into a chicken drumstick, announcing that it takes a while for meat to go bad. Mama took another piece. The rest of us dug into the rice, mashed potato, hamburgers, pizzas, spaghetti and sausages. We drank dead Coke and melted ice creams all mixed up. With her teeth, Naema opened bottles of Tusker and Castle beers. None of us

thought to inflate the balloons or open the cards that Maisha had brought.

Then the twins fell over on their backs, laughing and vomiting. As soon as they were done, they went straight back to eating, laughing and screaming, their mouths pink and white and green from the ice-cream. We could not get them to keep quiet. A taxi pulled up and Mai-sha came out of the house, dragging her trunk behind her. Our parents paused as the driver helped her put the trunk in the car. My mother began to cry, Baba shouted at the streets. The car pulled away. The noise attracted kids from the gangs. They circled around the food, and we struggled to stuff the food in our mouths, to stuff the bags back into the house, but the kids made off with most of the food.

We remained with the balloons and cards and the faint smell of Maisha's trunk. The twins giggled and burped.

AboutThe Author

Uwem Akpan does not talk about himself easily; He is a Jesuit with a strong social conscience. We concur.k

©2003 SEPT 3
GADO
gadonet.com
WTO
CHEAP PATENT DRUGS
POOR COUNTRIES
IS THAT THE BEST HE CAN DO!?
MULTINATIONALS

HOLD IT... I'VE GOT MY OWN AXIS OF EVIL LIST!
The AXIS of EVIL
IRAQ
NORTH KOREA
IRAN
W
W
AIDS
POVERTY
WAR
AFRICA
©2002 FEB 15 GADO
GADOnet.com

HA-HA - HAAA !! HO-HO- HOOO!! I WARNED YOU MY FRIEND...!
©2004 JAN4 GADO
www.GADOnet.com
YOU SHOULD HAVE BOUGHT HER A CAR, A SHAMBA NA NG'OMBE, PUT UP A HOUSE AND A GSU GUARD FOR HER... KWISHA!!

AboutThe Author

Cartoonist Godfrey Mwampembwa, GADO was born in Dar es Salaam, Tanzania on August 6, 1969. In 1992 GADO left tanzania to become Editorial cartoonist and illustrator with Nation Media Group LTD. GADO is the most Syndicated Political/Editorial cartoonist in the East and Central Africa. He has won several local awards. In 1996 he was honored by the International Olympic Media Award in Print Media and in 1999 was named Kenya Cartoonist of the Year. He has exhibited his works in Tanzania, Kenya, France, Norway, Finland and Italy. Now a Freelancer, GADO continues to do editorial cartoons for the Daily and Sunday Nation.

Tony Mochama

Poems

CAMPTOR

The Sicilian Dragon Defence

When I was young,
Dragons came in green
With tails coiled
& pitched / like Satan's tongue
or Pinnochio's penis
yuh- I was a kid, hardboiled
alright,
but I was frightened...
also

When I was young,
Sicilians were scary men
With godfather hats
And voices like dragging cement
Over a dead man's grave
(this is a poem, inter-rupt-ed).

Now,

That I'm older

(although not as old. As my predecessor
Taban Lo Liyong)
Days are short- but nights are long-
And along
The office block where I work
(built in architecture/that is shapely oblong)
Sicilians and dragons
Are arranged in lines that obstruct the horizon
(and this is wrong)
my bizness-pardners, Wilfred and John
play a perpetual chess game, everyday
on the floor
(and this- this is all wrong)
and the washer woman

cannot wash it (the chess games) away :-
with her broom
that sweeps the room

Tony Mochama

WHAT'S LEFT OF US

For my siblings

Dad's death left what was left of us
Shell shocked
(even it if was all make believe)
like my poetry, or my trip to Russia
it came with that feeling of preja-vu
that I received the fictitious bad news
on Friday night, at Tanagier,
as me and we and my only sister
sipped whiskey, soda and tangerines

It's like when
In mid- year
She told me of the smell of air
That hangs over Croatia

(and I smelled it too). Gray, smoggy air
clear blue day
and the pictures of dead men
hanging in the air
the way, some days,
Benjamins spill out of your pockets.

That terrible air of preja vu
With its purple ting'ed hue
That disappeared at the stroke of midnight
As August crossed into September
It is as if/ seasons/ contain invinsible lines
Where,
If August is the front line
September is a no- bomb zone
(we can be safe there/ in the middle of September
Nevertheless, I keep the phone uncharged
In order that
No bad news/ may come my way.

Tony M © 2003.

Benjamin, the MaGiCiAN.
By Tony Mochama

My family is made up of magicians
I
Create realities, that Creak,
Out of thin Air
And if I pick up a little box
And press 'unlock'
And then press some secret number
There's my sister
On the other end.

Vivian is a vivacious enchantress
Pretty smart as a whip

Elaine is the little magician
Of the family
Still learning her tricks.

Andrew, too, is a magician
Tonight he'll get into thin air/one
A Box (and vanish into of life crum hoax.

Benjamin

By the ears

(just like a white wabbit)

It's Benjamin, though,
Who is the master Magician
He disappears, for years, into thin air
And then- miraculously- re- appears
For no apparent reason
Clean-out of the Horizon.

I've always wondered where's her's gone
When he does those 'disappearing acts'
Wallowed, in mt agon,
But I am too full of like a paragon tact
To ask him the facts/ of his magical act
And, besides,
I too am a magician
In my own right. Tony C. 2003.

GOING AWAY

By Tony Mochama

This is a bar
I am in –
In a state
Of potential sin.
To avoid temptation
I give in to the thought
Of writing poetry
Which is a little
Like mental masturbation

This is a bar
I'm sitting in
On the right
A man goes away
And
Lives to die
Another day
My pen
Is like poison-ivy
It will not
Let me write leave 'live'
Because it does not wish abandonment

This is a leaf
I hold it between my fingers
The way I held the pen like an ornament
I that rat- a- tat wrote this
Between my calloused fingers

Like a kiss from a callous stranger
A kiss that lingers
On my finger-tips
I trace
The shape of the leaf-tip
The way I traced
The shape of that stranger's lips

Then, a girl with bottoms, wide as a bus
Or a mad architect/ with grotesquely twisted oblong thoughts
Invading his head
And a couple-in love and a barmaid
And silence / forever interrupts.
Forever, interrupts.

Tony Mochama c.2003

AboutThe Author

Tony Mochama is a poet and oral poet a journalist and Kenya's leading expert on sleazy bars. He is a lawyer when he is not pontificating or gossip columning.

TEA
MIRAA
VICNDULA
2004

Miraa, Kahawa n' all that n' Jazz

bY USAMA

My upstairs apartment in New Orleans was like a tree house, a little Birdland where vinyl discs engraved with the blues and avant-garde jazz played around the clock. With immersion in this music, came a great curiosity about its sources. The university's course on the history of jazz defined the blue note as "a flattened fifth or seventh," associated with musicians of African origin in the rural south. But no one could account for its universal effect on the human soul; and although there is a science of jazz, underpinned by an evolving structure—explaining the lyrical intensity of a John Coltrane, or the primal complexity of a Pharaoh Sanders tune, remained beyond the critics' grasp.

Then home-grown New Orleans virtuoso, Earl Turbington, started playing in local clubs; each time I caught his act, at some point in the set he would put down his sax and chant, "Africa, Africa, music was born…in Africa!" I was scheduled to complete my BA: this refrain and all that jazz induced me to do explore Earl's hypothesis.

I arrived in Nairobi in September 1974, and quickly discovered Kenyans were not interested in chord clusters, blue notes, and the origins of polyrhythmic dissonance. Rather, everywhere I went the main topic was "development," and Kenya presented a diversity of variations on the theme. Moreover, it was clear that people saw people like me as natural agents of this creed. For me, this was confusing and problematic.

To begin with, in the social milieu I was coming from, 'development' was a dirty word: development was new tracts of cinder block houses, meadows paved over with strip malls and parking lots, and industrial pollution galore; it certainly had nothing to do with enhanced quality of life. In Kenya, as I quickly learned, development was the national religion—and also a brand, marketed through faithfully recited mantras: Uhuru na kazi, KANU yajenga nchi, and Harambee!

Secondly, I was wary—in Central America, where I had traveled the year before parachuting into Kenya, development, or dessarollos, in the Latin American discourse, was mostly used in the infrastructural sense—i.e. public works or progress in the evolutionary context. The kind of development popularized in the Kenya mantras, in contrast, could get one into trouble if you were not careful: e.g., uhuru

connoted revolutionary struggle; the cooperative movement and notions like harambee would have been viewed as communism in disguise.

In Kenya, development or maendeleo in Swahili—was literally "moving forward," straight forward and devoid of suspicious baggage—typically referred to rural development because most Kenyans lived in the countryside, where most of the services and opportunities most urbanites took for granted did not exist.

My fellow students and I were enrolled in a field studies program headquartered in Long Island, New York, called Friends World College (FWC). Friends were the Quakers, and World referred to the fact that we students, or "wandering scholars" in the FWC catalogue, were supposed to treat "the world as our classroom." To that end, the college maintained centres in Europe, Latin America, Japan, India, and Kenya. The African Centre was located at the Katheka Kai Farmers Cooperative. Katheka Kai covered 3,500 hectares on the slopes of Mua Hills, six miles from Machakos, and was home to two hundred member households scattered across the farm.

It was the ideal locale to learn about maendeleo. Large tracts of Arabica coffee generated income, a large herd of cattle produced milk for the members and some for sale, every homestead had a few acres on which to grow their maize and beans and there was a primary school for the children. Katheka Kai was formerly the property of a family called Webber. Old man Webber was a good man according to his former squatters, as was his son, whom they described as an "African," and not only because he had two English wives. Our campus comprised the several houses occupied by this sprawling household, and we lived in close symbiosis with the extended family that was Katheka Kai.

We had arrived on the local scene a decade after independence, after many issues still controversial in Latin America had been sorted out. Mzee Jomo Kenyatta, the "George Washington of Kenya," was the undisputed boss. Not only was capitalism good, it rhymed with "African Socialism," the officially endorsed guiding principle of Kenya's nation-building project. A civil servant who owned Highway Bar, a local oasis perched on the last hill before Machakos town, clarified it for me: "African socialism is simple—just like what we are doing here—we Africans get together, buy each other drinks, and socialise. The socialism in Tanzania is different—they call it Ujamaa, but it is really Marxism, which is totally un-African—Africans are natural capitalists!"

This was also the era of Modernisation. Modernisation was predicated upon the transfer from the first world to the third of the capital, technology, and skills needed to industrialise with the rural population as an unlimited pool of labour. This theory presumed that the educated elite, assisted by Western expatriates, would promptly lead their new nations into the modern world.

Marxist ideas which were then also popular in Africa advocated essentially the same centralised command economy, but one controlled by a revolutionary vanguard which would liberate the enterprises and resources controlled by comprador capitalists and manage them on behalf of the exploited masses.

The Government of Kenya did not have to buy either bill of goods, chiefly

because the introduction of the Swinnerton Plan in 1950 opened the way for peasant farmers to piggy back on agro-commercial developments pioneered by the settler estates. The Million Acres Scheme redistributed land to a mix of elite farmers, yeoman peasants, and landless poor, serving as a model for a host of other settlement schemes. Ministries concerned with rural production introduced programmes for smallholder production of tea and dairy products. Later on, a new set of entrepreneurial farmers initiated horticulture for export markets. Kenyan economic policy of this period both promoted commercial intensification and provided a safety valve for Kenya's sky rocketing population

By the mid 1970s, the Kenya exemplar was very much in style. As elsewhere, a new African elite monopolised state power, but their economic interests were served by sharing the prosperity with progressive farmers, and the host of civil servants, private sector employees, and entrepreneurs who straddled the urban and rural sectors. The cultural elite was listening to Jim Reeves, Skeeter Davis, and Roger Whitaker. Political trends, in contrast, were more problematic. Growing inequity, corruption, and heavy-handed governance fueled ideologically primed critics, mainly academics based at Nairobi University, opposed to the Kenyatta state's status quo. The murder of J.M. Kariuki and a string of political detentions confirmed the rot.

While Nairobi university students freely broadcast these sins, FWC students' involvement was confined to reading Petals of Blood. Many of us liberally imbibed the neo-Marxist jargon popular at that time, and some vied to impress with allusions to dependency and the conspiracies of neo-colonial compradors. But back on the farm, the wise men of Kai always set us straight. Although it seemed that Ukambani's power baron, Paul Ngei, was tainted if not an outright thug, they said, "Ngei ni simba wetu. He protects our interests and besides, he is the grandson of Masaku himself."

Siasa was dirty, but coffee prices were high. For the large-scale growers in the Mua Hills and the small-scale farmers of Iveti on the other side of the Machakos valley, life was good.

For the FWC "wandering scholars meanwhile," six weeks of lectures and Swahili training culminated in independent field studies which would focus on some kind of rural project.

A Dutch doctor organised the most memorable activity of our orientation. He sent us on a field trip which took us through fertile farmland and ended at a rural clinic in the much drier and poorer town of Mitaboni. He used this trip as a foil for our assumption that simply being who we were qualified us as agents of progress—a notion which dove tailed quite nicely with local expectations about our contribution to 'development'. I encountered this assumption so frequently whenever people learned I was traveling to Africa that I started referring to it as the Dr. Schweitzer complex.

The doctor described the years and the effort he had expended at a district hospital in Western Province only to see it all unravel after he left. He told us that although he was doing the same thing again in Machakos, he had no illusions about

the permanence of any of the improvements he had effected. "There is real poverty here—like you saw in Mitaboni—but the best use of your time here," he advised us, "is to learn everything you can about the real Africa."

This was exactly what I intended to do. True to the Friends World theme, I planned to wander as much as necessary before formalising my "study-project proposal." My first destination was Turkana, and a fellow student, Bibi Lynn, a young lady from New York City interested in photography, volunteered to accompany me on this trip.

Traveling with Bibi Lynn had its advantages. For one, it made hitching rides much easier. At the edge of the Eastern Rift Valley, a real live settler gave us a lift. Prior to this chance meeting, I considered such colonials to be the enemy, so to speak. But Mr. Hempstead was a wonderful man. He took us to his farm near the Menengai crater, and I learned much about Kenya during the three days we spent there.

He told us about his friend and neighbour, "the old man," and how Mzee was a traditionalist at heart and still danced all night whenever he visited Nakuru. He told us about the Kyukes, "hard working and jolly good blokes, as conspiratorial as they come." I learned about coffee, buni and parchment, soil and climate, coffee berry disease and how the Yanks had developed new chemicals that saved the day. He was in the process of selling the farm: "It was high time the Africans got their land back—I was ready to turn it over a long time ago, but waited for someone serious to come along—selling out to a telephone farmer just would not do." Yegods – he should have been a priest, so much noble sentiment….He thought the government capable and well run on the whole, though with the standard settler caveat, "The whole place might blow up when the old man passes away."

Upon arriving in Kitale, we were adopted by Jaspel Singh, a young contractor by trade. He lived in the house on a former settler coffee plantation on Mt. Elgon—now owned by a telephone farmer who "Had let the place go to hell." Jaspel drove like a maniac, and we spent a large portion of the two days before the lorry left for Lodwar in a mountain bar. I spent the first evening in this bar with a very unusual African. He loved trees, and for the next three hours my ancient Druidic genes vibrated as he described the virtues of trees and their importance for development. He waxed on about how he was going to plant ten thousand trees. Man, was I impressed.

"Yeah, you bet," Jaspel said, to my ravings about how cool his friend was.

The next day Jaspel took us to a high mountain clearing where his machines were working. A shot rang out, and then another. We dived behind the bulldozer. A few uneventful minutes later, Jaspel shouted, "Rudi kazini!"

"What was that about?" I asked.

"The squatters are pissed."

"What are they angry about?"

"They think we're clearing their forest."

I mentioned the incident to my forester friend back in the mountain bar. He said something about anti-development hooligans, but that they couldn't stand in the way of progress.

"But what about the forest?" I asked. "It looks like it's being cleared."

"Not really," he said. "That's where I'm going to plant my trees. They will grow very fast, and then I will make lots of money! Trees are money, and money is development."

He ordered another three rounds of beer for everyone. Now in the initial stages of withdrawal from African Socialism, I protested that I couldn't drink them. Jaspel corrected this breach of protocol by informing me that one didn't refuse hospitality. "If you can't drink them, the bartender will put the bottles back on the shelf for the next time we are here!"

The next afternoon, the Shah Mohammed and Sons lorry left for Turkana. The lorry was crowded, but we perched comfortably enough on sacks of flour which gave us a commanding view of the spectacular landscape. The lorry descended through an expanse of large and small caldera scattered around Kacheliba, shot the gap between two jagged mountain ranges where a crude sign marked the border with Uganda, and then plunged back down the escarpment into Kenya, speeding across sandy tracts of Turkana. We would stop periodically in front of isolated shacks to unload a few boxes before continuing to Lodwar.

Our driver insisted that I join him for libations. It was 2:30 a.m, and the local bar was packed to the rafters with frolicking socialists. My companion taunted a posse of naked boys, pretending to press a coin into one of the many skinny hands extended through the windows. He allayed my apparent discomfort with a beaming smile, "Sijali, wako na njaa, lakini tumewabebea chakula." I slept under the lorry and woke up to a tableau of scattered acacia and thin people wrapped in dirty white togas.

Lodwar was two lines of wooden storefronts and closed doors. One opened up briefly and a Somali man motioned us inside where he served us black tea and dry bread and refused payment. My friend the driver said the lorry was going on to Kalokol, and advised us to join him. A crowd of stick people collected around us as we waited for the lorry to depart, withered arms extended.

Bibi Lynn was distraught; I watched an old man squatting to the side keel over. Impelled by a mix of compassion and discomfort, we started cutting up our travel stash—a basket of fruit, distributing strips of papaya and mango as the engine roared into life. The recipients of our largesse gave chase as the vehicle rolled forward. Then, as the lorry lurched into second gear, they pelted us with the fruit.

Conditions in Kalokol were better. Some Norwegians were teaching the nomads to fish. Bibi Lynn went back the next day. I stayed on and learned that Shah Mohammed had passed away the night we were on the road. I was stuck. I became

the ward of the Muriuki family. Mr. Muriuki was a gentleman who worked for NCCK.

I wandered around during the day, spent evenings listening to the BBC with my host, then slipped away to watch the Turkana as they sang and clapped late into the night. Some American missionaries I met said the dancing was pagan. They lived in a house that looked like something out of a Dallas suburb. Conscious of my dependent status in the missionary compound, I watched the dances from a respectful distance.

It was three weeks before the next lorry left for down-country. We took the same route but traveled during the day. The lorry stopped briefly at a laga in Uganda, giving several emaciated Karamojong men the chance to beg for food. This time, the upcountry people on the lorry tossed them some biscuit boxes, and enjoyed a hearty laugh when the pastoralists found them empty.

After returning to Machakos, I was recruited into plans to spend the Christmas-New Year holidays in Tanzania. Two of the planners dropped out on the day of departure, leaving Bibi Lynn and myself together again. After an unplanned deviation into the wilds of Maasailand, we arrived in Arusha

Here we met many friendly Africans, hospitable Swahili speakers keen to celebrate their home-grown approach to development. Some of them socialised Bibi's shillings, dollars, and travelers cheques all the way from Arusha to Musoma. It was easy enough to do since she was in the habit of leaving them unattended in a large kiondo. The first disappearance occurred in Ngorongoro. The rest vanished on the bus, during a tea break in Serengeti.

There was nothing to be done except obtain a police abstract, so we spent part of a morning in the Musoma police station, where I observed porters carry in many large loads of dry reddish stalks which bore a remarkable resemblance to marijuana. That afternoon we attended a public rally addressed by Mwalimu Nyerere. He seemed to connect with the large crowd of wananchi. They remained respectfully quiet. I went down to the lake. While I admired the pillars of delicately balanced giant boulders, an earnest young man answered my Swahili greeting by telling me that lugha ya taifa was OK, but Tanzanians needed to learn English if they were to going to get anywhere in the modern world.

The loss of currency had forced us to retrace our steps. I purchased tickets on the next bus back to Arusha, the agent stressing how lucky I was to get seats at all. I came to appreciate what he meant during the fifteen-hour journey. The bus left Musoma full and arrived in Arusha with passengers crammed into every possible space. We began to feel more guilty than lucky as the queues of well-dressed travelers waiting at every stop were left behind. Disembarking was swimming against the tide of people imploding through the windows before the bus rolled to a stop.

We decided to hitch-hike to Namanga. An outspoken young farmer picked us up and debriefed us during a detour to his family's farm on Mt. Moshi. "We are Chagga," he announced. It was meant to demonstrate that underneath the PC behavior, Tanzanians are as conscious of their tribes as anyone else. "The government doesn't like us," he continued. He described Nyerere as a fake who talked in code: ujamaa really means unyama while the economy is destroyed. Kujitegemea is a formu-

la for stifling any form of individual initiative. "We do OK," he told us, "but only because Mzee planted these 85 acres of coffee—and it takes fifty of them to keep this pick-up fueled and running."

Our next ride was an Asian who took us all the way to Machakos. He chuckled when we related our Chagga friend's views, while confiding to us that it didn't stop his people from making money—as long as they were careful not to show it. "I own a Mercedes," he confided, "but when I go to Arusha, I drive this VW bug."

****

As students in a unique 'experiential education' field programme, we often thought our insights were original and correct. In my case, after covering a large swathe of territory (including the coast), much of what was held up as development appeared to really be a crock. But rural development is as old as the hills. Other people had been studying the problem for a long time, and looking at the big picture too.

End Part I

II: An Brief History of Rural Development

The period spanning the 1970s and the mid 1980s was the golden age of developmental discourse; a heady time when people from all walks of life debated problems of the Third World and their causes. These were passionate discussions, often punctuated with high-minded venom.

In the beginning…there was Marx. Then came neo-colonialism, as popularised in Andre Gunder Frank's classic work, The Development of Underdevelopment. In this part of the world, Walter Rodney's How Europe Underdeveloped Africa was the bible. The Marxists of that era were prolific writers, and developing regions provided a vast playground for the study of capitalist parasitology. Over time, the basic premises of Marxism gave rise to multiple diagnoses of the disease that the West had infected developing nations with.

An annotated bibliography of this neo-Marxist literature would fill thousands of pages. However, a few salient features of this school of thought and how it operated are sufficient for our purposes.

Though concerned with exploitation of the common man (and woman), most seminal works of the era are almost as difficult to read as the writings of Karl Marx himself. But other factors enabled the Marxists to punch above their weight. To the degree that the world was screwed up and getting worse, it was as futile as it was unfashionable to argue against radical critique. Also, for a variety of reasons, places where theory had long informed practice (like the Soviet Union, North Korea, and Albania) did not count. It did not matter if the new interpretations were right or not

because they could not be wrong.

The neo-Marxists did however have a fatal flaw: they had ignored one of Marx's most fundamental principles, that is, that the development of capitalism proper is the prerequisite for the emergence of the internal contradictions that will destroy it. Even capitalist Kenya was populated largely by pre-proletarian tillers of the soil. Such conditions, as the British Marxist Bill Warren once pointed out, oblige true believers to support right of center political parties—like KANU.

This presented a real dilemma. Although everyone agreed upon the urgent need to liberate the African masses, there was little consensus on the method to be employed. Africa had spawned Tanzania's Ujamaa African Socialism, Siad Barre's scientific socialism in Somalia; Nkrumah's government driven industrialisation in Ghana, Ethiopia's Afro-Marxism, Sekou Toure's radical delinking from the metropole in Guinea.

When these theory-inspired applications went awry, the leaders who had spawned them clung to power anyway, playing the super powers off against each other to do so. On the other hand, opposition politicians and guerilla movements continued to exploit Marxist ideology well into the 1980s—even as an excuse for fighting each other.

In theory, objective conditions in Kenya, this 'country of many contrasts' presented more fertile soil for Marxism than most of the countries that had embraced it. In practice however, Kenya was one of Africa's best-known neo-colonial toadies, a fact eloquently illustrated in Colin Leys' 1969 book "Underdevelopment in Kenya." Because Leys was clever enough not to directly insult Kenyatta or to finger him as a capitalist high-roader, the book became one of the most widely read case studies of its kind.

Only when J.M Karikui called Kenya "a nation of ten millionaires and ten million paupers," did the authorities realise their blunder, and by then it was too late. Their attempt at damage control resulted in Kariuki's corpse turning up in the Ngong Hills and brought Kenya to the brink of revolution.

But Mzee saved the day, warning the chickens that they were being "watched by a big chicken-hawk in the sky."

In Nairobi, the chickens disregarded the warning. Kenya Air Force F-4s buzzed around the city as university students took to the streets earning themselves an extended vacation in their rural homes, where their revolutionary rhetoric did not play very well. Some university lecturers ended up in jail.

Kenyatta's death in 1978, and Daniel arap Moi's contested ascent to power, muddied the ideological waters. The abortive doctors' strike of 1979 proved to be the radicals' swan song. The day's events also confirmed the end of President Moi's honeymoon.

Student activists took up the striking medics cause, and organised a march in downtown Nairobi. The protesters waved branches and carried placards stating "A Luta Continua," and "Arise, Arise, Ye Wretched of the Earth." They recited these slogans in chorus as they proceeded down River Road. Unbeknownst to the noisy procession, a column of GSU armed with shields and clubs had massed on Tom Mboya street, and were advancing down Latema Road.

I watched both movements unfold from the balcony of the New Kenya Lodge, a veritable front row seat for the imminent collision that was to bring closure to the short happy life of Marxist praxis in Kenya. Protestors scurried into shops as River Road's petit bourgeoisie bolted their doors. Others turned heel, and a small core of hardened troopers dropped their placards and waded into the milling crowds of people sandwiched in between, shouting "no maize in Kenya, no maize in Kenya!" The goon squad focused on chasing the scattering students as they headed towards the city centre. I didn't witness any real violence, but over the next two hours numerous innocent by-standers got clobbered as students skirmished with the GSU. The doctors went back to work, and the basis of resistance to the Moi government underwent a basic shift: ethnic conspiracies displaced revolutionary ideology.

The run-up to the attempted coup d'etat of August 8, 1982 was a time of rumors and political intrigue. As it turned out, the trial of the Attorney General's cousin for arms smuggling and the Gor Mahia's inexplicable loss to Vital'O of Burundi were not unconnected. Then a cabal of non-coms in the Kenya Air force launched the planned putsch—prematurely, after a drunken Saturday night. The Sunday morning sun came up on scenes of inebriated airmen shouting "Power!" to gathering crowds of urban lumpen. During the next four hours Nairobi suffered more damage than Kampala under four years of Idi Amin.

The ideological motivation of the failed revolution was summed up thus by its leader: "If Ghana has Flight Lieutenant Rawlings and Liberia Staff Sergeant Samuel Doe, why not Senior Private Ochuka in Kenya?" Ochuka and his inner circle were Luo. In the Kenyan folk model of that era, the Luo featured as communist sympathisers owing to Oginga Odinga's flirtation with Soviet patronage during the 1960s. The Luo brain trust was considered to be a breeding ground for Marxist ideology by extension; the August Achiel disaster presented the state with force majeur to attack the problem at its source.

It was a bad time to be a Luo university professor. In any event, the Marxist threat was fading fast in Kenya and Africa in general. A decade after going into exile, Ngugi wa Thiong'o published his final novel, Matigari. In a hallucinatory preface, Ngugi claimed the police in Central Province believed the book's hero, a chokora mtangi urchin turned revolutionary, to be a real person. In reality, Matigari didn't raise a ripple in Kenya.

But in the West, the intellectual heat generated by the theoretical problematique remained largely undiminished. An international professoriate of epistemological Marxists still published weighty volumes, and its luminaries sat on the boards controlling most social science research funding.

The Structural Marxism associated with French anthropology, a neo-Marxist genre especially designed for African conditions, crossed the linguistic barrier and their modes of production analyses became hot for a while. Like Claude Levi-Strauss before them, they scraped away the surface in order to expose the deep structures underpinning all social relations. Research in West Africa for example, revealed that phenomena like gender discrimination and tribalism are actually manifestations of class conflict in pre-capitalist clothing.

In East Africa, by contrast, epistemological Marxism was firmly rooted in the British tradition. Researchers marshaled quantities of hard data to back up their interpretations. Their empiricism did not change the fact that theory is God. True believers were known to claim that only by raising one's consciousness could one appreciate the real scope and depth of Marx's Theory. Critics began to claim that Marxism was nothing more than the final stage of Western Christianity. Sometimes the dialectical contradiction between quasi-religious theory and life on earth induced a kind of intellectual schizophrenia. In the introduction to his study, Land and Economic Change in Kenya, Gavin Kitchings actually apologises for basing his analysis on empirical fact.

Twenty years later, it became fashionable to credit Marx for his incisive analysis of capitalism. The neo-Marxists' starting point was concern about the poverty the suffering rife in the Third World. For several decades they generated unprecedented intellectual ferment, and highlighted the problems of developing regions. By proposing alternatives to capitalism, they exerted a gravitational pull on orthodox developmental policy. Reinforced by the success of Viet Nam's rural insurgency, the neo-Marxists shifted their focus to the countryside. The World Bank replaced the trickle down approach with basic human needs. Unlike Marx himself, decision makers became interested in "the idiocy of rural life." Long the preserve of missionaries and the occasional anthropologist, the boondocks were back in style.

I had arrived in Kenya when the rural developmental juggernaut was gaining speed. Rural societies around the world are famous for being conservative, resistant to change, and suspicious of outsiders. The opposite appeared to obtain for most of Kenya's countryside—certainly in regard to the latter two qualities—and especially when white-skinned foreigners were the conveners of progress in the form of a project.

Maendeleo was by definition an imported commodity; a by-product of what Dennis Rondinelli calls "policy experiments. " And of all these, the integrated project was the Cadillac of rural development.

The integrated project had something for everyone. For the foreign government, much of the investment found its way back home. For the host government—the Treasury got foreign exchange, ministries got the leftover cars and flats, savvy civil servants got to go abroad for training, businessmen got contracts, the Party got to take the credit, and the beneficiaries got to feed off the scraps. The domestic taxpayers who paid the bill got to avoid guerilla war.

For a long time most everyone was happy with the arrangement though an iconoclastic few raved about conspiracy theories. I didn't want to interfere. African socialism was flourishing on Katheka Kai and upcountry in general, but this was not my

cup of tea. Instead, I headed for the coast, worked with Bajuni fishermen, and studied an Africa of wooden boats, inhabited by men of steel.

The Swahili are Africa's most accomplished indigenous mariners. I saw craftsmen equipped with three tools—adze, axe, and bow-drill—build two hundred ton vessels with homemade nails. We routinely sailed miniature versions of these jahazi to fishing grounds beyond the psychological barrier when land disappears from view. For two years, I pulled on ropes, waded into dark, dangerous waters with nets, gutted fish, rowed and poled becalmed boats, hauled mangrove out of swamps, prayed, married, and—except for reading a lot of books (and listening to jazz)—lived pretty much as the Lamu Bajuni live.

I met fisheries officers who ate tilapia but would not touch snapper, forestry officers charged with monitoring the archipelago's mangrove who could not set foot in a boat, nurses who would not nurse, hypocritical imams, clerks who demanded bribes, politicians who told lies, and experienced firsthand the idiocy of so called civilised life as the government effectively suffocated the maritime sector—but this is another story altogether.

End part II

Part III: The Gospel According to Mark

The 1980s was not called Africa's lost decade for nothing. As was the case in most of Africa, the Government of Kenya lost control over economic policy. The economy lost direction, many large coffee growers lost their farms, and by the end of the decade, many Kenyans had lost faith in the government.

Most economic sectors experienced slippage. The cost of energy and other production inputs increased. The Cadillacs of development ran out of petrol. When the neo-Marxist movement ran out of steam, the World Bank switched from basic human needs to the pro-market conditionalities of the IMF. The resulting growth of agricultural commodities glutted Kenya's traditional markets. The country's major demographic safety valve jammed shut as unsettled land for agricultural expansion began to run out.

After surviving the crises of 1982, Moi used the elections of 1983 to clean house. The government took control of the countryside by launching its Rural District Focus. The RDF was a cleverly designed decentralisation programme that, by granting control over district budgets to new district development committees, effectively diluted the power of entrenched ethnic power brokers while concentrating final decision-making power in the executive. To "bring government closer to the people," parallel "development" committees were established at the sub-location level, Kenya's basic grass-roots administrative unit. This intensified peasants' mistrust of the state.

But the picture was not all negative. Amidst the country's deteriorating infrastructure, the central Rift Valley highlands was the scene of major dessarrollos with new tarmac roads, improved schools, and expanded communications infrastructure consuming a disproportionate share of the Treasury's stagnating public revenues.

Kenyans naturally grumbled though grudgingly acknowledging that leaders are bound to build up their home areas. Nairobi got a night life. Everywhere else got evangelical churches—Pentecostal banks that exhorted the newly "saved" to deposit their savings in exchange for blessings, i.e. jobs, cars, money, and houses.

Individual Kenyans continued to excel in many domains, and sports continued to buoy the nation's morale. The greatest achievement, however, was sexual. The country's galloping growth rate peaked at 4.1 per annum in 1989. One team of demographers cited Kenya's net population increase over the last half of the twentieth century as the highest in known human history. These demographics mocked years of Rough Rider condom ads in the Daily Nation (paid for by USAID). The baby boom's economic ramifications were one more example of Kenyans defying the logic of donor rationality.

Granted, the donor logic problem was largely reducible to the expectations of stupid white men. In my own case, a decade later I was still trying to figure out why starving Turkana pelted us with food, why my Kamba friends wore sweaters and suits in blazing heat and a host of other hard to crack behavioral riddles. So I applied to graduate school.

I departed Kenya at the height of the severe drought of 1984. En route to the airport we passed a trail of carcasses dead and dying cattle lining the road to the Kenya Meat Commission abattoir.

In graduate school, I faced a choice among history, agricultural science, linguistics, and economics and then ended up taking all four by specialising in anthropology. I kept faith with the new neo-classical economic dispensation by undertaking research on the commercialisation of small-scale agriculture in Meru's Nyambene Hills for my dissertation.

The free wheeling free-marketeering of the Nyambene scene was quite a shift from the folksy communism of Katheka Kai.

Katheka Kai, under the leadership of Bwana Muthoka, Weber's coffee manager, was a well-run operation. The members considered the coop to be a large family; indeed, I doubt if I will ever see Karl Marx's maxim, "each according to one's need, each according to one's ability," better put into practice. The local sub-chief representing government was a member of a benign male gerontocracy that, for the majority of the inhabitants, was the only government they needed to know. These elders were active African socialists. Their wives provided the farm labor and most of their daughters joined their brothers in school after toting water for the home. The sick always received treatment, even if it required the coop's pick-up rushing them to town in the middle of the night. When a member got caught with hand in the till, the sum was repaid through payroll and coffee bonus deductions, like an interest free loan.

Katheka Kai entered Africa's Lost Decade on a high note. The coop had paid off the government loan used to purchase the farm from the Webers during the coffee boom of 1977-78. In 1980, they purchased Potha, an expansive 20,000-hectare ranch 'settled' by the Percival family during the early years of colonial rule. To commem-

orate the purchase, the coop organized a convoy of cars, trucks, and tractors to carry the adult members to the highest point on the ranch, Kya Mutheke, a large hill marking the Machakos turn-off on the Mombasa road. The picnic on the summit that day was a serene and happy occasion.

I recall taking in the extensive panorama, a territory spanning the line of eucalyptus crowning the Mua Hills to the plains adjacent to distant Katumani all of which was now owned by the wananchi of Katheka Kai farmers Cooperative Society. I also recall agreeing with Dan Schellenberg, a second generation Ukambani Baptist missionary who had joined us up top, that "this is about as good as it gets." Certainly at that moment in time, the success of this distinctively communal capitalism qualified as maendeleo at its best.

I faithfully checked in at Kai during my post-1984 summer visits to Kenya, and the coop appeared to be holding up well despite the downward movement of coffee prices. The loss of income was ostensibly a factor in the expansion of household land holdings from two to five acres sometime during the late 1980s—although the management vigorously resisted this modest privatisation of land when it was first proposed in 1983.

I discovered the unique environs of the Nyambene Hills quite by accident. A Jamhuri day holiday trip to Meru National Park in 1981 took us through a swathe of verdant Nyambene farmland, distinguished (to our untrained eyes) by the absence of crops. On the way back we stopped in Maua, then a modest hamlet even by the standards of Kenya's one street towns. There we came across a small but significant branch of Barclays Bank tucked away in the town's lower corner. Our search for some of the famous Meru miraa yielded only leafy bunches bearing little resemblance to the stems sold at Mwembe Tayari and River Road—until a young man guided us to Muringene. The turn-off to Kenya's premier hub for the distribution of Catha edulis was marked by a small wooden sign that gave "Muringene Market—Soko ya Miraa bila Ubagusi," miraa market open to all.

Elias Maitheta, a miraa trader who supplied Nairobi's rich and famous encouraged me to visit his homeland again. The following July I walked through the miraa heartland, home of the Igembe. Meru traditionalists educated me in their ethno-science. What we had mistaken for unkempt countryside was actually a land of compact agro-forests generating a range of food, fodder, medicines, and other household use products. A new 'farm' evolves over several generations into a mature agro-forest. The tree of paradise is the economic engine dragging these long-term projects into the modern era.

I was impressed—by the wonders of indigenous agriculture, by its contribution to local capital formation, and especially by the self-starting properties of Igembe culture. Unlike other areas of the highlands, the Igembe expected little from the government. Oral traditions describing a time of oppression on the coast by red-clothed antu beria made them wary of stupid white men. I was received as friend, and not agent of development.

The Igembe synthesis of biodiversity, prosperity and cultural integrity struck me as an exemplar of natural maendeleo. Like the Swahili maritime sector, it was based on local knowledge and indigenous economic dynamics. Then I met a highly

respected local entrepreneur, Julius Mbariu, during a stopover in Muringene. Mr. Mbariu confronted me with a stark hypothesis. "Yes," he admitted, "we have lots of money. But this only underscores our lack of development." Not for the first time, a riddle of rural development was challenging my basic assumptions.

My intellectual curiosity pricked, I continued to survey the Nyambene landscape on an annual basis after relocating to the University of Florida in 1984. This led to an article entitled, The Production and Marketing of Miraa in Kenya, which induced my professors to 'suggest' that I pursue the Igembe phenomenon for my doctoral research. After a lecture by Michael Lofchie, author of an influential book extolling Kenya's policy-driven agricultural success, I noted that Kenya's commercial agricultural success was exclusively a highland phenomenon, and asked the professor to comment on the prospects for commercial success repeating itself in Kenya's less endowed agro-ecological zones.

"That's a very good question, he replied, "but one that I can't answer. You have identified a critical area for further research."

Thus anointed to answer my own question, I returned to the field presuming that following the burgeoning Igembe population down the Nyambene slopes would take me beyond the orbit of the valuable herb. I was wrong. Everywhere smallholders were adapting miraa agroforestry to new conditions in the rocky and drought-prone lowlands. Catha edulis is a remarkably resilient plant. Its cultivation as a component of Igembe permaculture was proving environmentally adaptive in ecologically austere conditions, and the market for even low quality miraa favored it over millet and cotton.

After making me cut 60 pages of unacceptable (to them) theory, a committee of eminent scholars signed off on my dissertation. Its conclusions about sustainable agriculture sidestepped the Mbaaru hypothesis and its counter-intuitive implications which held the steady inflow of 'easy' money responsible for sabotaging the developmental process.

This is a complicated subject.

Miraa powers a modernising economy while blunting the impact of external forces of modernisation. While it has preserved adaptive indigenous institutions like the Njuri Ncheke council and conserved the indigenous agroforesty system, critics point to the expanding employment generated by the miraa industry as discouraging education. Though even some beneficiaries of the trade blame miraa prosperity for limiting social progress in general, miraa has conquered the opposition of the same educated elite, who grow it on their farms.

While coffee producers on Mt. Kenya, bound by the monocultural provisions of The Coffee Act, spent the lost decade tightening their belts to the tune of meal a day, the miraa economy percolated happily along. And while the 'modernised' Meru of Mt. Kenya often refer to their culturally conservative Nyambene brethren as "hillbillies," the emerging doctrine of sustainability—with its emphasis on agroforestry and environmental biodiversity, indigenous technical knowledge and local market initia-

tives—designated the hillbilly system as positively PC.

Not that the yeoman farmers of Kangetastan gave a damn. Oblivious to USAID's new testament, the gospel according to Bretton Woods or the writings of prophet Marx, —like Frank Sinatra, they did not care—as long as doing it their way put money in the bank.

This should not be construed as money substituting for brains. I have met unlettered entrepreneurs who articulate in their own words economic principles associated with Ricardo, Adam Smith, and Schumpeter. Still, from a socioeconomic perspective, Igembe's indigenous economy was generating its own set of what Marxian dialecticians love to call "internal contradictions."

Igembe agroforesters use the panga, not the hoe. They use these razor sharp tools to sculpt trees and shape the canopies of their agroforests in amazing ways. Pangas also come in handy for settling personal disputes with unfortunate results. Child labour is a serious problem, not because it is forced or the wages are unfair, but because juvenile income plus abysmal primary exam performance form a locked cycle discouraging others from going to school. The Nyambene Njuri Ncheke's developmental ideology will remain relevant as long the Meru live on the land. But the growing cadre of lawyers who now litigate the land disputes the elders' council used to arbitrate is steadily eroding the elders' role. Projecting these mixed socio-economic trends supports the Mbariu hypothesis.

Development is not a function of money. One scholar argued more would have been achieved if the money invested in development projects was deposited across the landscape by planes flying above. But the obverse hypothesis stating that development does not occur in the absence of money is also true. What is money but a modern substitute for the surplus generated by agrarian societies?

Anthropology treats development as a universal process set in motion by agricultural surplus. The surplus ends up being exchanged for other commodities and labor, which allows some food producers to begin making other products for use and trade. At a certain stage in the process powerful members of the society capture the surplus for their own use and for distribution to others. Typically, surplus capture begins with the source of protein, which reinforces leaders' physical and mental advantage. Institutionalisation of this arrangement marks the beginning of state organisation—it also explains Kenyan politicians and civil servants penchant for nyama choma (roast meat).

The development process, according to my academic tribe, proceeds through a number of such stages before undergoing the transition to capitalism. In Africa, however, historical circumstances and abundant supplies of animal protein conspired to see these stages become jumbled together.

On the brink of colonialism, most African societies were at different points on the pre-state continuum. Then, several generations later, Africa's new nations inherited full-blown replicas of the European state. Both the new clans of capital poor Westernised elites created to run them and the diverse ensembles of capital poor peasantries these nations encompassed deemed home-grown capitalism a non-

starter at that time. State capitalism was promoted in its place.

Kenya emerged as an exemplar of this quasi-capitalism where the natives associated development with the government; aspiring neo-capitalists sought access to its resources, and everyone else wanted its services. Insofar as political patronage went hand-in-hand with delivering 'development' to the people, being connected to the state was critical for private capital formation.

Neo-Marxists disparaged this system as the product of neo-colonial Uhuru. Marx himself considered the practice of extracting capital and property from the state primitive accumulation, a generic developmental phase leading to the establishment of capitalism proper. State capitalism, in contrast, was an oxymoronic term for a poorly thought-out concept: an ideologically neutral variation on the statism of the neo-Marxists, which ostensibly served the purpose of protecting the status quo.

The agricultural surplus modern Kenya was built on came from coffee. Foreign aid and fiscal constraint in the form of excluding minority access to the national pie helped sustain the nation building formula—as long as coffee prices remained high. But they started to drop after the boom of 1978. Two years into the Moi presidency, Treasury Minister Mwai Kibaki used budget day to announce that the era of easy options was over, as his boss quickly discovered.

If the government is a milk cow with a monopoly over the best grazing, it is only logical that the cow would get bigger and bigger over time and it did. Moi had appeared a reluctant 'capitalist' at first, but he nevertheless followed Kenyatta's footsteps to the land of primitive accumulation—with the caveat that if you wanted to milk the cow, loyalty was paramount.

The IMF prescribed structural adjustment of the economy. Kenya and other African countries became experimental plots for new theories. Cultivating the private sector was the objective, freeing up valuable nutrients consumed by bloated governments for its growth was the theory.

The ministries of rural development shed bulk, ministry of agriculture Land Rovers ran out of fuel by mid-month, public hospitals introduced cost sharing. Cooperatives and local authorities went bust. The purchasing power of civil service salaries continued to decline. Agricultural output proceeded to fuata nyayo. Kenya's economic planners argued that rainfall was the primary factor explaining the country's varying grain production, but the Club du Paris—said no. Fertiliser subsidies distort market forces, and so they were cut. A World Bank policy paper recommended that Kenya double the acreage under coffee whose production in 1989 was half that of its late 1970s high. State revenues dropped accordingly. Maize imports soared.

Although the Empire's excesses and its campaign against real or fictitious Mwakenya rebels grabbed most of the attention, kleptocracy and misplaced priorities of the one party state only partially explain what was going on. The African policy experiment wasn't working. The Bank guys doctored their statistics to show that it was. The Yanks said politics is undermining policy; the big guys are milking but not feeding the cow. USAID funded democracy and governance experts to build a better mousetrap. They called it civil society. President George H. Bush called it Ambassador Hempstone.

Many of Africa's predatory states were dying unnatural deaths. How was Moi to avoid the fate of other Big Men? He shed his skin and survived to preside over the revival of Kenya's multi-party democracy. Nyama Choma licked his fingers, and went home to write his memoirs. In an article in Finance magazine, Mr. Hempstone, apalled at Moi's continued employment suggested that Kenyans had never known a democratic institution until he arrived on the scene. He spoke too soon. Moi was a lousy dictator, but the final decade of the millennium was to be his finest hour as a politician. Kenya's multi-party democracy flourished—as recipe for liberalising the political marketplace.

The price of votes varies according to constituency, but they have always been one of the best buys available in Kenya's political marketplace. With the introduction of political pluralism, even parliamentarians could be bought—for as little as the title deed to a public urinal in Kiambu town. MPs were finding it difficult to both keep up appearances and appease thousands of poor constituents on 70,000 /- a month. Before long, freshman members of the Opposition began to negotiate with KANU while other political entrepreneurs shopped for deals in the rapidly commercialising political arena.

If the 1980s was the 'lost decade,' the 1990s theme was kikulacho ki nguoni mwako, or "we have seen the enemy, and it is ourselves." Tacit societal acceptance of this truth was a prelude to the real progress capitalism was to make as the decade progressed.

Privatisation in Kenya reminded me of Victor Borges' short story, The Gospel According to Mark. In the story, a Christian missionary goes off to a remote atoll to share the good news with its primitive inhabitants. He spends the better part of a year preaching in a simple wooden church. The natives duly attend, but otherwise remain dull eyed and show no sign that they comprehend the import of his sermons. Then, early one Friday morning in April, his pupils come to his house en masse. They are uncharacteristically excited and babbling in their language, which the missionary has yet to master. He recognises only a few localised words from the scriptures. They form a procession and escort him to the church. Their joy and enthusiasm increase. Perplexed, the missionary turns the corner, where with smiles and gesticulations—they point to the cross and the nails they have prepared especially for him, their foreign saviour.

For KANU's primitive capitalists, the Bretton Woods policy turned out to be very good news. Privatisation had created a real dilemma for President Daniel arap Moi. Most of the Kenyan citizens in a position to purchase the public assets he was being ordered to unload were Asians and the Gikuyu elite. But opening up the market to political capital in all its diverse forms made selling off state and parastatal assets considerably more democratic than the policy's proponents had envisioned.

The shift from the mashamba scams of the Kenyatta era to grabbing urban maploti under Moi symbolised the decline of the gentleman farmer 'mode of production' as get rich quickly liberalisation picked up speed. Powerless to stop the forces they had set in motion, the IMF mandarins turned off the taps and left capi-

talism in Kenya to sort itself out without them.

Kenya's combined economic reform and political democratisation came at a price. Procedures for cannibalising parastatals and other state institutions were standardised. A favourite one was run down the corporation, then use the purloined resources to buy it back a throw away price. If this was the preserve of state elites, others could pursue contracts for tendering supplies, or acquire public land for quick sale—some prime land was privatised only to be sold back to the government at highly inflated prices. The plot grabbing mania snowballed until schools, churches, and even private property became fair game. One especially bold privateer obtained the title for a plot at Embakasi that belonged to President Moi.

The diligence and diabolic creativity unleashed by this liberalisation was truly amazing. It seemed as if a whole generation of intelligent Kenyans grew up reading Chinua Achebe only to adopt as role model his "if-a-juicy morsel-falls-into-my-mouth, who-am-I-to-spit-it-out" Man of the People. It was good sport, punctuated by instances of poetic justice. A prominent grabber in Meru town propagated a rumor to the effect that the President's favorite son was shacking up with his daughter. Although this stayed his persecutors for a while, the county council managed to repossess the centrally located plot including the structure he had built on it before he was able to finalise its sale to another party.

Grabbing was only one of many streams feeding into the topsy-turvy decade of the 1990s. Most of the action was in Nairobi. It was a hot time in the city, which now had a character of its own. There were flashy matatus, clubs and discos, multiple local channels and satellite TV, gangsters and crooked cops, fast food, wealthy refugees, and new ways of getting high. Miraa underwent a makeover, emerging from its Swahili-Cushitic ghetto renamed as veve. Kuveveka entered the repertoire of the new manyanga generation, urbanites who occasionally visited their shags but no longer identified with a rural home. For expatriates, Nairobbery was still the posting of choice. Its bright lights made it hard to keep many a country girl down on the farm. School leavers found shining shoes in the city preferable to enrolling in polytechnics and teacher colleges in the sticks.

Some of the new trends born in the urban crucible took root in the boondocks: hair salons, handguns, and HIV, to name a few. The age of rural development had passed, the noble sentiments extolling equity and peasant progress gone with the wind. Love of cash money and institutional rot took its place. Like the forester in Kitale, people developed a love of trees and the forests came under siege. Young Turkana raised on famine relief picked up AK-47s. Pentecostal preachers toured the countryside, harvesting the peasantry's surplus. Reform of the Cooperatives Act sidelined the front-line ministry of rural development, leaving producers at the mercy of entrenched local mafias.

Mashambani, proverbial home of the blues, became a meaner, more dangerous—and for urban based elite, essentially foreign place—that had exhausted its fifteen minutes of fame.

The developmental debates once waged in the pages of Kenya's Sunday papers rated only passing reference in Phillip Ochieng's column. "Class" became high fashion and tips about how to wear underwear, urban neuroses and sexual dysfunction

are symptoms of its internal contradictions. Commodity fetishism dominates the centerfold magazines' mix of bad jokes, beauty tips, and reviews of upscale eateries and ecotourism lodges. Radical chic is the latest BMW. Rural Kenya barely registers a blip. Wahome Mutahi, may you rest in peace.

Marx was right about very many things. But the dirigiste theory of dependency turned out to be wrong. In 1986, two World Bank economists published data showing that rural Kenya enjoyed a positive net flow of resources, and not the other way around. This probably remained true into the 1990s, although the resource flow assumed new and unique forms—like the hijacked Toyotas the police discovered buried in Central Province farms, Trust condoms, and unruly city kids exiled to rural boarding schools.

Study of rural political economy has yielded to the drudgery of trial-and-error science, yet according to some experts, even this may be Sisyphean folly.

Jeffrey Sachs garnered kudos for his role in Poland's post 1989 transition to market economy. When The Economist showcased "Emerging Africa" on its cover in 1997, the editors invited Mr. Sachs to address Africa's unique developmental problems. Sachs, taking his cue from Adam Smith's observations on the critical importance of coastlines and navigable waterways for commerce, proceeds to declare Africa's inhospitable and isolated interior as an impediment to economic growth. He cites data from a study by Harvard's Institute of International Development to conclude that sub-Saharan Africa's poor soils, bad climate, and physical isolation impose an economic penalty that even market policies and good governance cannot surmount.

While conceding that the sheer numbers of practitioners make agriculture-led growth a logical premise, he cites low productivity and rampant infectious disease to dismiss it as a trap. "Sustained agriculture-led development, whether in the United States, Australia, Denmark, or Argentina, has always been a temperate-zone affair," he declares. Sachs advises Africa "to earn its way in the world" by promoting manufacturing and service exports, and recommends that donor aid target tropical diseases and improving public health.

His views are reflected in the monies committed to Africa by the past two US administrations, and the philanthropy of Microsoft magnate Bill Gates. But taken literally, this latest stupid white man theory advocates shifting large numbers of underproductive rural cultivators from the interior to disease-free manufacture for export zones on the coast. The Government of Kenya wisely pre-empted this policy experiment by allowing the Mombasa highway to fall apart.

For forty years Kenya has traveled a similarly narrow and increasingly potholed road. During the last ten, the country has weathered the cut-off of donor aid, declining value for its exports, tribal clashes, an El Nino of unprecedented proportions followed by an equally severe drought, the demographic bulge's coming of age, two major terrorist attacks, regional chaos, Goldenberg, the cypress aphid and Nairobi flies, Caroline Mutoko and an often unfriendly if not hostile relationship with its international partners.

During the same period Kenya was becoming a progressively jazzier society.

Problem-solving capacity is sprouting at the grass-roots, its urban core is spawning a cultural inflorescence, the shilling held its value after the last IMF cut-off, and the turbulent political arena witnessed the peaceful transfer of power. For a state accused of poor governance and numerous other sins, somebody must have been doing something right.

Postscript: Notes on the Fall

For a long touted exemplar of African capitalism, Kenya is not a very encouraging example of the efficacy of policies scripted by Breton Woods. Ask why Kenya has not come around and the Greek chorus wails, Moi, woi woi woi!

Perhaps the Opposition was predestined to split the votes in the 1992 elections; but President Moi improved his margin of victory in 1997. Either Kenyans are a nation of very confused democrats, stupid black men, or there are other reasons why at this juncture they did not take their hundred shilling notes and vote for someone else, like the nice guy in State House now. This requires explanation.

"Moi knows Kenyans," Mzee Kenyatta told his kitchen cabinet. "You only know Nairobi." Moi used his knowledge to evolve from "passing cloud" to the euphemistic Professor of African Politics. Nairobi may be cosmopolitan, but politically, rural Kenya still calls the tune. Jogoo wa shamba baado anawika mjini, as Raisi Moi understood so well.

The State House Moi was trickster and magician; Moi the Professor criss-crossed the country drumming his politically correct ideology into everyone's head. Rungu in hand, he persistently flogged his ecumenical political vision, connecting with the people in his familiar those-who-ride-in-the-back-of-lorries-should-not-throw-cookie-boxes style of speaking. Every Sunday, Kenya's head of state reverted to faithful choirboy attending church, missal in hand. The man presented a baffling mix of contrasts.

The epistemological Marxists deserve credit for many of the more penetrating insights into African developmental processes. While standard Big Man theories explain the behavior of the country's political class well enough, I only came to grips with Moi's Kenya after donning the conceptual lenses provided by John Illife and James C. Scott.

In his book, The Emergence of African Capitalism, Illife argues that the emergence of an indigenous and truly creative African capitalism will come about, not as the result of economic theories and policies, but through the skills of political leaders. He discusses distinctively African examples of economic success, but distinguishes them from capitalism proper. Rather, these hybrids represent "easily achieved precapitalist capitalist syntheses." The Igembe miraa juggernaut, Katheka Kai Farmers Cooperative Society, and indeed, many locally owned business enterprises fall into this category.

I came to realise this when the miraa industry went into to overdrive following the collapse of the State in Somalia. The new Somali Diaspora fueled a miraa boom reinforcing the biodiversity-based economic monoculture, while encouraging negatives like child labour, alcohol consumption, and the exploitative practice of renting

shambas. Before the decade ended, Somali exporters had taken over the lucrative international segment of the marketing chain. Igembe's agro-foresters began to experience what capitalism actually means as their agrarian moneymaking machine hit a glass ceiling, just as the Mbariu hypothesis predicted.

I returned to Katheka Kai in 1996 to find privatisation was well advanced. The shareholders farmland had been increased to twenty acres, the cattle herd was long gone. Some of my friends had sold off their land piece by piece until only their humble homesteads were left; the several incongruously large new houses down the hill belonged to "strangers" from Nairobi. Like the miraa farmers stuck in the shamba-renting trap, they had become what Kenya's scholar turned politician, Apollo Njonjo, once described as "proletarians on patches of land." When I visited again last year, Potha was being chopped up. Kya Mutheke hill, where we poured libations in 1980, was one of the first parcels to go, reportedly sold off for 11 million shillings.

I revisited Turkana in 1997. Kalokol's extensive aquaculture and fish processing infrastructure lay abandoned and desolate, windswept ruins of a not so ancient era when missionaries of development preached that it was 'better to teach a man to fish'. Most of the Turkana had moved with their cattle to the Western escarpment. The fishery was reduced to a party of Congolese fishermen encamped in the former tourist lodge.

We stop at Turkana's newest town, Lalorupe, near the turn-off to Lokitaung on the Kakuma road. Lalorupe is home to some Somali businessmen and a transient population of pastoral dropout gold diggers, or more accurately, burrowers. The gold fields begin as shallow depressions that give way to crude, un-reinforced tunnels penetrating over a hundred feet deep into the ground. Some of these dark holes fork off into equally long shafts running parallel to the ground, We watched karais of stony grey soil come out, ferried to the surface by a twenty man chain. The sight of these Turkana moles emerging into the light was an unforgettable testament—either to Kenyan perseverance or to human idiocy (or vice versa).

A glass of water cost ten bob in Lalorupe, but one small yellow nugget could finance a month of African socialism in Lodwar. My Somali friend showed us the latest shaft to collapse: eighteen proletarians were buried alive under a patch of land the size of a steel drum. It was not the first time.

Legally, any minerals found beyond the first four feet of topsoil belongs to the government. The law was not being enforced at Lalorupe, but we were chased away from an expansive fenced-in compound nearby, housing machinery that funneled the same earth into a large hopper. Our guide told us it was a South African operation, and that the Turkana had unsuccessfully tried to close it down, insinuating it enjoyed the blessings of the Bull of Auckland. This kind of riddle, not the Prime Minister versus President quagmire, is why Wanjiku screams for constitutional reform.

Several weeks later, I was crossing Harambee Avenue one afternoon when the Prezzy popped up in a land rover and spontaneously addressed the small crowd that had gathered. What I recall Moi saying that day was, "hiyo katiba tutarakebisha, lakini nataka nyinyi wananchi mukumbuke kwamba hata katiba haiwezi kuzuia shari ndani ya moyo wa binadamu."

James C. Scott entered the development debate with a book entitled The Moral Economy of the Peasant. He elaborated on this theme in Weapons Of The Weak, which explores class struggle as commonplace acts of resistance by the relatively powerless: "foot dragging, dissimulation, desertion, pilfering, feigned ignorance, false compliance, slander, arson, sabotage, and so on." Then he turned his attention to a thesis he calls "the hidden transcript." The hidden transcript records what political actors say, "when they are off-stage." One explanation for his command of the multi-party political arena is Moi's fluency in the idiom of Kenya's hidden transcript.

Such 'off-stage' conversations I have been privy to highlight an intriguing and potentially volatile mix of pre-capitalist economic morality, ethnocentric false consciousness cum personal opportunism, and capitalist political logic. There are also colourful unwritten local histories of Kenya buried in the hidden transcript, which is constantly updated to reflect shifts in the country's power map.

Moi the person was arguably weighted towards the precapitalist side of the transcript, but Moi the politician was forced to cope with pent-up capitalist forces. The first term President relied on a regional power sharing formula, and revived KANU to serve as vehicle for this KADU agenda. After liberalisation of the political sector, he switched his modus operandi. He compromised the predominantly ethnic-based opposition by skillfully manipulating the personal greed and ambition of its leaders. When faced with the choice, many politicians and other men of the people elected to swallow the juicy morsels served up at State House, and on the donors' plate.

The key to this strategy was a running discourse with the nation that kept the President continually on the stump. Moi polished the art of locating political issues, be it the ethnic chauvinism of opponents or his own regime's shortcomings, in a comparative perspective provided by subtle allusions to the hidden transcript—reinforced by references to regional violent manifestations of the evil in men's hearts. He offered an alternative social contract that bundled the politics of conflict mitigation together with the economics of the half-full cup. If urbanised and educated Kenyans took a cynical view of this pact, the risk averse rural population was more accepting of the devil they knew.

Regardless, such was his mastery of Kenya's body politic that after 1997, an enthralled nation spent millions of man-hours speculating on the Professor's succession strategy. We all wasted a lot of time. Some things can only be understood post-facto. Kenya's 4.1 per annum fertility rate, for example, began to make a lot more sense when the body count spiked as the Aids pandemic hit its stride.

By the end of the twentieth century Daniel arap Moi had undergone transformation from perceived stooge of Western powers to one of Africa's most radical critics of the West and their imposed solutions for African problems. Western critics may have mistaken Moi's stiff and halting English for a lesser intellect, but much of what he said after switching to Swahili was hard to refute: siasa mbaya, maisha mbaya—in the context of the transcript this can be translated as either we work out our problems politically, or we all get nailed to the cross.

****

Following the forced liberalisation of the 1990s, Kenya's economy was swamped with Castle beer, Pakistani rice, Malaysian batteries, Russian call girls, Chinese casinos, and an unregulated deluge of sundry other imports. In the everything-is-a-market milieu of that time, a miniscule fraction of the global capital looking for a local nest could have snapped up everything from Telkom Kenya to Kenya Railways to the family farm, with very hard to reverse long-term implications—but for the antics of KANU and friends.

Unlike many other social critics during the Industrial Revolution, Marx did not see capitalism as a moral problem. Time will tell if it was right or wrong, maendeleo or evolution by some other name, but forward-looking Kenyans are likely to concede that ex-President Moi bought valuable time for the emergence of the kind of dynamic and creative indigenous capitalism Illife talks about in Kenya.

In Samburu, Namunyak the lion laid down with the baby oryx. Then the Professor of Politics handed over a somehow calmer more confident nation to its most experienced economist.

AboutThe Author

Paul Goldsmith was born in New York City in 1952, grew up in central Florida, studied literature at Tulane University in New Orleans, helped build Disneyword, and financed his first trip to Kenya in 1974 by winning a workman1s compensation case against Mickey Mouse. Following two years of regional field studies, he returned to Kenya in 1978, working in a number of different capacities and studying diverse local domains since that time. Upon completion of a Ph.D. in anthropology from the University of Florida in 1994, he renewed his quest to explore the asymmetrical complexities of African society and environment via an eclectic range of research, consultancy, civil society activities, and unplanned experience.

A week passed before I was ready to go back to Rwanda. I was going with F. And the journey began badly. We were giving a convalescing RPF soldier a lift to the rebel headquarters at Mulindi, but as if that wasn't enough, we had to look for him and F couldn't remember his address. So it was not until mid-afternoon that we were able to leave. We left in a h urry, driving as fast as we could in order to reach the Gatuna border post before it shut down for the night. We were driven by a taciturn, nervous and unsteady driver called Juma. I was rather worried by his erratic driving. But the prospect of driving a t night through a country at war was even more worrying. It was completely dark when we reached the Rwandese border at Gatuna. And to our horror it was closed.

The Ethnic Trap

by Benjamin Sehene

The past is a foreign country, they do things differently there.
- L. P. Hartley: The Go-Between

A week passed before I was ready to go back to Rwanda. I was going with F. And the journey began badly. We were giving a convalescing RPF soldier a lift to the rebel headquarters at Mulindi, but as if that wasn't enough, we had to look for him and F couldn't remember his address. So it was not until mid-afternoon that we were able to leave. We left in a hurry, driving as fast as we could in order to reach the Gatuna border post before it shut down for the night. We were driven by a taciturn, nervous and unsteady driver called Juma. I was rather worried by his erratic driving. But the prospect of driving at night through a country at war was even more worrying. It was completely dark when we reached the Rwandese border at Gatuna. And to our horror it was closed.

It even seemed useless to bribe the somnolent but compliant guard, because the barrier was fastened with a huge padlock, and the person who had the key had apparently gone to Kabale several kilometres away. But F was a shrewd and dynamic businessman, always prepared to take a gamble. He was not one to brush aside a problem, he would dwell on it. He would brood over it, and become distracted as if doing mental arithmetic even as you talked to him. Soon he was engaged in discussion with the guard. From several minutes of palaver it transpired that the man with the key could be reached. At the sight of money, it turned out that the man had not yet left for Kabale.

We drove into the no-man's land, across the makeshift bridge which had been erected in place of one blown up by the Rwandan army (FAR) in 1990 to prevent an RPF advance. At the Rwanda border, the RPF guards knew F who for a long time had put his premises in Kampala at the disposal of the RPF, so they let us through without any hustle. We had intended to spend the night at Mulindi, but we found that the entire RPF administration had already moved to Kigali. So we drove to Byumba.

Rwanda at night was silent and featureless. The beams of our headlights cut through the black night like twin tunnels of light streaked with insects and dirt. Beyond the beam of our headlights, at the end of every curve in the road, I fancied an ambush. I remembered James Fenton's golden rule in Indochina: Never be on the roads after dark. Each time, the roadblocks along the road came as a relief. I have never felt as safe as I did that night, with African soldiers.

We spent the night at a dark RPF guest house manned by two sleepy soldiers. Byumba at an altitude of about 2,500 metres above sea level is chilly at night. In the darkness the guest house was shrouded in mystery, something, a shape, suggested

a grand black mansion set against a luxuriant black garden. But morning revealed a gutted, pockmarked house in a littered, overgrown garden.

Then begun the journey down to Kigali, past reforested hilltops of pine and eucalyptus, past abandoned villages set in banana plantations and a patchwork of well-tended fields rich with crops. The fields were often set upon terraced hills, the work of many years. Now they lay abandoned like fruits of wasted labour. Rwanda was a nation that had abandoned its land and many years of effort.

All along the road there was a continuous trail of devastation. Roofless houses, their rusted iron roofs caved into burnt out interiors. Collapsed houses lying in piles of overgrown rubble. This was not the indiscriminate destruction of war, but the surgical and systematic destruction of communal violence, destruction among neighbours. In some villages all houses were intact, while in others, particular houses had been destroyed without damage to the ones next door. Tutsi families had been dragged from those houses and hacked to death by their Hutu neighbours. Then they had destroyed the houses, either by burning them to the ground or by blowing them up with grenades, and sometimes they had even levelled the ground where the houses had stood. As if by destroying the Tutsi's houses, they hoped to erase the memory of their victims and all trace of their crime.

As we approached Kigali I felt elated at the prospect of seeing my birth place, a place of myth whose name had always made me quick with longing. And like all places of myth I knew it would not quite measure up to expectations. But nothing had prepared me for the ugly, deserted war torn city we drove into that morning. A city of empty, looted shops and houses, and the interminable trails of ragged returning refugees. For the traveller arriving by air, the refugees might have appeared like columns of black ants. They walked in single file, carrying their belongings on the head. We kept passing these lines of ragged returnees, as we tried to figure out our way through the littered streets, strewn with war rubble.

Kigali had been the heart of darkness, the epicentre of a genocidal cataclysm. There were spent ammunition casings, paper, concrete chunks, shards of glass, clothing, carcasses of abandoned, scavenged vehicles, broken furniture, packs of stray dogs and the occasional human skull or femur. When the shards of glass caught the mid-morning sun, they looked

like ice. There were dugouts surrounded with sandbags on many street corners or at strategic points throughout the city. The shell-marked streets spoke of the recent drama, of the butchery. Many buildings in Mateus, the commercial centre, were gutted, their iron roofs gnarled and ripped up by exploding shells, the walls bullet-riddled. And those that were intact had been looted clean.

There was little traffic but the numerous RPF roadblocks around the city managed to create a resemblance of traffic jams. The young soldiers came up to the car and politely asked for papers then asked you where you were coming from and going to. You never told them where you were really coming from or where you were going. You did not say you were coming from Uganda because if you did the soldiers would start searching your car. Sometimes this took ages and cars piled up behind the barricades.

Kigali is a slum, of dust-brown mud-brick houses, scattered over several hills. In

most of the residential areas the roads are not tar marked, they are just dust. There is dust everywhere you look, dust on roofs, dust on trees, dust in the hollow of satellite dishes, dust in your nostrils, dust on your tongue, dust in your spit. Then when it rains the dust coagulates into mud, a viscous brown sludge that has wheels spinning helplessly, digging in deeper and deeper.

On the narrow roads that crisscross Kigali it was hard to find one's way without a map. We got lost several times trying to find our way to a place called Remera, where the RPF was presently headquartered. And the young soldiers at the roadblocks were of no help to us, because most of them were also newcomers to Kigali, they were either born in Uganda, Burundi or Zaire; the sons of Tutsi refugees who fled the violence in 1959.

Much of the traffic was comprised of speeding military convoys and other military vehicles or madoadoa, RPF commandeered vehicles of the former regime, UNAMIR, or aid agencies that had been painted an impromptu camouflage. Most were dilapidated vehicles full of soldiers and driven by inexperienced drivers. Their brake-lights had been systematically

eviscerated to elude sniper fire. And on Kigali's narrow winding road s,

they were cause for some spectacular accidents. All the accident black spots were littered with madoadoas. I think in those initial days, the RPF lost more soldiers to car accidents than it did at the peak of the war.

In Remera, the first person we met was D, an acquaintance of mine from Toronto who had returned to Rwanda to work with the RPF. I was impressed by him, he seemed to know everyone on the street and most of them by name. He was bursting with enthusiasm, and was eager to show us the scenes of massacres, the places where the looting was still taking place, to take me to see my niece S who read the news in English on the RPF radio Muhavura-which was now radio Rwanda.

As the morning advanced, the prevailing chaos upon which D seemed to thrive, begun to impress itself. Kigali was like a Bujumbura surburb. Wherever one looked, there was a crowded car with Burundi number plates. The Tutsi refugees who fled to Burundi in 1959, now driven by mounting insecurity in Burundi had been the first to arrive after the fall of Kigali, those from Uganda would arrive much later. The refugees from Burundi drove around and around the city all day, sightseeing. When they met friends or relatives, they stopped to embrace, guhobera, in the middle of the road tying up the traffic. There was a lot of guhobera in those days, it was like a form of congratulatory accolade. Even people that had met earlier in the day, would embrace when they met again the same day. The prevailing atmosphere was one of a triumphant homecoming.

There was a sense of the unreal about being in Kigali. It was as if what was going on around me, was actually happening to someone else. I was completely disoriented, and from time to time, I caught myself turning around at the sound of people speaking Kinyarwanda, just as I had always done in Kampala, Nairobi or in that transit hall at Cairo airport. For the

first time in my adult life, I was in a place where everyone spoke Kinyarwanda. It was eerie.

The returnees from Burundi - the Barundi, as they were called - were busy grabbing shops and houses, looting cars, furniture and household appliances left by the dead or those who had fled to Zaire or Tanzania. The facades of many shops and houses carried this notice written in chalk or charcoal letters: Iyinzu yara fashwe - this house has been taken.

Kigali was a free-for-all, there was looting, called kubohoza, everywhere, at the embassies, government offices, the warehouses, schools,shops. All that had not been looted by the fleeing Hutus, was now being looted by the returning Tutsis. D had acquired an expensive, black leather set of furniture, and had taken over a beautiful bungalow. And almost everyone was involved in the looting except the RPF soldiers who just stood by and did nothing, since no formal orders had been given. But on the other hand RPF officers drove around in expensive looted cars, occupied opulent mansions or had set up their relatives in one of the appropriated shops. And the RPF civil administration was also busy auctioning off stocks of tea, second hand clothing, cooking oil and other imported goods left by the former administration at the bonded warehouses in Gikondo. At the warehouses, I watched labourers imported from Uganda, grunt under heavy bales of tea, while loading several trucks. There was a shortage of able bodied men in Kigali, many either being dead or in exile. In those days it was almost possible to do anything. Like the absurd case of a returnee family which was squatting the Swiss embassy.

Contrary to the returnee civilians, the RPF soldiers (Inkotanyi), were very disciplined. They were evidently the most disciplined African army I had ever seen. In spite of many loosing their entire families in the genocide, they had not carried out the revenge killings, rape and pillaging many had predicted. The Hutu leadership had for a long time demonized the RPF soldiers 'the Inkotanyi have fangs, pointed ears and a tail, and they kill wherever they pass,' they used to tell the poor Hutu peasants. Now at the roadblocks, old men, women and children, seeing the polite young RPF soldiers for the first time, were going up to them with questions.

'Was it true they had fangs, pointed ears and a tail? Would they gouge people's eyes out?' The fact that these peasants had believed this propaganda, goes to show their ignorance and credulity. The same credulity with which they had accepted to gang-rape, pillage and hack their neighbours to death.

For the returnees, the Inkotanyi were heroes. In bars people bought them drinks, and no one drove past an Inkotanyi without giving him a lift. And the Inkotanyi were very popular with the girls, there were always several girls lingering around every roadblock.

In Remera there was a flurry of activity. The RPF civilian administration, now the de facto government was busy trying to set up a coalition government. Faustin Twagiramungu, a Hutu opposition leader who had been designated prime minister by the Arusha peace accords, was mentioned as a likely candidate. There were lots of rumours and intrigue about ministerial appointments, a lot of jockeying for position. Outside each RPF official's house there were parked cars, madoadoas, armed military escorts and a small crowd of favour seekers waiting for a chance to present

their cases; lesser officials, Tutsi businessmen from Uganda or Burundi with favours to ask. The number of cars suggested the official's importance. These houses stood together across the road from the Centre Christus where several catholic monks had been slaughtered by the Interahamwe militias. Now the centre was being used to house foreign journalists, who could be seen being led away like a flock of sheep to sites of massacres by cadres from the RPF information department.

It was hard to avoid the atrocities committed by the Interahamwe militias. Everywhere there were reminders of massacres and rape. Kite-hawks and vultures circled above the city as if waiting for the massacres to resume. In the evening, a floral scent - that smell of African dusk - was compounded with the warm humid smell of putrefied bodies, and hung in the

air like an invisible curtain. On Gikondo road I saw a stray dog sniffing at the legless shrivelled remains of a man. The man's skull was still partly covered with hair, his rib cage was sheathed with shreds of what must have been a black jacket.

There were hundreds of these stray dogs and some of them were even pedigree. Dogs whose owners were either dead, in exile or evacuated European expatriates. At the height of the genocide, when the streets were still littered with dead bodies, these dogs had eaten and developed a taste for human flesh. Now they moved in fearless packs and would not hesitate to attack people, or moving vehicles. Such that on many streets it was common to find a dead dog run over by a motorist.

There were piles of incriminating documents and hate literature strewn about the streets. Official documents were scattered outside looted government offices. The tormented history of Rwanda was piled among the war rubble and dust on Kigali streets. Someone gave me a copy of Kangura (awaken), a Hutu extremist magazine, which contained the notorious 'Hutu Ten Commandments'.

Later we drove back into the town centre, to look for S at radio Rwanda. She was not at work but everyone knew where she lived and we took on a volunteer guide. She and a colleague from the radio had just been allocated a government house. But they had neither mattresses nor furniture apart from a dinning table and two chairs. They had no water, no electricity and were unable to cook the food rations they received from the RPF.

The house they had been given, used to belong to the director of radio Rwanda. The house, like Kigali, was a looted shell. All over the house, on the veranda and in the garden were scattered clothes, papers, family photos and other personal effects of the former occupants. Photos of chubby smiling children, a group of adults around a table, a lady in traditional dress, a church wedding in black and white. They lay there waiting to be swept away with the other debris; moments of happiness from shattered lives. The monster of hatred has no patience for personal memories of the happy moment lived and preserved on paper. And it was amidst these episodes from the former director's life that we improvised a meal of bread and corned beef.

Nyamirambo

That afternoon, we drove into Nyamirambo in search of, Antoine Mubirigi, the maternal uncle whose name I had got from my sister Helena. Nyamirambo is a vast slum crowded and cramped with back-to-back mud houses on narrow, dusty broken lanes and open stinking sewers. A city within a city. Nyamirambo is also the Muslim neighbourhood complete with two mosques. It is there that Arab traders from the East African coast had settled, and their descendants also called swahilis like those on the coast, are an ethnic group apart in today's Rwanda. A fact which perhaps explains why most people in Nyamirambo were spared by the genocide.

In Nyamirambo life seemed to thrive unabated in spite of the war, the genocide and the intense afternoon heat. Kite-hawks and vultures circled above. Among the ruins, the litter and war rubble there were many open bars teeming with people. There were open air vendors, selling the only food; roasted meat. People stood about in small groups. And there were the inevitable hoards of bare-chested children tripping about in the dust.

Naturally we got lost. Helen a had told me that Mubirigi lived near the market. But the market we were directed to was not the right one. We found ourselves near the Islamic cultural centre, a donation of the Libyan leader Colonel Muammar Qaddafi. That part of Nyamirambo is close to the Mount Kigali, the highest point in Kigali and up to the last moment a FAR stronghold. And it had come under heavy shelling. The mosque at the Islamic

centre was in ruins, its minaret bent at the top and holding on by the flimsy steel reinforcements. Its pillared arches were bullet-riddled and its green dome ripped open. Our car got stuck in a deep rut and we had to get out of the car and push. We also had to tread carefully for there were many unexploded shells and rockets strewn about.

In the vicinity of the second mosque, we asked a group of idle men wearing skullcaps and kanzu - an East African derivative of the djellaba, for directions to Antoine Mubirigi's house. One of the men knew Mubirigi. Yes, he was alive and well, said the man as he gave us directions. We went down a deeply gullied road which disintegrated into a narrow dusty lane,

past a deserted market to the furthest into a narrow dusty lane, past a deserted market to the furthest point accessible to a car. We left the car behind, went on foot passed a noisy bar, crossed a makeshift bridge over a large stinking water drain and stopped in front of a small shop.

The man's directions were so precise that the first house where we inquired was Mubirigi's shop.

Mubirigi was a thin, prematurely aged, dark, tall man with greying hair. My self introduction was met with astonishment.

'Benjamin? Coletta's son? Imana ishimwe (thank God),' exclaimed Mubirigi. He embraced me and I was veiled in the smell of alcohol on his breath.

Then the young woman standing next to him stepped forward.

'I am Mubirigi's daughter Venancia.' She said in a tremulous voice, then embraced me and begun to weep. And she would remain hysterical and on the verge of tears during our visit.

We were led from the bare shelved, certainly looted shop, across an inner courtyard and into a sitting room. The leatherette sofa set, their headrests covered with patterned lace cloth, and the family photographs between crossed arrows on the dirty whitewashed walls, reminded me of sitting rooms I had known throughout my childhood. And also hanging on the wall was the inevitable coloured poster of the Pope leftover from an outdated calendar, a favourite icon in Rwandese homes.

And almost as soon as we had sat down, Mubirigi and Venancia started fussing over us. Oh, they lamented, what will we offer you? We almost have nothing. Some tea perhaps? Maybe some beer or Fanta? For some reason in Rwanda all bottled soft drinks are called Fanta. And Venancia still on the verge of tears sent for some beer and Fanta from the bar next door.

Mubirigi's wife was a small woman, with an intense suspicious face. She sat at a distance from us in a manner which seemed to suggest that she did not want to intrude into our conversation: the traditional discretion of an African wife. In the general excitement I had failed to notice her, but once I begun taking photographs she called out to Mubirigi that he was being photographed, as if asking him to strike a pose. People in Rwanda do

not like being photographed without putting on their Sunday best.

In relay, father and daughter told us the story of how they had survived the genocide. At the beginning of the massacres, Mubirigi and his wife had sought refuge at Ruberi's house, Venancia's husband, because he was a Hutu and a government soldier. And for months they had hidden there while Ruberi went out to fight every day (and perhaps to participate in the killings). And here father and daughter chose to differ. According to Venancia they had also been forced run behind the Interahamwe to bury the bodies. Then when the war had gained most of Kigali, Ruberi and his fellow soldiers had come to use the house as a retreat, and shooting from there. Soon the house had come under fire...

But Mubirigi quickly interrupted her, and asked her why she was telling us that. Then he instead told us his version of the story. Apparently as the RPF had advanced, Ruberi along with his three children and Marie-Therese (my step sister) had fled towards Gisenyi. While Venancia and Mrs. Mubirigi had taken refugee at the Sainte Famille church. Mubirigi had come back to his shop, where the Interahamwe had looted his stock, stolen his refrigerator and threatened him with death. Then one afternoon they had tried to chop off his head with a machete, but he had raised his hand in defence.

Here he stopped to show us a scar which run across his left back hand. But he faltered a little when I asked him if they had not forced them to kill in order to be spared like many other Tutsis with Hutu relatives.

'Er, no,' he said.

About a year and a half later, I would learn that Mubirigi had died after a short illness. But I still wonder why he had prevented Venancia from telling us certain things. On successive visits to Kigali I would often meet Venancia in Nyamirambo drunk in broad daylight. I would ask her about her parents. But I could never bring myself to ask her what she had wanted to tell us that afternoon. Up to now I still wonder if she and her father had not been forced to participate in the killings, or about her husband and children languishing in a refugee camp in Goma. I wonder what deal she and her parents may have done to be spared. It was not unusual for Tutsis with Hutu relatives to strike bargains and take up a machete to kill on another hill in order to be spared.

The Barundi are very enterprising and had gone into the only viable business in Kigali at the time, the bar business. With spirits from looted stock, bee r imported from Bujumbura, and meat from God knows where; appropriated shops, butcheries, pharmacies, and residential homes were transformed into bars. It was surprising to discover that in a city short

of food, some businessmen had managed to import beer. I was able to count at least twenty bars. And business was booming. Prices were astronomical but still the bars were always packed at all hours. As there was no water, no food and nothing else to do, people be gun drinking early in the morning and went on until late in the evening. They had beer and roasted meat for breakfast, beer and roasted meat for lunch, then beer and roasted meat for

supper. The meat was tough, leathery, of uncertain origin and you had to eat it directly from the skewer. D., who was very fastidious about Tutsi food restrictions would later ask; 'How can you people eat meat whose origin you do not know? Do you realise that you could be eating anything, mutton, or one of the many stray dogs? Who knows you actually may be eating human flesh; a Tutsi relative you never met.' He was right, there was absolutely no way of knowing where the meat came from, the cows had all been looted and eaten by the Interahamwe. I never touched that meat again.

Even in those early days, the Barundi exclusively patronised bars run by fellow Barundi and the Bagande - returnees from Uganda - patronised Bagande bars. Burundi francs, Rwandese francs or dollars were accepted at Barundi establishments, but not the Uganda shilling, that was only accepted by Ugandan establishments. Seeds for future division were already being sown.

AboutThe Author

Benjamin Sehene is a Canadian writer, born in Kigali, Rwanda in 1959. At the age of four his family was forced to flee into exile. He grew up and went to school in Uganda. In 1984 he immigrated to Canada where he started writing in 1988. In 1994, he was living in Paris, France when the genocide begun in Rwanda. He travelled to the country of his birth in the midst of the genocide and civil war about which he was to write his monumental book called: Rwanda the Ethnic Trap.

Rwanda.

Our thoughts and Prayers are with you

photo: Sven Torfinn
Rwanda, Kigali, Nyamata, 08-2003
Two bag with bones and skulls against a wall of the small church of Nyamata, where according to the government 5000 peopl had been killed during the genocide in 1994. For nine years the church and remains of the victims had been left undisturbed an had been a place of commemoration. It made a deep impression on many, especially foreign visitors. For unknown reasons, th year people have begun to clear the bones and skulls from the church.

oto: Sven Torfinn

anda, Nyamata, April 2004

ring the commemoration period this year, many people visit genocide memorial site such as this one in Nyamata. A young man, a survivor, with scars on her head, walks past the skulls.

photo: Sven Torfinn
Rwanda, Kigali, April 2004
Women are washing bones, skulls, remains of victims of the 1994 genocide, appeared in a newly discovered mass grave in Kiga where allegedly 300 bodies of victims of the genocide were discovered. Still, ten years after the genocide, buried bodies are foun During the excavations attempts are made to identify lost family members, using teeth, jewellery and skull characteristics. Durir the coming 100 days (the duration of the genocide), in a lot of places all over Rwanda excavated remains of victims will be cerem nially re-buried commemorating the 10 th anniversary of the genocide.

oto: Sven Torfinn
vanda, Kigali, April 2004
omen are washing bones, skulls, remains of victims of the 1994 genocide, appeared in a newly discovered mass grave in Kigali ere allegedly 300 bodies of victims of the genocide were discovered. Still, ten years after the genocide, buried bodies are found. ring the excavations attempts are made to identify lost family members, using teeth, jewellery and skull characteristics. During coming 100 days (the duration of the genocide), in a lot of places all over Rwanda excavated remains of victims will be cere- nially re-buried commemorating the 10 th anniversary of the genocide.

photo: Sven Torfinn
Rwanda, Nyamata, april 2004
After the end of the genocide, a monument has been built next to the church in Nyamata where in 1994 a few thousand people w killed. Bones and skulls, the remains of the victims that were displayed there for the last years, are now washed, cleared away some of them buried in special commemoration ceremonies.

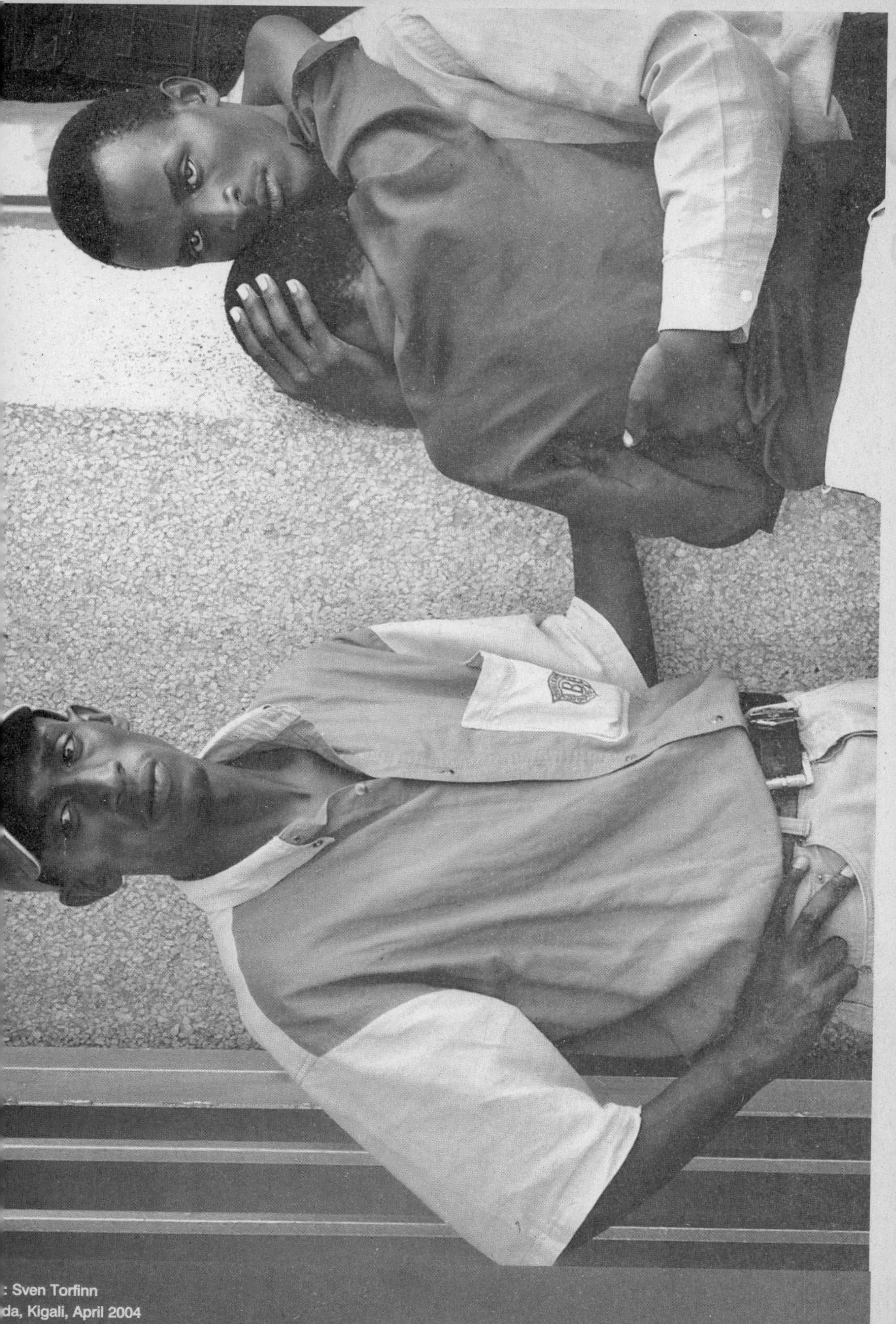

: Sven Torfinn
da, Kigali, April 2004
rothers are consoling their sister during a commemoration gathering in the stadium of Kigali. For many people, the commemo-
of the beginning of the genocide on April 7 th 1994 ten years ago, was very emotional.

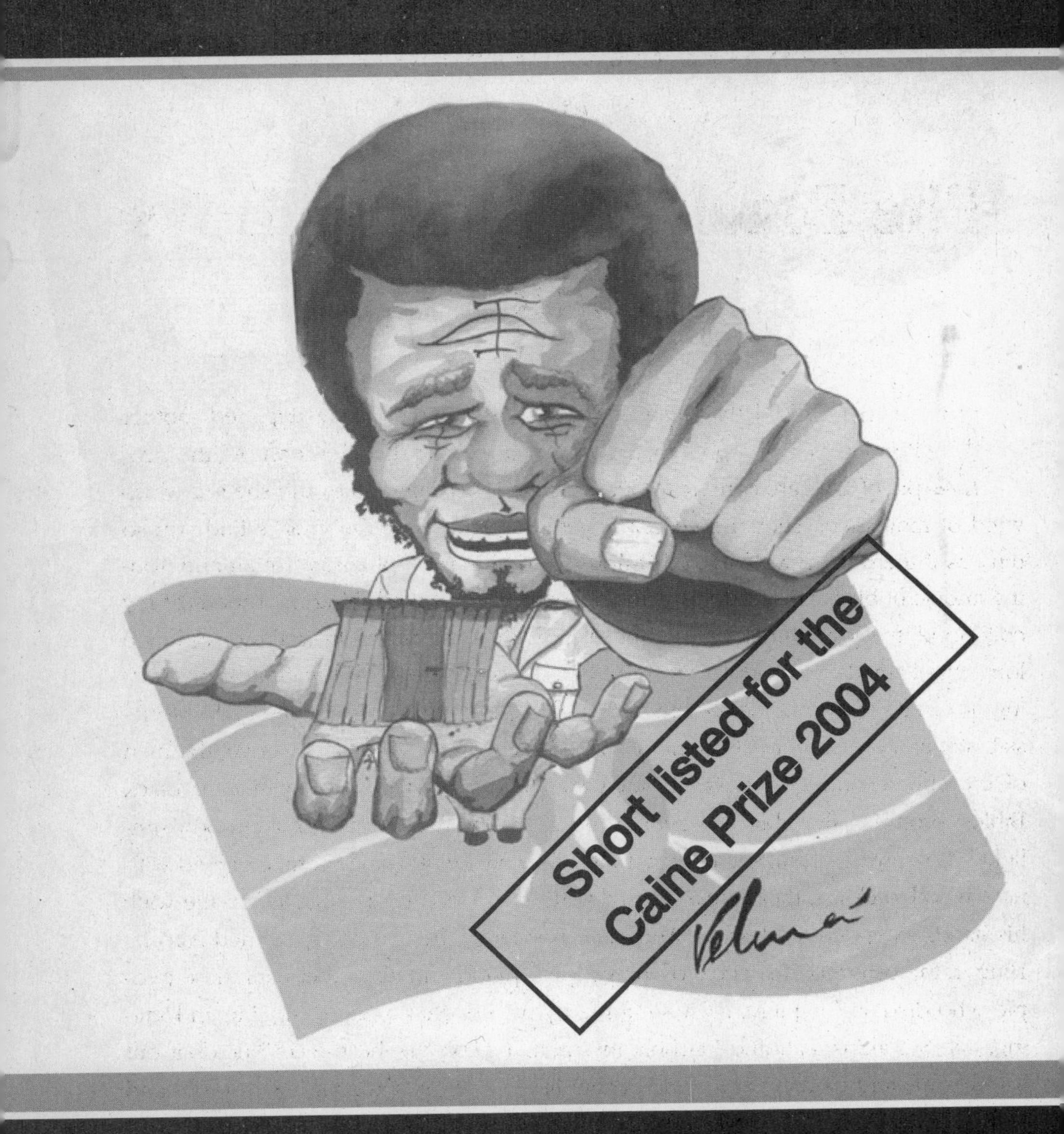
Short listed for the
Caine Prize 2004

Last night I had the dream of fish again, in which my departed mother Petrobia is a young woman throwing a party in the afternoon. All the people of God are coming to our house in Jerusalem estate, and she is a whirlwind of movement, shouting get-ready get-ready, how can the visitors find you so dirty as if there is no woman in this house and you are orphans, washing and ironing and scrubbing the courtyard with soap and water, brandishing the broom of my childhood, the long thin sticks tied together with strips of tyre from the abandoned lorry that leaned drunkenly against the outside of the courtyard wall, its axles resting on crumbling construction bricks. The smell of frying fish on the fire in the stone-slab stove in the corner tickles my nostrils.

Comrade Lemma & The Black Jerusalem Boys Band

Last night I had the dream of fish again, in which my departed mother Petrobia is a young woman throwing a party in the afternoon. All the people of God are coming to our house in Jerusalem estate, and she is a whirlwind of movement, shouting get-ready get-ready, how can the visitors find you so dirty as if there is no woman in this house and you are orphans, washing and ironing and scrubbing the courtyard with soap and water, brandishing the broom of my childhood, the long thin sticks tied together with strips of tyre from the abandoned lorry that leaned drunkenly against the outside of the courtyard wall, its axles resting on crumbling construction bricks. The smell of frying fish on the fire in the stone-slab stove in the corner tickles my nostrils. Then the guests begin to arrive, the men of the church and their wives in their stiff Salvation Army suits with their black Bibles, propping their bicycles against the courtyard wall in the hot afternoon sunlight. The only place the sun does not intrude is our small living room, crowded with new wooden chairs, their backs draped with crocheted vitambaa, Jesus on the wall, his hands extended in blessing. And there is singing and clapping, the fried fish sizzling in the centre of this circle of the people of God and all of them, all these people who died so long ago, are calling me by my childhood name, smiling and saying, eat, Sylvanius, eat, and Petrobia my mother picks up the fish and holds it out towards me and I am ravenous and radiant like her in my spanking new clothes and I reach for it. And then, suddenly, I am an old man again, my face sagging and creased, my guitar-playing fingers gnarled and bent, and there are blue-bottle flies buzzing over the fish, and Martha is sitting next to me. The people of God are still smiling kindly and saying eat, Sylvanius, eat. Then their faces melt, become skeletal. Even in the dream, it is at this point that I know I am going to die soon.

I was woken up this morning, the eve of our nation's 40th independence anniversary, with the gift of an old jacket and a song of freedom. A delegation from the community arrived at my front door, surprising me with a long-forgotten song I had composed in my youth as the leader, lead vocalist and lead guitarist of our neighbourhood group, Comrade Lemma and the Black Jerusalem Boys Band. They were

singing Joka, a song I stitched together from sleepless nights spent with my ear against my departed mother Petrobia's shortwave radio, when the shrrr-shrrr of static would part like clouds after the rain and allow some music through, the little transistor shivering at the forbidden sounds coming from a thousand miles away with the shaky faraway voice from a sad, sweet heavenly place singing: "Ayeee Afrika-e/Ayee Afrika-e..." Then you couldn't hear the rest because of the shrrr-shrrr of radio quarrels and the announcer's Queen's English interrupting them in an in-out whisper, like a man calling out from a well that is being opened and shut.

Among those forbidden faraway songs called up by my mother Petrobia's transistor radio, there was one in particular that had me in fits and sweats of how can this be? Who is this god of music whom I have never heard of? Every night at the same time, the transistor clouds would part for long enough to allow a voice from the pits of hell to cry out in the accents of the damned:

There is a train from Beira!/
There is a train from Namibia!/
There is a train from Zimbabwe!/

And then the voice would make the choo-choo sounds of a train and the clouds would close again, the train's shrieking whistle fading into shrrr-shrrr-shrrr-you-are listening-to-shrrr-shrrr. As the train sounds faded, I would close my eyes tight and travel to lands I had only heard of in my geography class in Primary 6, from which I dropped out because Mr Clarke, the headmaster wanted to separate me from my departed mother Petrobia and send me away to a boarding school, and then who would take care of my sickly departed mother who had already lost so many children to small-pox and influenza? I would soar over the clouds and find myself riding in a train of doom from Beira, the wailing voice chasing behind, like so many demons escaped from hell.

It was a time when words were heavy as stones and could get you into trouble. Certain words especially, certain names, were only whispered. Dedan Kimathi Waciuri, General Mathenge. But most of all it was Comrade Lemma, the founder of the liberation struggle, who strode into our boyhood games of war, carrying away the children, the cowards, the irritating little girls who wanted to play boy games on the street on which our dusty, pink mud-brick flats were located in Nairobi's African quarter. Our mothers used his name as weapons against us, as in if you don't come in now Comrade Lemma will come and take you to the forest and eat you up. At night he would invade my dreams wearing his long, brown leather jacket, his shaggy knotted hair obscuring his face.

The delegation from the community was chanting in rapid verse, their younger members cutting the air like those exponents of martial arts in the makeshift cinema halls in my neighbourhood, cutting the air and chanting 'Nairobi Kambi ya Watumwa', and in doing so, taking me back to a long time ago.

We heard of other places that people went to; and they would return dispossessed of the gift of speech during the day so that only during their nightmares could they tell stories of the quicksand torture of the prison camps, of how the earth had swallowed them, them and the stranger next to you, Prisoner Number 1234 - No Afande Sir I am not belonging to the proscribed group otherwise known as Mau Mau, Afande - and all you saw was an acre of heads and eyes, heads and eyes, and all the time the earth sucking and swallowing, like shitting in reverse. One night my father failed to come home and my mother started to grow old.

So I became a musician, leader, lead vocalist and lead guitarist of Comrade Lemma and the Black Jerusalem Boys Band, and composer of Joka, the song that the nation has long forgotten after so many years of its being banned. And now I wake up to hear my neighbours singing it as if to mock me first thing in the morning after my premonition of my own death. Franco and Stish, the grandsons of Martha, my next door neighbour and friend indeed over these gruesome years, are a pair of teenage poets whose rapid verses of our life here beneath the bridge, beside the river, regularly bring tears to my eyes when I remember my own youth of saying heavy things from the side of my mouth. I usually treat the sounds of their rapid verse with the contempt they deserve because it is a parody of music and to encourage it is to repudiate all those years of my youth. And so I am especially wounded by their mannerless mistreatment of Joka:

Kutoka Kwale hadi Kampala/From Kwale to Kampala
Mwendo wa Joka siyo halaka/The giant snake moves slowly/
Kutoka Kisumu hadi Kisauni/From Kisumu to Kisauni
Joka linanyonya nyinyi wahuni/The giant snake sucks up you criminals/
Linatambaa, hili gari la moshi/It crawls, this train
Linasafisha Reserve,linakausha ardhi /It purifies the Reserves, it petrifies the earth
Linawabwaga wahuni jijini/ It vomits the criminals in the city /
Huku Nairobi kampi ya utumwa/In Nairobi, this camp for slaves

I remember how I became a musician as clearly as the evening of our nation's independence day, when my departed mother Petrobia was ex-communicated from the Army of God for forgetting herself and simulating the tribal dancing of her people from the west, thus forcing us to leave our one-roomed Jerusalem flat in disgrace and begin our journey to the banks of the river where I buried her. But that was much later, when my musical career was already flourishing. My career began on the same day that we saw Comrade Lemma for the first time. A photograph on the front page of the East African Standard, showed a man of about 40, his head resting peacefully beside his bullet-riddled torso in the Ngong Hills, the victim, said the report, of a group dispute over dinner.

As usual on that night – I must have been 15 or 16 years old -- I had my mother Petrobia's radio glued to my ear, my borrowed Salvation Army guitar cradled in my arms, a tentative Ten Cent cigarette drooping from my mouth and pen and paper at the ready just in case the clouds parted long enough for me to decipher the music beyond. The god of music began speaking in my ear in that terrible voice of there

is a train from Zimbabwe. But he was not taking me to the mines of Johannesburg. Instead, as he chased me through the clouds, his voice ripping through the heavenly peace, and I watched down below my fellow Africans from Kisumu to Kwale and Kampala to Kisauni climbing into train carriages. Regard them, said the voice, with their life's possessions wrapped in bedsheets, arriving in the city for a better life. But that was not yet a song but my heart damn near burst out of my chest.

Then I was back in my room writing to the music coming from the transistor, the strident church voices of Southern Africa accompanied by the penny-whistle tunes that evoked so much sadness. I also wrote to the hypnotic guitar rhythms of Dr Nico and Le Grand Kalle, those Congolese gentlemen who were especially favoured on the transistor. I wrote a chanting chorus from the drum beats of my childhood which I spent under the umbrella of the Salvation Army, which promised hell on earth and victory in heaven. My words burned with blasphemy. I woke up in the morning full of the joy of a religious conversion and the realisation that my voice had been transformed overnight from the lilt of puberty into the deep tones of my lost father's Salvation Army choir's voice.

It was Humphrey, one of those bullies from my childhood who, together with Tairero and Solomon now constituted the popular neighbourhood band known as the Black Jerusalem Boys Band, saw the possibilities of my song Joka. In fact, it was he who intervened when Tairero threatened to beat me up when I suggested that I join the band. Humphrey was the vocalist, both Solomon and Tairero played guitar in the frenzied high-pitched tunes of those days.

"Hold on," he said lazily, leaning against the old lorry next to our courtyard wall. Humphrey and I were neighbours. Our mothers detested each other. They waged a never-ending war over which religion was superior and you Salvation Army people are so primitive, marching about like a herd of sheep and you Catholics pray in unwashed clothes, we are God's true army, we wear uniforms.

"Let him sing his song at the end of our show tonight," Humphrey said. "The crowd will laugh him out of Jerusalem. That will teach him."

Mr Ben's bar in the shopping centre had the dubious reputation of staying open long after Curfew. Mr Ben was partners with a police sergeant who made sure that his men went deaf to the noisy bands that played in the bar after the 6.00 pm Curfew. Mr Ben was a respected member of the community, being the only African licensed to sell beer.

I was quite nervous. The small bar was packed. There were customers squeezed on the narrow, wooden benches, standing and smoking at the dimly-lit counter, leaning against the dirty windows, blocking the corridor that led to the toilet at the back. I gagged on account of the pungent scents of Ten Cent cigarettes and Roosters, and the odours that blended with the flavours of beer and urine. The fat barmaids sweat-

ed as they delivered orders, and would scream dramatically when the drunken men reached for their breasts. Behind the counter, Mr Ben was yelling orders to his skinny assistant, his balding head glistening.

People were calling out Francisca, another round here, and don't forget my change this time, Anna. Nobody saw how uncertainly I held Humphrey's guitar. I closed my eyes and went to Beira.

It was the sound of a man weeping that made me realise that something strange was happening on that night in Mr Ben's bar. My fingers were racing over the guitar strings like a reckless guerrilla on the run. Then I was in Nairobi and there were people weeping and clapping, weeping and clapping and I was singing Joka again. After that night, Joka was always the last song we played because, as Mr Ben, whose paunch grew steadily bigger, once said, it keeps the customers drinking.

Humphrey disappeared after that night. We heard he had got a job as a music librarian at the Voice of Kenya.

I took the name Comrade Lemma, not so much to honour that man with the burning eyes in the newspaper photograph, but to prevent my mother Petrobia from hearing that her son was a bar-room singer on Saturday nights. Every Saturday people came to Mr Ben's to weep, people from all over the African quarter, from Pangani and Kaloleni and Ziwani and Bahati. Mr Ben continued to insist that it was a mortal sin, boys, a mortal sin, to pay musicians any more than they could reasonably drink on a single night.

Rumours about me grew. I was a Mau Mau leader disguised as a musician. No, no, no, he is actually a South African who sailed to Mombasa where he learned Kiswahili from the ghosts in the Old Town and come to Nairobi to steal the souls of respectable city residents, like us. And on and on. I wore my black cap lower, fearing my mother's wrath.

When we began to smell freedom, Joka was being seriously discussed as a contender for the new national anthem. By this time, however, I had been cut loose from the song.

Within the first year of the new independent government's life, the song was banned. It was said that the song's disturbing lyrics had annoyed the new leader.

Mr Ben became uncomfortable with us, and paid us off with enough money to launch Tairero's career as a drunk finance Solomon's trip back home to Uganda, and transform me into a vegetable dealer who, during those slow times in between customers, would read anything he could get his hands on and especially the classics of Charles Dickens. Then my mother Petrobia danced in church. We moved to the empty land by the river.

II.

I was therefore in a furious mood this morning by the time I had put on my usual trousers, my brilliant white kanzu from those days of Rehema, an old flame of my active years who had come to comfort me as I mourned my poor departed mother Petrobia's death from tuberculosis and shame, and who had left a few months ago convinced that my mourning period was over, and my sandals which I designed myself from strips of abandoned lorry tyres to accommodate the crisis of my twisted feet. I have a distaste for mimics as I have suffered greatly because of them, and I therefore intended to reprimand these young men. I was instead met by cheers of 'Comrade Lemma! Comrade Lemma!' and Martha herself staining the newspaper page in her hand with her tears.

"Look at you!" she exclaims accusingly, her voice quivering with an emotion I have never witnessed in all these years of our friendship. She brings the page close to my eyes as only she and a very select few know of the special problems of my eyes. There is a grainy picture of three young men, dressed in the band outfits of my youth. Next to it, incredibly, is a passport-sized photo of myself with my Comrade Lemma locks and all the stains and distortions of my advancing years. The headline reads: COMRADE LEMMA FOUND! And then there is a sentence below that takes me a moment to decipher because of the special problems of my eyes and the fact that my spectacles have been missing ever since the mysterious early morning departure of Rehema some years back. I am just able to make out the sentence below: 'Independence Musician and National Hero Lives In Nairobi Slum Squalor'.

Around me are the shining faces of my neighbours, regarding me as if I were a stranger, even after all these years of our collective struggle for a better life. I was once told, in private, that when reading, an amused expression comes to my face, as if I were laughing at a private joke. I can feel Martha's gaze boring into me, confusing, like she always does, my squint for a smile, because why else would you be smiling if you were not staring at that picture and recalling the heroic years of your youth.

There is a long pause. They peer at me. I squint my way across the tear-stained page, recognising, in one paragraph the lyrics of Joka that I wrote those many years ago, and how my poor departed mother Petrobia, on discovering that I was Comrade Lemma on the day of our country's independence, had begun her retreat into shame and silence.

"Ni yeye!" It's him, declares Martha, her voice quivering, fading eyes alight with something I shall have to investigate later. There is a roar of approval. Franco and Stish, her poetic grandsons, are already chanting, in their youthful rapid verse, Joka! Joka! and it is soon answered by the feminine response of 'Mwendo wa Com-ra-dé siyo halaka' and an impromptu festival of cheering and rapid verse takes over the normal morning noises of my narrow street. Another young man has taken up a tin

and a stick and is beating out a rhythm, and I find myself hoisted up in the air, on the shoulders of my neighbours, my kanzu flapping ridiculously about me like a flag that is looking for an anthem.

They put me down long enough for Martha to hold an old black jacket against me. "It fits you," she says. Inakushika. The way she undresses the word provokes a stir in me that I last experienced with Rehema. These days, I rarely succumb to the sin of Onan, to the agony of my adolescence, a little soap and a little water in the quiet of the night. It was much worse in the aftermath of Rehema's departure when I was borrowing so much soap from Martha that I begun to suspect that she suspected.

"It's from Marehemu George," Martha says, two youthful, sultry dancers gyrating so suggestively in her widely-set pupils that the stirring in my loins becomes uncomfortable. "It's a present for you." She is dressing me with her deft housewife's hands and undressing me with her look. "He says you must look presentable for today's meeting." Her fingers on my back are like little electric currents. She slides them over my shoulders so that she is now holding my lapels, standing very close and looking straight at me. Her oval-shaped face, with the tight wrinkles around her mouth, belies her age, betrays her grief. I am appalled at myself, looking at my friend and neighbour of many years in this way (and at my age!). But this morning, I fear, shy, retiring Martha is suggesting things that would lead to riots when she was younger and the unintended tormentor of young men.

I am hoisted up again. And so I begin a new journey with my old song.

Marehemu George has pulled out another miracle from his little bag of imported hand-me-downs. A year ago, he arrived on foot in our neighbourhood with a bale of second-hand clothes. They were a donation, he said, from a rich American, recently deceased, named George, for whom he acted as a special local agent. And so we took to calling this young man Marehemu, the late George, who provided us with dead people's clothes at a discount price. But a resurrection has taken place in Marehemu George's personal circumstances in the months since he embarked on a new project to dispense free condoms to poor people. He is now an evangelist of new afflictions and beware the next victim could be you, you are never too young to die.

It is only from my perch on the shoulders of friends and neighbours that I realise how my neighbourhood has grown in the years since I moved here to bury my departed mother Petrobia near the river so that her soul would be carried away from this city of misfortune. We head deeper into this valley of cardboard walls and tin roofs and the greenish sludge of sewers running like snot-nosed kids on a Saturday morning. It occurs to me that all these years, my world of narrow streets and afternoon chats with Martha about how are your late daughter's boys doing, that is a good colour for a growing boy's cardigan, have been this neighbourhood that is Kwa Lemma, where the city's newest immigrants have always settled.

I was the first one here, so they named it after me. Now I can see at least eight distinct Kwa Lemmas, collapsing against each other like a completed game of dominoes. There is the bridge, belching with the arrogance of city traffic, the old stadium in the smoky distance where all those years ago they played the first football match of an independent nation. We are singing Joka, and the women with their clutched babies hanging from them like an extra, cheering hand, are peeping out of their tin-roofed shacks. Spirals of charcoal smoke rise in the early morning air. In my present mood of a conquering neighbourhood hero and without my spectacles, I see a phoenix rising from the ashes. For the first time in many years, I welcome the chemicals and plastic stench of the river.

Parked by the smart wooden office at the end of the street, I recognise the immaculate four-wheel-drive vehicle that Marehemu George has taken to driving. Then I see other vehicles, untidily parked. Suddenly, my narrow street has become a cul-de-sac: unmarked saloons and pick-ups, dark blue Government of Kenya vehicles block off the side that leads to the open field where we have our football matches. A small horde of journalists brandishing biros, notebooks, cameras and complicated electronic equipment. This unexpected sight has the quite embarrassing effect of making me fart, briefly and pungently, on my new porters.

I realise Marehemu George has a hand in this morning's unexpected events. I had mentioned to him on several occasions that while condoms were very much appreciated, we must also bring to the attention of the authorities that many people here also fall victim, often even die, to the hidden diseases of our polluted river water. That it is not enough to dispense rubber for the protection of our people during their nocturnal embraces when the same prophylactics end up clogging our already overworked drains in the morning and floating on our river in a most unacceptable manner, especially as this is the same river we all depend on for our domestic needs. It is a subject that I have, in fact, written extensively about. Being one of the more literate individuals in our community, I took it upon myself some time ago to agitate, through the press, for external assistance to help us resolve this problem. Curiously, and it might have something to do with the deteriorating handwriting of an old man with special problems of the eyes, these lengthy articles were never published.

We were seated in my darkened parlour, Marehemu George and I, sipping his mineral water on the evening of our potable water discussion when his attention was diverted to the collection of framed photographs by my bed honouring my departed mother Petrobia. Among them is a misplaced photo of the band outside Mr Ben's bar and it is the one that has Marehemu George's attention.

"Who are these people, Mzee?"
"Oh, nobody really. It's just an old picture."
"Yes, a very old picture. Is one of these young men you?"

I wanted to get back to the subject at hand so I told him impatiently that, yes, I was one of them.

"Which one?" Marehemu can be very persistent.

"Isn't it obvious? The one in the middle, with the guitar and the hat."

"That's you? Mzee, I never would have…"

"What was the name of your band?"

"Comrade Lemma and…"

"… The Black Jerusalem Boys Band! My God, I've found you!"

Marehemu George is a big, imposing figure, a man of quick ideas. He has put on a lot of weight since he joined us. Now he is excited like a little boy. He is gesticulating hugely, so that his fingertips brush the walls, telling me how till the day he died, Mzee, my late father always talked about your band.

"Especially that song of yours, remind me, Mzee what it was called…"

"Joka."

"That's it!" He snaps his fingers. "He said Joka had changed the way he looked at the world. My family owes you a debt, Mzee. Which one were you, if I may ask?"

"I am Comrade Lemma."

He looked at me intently for a few moments, then, I am afraid, he removed his scented, white handkerchief and carefully wiped a waiting tear at the base of one of his eyes. Then he said in the voice of a man in a Charles Dickens novel: "And so, this is what it comes to."

He kept on repeating, "So you are the Comrade Lemma?" and standing up and sitting down, trying to catch up with his accelerating thoughts. By the time he was leaving, he had the look of a man who has found his destiny.

Next day, in the afternoon, when the light is especially good by the river at the back of my house, Marehemu George took me to meet a straggly-bearded man with dead eyes, a bush-jacket and a camera. You must look broken, Comrade, Marehemu George had said, with all the years of suffering etched on your face.

Marehemu George appeared at my door the following evening with a copy of the newspaper under his arm and a knowing smile. As we sat down to our drink of mineral water, Marehemu George spread out the newspaper. On one of the inside pages was a photograph of me the day before, the shimmering river hiding its dirty secrets through a trick of sunlight so that we appeared to be in a better part of town, out in the countryside. Above my name was the question of 'Who is this Man?'

"Even as we speak, Comrade, the nation is scratching its head in bafflement. Who is this man, indeed, Comrade, indeed," said Marehemu George, tapping the photograph with his hand of shiny rings. Underneath the photograph, there was the hint of amazing prizes to be won, and you could be the lucky winner of a year's supply of Careful Love condoms, a donation from the American organisation Marehemu George represented.

The next day, I was visited by an overweight and sweating young woman clearly experiencing difficulty with her luggage. She spoke with a strange accent, a little like Marehemu George in those first day when he was explaining "No folks, you just don't get it, I've just come home from America. I've been living there for the last two years!". She described herself with the curious statement that she was "in radio". I invited her into my house where she took out a complicated array of electronic gadgets, attached one to my kanzu and asked me to laugh. I finally managed to emit a long drawn out croak. She said thank you and left.

A little boy woke me the following evening with the message that Marehemu George wanted to see me. The big desk in his office had been cleared of everything but a big radio, from which a young lady whom I thought sounded like my visitor of the previous morning was shouting as if her house was being robbed, saying you are listening to Clouds-Aif-Aim-Ninety-Eight-Point-Five and reporting on the chaos of evening traffic. Marehemu George told me to sit down, Comrade, our plan is taking shape.

There was a pause in the music. Then a machine voice said, "Whose laugh is this?"

And the woman said: "Okay-so-it's-the-moment-you've-all-been-waiting-for. It's time for 'Whose Laugh is This?" There was the sound of clapping and cheering from the audience. "For two-thousand-five-hundred-shillings, a year's supply of condoms from Careful Lurve condoms, two bottles of Count Pushkin Vodka, a Coke and a Smile, can you guess which celebrity is laughing?"

There was a drum roll and then the sound of a frog in distress.

"That's right, folks. Call me on foar-foar-foar-foar-double-foar and tell me 'Whose Laugh is This'" Again there was the sound of clapping and cheering from the studio audience.

Moments later, there was a telephone call and an uncertain voice said: "Could it be the President?"

A sheep bleated and the audience laughed mockingly. Then the disembodied voice of the machine said: "Kondoo! You-are-as-dumb-as-a-sheep."

And the young lady said dismissively: "Wrong! Next caller, please." I had the impression of a long line of people at a telephone booth, waiting patiently for their chance to call in and become sheep.

The next caller suffered the same fate when he suggested the laugh belonged to the Minister of Finance. The prize went up to for five thousand shillings tomorrow, a year's supply of Careful Lurve condoms, four bottles of Count Pushkin Vodka, a Coke and a Smile, whose laugh-is-this?

Marehemu George's teeth flashed in the evening gloom, like a block of white flats in a run-down neighbourhood.

"Comrade, you outdid yourself!" he said. "Even I wouldn't have recognised that laugh as yours."

"Is that me?"

"But of course, Comrade. You remember laughing for a pretty lady yesterday morning?"

Marehemu George informed me that I was now officially on the nation's celebrity list. For the modest sum of ten thousand shillings, which he had personally pledged, my laugh of a frog in labour would be identified in a few days when he, Marehemu George, made a call to the studio and became the surprise winner of 'Whose-Laugh-Is-This?'.

"It is all about knowing people, Comrade. But I digress. At that point, Comrade, the whole nation will be asking, 'Who is Comrade Lemma?' On that very day, my friend the editor assures me that your identity in the photograph competition will also be revealed. Then the action will really begin." Later, as we sat there on his veranda, he wondered aloud what it would take to mobilise the community, Comrade, you know these people better than anyone else, then reached into his pocket and presented me with some money, saying, no please accept it, Comrade, as a small token of my respect for a figure of national importance.

Things started to happen very fast from the time we got back to my street. The newspeople moved quickly towards our party of throbbing, gyrating youths honouring an old man in his hour of glory. For a moment, I forgot my aching back, twisted feet and fading eyesight in the flash of lights, the click and whirr of cameras and rapid-fire orders, of stop there so that we can take a picture, sir, no right there so that these shacks form a backdrop for your remarkable face, isn't it remarkable, and more calls of exactly like that, Comrade, yes, that's right, that's perfect, sir. The years of heaviness, and the price paid for saying heavy things, fell away as I recognised

that I, Comrade Lemma, was being honoured, finally, for services rendered to the republic. I stood alone, in this broken down neighbourhood that had been my home for all these years, in my old kanzu and my morning gift of a black jacket, and shed tears.

When I opened my eyes, I was alone in the middle of my narrow street, the glorious vision replaced by dust, screaming and chaos and the throb of a helicopter overhead. I could dimly discern that the crowd, as well as the newspeople, had diverted their attention to the helicopter landing in the dusty field next to our neighbourhood.

"Marehemu George said he was expecting a Cabinet Minister." I was startled by Martha's voice behind me. I turned to face her. She was smiling.

"I wonder which Minister. I lost track of them in the late `60s." I must admit, I was putting on a brave face. I had not expected that my moment of glory would be so brief.

"Marehemu said maybe the Minister of Culture. But it doesn't matter. You are the man of the moment. Even the Minister is here to honour you." I found her hand in mine for the first time in all the years I had known her. I was astonished to discover how tender her spirit could become, how in moments like this, her eyes could defy her grief of burying your own daughter, this world can be cruel.

"Don't forget your neighbours now that you are famous. I will cook your favourite meal tonight. Come." And she was gone, leaving me to contemplate the possibility of two lonely people keeping each other company in their sunset years. In front of me, the surging mass of people were trying to get a glimpse of the Minister and meeting instead the solid resistance of the police, who were clearing the way for the Minister with threats of whipping and shouts of 'Ondokeni! Ondokeni!, and arranging the crowd into a wave of placards in front of Marehemu George's office.

Our veranda of the radio broadcast had been turned into a museum in my honour. The photograph of me by our shimmering river taken the other day was a huge poster covering the main window of the office and overlooking the table, now draped in a brilliant red cloth. The poster said in big, bold lettering: 'Careful Lover presents Comrade Lemma, a genuine Kenyan hero. Careful Lovers Last Longest'. Then there was a line at the bottom: 'Careful Lover Condoms Supports the Search for a National Hero'.

There were smaller posters on the walls and windows, all with 'Careful Lovers Last Longest' emblazoned beneath my photograph. This irritated me because I have sometimes suspected that Rehema of my active years left out of frustration at my brevity during our nocturnal unions.

The Minister of Culture is a gentleman of the first order. To the utter astonishment of Marehemu George and others, he refused to take the high chair reserved for him and instead left it for me, saying that this was my day and besides, I was the older man.

I was unsure of how to behave after so many years out of the limelight. I was the hero, the man of the moment, and yet I had the distinct impression of being a servant to this event amid all the clicks and whirrs and like that, mzee, right there, and the attending minister and the welcoming flash of teeth of a grave and resplendent Marehemu George, more spectacularly dressed than ever. My face felt tight and dry with the effort of suppressing my need for the toilet. His ease around all these strangers and their gadgets acted like an anti-laxative and I relaxed beside him. I was, however, struck by the unnecessary thought that his lips were so close to the cluster of microphones that he appeared to be performing unspeakable acts to several men at the same time, without the protection of Careful Lover condoms.

When he started speaking, the veranda went quiet. Even the crowd on the street strained to hear what he was saying.

"There was once a young man who wanted to change the world through music. At the time, there was a war on and his people were dying in their hundreds and being detained for their opinions and their defence of a struggle for national liberation. Yet this young man ignored the dangers of subversion and sang his heart out…"

The exertion is affecting me. Look at me, the hero of the nation, the old warrior battling to stay awake. My eyes won't remain open and my mouth hangs embarrassingly open as Marehemu George weaves his way in and out of my story.

And I can see Humphrey that night so long ago when he surprised me after so many months of being away, in that suit of the new, upcoming African manager, made to measure by the Indian tailors on Biashara street.

"Comrade Lemma," he announced grandly, "I am going to get you on radio. You will be a national hero. I will make you rich beyond your dreams." As he was leaving, he asked me for the words of Joka. "It has become my favourite song. I hum it on my drive to work. Now I want to be able to sing it." I wrote them down for him. And he was gone. And then later, on that first morning as an independent nation, putting on the radio to hear: "And now the song the nation is dancing to, Joka, by Humphrey W., the man of the moment…".

My eyes jerk open to find Marehemu George killing off all my old friends and band members.

"…Save for Comrade Lemma, who survived death on numerous occasions, all the other members of the Black Jerusalem Boys Band died heroically in the service

of the nation. For two years he was a detainee in Hola..."

He talks of my long and traumatic experience in several detention camps, where quicksand torture was liberally applied (I was considering suing the British Government, he said gravely, for the crimes of torture and illegal confinement), of how Tairero Omondi died at the hands of thugs after a Comrade Lemma concert in the City Stadium; of how Solomon Olimba died trying to escape during a Colonial police interrogation after his arrest for subversion; and Humphrey W., in a British Army bombing raid in the Aberdares as Mau Mau soldiers wept with sheer joy at his vocal talents.

"Now on the eve of our 40th anniversary as a free nation, and under the new leader of a truly democratic government, Careful Love condoms is proud to return a national hero to his rightful place in society!"

The smell of fish begins to invade my nostrils.

I have difficulty recalling in exact detail what happened when I stood up during the question and answer session on Careful Lover condoms' role in the search for a national hero, and went looking into the eyes of the seated newspeople, of the Minister for Culture, for the owner of the fish, my muttering growing louder and louder until I was screaming in my hoarse, old man's voice, I am not Comrade Lemma, Comrade Lemma is dead, over and over and there was a roaring in my ears like that of the doomed train from Beira. And I was seizing one of the microphones from Marehemu George and I could see them as if they were written in the air in front of me, those words of the last verse of Joka, which had eluded me for all these years and the sound of an old man who is speaking out after so many decades of silence, was fading in and out as if from a well that is being opened and shut. And I was saying kifo ni rahisi, death is easy, it is living in silence that is difficult, which one will you choose my brother, in these days of bondage, don't be an old man who can't explain why he didn't die young or why his children walk in chains. And I remember seeing Martha's eyes so clearly in the middle of that surging crowd, please understand why I have to do this, and hearing the commotion of chairs falling over and the smell of gunpowder and asking why were you there, Martha, in the dream of fish.

My own understanding of the riot, as I told the police later, is as follows: as the event wore on and the people began to tire, Martha's grandson, Franco, decided to check that his money from Marehemu George's early morning payment was still intact, and realised that his pocket had been picked. It is therefore incorrect to assume that the ensuing cry of 'Mwizi' 'thief' and all the commotion had anything to do with accusations levelled against me on the podium by Marehemu George that why did I want to wreck his event after he had paid me such a large advance. The late Martha, being an elderly woman and ignorant of how to get out of the way during a stampede, was therefore a victim of circumstances.

Martha is dead. I am still alive. The stench of rotting fish is everywhere now.

AboutThe Author

Parsalelo Kantai: Parsalelo Kantai is co-editor of Ecoforum, an environmental journal. He is a recovering vegetarian. This is his first foray into the world of fiction. He has recently won a Reuters Foundation fellowship to go to Oxford University for a year. Corrupt Big Men and Neocolon KC's quake when they hear his name.

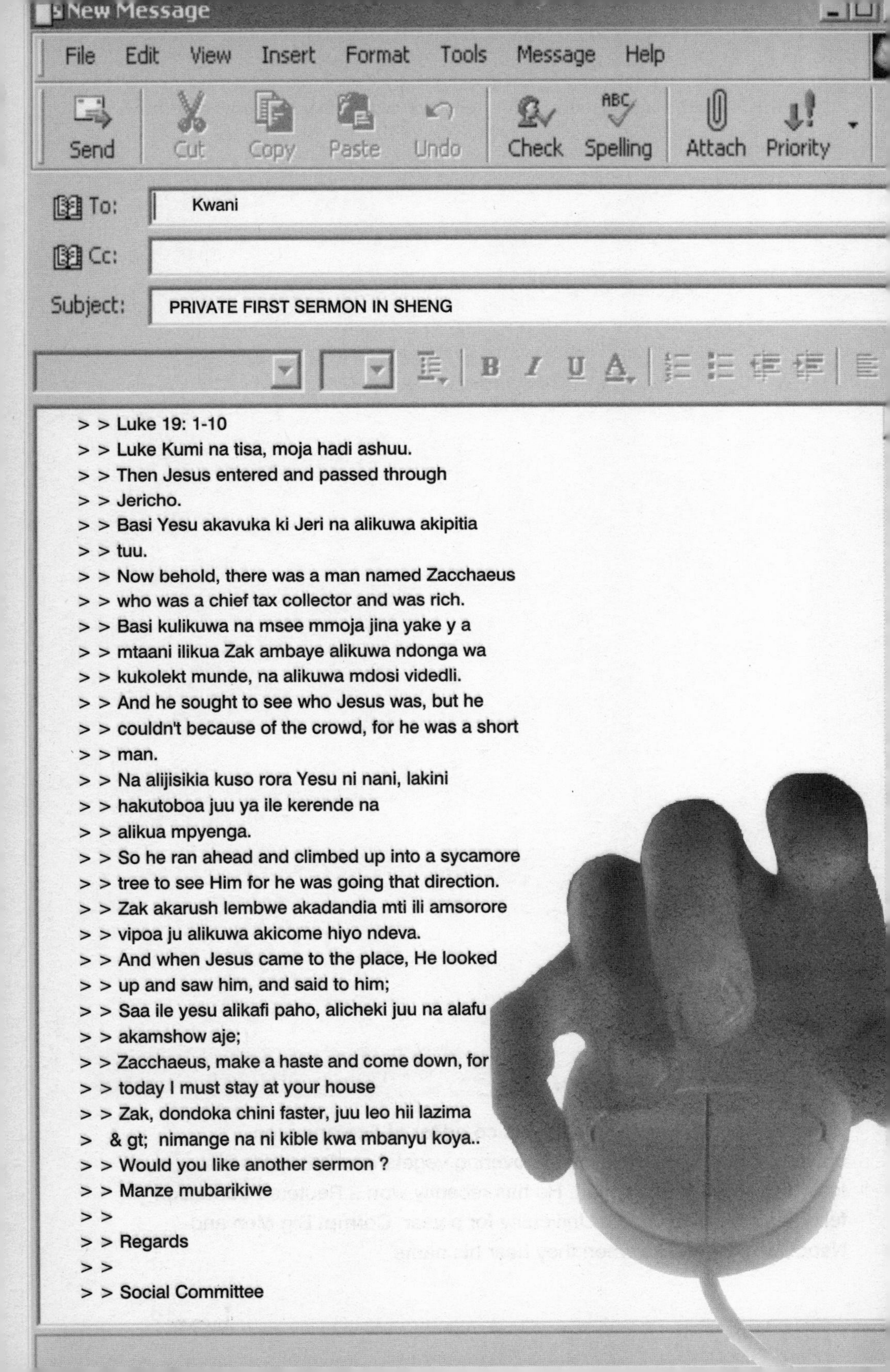

New Message

File Edit View Insert Format Tools Message Help

Send Cut Copy Paste Undo Check Spelling Attach Priority

To: Kwani

Cc:

Subject: PRIVATE FIRST SERMON IN SHENG

> > Luke 19: 1-10
> > Luke Kumi na tisa, moja hadi ashuu.
> > Then Jesus entered and passed through
> > Jericho.
> > Basi Yesu akavuka ki Jeri na alikuwa akipitia
> > tuu.
> > Now behold, there was a man named Zacchaeus
> > who was a chief tax collector and was rich.
> > Basi kulikuwa na msee mmoja jina yake y a
> > mtaani ilikua Zak ambaye alikuwa ndonga wa
> > kukolekt munde, na alikuwa mdosi videdli.
> > And he sought to see who Jesus was, but he
> > couldn't because of the crowd, for he was a short
> > man.
> > Na alijisikia kuso rora Yesu ni nani, lakini
> > hakutoboa juu ya ile kerende na
> > alikua mpyenga.
> > So he ran ahead and climbed up into a sycamore
> > tree to see Him for he was going that direction.
> > Zak akarush lembwe akadandia mti ili amsorore
> > vipoa ju alikuwa akicome hiyo ndeva.
> > And when Jesus came to the place, He looked
> > up and saw him, and said to him;
> > Saa ile yesu alikafi paho, alicheki juu na alafu
> > akamshow aje;
> > Zacchaeus, make a haste and come down, for
> > today I must stay at your house
> > Zak, dondoka chini faster, juu leo hii lazima
> & gt; nimange na ni kible kwa mbanyu koya..
> > Would you like another sermon ?
> > Manze mubarikiwe
> >
> > Regards
> >
> > Social Committee

Kenyan definition email forward

Written by Anon

1. You unwrap all your gifts carefully, so that you can re-use the wrapping. (I still have mine for Christmas '98 na usinicheke!).

2. You don't have genuine containers or executive utensils, you only use margarine, ice-cream and yoghurt mikebes. (Blue Band, Kasuku, Kimbo, Mallo, Lyons Maid serve me well).

3. You call an older person you've never met before 'uncle' or 'aunty/auntie'. (unashuka? uncle si nikuvukishe baro?)

4. More than 90, sorry 95% of the music CD's and cassettes in your home are illegal or pirated copies. (done in Dubai, Kariokor base or Rivarori).

5. Your backyard or store is always full of stuff because you never throw anything away, just in case you need it someday. (a gum boot without a partner, njumu ya left ya sandak zile za tenee and the baby walker - the baby now 12 and you are 40).

6. You have a collection of miniature shampoo bottle (mikebe tupu) from your stays at hotels (Sarova Shaba, Sirikwa...) and also the tu flamingo sachet soaps that are usually offered in the lodges. Most of them ni zile umechanua. It's Kenya anyway.

7. You have almost always overweight baggage when traveling by plane. (Taking unga ya Jogoo, Omena, Royco, sugarcane, arrowroots and githeri to 'uncle' Paul in the U.S.!).

8. If a store has a limit on the quantity of a product, then each member of the family will join separate queues to purchase the maximum quantity possible. (Mumias sugar during a shortage).

9. All children have annoying nicknames. (bebi, toi, boi, kadogo, yako,

rembo, doli, mamie, dadie, toto, kanono, twig).

10. Nobody in your family informs you that they are coming over for a visit. (uncle, wife, sis-in-law, two nephews and mboch have camped at home from Wesdan-Western).

11. You stuff your pockets with mints and toothpicks at restaurants. (Murray mints, wrappers, and salt shakers, serviettes!).

12. Your mother has a minor disagreement with her sister and she has not talked to her for almost 10 years. (nisikie mkiongea ama mkicheza na watoto wake - mtaniona).

13. You only make telephone calls at a cheaper rate at night. (Eti economy ni mbaya!)

14. You teach your friends swear words in your language. (jinga, fala, shenzi, wallahibillahi, aki ya ngai, nyasai kende, mlembe muno ingokho!).

15. You never have less than 50 people to meet you at the airport or see you off even if it is a local flight. (Yeah, my relas from Gatanga have hired a minibus to see me off to Lokichoggio. - 1st person to fly in the family, that's why).

16. You keep changing your Internet Service Provider. Because the first month is free you surf for the first free month and then when it is time to start paying, you disappear (I have prove, I know some jamaas.....).

17. Office supplies mysteriously find their way to your home. (Yes, scissors, biros,post-its, stapler ya mdosi, paper glue etc, etc.)

18. You don't buy a printer because it is cheaper to do it at your work place where it is free. (Yenyewe).

19. You wash your car on a Sunday. (Yeah reading the paper sitting on a kamawe in tu baggy shorts) even if you don't have, you usually spend most of your time imagining that you have one.

20. Weddings never start at the appointed time. [Three hours later {African time: Better late than never)], food is majimaji (kitoweo), salt is NEVER enough).

21. You always lie about the ages of your children if they have to pay higher

admission fees. "Hapana, haka katoto kangu ni kasweet sixteen", and yet he has beards all over. (Nairobi Show).

22. When you are young, your parents buy you clothes at least two types and too big so that they would last longer. (Especially the lacy nylon ones in exhibitions when they are on promotion or end of month sales, with weird hats - yuk!).

23. At least one of your uncles is a teacher. (Yeah Jaduong Obondo)

24. You have a 10 kg bag of rice in the kitchen. (Basmati from Mwea)

25. You always read the Sport sections of the Sunday newspapers first. (Especially men!)

26. You always love shopping at Uchumi strictly during the End month and at the mid month. Reason: End of month sales. Mapromo!

So then am a real Kenyan and am proud of that. Are you...? If you are, prove this to me by forwarding this message to five of your friends and hopefully you will make someone's day better just like I have. Ama?

Have a nice day.

Song of Kapuki

by Victor Iugala

I want to taste the wine of insanity

I am fed up
I am fed up.
I desire for
Only one thing
Before I die:
I want to run
Mad, period.
I want to run
Totally mad
So that I will parade
My nakedness
In the street
If I offend anybody
Curse my stupid cunt.

I want to smear myself
With wet ash
And human excrement
So that nobody
Will arrest me.
I want to run amok
And wild like a warrior.
I want to arm myself
With a spiked club
And run in the streets of Juba
To hunt for the enemies

Of the black people.
I will go to the army barracks
And police barracks.
I will sort out
All the informers
And clobber their skulls
To pulp.
I will run
To Konyokonyo market
And burn the food stores
Of the petty traders
Who fleece the black people
In the black-market.
I will hunt for the C.I.D man
Who killed my brother.
I will lift my flabby breasts to him
And torch his house.

I will go to downtown Juba
And smear the potbellied
Enemy merchants
With human excrement.
I will tell them
To pack and go
To their homes of origin
In the desert.

I want to sleep rough
In the streets
So that I don't pay
The house rent.
I want to visit
All the rubbish heaps
In Juba
And eat all the bones
And rotten food there;
I will not

Buy food again.
I will not buy
Water again,
I will piss
In a pale
And drink
And bathe
In my own urine.
I want the urine
To make my skin
Itch with madness.

I want to be
afflicted with insanity.
I want to tear apart
My dog life.
I want to live
In a world of madness
I want to forget
That I exist.
I want to forget
That I am a widow
I want to forget
That my children
Are street beggars.
I want to forget
That my daughter
was raped by the enemy.

I have tasted
All the beers in Juba:
But I am still sober.
I want to taste
The wine of insanity
In order to get
Drunk for life
And be in perpetual stupor.

I want to learn
The language
Of mad people
To speak
In coded monologue
With the spirit
In me.
I want to bury myself
In a cocoon.
I want to shut
All the windows
To the world.

AboutThe Author

Victor Lugala is a poet, activist. He is from Yei, Sudan and lives in Nairobi. He works for the Sudan Council of Churches. Song of Kapuki

THE TORTURE
CHAMBERS
OF NYAYO HOUSE
WHITE
WASH
VICNDULA
2004

Nyayo House: The Event

There is a problem. Some one has locked the door to the Nyayo House basement cells. No one knows where he is or indeed who it is.

It is Wednesday the 3rd of December 2003, Human Rights Day, and Citizens for Justice, a group of former Nyayo House inmates are about to launch a book called "They Lived to Tell the Tale: Tales From the Nyayo Torture Chamber."

Earlier in the day when Kangethe Mungai from Release Political Prisoners spoke with the Nyayo House officials, every assurance was given that access would be granted. Now at three O'clock in the afternoon, the officials are singing a different tune. Two administration policemen stand at the Nyayo House gates having a surprisingly civil conversation with a group of human rights activists. The message being put across with utmost politeness is that there is no way anyone is going down to the cells. The deputy P.C comes down. He too is an eminently reasonable man. We will be allowed into the basement area, he tells us, but the keys to the cells....

So a group of about fifty men and women, banners before them walk down a ramp into the basement parking at Nyayo House which many of them know only too well. The deputy P.C disappears. The door remains locked. What was meant to be a revisiting of the past and past horrors fizzles into two brief and rather anticlimactic interdenominational prayers.

But maybe that is just as well. We hear that what were once the infamous government torture chambers have now been converted into a store room. Where once there were broken bodies and blood splashed walls, there are now the excrescences of officialdom: well used desks, broken bits of furniture, filing cabinets and such. No sign of the memorial, the reminder of a sordid and brutal past that our minister for Justice and Constitutional Affairs promised us when the torture chambers were first opened to the public on February the 11th.

The locked door is an electronically operated iron door. It has been newly painted a soothing dove grey. There is a peephole in it just above my eye level. I look through it but see nothing. Through a gap between the door and the wall, I peer onto the other side. The whitewashing of the past has begun. Literally. Gone are the jet black walls of February. The walls on the other side are newly painted as well, in white no less. There is a lot of light. The whole place looks airy and bright. A few odds and ends are littered on the floor. It looks positively welcoming. I know more than a few Kenyans who would trade their sordid digs for a place like that.

When the prayers are over, the party moves in procession down Kenyatta Avenue towards the Sixeighty Hotel where the book is to be launched, moves behind a huge

banner emblazoned with the Friedrich Ebert Stiftung logo. "Brand the revolution, why don't you," I think.

The afternoon's events begin after more prayers and the singing of the "national anthem," taken from Ngugi's "The Trial of Dedan Kimathi" and sung to the tune of Nkosi Sikeleli Africa. A member of parliament gets up and launches into officialese. He begins by thanking the Minister for Justice and Constitutional Affairs, without whom "the Nyayo House cells might still be closed," he says. Did he miss something? Did I? They are closed! Some one behind me laughs. "Don't worry," he says under his breath, "he's just doing his job."

Mr. Murungi, the said minister who was to have presided over the book launch had made his apologies. Maybe he had more pressing matters of the state to attend to. At any rate, it was a prudent decision. There were lots of claws being sharpened among the audience. As it is, he has left the task to his adjutant who has his work cut out talking around the foot in his mouth.

Njeru Githae, the assistant minister tells us that he is saddened to hear that the cells are locked and that they have been converted into a silo because in his opinion, they should be accessible to the public. And what a public he has in mind! In his view, the Nyayo House cells could be turned into a tourist attraction to rival the fabled "dungeons of London." After removing the furniture of course, and perhaps giving them a fresh coat of more forbidding black paint with perhaps a splash or two of crimson thrown in for good measure.

And as a final mark of solidarity with the survivors of torture: "I can't believe," quoth he, "that the government could ever have thought that people as innocent as you could ever have overthrown the government."

Indeed.

Vive la revolution.

AboutThe Author

Andia Kisia: Andia Kisia is still not fond of giving out her bio. She likes to enter and win BBC radio plays using pseudonyms. Her last incarnation, almost a year ago, was as an Igbo male person with a promising theatre career. We don't know where she is and who she is currently.

We are on the way from Nakuru and my wife says, "Should we stop and pick up some vegetables… maybe even some rhubarb?" I clench my jaw to try to restrain a deep-seated desire to extract painful retribution for this proposal that we stop by the roadside and waste valuable time inspecting a fruit that at best should be ingested by beasts with stubborn, all accepting constitutions like pigs. "Rhubarb?" I ask. "Why rhubarb?"

Rhubarbism: Reeks of 40

By Jimmy Kibera

We are on the way from Nakuru and my wife says, "Should we stop and pick up some vegetables... maybe even some rhubarb?" I clench my jaw to try to restrain a deep-seated desire to extract painful retribution for this proposal that we stop by the roadside and waste valuable time inspecting a fruit that at best should be ingested by beasts with stubborn, all accepting constitutions like pigs. "Rhubarb?" I ask. "Why rhubarb?"

Why anybody in this country should be interested in rhubarb is a mystery to me. The last time we bought this harmless looking fruit I was quite excited, for although I had heard much about the plant I had never been involved in its preparation. Rhubarb is one fruit that requires an inordinate amount of preparation. In fact, the preparation of rhubarb must be the invention of someone who accidentally stockpiled the stuff and was snowed in for a month. Preparing rhubarb involves over six hours of boiling the plant in water, followed by adding almost its equivalent weight in sugar. The result is a stringy white substance that I was made to understand provides a good stock for pie.

My opinion now is that perhaps there is another foodstuff that could be more easily applied to the making of pie. It is also my strong suspicion that this process is reflective of the advanced marketing and brand creation that has resulted in Africa producing over 30% of the world's resources but trading values of less than 1%.

The idea that people in the countryside who sell rhubarb go through a similar process was too much to bear, and I have not had the stomach to ask what they actually do with the stuff. It is my hope that perhaps it tastes good roasted with a slice of banana; it pains me too much to contemplate people around the country preparing pie with it. Rhubarb preparation is to me a good analogy of a culture that has developed with too much of something else – with not enough of us asking why. To me, such 'rhubarbism' represents that part of us that is conditioned against all logic and rationale, to accept a way of doing things that is alien or foreign for no articulated reason. It represents that part of us that is weak and seeks acceptance by doing things simply because we feel we will be better accepted for them – even though we rarely are. Conversely, it also represents a dedication to a process no matter how mindless, and attracts and creates value for it. Hmmm... how I love rhubarb pie!

"Perhaps we are running a little late," I reply. "Instead of spending time buying fruit, we had better hurry back and pick some rhubarb and things next time we're

on this road." Immediately I say it, I regret it. There was no reason to punish everyone in the car; we have all the time in the world. Even such a small thing as grocery shopping is dragged into the raging debate on identity firing away in the oven of my mind. But looking at my wife out of the corner of my eye, I realise that she understands that this has nothing to do with anything but my own tortured thought processes. My wife's understanding is one of those beautiful gifts in life, which pairs us with people who can put up with our most irrational outbursts – nay, even enjoy them. I guess it is just the mongrel in my background that brings all this out in me. I say mongrel because I have been in enough places for it to have influenced me without leaving a single dominant influence, so I tend to be a little drifty. By drifty, I mean silly things like changing one's accent depending on who one's talking to, jumbling up spelling and language when writing, shaking hands, kissing or hugging when everyone else is doing something else. Anyhow, as we are about to get to Nairobi and are passing the Bata Shoe Factory, I am reminded of an old story that perfectly encapsulates my resentment towards rhurbarbism...

The story was from a dear late uncle who nearly came to his death in the then stinking lake near the Bata Shoe Factory. Apparently he and his friends had had an excellent excursion and were on their way back to Nairobi at some point in the afternoon by motor vehicle. For some unexplained reason, perhaps related to the liquid refreshments consumed earlier in the day, they ended up losing control and driving straight into the lake. Unaware that one can only roll down the window in a sinking car, they unsuccessfully attempted to open the doors and break the windows with their hands, while a small group of spectators quickly gathered by the lakeside. In the crowd were two old ladies who were busy issuing sympathetic comments about the forgone conclusion playing out before them. Given that the car was still not underwater, the occupants were able to hear what they thought to be an ill-fitting epitaph to their lives: "Kai asho ne ma kua kioru eh." Literally translated, this means: "Those ones have really died badly." Not "let's help them." Not "let's try and change their terrible fate." Luckily for them, a passerby – in my uncle's words, a "clever mzungu" – managed to overcome the revulsion of the smell to stop, dive into the murk and smash the back window with a spanner, dragging the occupants out to safety and back to life. Life and death were decided by different attitudes of acceptance and challenge.

It is Sunday and I am travelling again. I am happy, although it only 'next door' to Harare. Standing with my colleague in the airport queue, my colleague's outfit brings my own sharply into focus. I have on a casual pair of shoes, tracksuit bottoms, and a T-shirt. I can be and often am mistaken for a college student when I travel (to my delight, I might add, given that I left college more than a dozen years ago). My colleague, by contrast, is in full business attire, with a briefcase to boot. Granted, he is older than I, but to be honest I cannot see what on earth can be gained by wearing such attire. The man just cannot be comfortable: there he is with one of those stomachs that makes even me feel fit, and makes others enquire about terms of pregnancy. His trousers are pulled high over his stomach, which is contort-

ed by a leather belt, and his briefcase jabs him methodically as he walks. What is it about a way of being that makes one dress so painfully, purely for the idea of acceptance? Here too, clearly, is another unwitting victim of rhubarbism...

When I think back to my childhood and my first travels for study, one of the things I recall was the necessity of wearing a suit and carrying a briefcase. It did not strike me again for a long time afterwards, but since then my habits have (thankfully) changed. Why is it that, when one attends a public occasion, casual or formal, there is always an obligation to wear a suit, or at least a blazer? Why does one feel the need to go through such an elaborate and uncomfortable ritual? Is it force of habit, or an inbuilt desire to impress? I think the process and its drawn-outness is fuelled by that part of us that wants to be modern, but still feels rural. It is – literally and metaphorically – a cover-up. A cover-up similar to rhubarb preparation, where we have an awful tasting fruit that we feel compelled to boil and sweeten so the world will love it – and us – much better.

I remember once asking someone, an elderly doctor, why he always dressed so formally. The first level of response was about dressing in keeping with one's status, being a respected public figure who people naturally expected to dress in a certain way. While this amply explained those situations in which he was meeting colleagues or clients, it did not explain the reason why he chose to wear a suit in the company of close friends. After some years of prodding, however, it finally came out: it was not so much inspired by his appearance to others as by how he himself felt changed.

"He was born of a humble background..." – how often do we see this phrase on a funeral programme? I find it interesting that we choose such a term, while everyone in Kenya over 50 has invariably come from such a background. Why do we never use terms like "simple," "rural," "agrarian"? Is there a sense of shame associated with these words? Our "humble backgrounds" are, after all, representative of virtually everyone born at the time. That we all came from such a lifestyle undoubtedly made it all the more pointed when one left for college or found a job in Nairobi, beginning a metamorphosis akin to the worm transforming itself into a butterfly. And in Kenya, the mark of this metamorphosis was the wearing of a suit – however much inside remained the same.

This metamorphosis from one background to another was represented first in dress and then in forms of transportation and accommodation. The response that I finally wrested from the elderly doctor was simply that he did not want "to be mistaken for another villager." It sounded harsh to me at first, even condescending, until I realised that perhaps he felt more of a villager than a doctor, that his suit was his costume and passport to his exotic new life.

Shit, shit, shitting... I am on the plane back to Nairobi and have just remembered Binyavanga and his request that I write something for his wretched magazine. I am

two months' late and have not a clue what I am supposed to write about. Binya's brief ('brief' being the word) was to write what I think about us Kenyans as we move into our defining 'middle age' at 40. I really am not too sure about this. In a Biblical sense, there is much to portend about the number four that signifies completion. The Israelites spent 40 years in the wilderness and 400 years in bondage, so we are made to understand that this was a point of maturity at which God could at last bring them to their destiny. Maybe I could use that as an allegory for where Kenya is: coming into its destiny, giving up the things of its past, being at last capable of being released into its future. But how do I get to the point at which I can describe Kenya in a manner that is accessible? How do I divide the truth and the lie? The truth is surely somewhere in between: that Kenya is maturing, but is still young and vulnerable to the influences and opinions of others.

Speaking for myself, as a 30-something businessman conversing on occasion with Government, there is many a time in these past few months that I have wished to be over 40. I even played briefly with the idea of accentuating my appearance with a careful sprinkling of baking powder in my hair – dyeing for stature! The truth about Kenya's current situation is that we are still not a people who are able in large measure to value ability entirely separately from packaging, results from reputation, succinct thought from stature. Can any whole people or culture really do this? Of course not!

Nonetheless, there is a time and place for a new discovery, and a confidence to emerge that is more truthful about who we are than who we were. I remember the early part of my career, before I became a little more sensible, when I thought that all one had to do was to walk into an office, define a need, and then make something of yourself. I was younger then, all of 21, and I was certain that all you had to do was to create value and the market would automatically recognise it. Thank God for friends: friends who pointed me in the right direction, who said "Get a job, and then see what happens." For the difficulty of dealing with a place that is indeterminate, is that the main decision makers are so often external, outside of us – perhaps hidden somewhere in the depths of a rhubarb pie...

AboutThe Author

Jimmy Kibinge is a finance consultant with a soul. It is his hope that the rhuburb industry will crumble.

MARA CONSERVANC

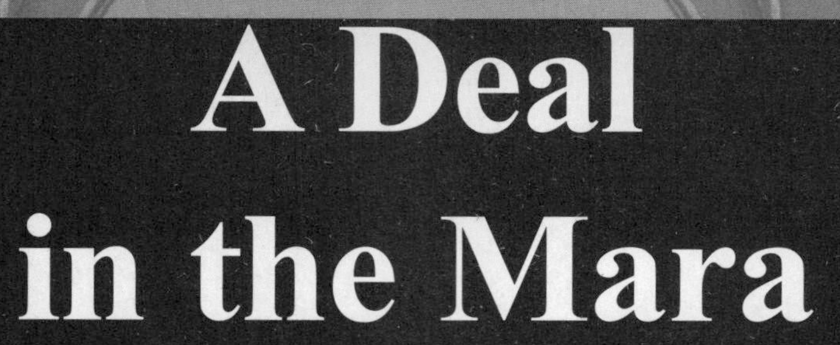
A Deal
in the Mara

A Deal in the Mara

by Parselelo Kantai

``Kwani decided to reprint this story which was first run in Ecoforum. We feel this is the finest piece of investigative journalism we have seen in Kenya in some years. The story took months to reconstruct, and has explosive implications...read and be astonished..."

Editor.

Prologue

About two years ago, I travelled to the Maasai Mara to research a story for Ecoforum magazine. A private company, known as the Mara Conservancy had taken over the management of the Mara Triangle. In the conservation circles where such developments immediately become the subject of casual debate (post-lunch, between-workshop, after-dinner), opinion was divided. Many hailed the coming of the Mara Conservancy as just what the doctor ordered. The Mara needed professional help, what with all the poaching, the broken-down infrastructure and the massive looting of revenues. Others felt, with little to back their suspicions, that the Mara Conservancy was just another mzungu conservationist land-grab. I myself was very suspicious of the whole arrangement. The 20th century was nothing if it wasn't deal, after deal after deal in which Maasai lands were systematically stolen. This latest development in the Mara smelled very familiar.

But on the ground the results spoke for themselves. Crossing the Mara River and entering the Mara Triangle was like entering a stable, democratic and upwardly mobile country of wildlife conservation from the decrepit, war-torn republic on the other side of the river. Whereas the Narok County Council had for years mismanaged, neglected and looted the Sis-Mara, the Mara Conservancy had transformed the Mara Triangle. While it was illegal, you could do 100 km/ph on the newly-repaired roads within the Conservancy. The rangers at the gate greeted you with a smile, gave you a real feeling of professionalism, of a park being in good hands. Gate collection fees, previously a major source of 'eating' for park rangers, local councillors and council bureaucrats , were up and being delivered to the authorities. In short, the Conservancy was finally delivering.

So why was there so much opposition to it?

I. The Cheetah Hunt

We are looking for a wounded, female cheetah in August 2001, at the beginning of the great wildebeest migration/Mara Crossing. "It lost its eye to poachers a few days ago," says Brian Heath, in his quiet way, voice raised slightly above the roar of the green long-chassis Landrover. There are four of us in the vehicle. At the wheel is Brian Heath, the Chief Executive Officer of the Mara Conservancy, the company that has been managing the Mara Triangle for the past 14 months. Next to him sits the company's consultant veterinarian, a Kenyan Asian with a practice in Mombasa. At some point during the drive he accepted the imperative of sleep. He is now dozing off the buffet lunch we had at the Mara Serena. Then there's myself and Japheth Muok, who works for the Mara Serena as a guide.

The Mara Triangle is in Kenya's Transmara district. It is a 690 sq. km triangular-shaped section of the 5520sq.km Maasai Mara Game Reserve, arguably the richest wildlife arena in the world. Until 1994, when Transmara was made into a district by Presidential decree, the game reserve was managed by the Narok County Council. Following the creation of the new district, the management of the Triangle, an eighth of the size of the entire game reserve went to the Transmara County Council.

The Triangle was the new district's jewel, the proceeds from tourism potentially a windfall. But the new administration lacked the infrastructure to turn potential into profit. The Narok County Council refused to hand over equipment to the new council. Revenue collection in the Triangle was inefficient. The old administration left a decaying road network;it decayed further. Staff salaries went unpaid, often for months, sometimes, according to the Mara Conservancy, for years. As a result, staff morale was low, poaching steadily approaching epidemic levels and tourism on the decline.

After an hour of driving everything on this mostly flat landscape begins to look the same. I ask where we are. "Milima Tatu," says Japheth. It means nothing to me. The names of landmarks here speak more about the ascendancy of interest groups in the Triangle than about actual place.; Bbefore tourism, those three hills in the distance probably had local names. Today, the landmarks bear tour guide nomenclature: Milima Tatu, Mlima wa Nyoka, Sundowner. Closer to the Tanzania border, local names predominate. Masanja, a low-rising hill with a huge thicket, or Nyanguki, the low saucer-shaped hill across which the poachers like to make their way into the Triangle and begin yet another bout of snaring and hunting.

Japeth is saying: "Since the Mara Conservancy took over there has been a tremendous change in infrastructure and security. At least now we can see where the roads are and it's easier to get to certain destinations. The same applies to security, there's no more poaching going on. The authorities didn't have the capacity to deal with it."

He is exaggerating (how did the cheetah lose its eye?), but since the Mara Conservancy took over the management of the Mara Triangle about 14 months pre-

viously, poaching has been drastically reduced. The Conservancy's PR machine, which has been crucial in getting the word out, lists the achievements: the seizure of 800 snares; the arrest of 130 poachers; the vast improvement in security accompanying the introduction of two-way radios and the boosting of rangers' morale – "they are now paid monthly and have new uniforms." The Conservancy says it has repaired 120 km of the previously dilapidated road network, added 60 km of tracks and re-opened several transit roads. It is a far cry from the sorry situation across the Mara River, managed by the Narok County Council. The lack of maintenance of the roads in that part of the Mara seemed almost deliberate, as if somebody decided that the sudden boulders in the middle of the road and the black-cotton-soil filled ruts add to the tourist experience – heightening the 'African bush' feeling.

One of the Conservancy's most notable achievements, as emphasised by numerous press statements, is regular payments to the Maasai communities living on Group Ranches bordering the Reserve. The Conservancy had always recognized the local Maasai as custodians of the park and , very early on made a commitment to share benefits with them. It was one of the key benchmarks they set for themselves. The others were transparency (they would be open to public scrutiny); accountability (they would account for every cent spent); and delivery (they would do what they set out to do).

Although the law stipulates that communities bordering wildlife protected areas must receive 19% of total revenues from the protected area, the Transmara County Council had, according to the Mara Conservancy's public relations consultant, Gavin Bennett, repeatedly failed to keep up their end of this bargain. Now, with the Conservancy in charge, payments to group ranches, says Bennett, tripled and quadrupled. By June 2002, the Conservancy announced that it had paid out Ksh 10.5 million to the three Group Ranches, namely Kerinkani, Kimintet and Oloirien.

"If you send out an ambush or a night patrol around 7.30 pm you can watch the torches coming down the hill," says Brian Heath. The vehicle has stopped a few metres from the Tanzania border, an unmanned beacon in the undulating landscape. My first impression of Heath was of a soft-spoken, slightly anxious middle-aged man. But there is something else there, a certain assurance brought on by years of experience. Born in Kenya, he has been around. In the `80s he managed the 1.6 million acre, 30,000 head-of-cattle Galana ranch before it was nationalised by the government. He then worked in Nanyuki for Farm Africa, an NGO specialising in arid lands issues. He also had a Masters degree in Rangeland Management. When Willy Roberts, the Mara Conservancy chairman was shopping around for a CEO, Brian Heath was clearly ahead of the pack.

"At this time of the year the poachers come down the hill with their snares and their dogs, probably cooking a meal in the low hills in the distance. They then cross the river and set snares on the other side. Their operations last usually five or six days can be quite effective. In ten minutes we've seen them kill 10 or 15 Thompsons

gazelle. The poachers are all waKuria from Tanzania." Heath has a special dislike for the waKuria. Recently his men arrested two poachers, both Kuria, with over 200 kg of dried game meat. He believes that poaching is part of their culture. "To them it's something they really enjoy doing. They all say it's because of poverty but they actually come from quite a high potential agricultural area."

Later, he makes comparisons between his present job and the previous ones. "We are a political organisation. It's been difficult to come to terms with this. The way things are managed in the public sector especially when you are dealing with politicians is very different from how they would be managed in the private sector. We don't have the kind of control and autonomy that we would have in the private sector." He insists that there is no political interference in the Conservancy's day-to-day operations. "Initially there was quite a lot of interference. But the longer we are here, the more we become part of the scenery, and the more people can see we have made a big change the less political interference we are going to get."

As we speak, a court case hangs over his head, challenging the legitimacy of the Conservancy. But driving around the 690 sq.km Conservancy-run part of the park, he is almost dismissive about it. He absolves the Conservancy from any blame, apolitical as it is: "All the antagonism is not about us per se but about the individuals around us and this longstanding feud between two different factions of Transmara leadership."

It has been a long, hard road since he got involved in the Conservancy two years ago, when it was just an idea. Wary of politics, Heath however sees nothing strange about the fact that his organisation is strongly associated with politicians in the area, not least Julius Sunkuli, whose reputation is anything but clean. In fact, he pours praise on the local leadership. This is August, 2002. KANU still looks like it could win the forthcoming elections. Sunkuli's protection is important. And he is after all, the area MP. His patronage is essential for the Conservancy to continue to exist. "Without [Sunkuli's] support and commitment we would not be where we are today," he says. Until recently, Sunkuli's sister sat on the Conservancy board. Sunkuli replaced her once he felt bold enough to install himself. He had previously denied any involvement with the Conservancy. And then there is councillor Kijabe Kuya ole Tunai, a close Sunkuli ally and another Conservancy director implicated in questionable dealings. As if conscious of what I am thinking, Brian Heath turns and looks directly at me: "Without Kijabe's vision none of this would have been possible."

That, according to many people, is the problem.

II.

Miscellaneous Civil Application No. 686 was filed on June 22, 2001 by 20 out of

the 37 Transmara councillors in the High Court in Nairobi. It sought, among other things, to terminate the operations of the Mara Conservancy. The suit claimed that the appointment of the Conservancy contravened the Local Government Act, that the full council meeting "purportedly held" to vote on the hiring of the Conservancy had actually not taken place, and that even if it had, was convened irregularly as no notice had been given as stipulated by the law.

On June 11, 2001, less than two weeks earlier, the Transmara County Council had signed a management agreement with the Mara Conservancy at a ceremony held, curiously, at Nairobi's Serena Hotel. It is not clear how many Transmara County Councillors were present. A Conservancy press release said of the deal: "The new arrangement has the blessing of central government, and could set the standard in the management of community wealth throughout the country."

Under the terms of the management agreement, the Mara Conservancy would manage the Triangle for five years – the company had initially proposed a ten-year renewable contract -- with an option to renew "if the [Conservancy is so] desirous". As manager, the Conservancy plays three roles: security provision, infrastructure maintenance, and revenue collection.

Revenues -- and this is partly why accusations that the Council had sold off the Mara Triangle would soon emerge -- would be split three ways. 40.5% each to the County Council and the Conservancy, and 19% to the communities living on the group ranches. Both the Council and the Conservancy pay 9.5% into a fund, from which the group ranch payments are made. Although there is no mention of the Group Ranches in the agreement, these are the figures quoted by both Conservancy officials and group ranch members. The Mara Conservancy sub-contracted a private firm, Earthview Ltd, to collect revenues on its behalf, initially for a 5% commission, which was later increased to 8%.

It is not clear why the Council did not insist on paying the Conservancy a flat fee, or a commission as is typical of most arrangements in which an organization outsources some of its functions to a private company. Instead, considerable effort is put into detailing just how revenues would be collected and divided between the Council and the Conservancy. The Conservancy would collect revenues, and share the earnings with the Council but also deduct any costs incurred during collection. For instance, whereas the Council receives 100% of all ground rent monies – rent from lodges and tented camps – the Conservancy receives, under the agreement, 100% of all vehicle fees entering the Triangle. It, of course, collects those fees itself. The Conservancy says that its share of the revenues is ploughed back into managing the Triangle. Interestingly enough there is only one instance where the Council is obligated to collect revenues – in the case of ground rent.

And there is a disturbing omission. The agreement does not contain any mini-

mum performance requirements for the Conservancy; it was generally assumed that the Conservancy would set mutually acceptable standards and evaluateof its own performance as it went along. It is as if, because the Conservancy appeared well-intentioned, the most basic rules governing contracts could be disregarded.

A Nairobi High Court granted the 20 councillors an injunction quite soon after their June 22nd application against the Mara Conservancy. Then in early July 2001, the court lifted it following a counter application made jointly by the Transmara County Council and the Mara Conservancy.

37 councillors constitute the Transmara County Council. 20 had taken the council to Court. The County Council was able to get the injunction against the Conservancy lifted when they submitted sworn affidavits by 20 councillors testifying that they had indeed attended the May 21, 2001 meeting. Five councillors who had previously fallen on the opposing side had changed their minds and said that their names were included in the suit without their consent.

Since then, the case has has yet to be heard, bogged down by delays and adjournments. There are suspicions that the delays are deliberate.

But the story refused to die. In November the same year, the issue was raised in Parliament. Responding, the then Local Government minister, JJ Kamotho contradicted the Conservancy's June statement that the initiative had the blessings of the central government. He said, in part: "The contract...did not receive the requisite ministerial approval in accordance with Section 143 of the Local Government Act, Cap 265..." In other words, the Conservancy was operating illegally. Even so, the government took no action against the Conservancy.

Clearly, the Conservancy was enjoying patronage from a powerful source. "The initiative has the blessings of State House," said Gavin Bennett, during an interview in July 2002.

"The President has always been a great conservationist and he has taken awards for conservation," said the company's chairman, Willy Roberts, without a trace of irony, during an interview with Ecoforum in October 2002. "He did not muscle the idea through. He needed to know about the whole idea. He just liked the idea and openly said 'I support this idea I think it's a great idea, a great initiative and try your best, good luck'. He supported it as the President."

Others tell a different story. In his sworn affidavit of July 5, 2002, former Transmara Council Deputy Clerk, Samuel ole Morintat avers that the meeting endorsing the Mara Conservancy never took place. "I do not recollect preparing, issuing or seeing any notices to the Council members of the time, place and business proposed to be transacted at the full Council meeting allegedly held on 21st May, 2001," he wrote. "The County Hall where the meeting was allegedly held is approximately 300 metres from my office and no full council meeting would be held there without my knowledge. In fact on 21st May, 2001, the Resident Magistrate was conducting her

court sessions at the said County Hall, Kilgoris." It would have been, he says, impossible for a council meeting to take place while the court was in session. Morintat's testimony has an interesting footnote: "As at 21st May 2001 the respondent Council had not acquired a computer and laser printer with which the minutes of the alleged full council meeting have been typed and printed."

It was during this period that the Conservancy's public relations machine went into overdrive. Press statements gave the impression of overwhelming community support; the Conservancy described its detractors as a "small clique of individuals" unhappy with the Conservancy's presence because it brought an end to the "gravy train network".

The Conservancy published monthly financial statements in the press as proof of its commitment to transparency and accountability. None of them had been subjected to an external audit. Periodically it was also sending out press releases announcing payments made to the group ranches. These were spiced with quotes from community leaders. Curiously, these turned out to be individuals either sitting on the Conservancy's board of directors, or people known to be close to the Conservancy. Like Kijabe ole Tunai, a Transmara councillor but also a Conservancy director whose expressions of happy astonishment at yet another payment to the community frequently accompanied a Mara Conservancy press statement. Or the Council chairman, Chari ole Saiwa, an active supporter of the Conservancy, expressing approval at the early successes of the new company.

The Mara Conservancy was also receiving excellent international press coverage. Stories appearing in online publications praised the new idea, rolled out its successes and, echoing the Conservancy, talked about the fact that it was a bold new direction in the management of wildlife protected areas. Not a single story raised the issue of the Conservancy's legitimacy. "The Mara Conservancy has been established through a fully democratic process involving all the stakeholders," one press release said. Nobody disputed this. Yet the reality on the ground told a different story.

IV. Blurred lines

"We are prepared to die fighting this Mara Conservancy!" Peter ole Tompoi's face is a study in indignation. He is a former tour operator, a Parliamentary aspirant for Sunkuli's seat, and a member of Kimintet group ranch. He gesticulates furiously as if his vehemence needs several outlets in order to be properly expressed. "Nobody was told about the Conservancy before it was established. This is something that was done without our knowledge. They have done it using force and we are prepared to die fighting it." I met ole Tompoi for the first time half an hour ago in Lolgorian, a town made famous by the dissidence of the late Fr. John Kaiser. He is one of 500 members of Kimintet group ranch, which borders the Mara Triangle. None of the members, he says, have seen a cent from the Mara Conservancy.

If his sentiments are those of a politician looking for publicity, those of Daniel Leteipa ole Maaki are not. Maaki has worked in Lolgorian with the German development agency, GTZ, since 1992. He tells me: "Just step out of this compound and stop anybody you meet, anybody at all, and ask what they think of the Conservancy. Everybody is opposed to it. One reason for this is that they have never paid out any money to the group ranches."

Conservancy officials respond to this charge by saying that they have made the payments. It is, they say, none of their business how that money travels once it is out of their hands. "The Mara conservancy," says chairman Willy Roberts, "is not officially responsible for the group ranches. That is the Council's responsibility because the county council is the elected representative body of those communities. The money has been paid to those communities through the council." "I think there is a problem as to how it is spent, amongst the communities. It's really outside our jurisdiction. It's not our business to be involved with that."

Like so many things about the Mara Conservancy, the denial sounds good. Beyond the PR hype, the distinction between the Conservancy as a professional outfit and as a political organisation are a lot more blurred than its officials would care to admit.

The controversy around the group ranch payments illustrates this. Payments to group ranches are made into accounts jointly held by the Transmara County Council and individual group ranches. All payments to the group ranches are authorised by the County Council clerk and chairman. Often, councillors are also group ranch chairmen and are therefore signatories to the group ranch accounts. At least one group ranch chairman, Cllr. Kijabe ole Tunai sits on the Mara Conservancy board and another, Tiampati ole Lempeshua is closely associated with it. Also, according to minutes held at the first Mara Conservancy board meeting on January 24, 2001, there were plans to invite Council clerk John Naiguran to the Conservancy board as an ex-officio member. Naiguran has had a close working relationship with Brian Heath ever since the Council hired the Conservancy to manage the Triangle. So close, in fact, that the relationship between the Mara Conservancy and the Transmara County Council could be said to run on the working relationship between the two men.

After a point it is difficult to tell where the Conservancy ends and where the County Council begins. On May 29, 2001, eight days after the Transmara County Council allegedly held a full council meeting hiring the Conservancy, John Naiguran, wrote by hand, a letter to Brian Heath requesting that the Conservancy to purchase two vehicles on the Council's behalf and deduct the purchase costs from future payments the Conservancy would make to the Council. It would be another two weeks before the Mara Conservancy began operations. "The Council requests that you make arrangements to procure two vehicles on our behalf," wrote Naiguran. "We request that a moratorium of six months be given to us and thereafter the deductions be made for 12 months from our collections. We request this be done soonest

as the Council now is grounded..."

The next day, in a letter jointly signed by Heath and Naiguran, the two wrote to one MH Forster, the Group Chief Executive of CMC Holdings requesting the purchase of two Land Rover station wagons, "on the same terms you have offered the Mara Conservancy". The vehicles were worth a total of Ksh 6.4 million. Under the Local Government Act (cap 265), county councils are forbidden to procure goods worth more than Ksh 10,000 without inviting tenders and without the authority of a full council meeting. In the case of an emergency, such a purchase can only be authorised by the Council's finance committee. There is no evidence that either a full council meeting or the council's finance committee authorised the purchase of the vehicles.

And the symbiosis reaches down to the very origins of the Mara Conservancy. For many in Transmara, the Mara Conservancy is more a political project than a conservation initiative. The Conservancy says this is a result of a campaign of "disinformation" put out by politicians opposed to the Conservancy. However, even this denial cannot hide the fact that the Conservancy used its political allies within the Council and beyond to establish itself. Peter ole Tompoi's allegation that the Mara Conservancy was established using force stems from a series of abortive and violent meetings between community leaders and Mara Conservancy officials in late 2001. One incident is especially telling. In September 2001, the Mara Conservancy along with then Minister Julius Sunkuli wanted to present publicly group ranch cheques as a way of drumming community support for the Conservancy. They convened a meeting in a place called Kawai, not far from the Kichwa Tembo, the biggest lodge in the Triangle.

"We were informed of the meeting by the District Officer here in Kilgoris," says ole Tompoi. "He went around telling people about the meeting the night before it was to take place. I believe the intention was for us not to attend it because of the distance between Lolgorian and Kawai. But we mobilised people and vehicles and travelled the whole night. We were there on time. Sunkuli, Kijabe and Brian Heath were at Kichwa Tembo. When Sunkuli, then Minister in charge of internal security, got word that there were about 400 people waiting for him and that we wanted to know why he had sold the Mara without our knowledge he refused to come and address us." There was a demonstration. The crowd marched to Kichwa Tembo. Security personnel were called in. The meeting was dispersed. A press statement by the Mara Conservancy described the demonstrators as a "rent-a-mob".

"Whenever these people call a meeting, there are administration policemen," Ratik ole Kuyana, a Transmara resident and a tour guide had told me. "When you ask them why they are there they say they have orders from above."

V. Whose idea was it?

Many supporters of the Conservancy are blissfully oblivious to local protests.

"Whose idea was it?" Alison Parker echoes my question about the origins of the Mara Conservancy. "Willy Roberts, I guess," she pronounces 'Roberts' the way only Americans can, turning the 'ro' into a 'ra', then stretching it for a brief eternity before crunching into the last syllable. I have a vision of her gently dabbing at her mouth for any stray crumbs. "He was the one who was approached by the community leaders. He brought everybody together."

Her friend Lesley Roach also middle-aged and similarly attired in that casual way of money, picks up the story. "In 1999 I was out in Southern Tanzania, on a walking tour with my husband and two other couples."James Robertson, on whose Karen veranda we are sitting, was their tour operator. "We spent our last few days in the Serengeti, in the North East. We saw evidence of poaching on the border with the Mara. We wanted to do something about it." She looks at me briefly, searching my face for comprehension. "We're supporting the animals' cause."

Alison chimes in:"So we said to James that if there was ever a change in focus, any initiative worth supporting that can support the animals cause to please call us. Then in November 1999 he called us and said, 'Come out. I am hearing talk of a new initiative. At that time, I don't even think it was called the Mara Conservancy."

James Robertson is a tour operator with Kerr and Downey Ltd, and a conservationist. He has worked in the Mara since 1978. He witnessed the tourism boom of the 1980s, saw the degradation of the ecosystem and the decimation of wildlife and as a result, he says, has been actively engaged with Maasai communities and group ranches outside the park. Lesley Roach and Alison Parker have been his clients for years. Alison Parker is a cultural anthropologist/photographer. When Robertson told the two women of the idea to establish a private company to manage the Mara Triangle, they immediately gave a US$ 300,000 loan, the start-up money for the Conservancy, to be paid when the Conservancy could afford to.

Alison Parker is beside herself with admiration for the Conservancy's work. She has just returned from the Mara Triangle and witnessed yet again, the wildebeest migration. "I've been in the migration before and the wildebeest are all going 'grunt-grunt-grunt' all the time." The animal-rights activist in her surges forward. "This time we go up there and I am like 'Wow! What's happened to all the noise, I was so looking forward to hearing it!' and the feeling is -- and this isn't the least bit scientific – that the wildebeest are at peace. They are not scared, worried or jittery! That symbolised for me what has happened out there."

What *did* happen out there?

"[Cllr] Kijabe and several of the others [who come from] the top of the escarpment came along," explains Willy Roberts. "They said they needed help [managing

the park] and will you be having a solution to get this going better? So I said okay and I'll write a proposal and it's over to you. If you think you can convince your board, which is the council, and your MP then we'll have further meetings, which we did, and they called us and we met in Nairobi for two meetings with the county council and the minister."

(blacked out parts removed for legal reasons) Depending on who you talk to in the Maasai Mara, filled as it is with so much rumour and wrangling, Willy Roberts is either a great visionary of wildlife conservation, or a **xxxxx**. He lays out his own credentials. He was a wheat farmer just outside the Mara for years before he realised that the Maasai were being short-changed, not substantially benefiting from the proceeds of tourism. He then approached the late Chief ole Ntutu of Narok South with the idea of introducing game viewing charges on private ranches. After much struggle – including a long precedent-setting court case-- the idea came to fruition on a ranch known as Olchoro Orouwa. It has since become a model for community-based conservation, replicated as far away as Il Ng'wesi in Northern Kenya.

When I tell him that people say he left in disgrace, he remains calm: "They said that? Well that depends on who you talk to. Disgrace, I don't know." He asks me whether I have talked to Ntutu, the area MP at the time and a son of the late chief.

The association between Willy Roberts and Kijabe ole Tunai is at the heart of the Mara Conservancy deal. And the community's opposition to it. If Roberts' reputation among many in the Mara is tainted, then Kijabe's is enough to provoke a brawl. When Transmara became a district, the story goes, he took advantage of the confusion of boundaries and acquired the land on which the lucrative Kichwa Tembo lodge sits. The lodge was built on a 10-km corridor excised from the Mara Game Reserve to allow Maasai cattle to access the Mara River and the salt-lick nearby. Kijabe managed to get a title deed to the land, registered a group ranch now known as Oloololo, then went to the lodge owners and told them they were to pay rent to the group ranch not the County Council. Kichwa Tembo now pays Oloololo group ranch Ksh 1 million per month, Ksh 300,000 of which is supposed to be remitted to the council as rent (Kijabe's opponents say the group ranch hasn't paid the council in years). Repeated attempts by the local community to get the land back from Kijabe has taken the matter to court. On each occasion, Kijabe has emerged victorious.

"You must understand," Brian Heath had said, "The people who are trying to derail what we are doing are Kijabe's opponents. They are not opposed to the Mara Conservancy per se. In fact some have even approached the Conservancy and said 'we support you but we are against certain people on your board'."

The incident at Kawai forced the Mara Conservancy into an honest reassessment of itself. In an effort to build a bridge across the damaged relations with the community, it hired a community relations consultant, David Nkedianye, a Maasai and a conservationist working in Kajiado., Nkedianye was approached by Chris Thouless, a Conservancy director who told him the Conservancy wanted to find out how a more equitable distribution of revenues could be achieved. He accepted a 60-day contract with the C onservancy and started work in 2001.

"People were very unhappy with the way the Conservancy was established," Nkedianye told me when we met in Nairobi in November last year. "It was so abrupt. They didn't understand how it had been brought in. They thought it was being pushed by a small clique of politically-connected people." Nkedianye went around the three group ranches listening to people and collecting views. "People expressed reservations that somebody like Sunkuli was a director. They felt that he was colluding with Kijabe for political reasons and also to gain access to group ranch and county council money." Nkedianye's efforts to create an understanding within the community of the Mara Conservancy ended in failure. "He was chased out by the faction leaders opposed to the Kijabe," says Heath.

A year after he left, David Nkedianye's analysis of what was wrong with the Mara Conservancy is still fresh in his mind. "The Conservancy must put in place fairer structures that will oversee benefit-sharing with communities. These structures must be centred on community participation, not the kind of top-down affair you're seeing even now. Without that I can see the Mara Conservancy having a lot of problems in future."

VI. Illusions

At night in the Mara during the wildebeest migration, the landscape appears populated by the lights of a distant city. Reflecting the headlights of oncoming vehicles, the eyes of the grazing wildebeest form a million red dots on the horizon. It is an illusion. It is beautiful up to the point when you realize that your vehicle is blocked by hundreds of grunting bovines.

Strange things begin to happen when a system stops believing in itself. The first offered suggestion for redemption is confused with a good idea; illusions become attractive. Compromises are made between well-intentioned people and greedy men by the end of which it is impossible to tell the difference between the two. Old rules are disregarded, broken. A few people see possibilities, latch onto the new idea,

dress it up in the language of progress, and run away with it.

At some point during the cheetah hunt, Brian Heath had hinted at the long-term objectives of the Mara Conservancy. "If we can do this successfully," he had said. "We can then do this on the other side of the river, in Samburu, Shaba and so on. Publicly-run game reserves could really benefit from this kind of arrangement." In the Moi era, the idea behind local government - to democratise the delivery of services and the benefits of local resources - gradually faded, became an illusion in the landscape of corruption and greed. The practice of local government had become an exercise in diverting money into private hands while keeping the public engrossed in the divisions of the local politics. What the Mara Conservancy was offering - to maximise benefits from a valuable resource while keeping local politicians atr arms length -- appeared to be a bold new step in the right direction. But it had proved impossible, an illusion of redemption. And then again, maybe the whole plan was to benefit both the conservationists and the politicians - to 'mainstream' the conservation agenda by co-opting the politicians.

Late in October 2002, I call up the Conservancy's public relations consultant, Gavin Bennett, seeking clarification on several issues. I had first interviewed him in August 2002 before I travelled to the Mara. He had been emphatic on the Conservancy's commitment to transparency and accountability, its commitment to community. He had said that when he was hired he made it very clear to the Conservancy board that if there was any funny business he would pull out and, in fact, expose them. Now armed with what I know, I want an explanation: why didn't he pull out? He tells me that he has, in fact, 'withdrawn', and only offers his services in an advisory capacity. He is optimistic, however, that, that things would change after the 2002 election - that the politicos will be shorn of power and will therefore not be able to exert any influence on the Conservancy's operations. You saw what the Conservancy has achieved, he says. We should be working towards improving it, it's a good idea. Don't destroy it. Don't throw the baby out with the bathwater, he says. Things will improve after the elections. Later, I learn that he has stopped representing the Mara Conservancy altogether.

On the same day, I conduct my last interview with Brian Heath. I meet him at the Conservancy's offices in Triad House, Muthaiga. He is in the middle of a meeting with officials and councillors of the Council, including the Council Clerk, the chairman, Kijabe, Tiampati and others. He comes out to the lobby to talk to me. "Those people in there know where the group ranch money goes," he tells me. I suddenly see another quality in him. Some call it pragmatism. There are other, far less charitable terms for it. "Don't be too hard on us," he says as I leave. His eyes are always smiling. "I'll report the facts," I tell him. The election came and KANU lost the elections, Sunkuli his parliamentary seat. Although Kijabe is re-elected unopposed as a councillor but the NARC party which shood KANU out of power, has a majority in the Council. There is talk of reviewing the Mara Conservancy contract.

Aftermath

A number of things happened after the story was published. Weeks before, we'd heard rumours that certain quarters in the conservation community were worried about the direction our story would take. Then the magazine came out. On the cover was a photo of a handshake between a white and a black man with the Mara as a backdrop. The cover said "A Deal in the Mara". There was no doubt what direction the story had taken. The storm of protest, mostly from whites in and around things conservation, was almost frightening in its intensity. Ecoforum received letters – have a look at the sample published alongside the main story -- that made no pretence of the disgust many readers felt. There were rumours that the Conservancy was going to sue. We hired a lawyer.

People from the area, both professionals and non-professionals alike, praised the story. Some even attributed it to being a factor in former Kilgoris MP, Julius Sunkuli's defeat. This was a bit of an exaggeration considering the story hadn't been published by then. What was true, however, is that Sunkuli's support for the Mara Conservancy was perhaps the main reason why he lost the 2002 General Elections to NARC's Gideon Konchellah. For many, Sunkuli had sold the Mara Triangle to KANU bigwigs who had then hired their white conservationist friends to run it.

Just weeks after his election, the new Kilgoris MP, Gideon Konchellah, acting with the Transmara County Council, ordered an investigation of the "circumstances leading to the formation of the Mara Conservancy" and a review of the management agreement it had signed with the Council. The team appointed to carry out the investigation were all professionals from Transmara.

The team did a thorough job, going to the origins of formation of the Mara Conservancy and charting out the reasons why it was so unpopular in Transmara. The report was presented at a workshop in Nairobi in August, 2003. Among its many recommendations was that while the idea of professionalizing the management of the Mara Triangle was an idea whose time had come, it had been carried out by the "wrong" people; if the Mara Conservancy were to co-exist harmoniously with the Transmara people it needed to rid itself of directors who were known to be corrupt. The report's findings were accepted by all major interest groups in Transmara, including, surprisingly, the Mara Conservancy. The new MP gave cautious approval.

THE REPLIES: FROM OUTRAGED SUPPORTERS OF THE MARA CONSERVANCY WRITING TO ECOFORUM

Outraged in the Mara

Parselelo Kantai's article, "A Deal in the Mara" (Vol 26 No. 1, 2003) is as revealing as it is biased. Whereas the writer expounded on the current affairs of the Western Mara, otherwise known as 'The Triangle', certain issues must be put in their

proper perspective, otherwise the facts will never be known.

The writer mentions the role of Willy Roberts in setting up the Ol Choro Oiroua Wildlife Management & Conservation Association and implied that he had misappropriated money from the Association. Nothing could be further from the truth, and the Ol Choro management should have been contacted before such accusations were made.

Together with my father, Paramount Chief Lerionka Ole Ntutu, Willy played a pivotal role in setting up the Association, which opened the way to community conservation in Kenya. Willy started as a wheat farmer in the area around Mara Safari Club, on land that was owned by individual Maasai. He realised that ever-increasing conflicts with wildlife were leading nowhere, and that if properly managed, wildlife and tourism could bring greater financial benefits to the landowners, while allowing them to continue their traditional husbandry on the same land. The idea that landowners should be able to benefit from the wildlife on their land was a new concept in the Mara, and we had many battles in the High Court before this right was established. As a result of these initiatives a critical part of the northern Mara-Serengeti ecosystem that was formerly farmland has been returned to wildlife and cattle.

Ol Choro was founded in 1993, and Willy Roberts was its first executive director, while I was his deputy. It was run on a professional basis and its accounts were professionally prepared by Khalid & Associates to the satisfaction of its directors. When Willy left in 1996, he left because there were now local accountants and game rangers who could take over from him. His family still has a home there and the Ol Choro management consults with Willy on strategic matters of conservation.

To us Willy Roberts is a great Conservationist, a transparent and accountable person. When he left Ol Choro he did not stop conservation work, and he still spends a great deal of his own time and money assisting with conservation in the Mara area. In particular, he helped found the Mara Conservancy, which to the best of our knowledge is among the most efficient wildlife management entities in both Narok and Trans Mara districts.

There are many differences between the Mara Conservancy and Ol Choro Oiroua, which the author should have considered for a more informed and balanced assessment for the 'deal' he laments about. There are powerful vested interests in the Mara Triangle and the Conservancy managers have done a skillful job to come this far in managing the area effectively and bringing a much greater degree of transparency into the revenue collecting process.

EcoForum should apologise to Willy Roberts and the Maasai Mara community for unsubstantiated allegations against one of the true founders of community conservation.

Stephen Ole Ntutu
Member of Parliament, Narok South

Let me declare my interest. I am a director of the Mara Conservancy, the forward-looking organisation that you recently attacked in a manner more associated with

British tabloids. I understand that the Conservancy's detailed reply is to be published and will, I trust, go some way towards rectifying the injustice done to the Conservancy by that article.

So let me declare my other interest. I would like to set the record straight as far as one of the individuals named in the article is concerned – Willy Roberts.

I am a lifelong friend of Willy Roberts and know him to be a man of principle and integrity, without whose vision, dedication, huge expenditure of energy and considerable sums of personal funding, the Ol Choro and Mara Conservancy experiments would never have got off the ground.It is not a question of deals, but of ideals.

In the minefield that is the Mara only someone well trusted by the people could have initiated, and brought to fruition, those two projects with all their positive features. Willy has done that with great patience and skill and with his integrity intact. The records of fact show that he has never betrayed the trust that was bestowed upon him.

The long history of political machinations in the Mara is well known and needs no repetition here. Those of your readers who know something of the area will not be surprised that there has been endless 'fitina' over who should get what. It is an extraordinary feat that out of this chaos some semblance of order and good management has emerged, and it is Willy Roberts who must take credit for this.

It is very disappointing that your magazine, with its reputation for a high standard of journalism and impartiality, should have descended to mudslinging, seemingly on the basis that the more you throw the greater the chance of something sticking.

In the past you have published informative articles telling your readers how to dispose of sewage and other noxious waste. May I suggest you re-read that advice and apply it in your own backyard. It stinks.

Alan Root, Nairobi

I am genuinely shocked by your seemingly malicious allegations against those of us associated with Ol Choro Oiroua. There was obviously no attempt to obtain any facts before you issued the article. You couldn't even spell their name right!

The biggest beneficiaries of Ol Choro were the land owners who received all of the revenues from Ol Choro, which was a not-for-profit company. In fact, Ol Choro was not allowed to make a profit as all of the revenue had to be distributed to the land owners. Financial statements were produced every month and there was an annual audit performed and duly signed by the chairman, Paramount Chief Lerionka Ole Ntutu, and another director.

To even imply that W. Roberts, or any employee, myself or any director ran away with the "profits" is just too shocking to imagine, plain untrue and I consider this implication insulting.

To print such defamatory remarks about people and companies without any evidence is just beyond comprehension. Am I allowed to say in print that "I have heard people say that EcoForum is going bankrupt and that they are beginning to fabricate

their own sensational news to increase their circulation"?

Having myself been a required signatory on every cheque written by Ol Choro (W. Roberts not being a signatory on any account, not even being entitled to an imprest account but rather spending his own money and being required to invoice and receive board approval for reimbursement) I am in the position to be able to speak fact rather than vindictive rumour.

On a personal note, I resented you calling Mzee L. Ole Ntutu "old man". You obviously never knew him nor will be presented with an Order of the Burning Spear, as he was.

George Orr, Nairobi

An article appearing in your EcoForum, Short Rains 2003 issue under the heading, "A Deal in the Mara" begs some correction. Yes, it is true as Mr Kantai reports, that I was hired by the Mara Conservancy to link them up with the people in the three Group ranches adjacent to the Mara Triangle. Essentially, my work was to find out how better mechanisms of sharing out income with the community would be put in place, and how to foster the spirit of good neighbourliness between the community and the Conservancy. My feeling is that I tried hard to do my work according to my terms of reference. As to whether I was very successful is a matter I leave to both the Mara Conservancy and the community to assess. I was aware that it was impossible to please everyone, and so I just embarked on my work and refused to be influenced or manipulated so as to see the problem from only one perspective.

The article quoted Mr Heath as saying in reference to my leaving: "he was chased out by the faction leaders opposed to Kijabe." That statement is outrightly untrue. The truth is that I disagreed with Councillor ole Kijabe, whose line I could not toe. I opted to leave rather than be compromised and possibly sacrificed at the altar of personal and political expediency.

David Ole Nkedianye via e-mail

Mara Conservancy report now out

In our last issue we reported that the new leadership in the Transmara County Council had commissioned a review team to investigate the terms and conditions of the agreement made between the County Council and the Mara Conservancy.

In August, the review team published its findings, a 47-page report that makes a number of far-reaching recommendations regarding the future relationship between the TMCC and the Mara Conservancy, and sheds light on the circumstances in which the Mara Conservancy was hired. The report was initially endorsed by all the key interest groups, including the Mara Conservancy. EcoForum will be interviewing the review team members and publishing excerpts of the report in the next issue…

Mara Conservancy's full and unabridged response, through their lawyers, to the article 'Deal in the Mara

This report is in response to an article entitled 'A Deal in the

Mara' published by EcoForum (1st quarter 2003) and represents the right of reply given to defamed parties under the Defamation Act.

The author of 'A Deal in the Mara' obviously dislikes the Mara Conservancy. No brownie points for readers who spotted that. What readers will still be looking for is some substantive fact or argument to justify that position.

For the EF article troubled itself very little with objective information, and even less with balance or the damage that it would do to reputations under the laws of libel. It contained not one syllable of evidence or logic to support its position and, most disappointingly, it presented no constructive suggestion of any kind on any subject.

Above all, it measured and maligned the Mara Conservancy on completely fallacious criteria.

A letter in the subsequent edition of EcoForum summarised well why the "Deal in the Mara" article was shameful, and this hopefully reflected the general reaction of readers.

In response to that letter the author has once again made assertions, claims and assumptions that suggest his real agenda cannot be the conservation of the Mara Triangle (which the Mara Conservancy has done much to secure and improve) nor the welfare of the neighbouring communities (for whom the Mara Conservancy has generated unprecedentedly large and consistent royalties).

It is still not clear why the author condemns the organisation that is responsible for those achievements, nor why he works so hard to put them on the 'butcher's block' of political intrigue. Yet in the process his words have done damage to two cardinal and legitimate objectives: conservation and community welfare.

It is important that the real position is now made clear: The Mara Conservancy has a five-year contract to manage the Mara Triangle. Its remit is:

* To secure the area for wildlife and tourism
* To repair and improve the infrastructure for those purposes
* To sustainably develop the environment for those purposes
* To optimise tourism revenues, collect and account for those revenues
* To self-finance its work on 40.5% of those revenues
* To deliver a further 40.5% to TransMara County Council ('TMCC')
* To deliver the balance of 19% to local communities, in whatever way the TMCC (its 'employer', and the elected representative of the people) directs.

The Mara Conservancy has an obligation to do no less, but no authority to do more. So, how can the Conservancy be judged when tested against these benchmarks?

The overwhelming physical proof is that it has done its job with a high degree of professionalism, efficiency and positive effect. In two years it has transformed an area from a calamitous state of disrepair and degradation into a fully functional,

viable and sustainable conservation/tourism resource of high value to its owners - the people of Kenya, under the jurisdiction of Government mechanisms, which are run by officials elected by local communities. This is patently obvious to both visitor and resident alike.

Among many spontaneous accolades, the Mara Conservancy has been endorsed by the Durrell Institute and the world renowned Nature magazine as 'achieving a dramatic turn-around' in revenue collection, security, equipment and management efficiency. They concluded that Mara Conservancy 'could become a model for tourism-based, integrated conservation through public-private partnerships'.

The Mara Conservancy has vastly increased revenues from the Mara Triangle resource, and has accounted for and delivered every cent of them in strict accordance with its contractual obligations. It has paid, promptly, fully and accountably, 40.5% to the TMCC (less the shared costs of revenue collection), and 19% to the official Group Ranch bank accounts of Kemintet, Oloirien, and Kerenkani.

In fact the cost of what it has achieved on the ground is far higher than the remaining 40.5% share allocated to the task. Bear in mind that, worldwide, few Conservancy operations are self-financing even on 100% of revenue. But on less that half that, and now with a huge plunge in tourism levels nationally, the Mara Conservancy has nevertheless managed without sacrificing on the quality of the service it provides, nor any reduction in the 59.5% paid to the council and community accounts. The Conservancy has bridged the funding gap by mobilising international donor support, at no cost to the Council or local communities, and it has wholly and solely employed these funds for conservation/tourism development. The EF article insults and jeopardises that support, too.

These are the FACTS. They are as solid as concrete. What is so disappointing is that the author of the EF article was given not only full access, but open invitation, to ask, inspect, check and ferret, and had he done this with the degree of objectivity one is entitled to expect from a journalist writing in a publication of the stature of EcoForum, there is little doubt that he would have established beyond doubt that the Mara Conservancy itself has honoured all its obligations and made no "deal", agreed no contractual clause, and committed no act which usurped or deprived any other legitimate interest.

Conservation and Community Welfare are its objectives, and if the Mara Conservancy is measured against those objectives, whilst absolute perfection may have to wait a while, it is clear that its performance is exceptionally good and its presence in the region is an overwhelmingly positive development.

Yet, in an about-face that would, we suggest, cripple even the most lithe contortionist, the author of 'A Deal in the Mara' chose to write, and EcoForum elected to publish, a diatribe of distortions which sought to condemn the Conservancy idea, belittle its achievements, and defame anyone involved with or supportive of it.

And what a fine demonstration of contortion it proved to be; moving smoothly and selectively between fact, opinion, conjecture, and rumour without drawing any flicker of distinction.

Without a single exception throughout the piece, anyone who speaks against the Conservancy is ennobled by the author with no substantiation being asked from

them to underpin any accusation made. Their credentials are not questioned.

And yet, almost without exception, anyone who speaks for the Conservancy is condemned by innuendo; suddenly, statements are interlaced with the author's own strong and often cynical opinions, quotes are manipulated out of context and abridged to change their meaning.

It's all about as subtle as a sledgehammer. In addition to these distortions, the article also contained numerous errors of fact. 'Terminologically inexact', being 'economic with the actualité' call it what you may, there is little doubt that these statements succeeded in creating an impression diametrically opposite to the real situation.

For example, it refers to one man as 'a thief' without offering a shred of evidence (never mind proof) that he stole, nor how, nor when, nor what, nor from whom. Defamation does not get much stronger than that.

It accuses another of double-standards because he refuses to represent but continues to advise the Conservancy, and yet the article does not say what advice he is giving - far from being spurious, his action may indicate the very highest standards of integrity. Why did the author not look into this further?

The article talks of the Conservancy's 'well-oiled PR machine', when the fact is it has no PR function at all, and has spent less on PR counsel in its first two years of operation than, we suggest, the article's author may have spent on a single trip to the site. The reality is that much of the good press that emanated at the outset was the spontaneous reaction of independent observers who saw the value of the concept and the quality of performance.

And there again, if the PR was so slick, why does he then go on to say in his follow up notes that the Conservancy suffered 'a series of PR disasters.' That's the sort of mumbo-jumbo that arises when a writer tries to fit facts to an opinion, instead of drawing an opinion from the facts.

The author would have us believe that there is nigh-universal public opposition to the Conservancy and equal measure of public support for the MP's Review Team. This does not accord with what the Conservancy hears from the grass roots up.

The author makes heavy play of 'family connections' linked to the Conservancy Board, and yet does not mention that his primary targets are in fact ex officio appointments - the Conservancy did not hand-pick them: they were appointed purely by virtue of being the holders of specific public offices and were elected to those offices by the people!

The FACT is that the Conservancy has progressively developed Terms of Reference for the Board which run to 10,000 words, in an ever-increasing buttress against potential interference from any quarter, and strenuously insisting on good corporate governance from all its office holders.

The TOR's guarantee the widest and most democratic possible representation of all public and community interests; they have managed - in a short time against daunting odds - to make it impossible for any one faction to be silenced or any other to railroad policy. There can be few organisations of any kind in any sector on Kenya that have such comprehensive and built-in checks and controls against abuse.

In his follow-up the author begs his own begged question by asking us to con-

sider to whom the Mara Conservancy promised the objectives of Conservation and Community Welfare. The answer is it promised itself, it performed its obligations as promised contractually to the TMCC , and it promised the people.

The author asserts that the people did not know it existed. Oh? In that case how did so many of the people's elected leaders end up on the Board? And by the way, when the author says ' 'the jury is still out' on the legitimacy of the Mara Conservancy's appointment', he sets himself above a ruling of the High Court of Kenya.

The article may play well to fuel popular prejudices and feed a public appetite for intrigue, but such commentary does not constitute - nor represent - the truth.

These are the tools of a particular style of journalism which does not let the facts interfere with a good story. The fact that EcoForum should choose to print his product is surprising, for in our view it demonstrates a profound lack of respect for the real welfare of conservation and the Mara communities, and is insulting to the intelligence of its own readers.

In condemning the Mara Conservancy by innuendo, the article does not offer any alternative system that would better serve the interests of conservation or community welfare. The open-minded may consider that as slightly more than an oversight in a publication which purports to champion those two purposes.

The Conservancy on the other hand believes that the majority of people have a serious concern for and genuine interest in the Mara and its neighbouring communities in general, and the concept and performance of the Mara Conservancy in particular.

The question they will be asking is why would a writer, in possession of the full and correct facts, take such a negative position?

Those who sifted out the article's chaff will have found that its principal grievance rested on the notion that the local communities are not receiving their share of the money.

If that were true, it would be a valid and even vital concern. And the article did give us a glimpse of the strength of feeling, the jaundiced perspectives, the disinformation, the political patronage, the conflicting clanism, and deep suspicions of electoral manipulation and fiscal mismanagement that have bedevilled the Mara and its hinterland for decades.

Certainly the Mara Triangle is a spaghetti junction of criss-crossing jurisdictions with vested and often competing interests. The potential for direct conflicts of interest and confusion are therefore considerable, and indeed that potential has for too long been a notorious reality.

For many reasons by the late 1990s the Mara Triangle was in peril of complete disintegration and destruction. Political and fiscal 'shenanigans' were rife before the Mara Conservancy was established, and they did not suddenly go away. It was always apparent that the blur between personal and public interest was going to be a long-established fog the Conservancy would unavoidably have to find its way through.

So how would the Conservancy be able to ensure greater levels of fiscal integrity and discipline in such a gnarled political environment, when its very appointment

required political endorsement? Could its arrival derail one gravy train but merely set another one in motion?

Yes, that was always a possibility. And therein lies the Conservancy's greatest problem and the EcoForum article's greatest fallacy.

The 'Deal in the Mara' piece sought to brand the Conservancy as a conspirator and culprit in the mismanagement of money matters in Council and Community affairs. It conveniently overlooks the fact that to do this, the Conservancy would need to have some influence or control over the Council, Group Ranch and Community finances. IT DOES NOT.

To even stand accused, the Conservancy would need to have some responsibility for finances outside its own remit and budget. IT DOES NOT.

The Mara Conservancy is unable to influence how the Council or Community funds are dealt with. It cannot stipulate who manages those funds or how they are distributed or spent. The only thing it is required to do, the only thing it is allowed to do, is to maximize revenue collection from tourism in the Mara Triangle and to hand over the agreed proportions to TMCC and the Group Ranches. AND.IT.HAS.DONE.SO! And that was repeatedly explained and substantively demonstrated to the author of the EcoForum article.

Much as the Conservancy (and others) may wish for systems that guarantee the equitable distribution of community funds more transparently and accountably, it is not in a position to impose such systems on third parties. That power rests with elected officials. And they are chosen by the people themselves.

In this regard the Conservancy can do no more than hope that those people already possess or soon acquire the wisdom and courage to make good electoral choices, and at the same time the Mara Conservancy will do all that it can to ensure that there are at least some funds to distribute - by managing the Mara Triangle professionally, sustainably and optimally to maximise tourism revenues, by collecting them diligently and accountably, and by delivering them to the people's elected representatives.

Mr Kantai was certainly right about one thing. There would be no problem with the distribution of tourism revenues from the Triangle if the Conservancy had not been appointed or if it was now expelled. Because there would be no revenues to have a problem with.

Issued on behalf of Mara Conservancy, through Kaplan & Stratton, Advocates

Letter From Forster .....

Mara Controversy

EcoForum's article on the Mara Conservancy does no credit to its author, editor or publisher. It damages the very conservation cause and the Maasai communities it purports to represent.

I will not dwell on the errors of fact, half-truths, misconstructions and prejudiced innuendo of the report. These insult many good and committed people, but they will take that on the chin or to court, as they see fit.

What most concerns them I believe and myself, is the article's negative assault on the concept of professionally managed community conservation, which is so vital to a positive future for wildlife in combination with the welfare of neighbouring people.

Mara Conservancy pilots the formula and there is irrefutable physical evidence that it has performed with excellence DESPITE attempts at political interference from many quarters. The Conservancy has manifestly delivered on every one of its promises to safeguard and nurture the habitat, to effectively tackle poaching, to husband the wildlife, to restore and improve the infrastructure, to increase and diligently account for revenue collection, and to pay a guaranteed proportion (and unprecedented sum) of income to the neighbouring communities and the council. Transparently (in the national press!) and accountably (renowned international audit!).

To relegate those achievements is to entirely miss the cardinal point. To bury and muddy them in the quite separate issues of local government is wanton mischief.

EcoForum's professionals and principals are well aware of centuries-old factionalism in the TransMara and Narok region; well aware of the methods, motives and rivalries of political leaders and almost universal mismanagement of local government finances in the last government. It would be naïve to imagine that the Mara Conservancy would not be under constant attack from these factors. This certainty, and empirical evidence of the performance achieved, warrants sympathy (if you like) and support (come what may) for the Conservancy's efforts to resist these forces while first saving the resource from total destruction, and then delivering its values to neighbouring communities and all Mankind.

Significantly, the EcoForum article did not offer any realistic assessment of how much worse the state of the Triangle and its communities was before the Conservancy was appointed, nor any constructive suggestion of what better prospect would be revealed if the Conservancy was now disbanded.

The project may be less than perfect but it is far the best available option. EcoForum was in a position to help. It chose to do harm. Shame on you.

Martin Forster Nairobi, KENYA

Parselelo Kantai's reply to Forster….

There is no dispute over what the Mara Conservancy has achieved in the short time it has been in existence. The first part of my article documents this. It is unfortunate if the impression given is that Ecoforum was "doing a job" on an individual organisation. Granted, as well, the article did not outline any specific solutions. Thankfully, the residents of Transmara are now in deep discussions with their new MP about how to rehabilitate their area after years of KANU rule in which their input was often ignored, the value of their suggestions "relegated". It is from this discussion that practical, lasting solutions will arise

However, the notion that the Conservancy either represents or is acting in the interests of the community is a fiction that the Conservancy's architects themselves recognised, albeit only after a series of community/public relations disasters.

Like many of the Conservancy's directors I interviewed, Mr Forster believes that the community opposition to the Mara Conservancy has more to do with "centuries-old factionalism in the Transmara and the Narok region" than with the Conservancy per se. Again, this is a fiction. Mr Forster implicitly makes the distinction between the 'professionals" on the Conservancy's board and local Maasai politicians. The latter happen to be not just Conservancy directors but, according to both Mr Willy Roberts and Mr Brian Heath, the real inspiration behind the Mara Conservancy. It is imprecise, even dishonest, to explain community opposition to the Mara Conservancy as an extension of intra-tribal rivalry in Transmara. In fact, the vast majority of Transmara residents that I interviewed were opposed to the Conservancy primarily because they saw it as an imposition subjected on them by KANU politicians. They were only informed about it after it had been established. Why?

My article was not so much a "negative assault" on the Mara Conservancy concept as an inquiry into why a project loaded with good intentions was provoking so much opposition. To say that the Conservancy has delivered on its promises begs the question: to whom did it make these promises if it hadn't even informed 'the promised' of its existence in the first place? As I made clear in the article, the jury, literally, is still out on whether the County Council actually met to deliberate on whether to allow the Mara Conservancy into Transmara.
-Parsalelo Kantai

In August 2003, the review team published its findings, a 47-page report that makes a number of far-reaching recommendations regarding the future relationship between the TMCC and the Mara Conservancy, and sheds light on the circumstances in which the Mara Conservancy was hired. The report was initially endorsed by all the key interest groups, including the Mara Conservancy. EcoForum will be interviewing the review team members and publishing excerpts of the report in the next issue...

Just weeks after his election, the new Kilgoris MP, Gideon Konchellah, acting with the Transmara County Council, ordered an investigation of the "circumstances leading to the formation of the Mara Conservancy" and a review of the management agreement it had signed with the Council. The team appointed to carry out the investigation were all professionals from Transmara.

The team did a thorough job, going to the origins of formation of the Mara Conservancy and charting out the reasons why it was so unpopular in Transmara. The report was presented at a workshop in Nairobi in August, 2003. Among its many

recommendations was that while the idea of professionalizing the management of the Mara Triangle was an idea whose time had come, it had been carried out by the "wrong" people; if the Mara Conservancy were to co-exist harmoniously with the Transmara people it needed to rid itself of directors who were known to be corrupt. The report's findings were accepted by all major interest groups in Transmara, including, surprisingly, the Mara Conservancy. The new MP gave cautious approval.

Here is an extract of the report:

"Regardless of the real intentions and motivation, the genesis of MC as a concept and finally as an entity is perhaps the single most important factor responsible for the current stalemate. >From accounts of the various stakeholders, there was a general consensus on events leading to the formation of the company, although admittedly there were many behind-the-scenes consultations that never came into the public domain. Because of these behind the scenes meetings that could have taken place at various points in time, it is difficult to place an exact time line when the idea of forming the entity could have been mooted. However, within the Transmara County Council (TCC), formation of MC could be traced backed to 1997/98. Ever since Transmara was carved out of Narok district and could collect and management its own revenues, there has never been a clear and transparent system used to maximize revenues to the council. From the account of the former Clerk to the County Council, the council was losing so much revenue through blatant diversion of council money by revenue collectors in collusion with local leaders. In fact some Councillors admitted to the review team that some of them had their own receipts to collect the funds. A survey on potential revenue that could go to the council in 1997/98 revealed that up to Kshs. 126 million per year could be collected compared to the meager amount of only Kshs. 48-50 m that was actually being collected."

"Meanwhile, the idea of MC was mooted and considerable behind-the-scenes discussion took place on various unspecified dates. This was between key originators of the idea namely Mr. William Roberts, Cllr. Kuya Ole Tunai Kijabe, Mr. Samuel K. Tunai and the former area MP and Minister in the Office of the President, Mr. Julius L. Ole Sunkuli on one hand, and TCC representatives on the other. Depending on who you talk to, there were discrepancies in the accounts of the exact series of events that led to the formation of MC. It was evident that the decision to form MC was reached sometime in early to mid 2000, if not earlier between the key originators with full backing of the political establishment. By August 2000, things were moving very fast and Mr. William Roberts (the main driver of the process and key political negotiator) was already looking for a Chief Executive Officer – and identified Mr. Brian Heath, who himself took an interest in the idea."

"Through political manipulation, the recommendation to have TMIS as revenue

collector was opposed and it was alleged that Clerk to TCC had denied MC the tender. Then around this time, the pushers of MC decided to declare the real intention – that indeed, what they really wanted was MC to take over the management of the Mara Triangle and hopefully the whole of the Mara and maybe even extend the model to other parts of the country. The idea was formally proposed in a meeting attended by Kilgoris and Narok South MPs, and key representatives of both Narok and Transmara county councils (clerks and deputies, chairmen and MC representatives Cllr. Kuya Kijabe, Samuel Tunai, Willy Roberts)."

"On the other side, resistance was building up on the ground spearheaded by some Councillors who read mischief into the whole deal. Based on available information, once the founders of MC got the political go ahead and support with powerful forces within the KANU political establishment (led by then area MP), a multi track approach was taken to deal with opposition to MC and bring the idea to fruition. There was the political side of things to handle through local Councillors, and legal aspects in which the Clerk to the Council seemed to merely go along (if he was not party to the whole deal) and the community aspects were left to Cllr. Kijabe and Samuel Tunai. It was necessary to deal with politics by bringing as many Councillors as necessary on board. This proved difficult as a considerable number (as many if not slightly more than the number in favour) were opposed to the idea. On 22nd of May 2001, MC was informed that a full Council meeting had endorsed the transfer of management of Mara Triangle from TCC to MC. The purported full Council meeting held on May 21 (May 22nd?), to endorse the decision, in reality never took place. It can only be said that whatever authorization was received on the issue came from a group of Councillors who were taken to Nairobi to meet the Head of State (former President Moi), and who informed the President that they supported the idea."

Highlights of the recommendations

(a) The no-conflict of interest principle: elected leaders of Transmara, the Provincial administration, officers of the TCC must not engage or be allowed to be involved in activities that would create or may give an impression in the eyes of the public that their position is compromised or that the leader (or leaders) are taking advantage of their public position. This means that leaders who can influence decision making within the Council or at district level should not float their companies for competitive bidding in matters related to a sensitive resource such management of the Maasai Mara National Game Reserve. The role of leaders, is primarily that of guardians of the public good.

(1) Restructure MC into a professional entity, with clearly and simply defined membership and directorship of the Board as well as clear mandates within and outside the Mara

1) Under the present setup, it is very clear that the ultimate and legal powers rest with the Members. The Board can be changed any day, but the composition of the members will remain. It is this power of the Members that stands out as a major contentious issue. If the management agreement is renegotiated as proposed above, it will be extremely desirable that MC re-packages its image by getting professional and people of integrity on their board.

Aftermath

A number of things happened after the story was published. Weeks before, we'd heard rumours that certain quarters in the conservation community were worried about the direction our story would take. Then the magazine came out. On the cover was a photo of a handshake between a white and a black man with the Mara as a backdrop. The cover said "A Deal in the Mara". There was no doubt what direction the story had taken. The storm of protest, mostly from whites in and around things conservation, was almost frightening in its intensity. Ecoforum received letters – have a look at the sample published alongside the main story -- that made no pretence of the disgust many readers felt. There were rumours that the Conservancy was going to sue. We hired a lawyer.

People from the area, both professionals and non-professionals alike, praised the story. Some even attributed it to being a factor in former Kilgoris MP, Julius Sunkuli's defeat. This was a bit of an exaggeration considering the story hadn't been published by then. What was true, however, is that Sunkuli's support for the Mara Conservancy was perhaps the main reason why he lost the 2002 General Elections to NARC's Gideon Konchellah. For many, Sunkuli had sold the Mara Triangle to KANU bigwigs who had then hired their white conservationist friends to run it.

Just weeks after his election, the new Kilgoris MP, Gideon Konchellah, acting with the Transmara County Council, ordered an investigation of the "circumstances leading to the formation of the Mara Conservancy" and a review of the management agreement it had signed with the Council. The team appointed to carry out the investigation were all professionals from Transmara.

The team did a thorough job, going to the origins of formation of the Mara Conservancy and charting out the reasons why it was so unpopular in Transmara. The report was presented at a workshop in Nairobi in August, 2003. Among its many recommendations was that while the idea of professionalizing the management of the Mara Triangle was an idea whose time had come, it had been carried out by the "wrong" people; if the Mara Conservancy were to co-exist harmoniously with the Transmara people it needed to rid itself of directors who were known to be corrupt. The report's findings were accepted by all major interest groups in Transmara, including, surprisingly, the Mara Conservancy. The new MP gave cautious approval.

Eight months later, none of the recommendations have been implemented by the Council. In fact, a new management agreement -- its wording is practically unchanged from the previous one -- has been drafted and awaits County Council approval. The new agreement, if signed, will last 10 years. Clearly, the mood at the Council has changed. Recently, the County Clerk, Ms Grace Mulisho, warned us not to publish any extract of the investigation report "because it is the property of the Council". There are complaints that the new MP has changed tune and is now very close to certain Mara Conservancy directors. Then at about 3.00 pm on March 12, 2004, Hon. Konchellah, accompanied by the OCPD Kilgoris, the Transmara DC, Mara Conservancy directors Willy Roberts, Kijabe Kuya ole Tunai and Samuel Tunai, his nephew, marched into Mara Conservancy CEO Brian Heath's office and told him: "I can no longer work with you. I am giving you 24 hours to vacate the premises peacefully."

In the forthcoming issue of Ecoforum Magazine we investigate the reasons for this change of affairs in the Mara Conservancy.

Parseleleo Kantai

AboutThe Author

Parsalelo Kantai is co-editor of Ecoforum, an environmental journal. He is a recovering vegetarian. This is his first foray into the world of fiction. He has recently won a Reuters Foundation fellowship to go to Oxford University for a year. Corrupt Big Men and Neocolon KC's quake when they hear his name.

Deer Mrs God

By Muthoni wa Gatumo

WRITER'S NOTE:

DEER MRS GOD is the story of a dysfunctional mother/daughter relationship from the daughter's point of view. Since she's semi illiterate she writes words as she hears them and since she alteast went up to std. 3, she makes good use of the alphabet, although not in the so called 'correct' manner. MAMY is the most important force in kamamy's world and this is why her name and all her spoken words are written in capital letters like the God Almighty she really is to her child. Kamamy's words are supposed to be all written in small letters to show her low self esteem and where she stands in the food chain, so to speak. When kamamy gets a devine intervention and decides that since her own MAMY doesn't care for her she's going to get her very own ally from the highest possible quarters; namely Mrs. God Herself.

Wen I hatted my finga wen I was littil wan dey wid my smalla cazeen, I cry end cry end cry veery lawdly end so my smalla cazen goed end telled my MAMY wat have happen.

My MAMY maked sam small waters hin a sospan 2 bowil end bowil end bowil. It bowilt veery mach end so my MAMY maked me to poot my finga hinna hot bowilt waters wid sam small solt insyd. Oh! Hit hatted me end hatted me! Bat I was brev, veery brev. I baited my tang til blad deed comed hout hin wom biig drops dat test jas laik a bant tee leeved 2 loong hin de faya.

PLEESE JESAS MY GOD FADHA HOLEY SPIREET HINNA HEVEN! I BESEECH U! I PREY U DEER GOD 2 HEAL KAMAMY FINGA! OH GOD! I BIND OL DE DEMONS TRY 2 TES MY FAITH THROUGH MY DOTA RIGHT NAW! I CAS DEM OL 2 DE DEEPEST DAKEST EATANAL PIT FAYA OV DE DEVALS! AMEEN!!!

Leta smalla cazeen; coaled dadee, end me was gived sam banana 2 it by MAMY. She goed bak 2 her wak hin mzungu hows. BOWIL WATER 4 UGALI she sey 2 me. I WILL MAKE SAPA WEN I COME . MAKE DE STEW B4 I COME. DERE'S ENAF CARROT END ONION. Mzungu man wid milk cala skeen end banny faya hare hon is roun ead.

Wen I seed im fas; mzungu man employ MAMY hin is biig hows neer de littil riva hon grasses cat smoot laik a capet wid cizas. MAMY sey KAMAMY GREET MR WILLYSOON SICELY. SA DIS HIS MY DOTA KAMAMY. SHE BE HELPIN ME HON OL SATADEY.

Sekend taim I seed im mzungu man hin de biig hows 4 im, was hon dey smalla cazeen dint wake up neva agen. I try 2 wake imap, shookin im. I call im lawdly hon is slipy fase – bat e onley slipy end slipy not wake-upin. Slipin hin is smalla red bed bliidin end bliidin wid is blad.

WAT U DONE DONE 2 IM U DEVAL GAL?!! EH?!! WAT U DEED 2 DADEE?! Slap. U DEED SAMTIN 2 IM!! Slap. Slap. U DEED!! Slap. Slap. Slap. O JESAS! O JESAS! O JESAS! MAMY skreem hon my fase wen I goed 2 tell her wat have happen. End she brake sosa she washy hon sink hin de keychen hin mzungu man hows. End she comed hout ranny end ranny end ranny hout ov door, hout ov get, dawn rod, kros rod hat kona end ap hill til she comed 2 hour hows hinsyd wid smalla cazeen haslip 4 eva end eva ameen hin is small red bed bliidin end bliidin wid is blad.

We bareed smalla cazeen hin langata semetree hinsyd fas get, hinsyd 2 get end hinsyd 3 get hat de veery veery las kona neer 2 weer maasai cow his itting grasses end goats his dropin black shits hon krak brown groun wid littil yello dry grasses grown onley. 5 peepoles come onley. 1 stat 2 seeng gloree gloree gloree haleluya we will meat hat de pissful sho end we seeng end seeng end seeng.

MAMY she onley look hon de groun hat krak groun wid a black klots end eadskaf sweengy hin de wind dat blow januari dast hon as. Preecha gal hin preechaman ty hon a long nek fram bibol school end mama james de onna ov hour hows seesta dota, she speek samtin hin engleesh fram de holey book. Sam semetree mans help plant smalla cazeen bosked hinsyd de hole. We beat de bosk wid hot januari soils. Ash 2 ash 2 dast 2 dast retan, preecha gal sey, dey powa de hot soils hon smalla cazeen hinsyd de holed bosk. We seeng agen gloree gloree gloree gloree gloree gloree …

De matatu bas we klamb his smoky fram semetree get til neer Nairobi west jankshon weer hit coff, sneeze end den dai. Dai hin de middol ov de rod. U bastaads!! Foleesh sheeps!! Seelee fulls!! Honk. Honk. Honk. Pee – pee – pee – peeee!!!! De dryva hin goodlokin kas end lorry end anadha matatus skreem hat as annoy we maked dem B let 4 wak end dey busynessis. MAMY, mama james, preecha gal coaled sofia, mama ken ov las door fram hour door end me , we was standy dere hat syd ov rod wid pasenja peepoles looking hon dryva try 2 treet is ka hin de enjinn poking end poking hit end pootin waters hinsyd, bat zero, natin have happen, onley hot hot januari son ban bake end bowil as standy til sam peepole sey go 2 tawn senta footin.

We wok end wok end ol de footin-footin hin de rod ban smoking raba hon my feets end my sleepas shoos cat. CARI DEM SHOOS HON U HAND FOOLISH GAL! My MAMY sey hat me slow wokin end make eveerybodi get let. Bat de bowily rod hon neked feets hat badly hon every step. I seen steem steemin fram my feets has I look dawn countin every step 1 to 1 to 1 to.

Countin eveery step 1 feet den anadha feet den jamp!

Countin eveery step 1 feet den anadha feet den jamp!

Countin eveery step 1 feet den anadha feet den jamp! Dis best game he end me was playin wokin fram school hin lanjtaim ol de taim every dey.

Kamamy! Smalla cazeen roun fase done shin hat me.

I deed count 50 step feet 2 feet fram my deks 2 de door ov de klas!

50 step ?

yas! End 100 step fram klas door 2 get door. Count. U C!

hit was 3 end a haf our step feet 2 feet 2 hour hows fram school get door, lanjtaim 2 aftanoon hat 5.30.

MAMY so angree we parked hinsyd de cabad hin hour hows dat mrs willysoon giva. Ol a klots throw hon flo end shoos end pepas end leepstik end poda 4 pootin hinda fase, teen, rop, bosk, eveerytin atsyd end as hinsyd til nest morny. No sapa. No tee. No banana. No natin. O JESAS! I BESEECH U! AM CALL U NAW HEER ME! ME JAS POOR HELPLESS WOMAN! A SINA! A ANWATHY SINA ANFEET 2 STAND INFRON OV U! BLACK AS BLACKEST SIN! HAVE MASY HON ME O MY FADHA HIN HEVEN! HELP DESE SINFOOL CHILDS DEER GOD! WOSH AWEY DERE BLACK BLACK SIN O GOD! MAKE DEM WHITE AS SNO AGEN!!! YAS!! WHITE LAIK U SWEET SWEET SAVIYA!!!!

Kamamy, wispa smalla cazeen afta MAMY she gone awey afta preyin 4 as. I want 2 soosoo, weer I go soosoo inna cabad kamamy? I fill laik soosooin 2, bat cabad door his lok, hold u stomak had, I wispa bak. Pres leg 2gedha had! Count 2 wan handread hin u ead. Bat I've count til 100 3ree taim kamamy! I've count til 100 3ree taim oredy!!

DON'T CRY GAL! U NO HIT SINNIN 2 DO HIT! GOD TAKE WAT GOD GIVE! Slap. SHARRAP U MOUT CRYIN! Slap. Slap. Her had and sqweeze my sholda laik rok end nels. GOD TAKE WAT GOD GIVE!!!

I wish I telled MAMY am not cry 4 smalla cazeen dai. Dat my feets hattin laik hell bowilin 4 devals. Meet comin at fram unda de feets from hot groun hon my neked feets. I wish I am tell MAMY dat. Bat mama james reemov MAMY had finga roun my panin sholda. Alice! Leeve her B! leeve kamamy B!! she stop wokin end peek my sleepas end poot dem inna sholda bag she carin. She peek me ap end poot me hon her biig sof bak end cari me wokin end wokin steel. MAMY gived me anadha dati looks.

* * * * * * *

de taim I seen mzungu man thad taim wan satadey, he come hin keychen hin is hows 2 get kofi fram speshal kofi masheen hon de tebol.

"Well, well, well young lady", he sey hin a lawd nosey voyces. "You've become quite a pretty young lady now haven't ya?" mzungu man look at me wid is green grass eyes fram top ov my ead 2 sleepased feets. Stopin hat chest. MAMY his hin de adha room dawn de korido hat de kona ov mzungu hows. E so biig – mzungu man – jas laki MAMY taims 3, milk calad, grass eyes, end banny faya hare hon is biig roun ead.

"You'll be just as beautiful as your mother, obviously", de man sey. E smailin end shiny long white tooths hat me. I fill fani laik neked wid no klots standy dere hin keychen sink dry deeshes 4 MAMY. I hopen my mout 2 sey dhank-u sa, laik MAMY sey I sey. Dhank-u sa civilise peepoles sey MAMY sey 2 me end smalla cazeen.

Dhank-u sa, pleese sa, no sa, yas sa. I heer dis wad play hon de redio hinsyd my ead. Dhank-u sa, please sa, no sa, yas sa ..... bat no wad kan come hout fram my hopen leeps. My brayn redio his dai. Dai laik smalla cazeen coaled dadee. I klos my mout end mzungu man coaled mr willysoon jas keep looking end looking hat me. I fill wom laik son shiny hon me. I fill coiled laik rain rainin hon me.

Sosage.

"What?" he shiny is eyes hon me, salplysed. "You talk?" he lafin. "What'd you say then?"

sosage. I repeet. Sosage. I look hat im wid is eye shiny end ranny water comehoutin fram dem Bcos e shookin end shookin end shookin wid de lawd lafta.

MR WILLYSOON SORRY! SORRY! WAT SHE DONE DONE NOW?! WAT KAMAMY DONE DONE AGEN?! AM SORI!! SORI SA!!

She got a apron steel, wid pinq glav end brash 4 brashin de capet. A hare peeps fram flawa calad sof smoot skaf fram mrs willysoon 4 chreesmass las yeer 4 wakin hon de satadey onley. B4 mr willysoon devoiced mrs willysoon. MAMY eyes his smoking laik a tobako mzungu man smoke olweys. A mout hopen hin strayt line cav hat hits end. She preety preety laik a flawa hin de houtsyd gaden. Preety even wen she giv me sam aglee looks.

Smoot smoot skeen shiny laik a chocolat mrs willysoon gived me B4 she been devoiced. Small shap nos laik mzungu man. Long theen finga. Long roun leg. Long long hare hon my MAMY hoval ead.

"She ain't done nothin' Alice!" mzungu man boom.
MAMY lost de aglee looks hon a mout.
"She's a bright kid, your daughter. What class is she in any way? She go to school?"
standaddy 3ree. Nest yeer standaddy fo.

* * * * * * *

wen dadee comed bak fram de hospeetol e sey dat de dokta wid de orenj ty end black biig beered have catted is dingdong a littil 2 tan im inna reel man. Wat?! Yas. A littil beet. I dint cry. I was brev. Veery brev. Anty MAMY sey GOOD BOYEE 2 me. She do!! Yas!! She sey!! She buyed 4 me sweet end chocolat end sosage end soda

inna Nairobi tawn shop. She buyed 4 ne toi ka 2 play wen I get beta. Ka laik 4 biig man Bcos she sey I amma biig man now! Smalla cazeen biig man now.

* * * * * * *

mzungu man taked is biig cap end feeled hit wid kofi end a honey.

LET ME TAKE HIT 4 U HIN DE STUDY ROOM SA! AV FINISH KLEEN DE SEETY ROOM. KAMAMY! CARI DIS KOFI CAP 4 SA HIN DE STUDY ROOM NAW! DON'T DROPEET! She smail hat mzungu man end e shine a wan smail 2.

* * * * * * *

samtaim dey tooked even iskreem, hin de study room. End dat taim dey tooked a weep end I hered MAMY cry end cry hin mzungu man bedroom wen I sapost 2B aslip hin keychen flo donstare. A moskwito reefus me 2 slip iiiii, iiiii, iiiii hit maked noyce around my years hin de dak .... Tomi de dog e bak end bak hout hin de nayeet. End I scarey hon de matrace tryin end tryin 2 slip. Iv I goed 2 seety room mey B moskwito dint come 2 iiiii neer me. Seet wid de small peelos his sof, end I cari my blaket wid me 2. I hopen de door end snek slo 2 korido , hit so dak I klos my eyes 2 C gooda hin de dak wid my fingas. Soon I kach a door hon de wall, end tan hit hopen – bat I heer samtin fani. MAMY she cryin O SA! MY GOD JESAS SA!! O SA!! YAS SA!!! Samwan make a noyce laik a annoy animol wantin 2 bayeet U hon de leg. Bat tomi de dog hin de black dak end bakkin end bakkin houtsyd.

* * * * * * *

mama james de onna ov hour hows seesta dota coaled preecha gal sofia done comed 2 de hows ol de taim naw smalla cazzen done dai.

She reed fram holey book, seeng fram song book end tel ov a heven wid de God en de Jesas en enjells n a profet moses en isaya en jon de bateez en smalla cazeen seengy song haleluya haleluya, 4 eva end eva ameen.

She sey dat wan dey wil C ol ov dem seengy hin de klaud.

MAMY leesen end sey AMEEN!! YAS LOD!! YAS JESAS!! HALELUYA!! End she pooted a and hon de eya poyntin' hon de roof ov hour hows looking hat heven wid klos eyes. She seen smalla cazeen dere hin heven she sey. Hin drem she sey smalla cazeen seengy hin heven wid white enjell wid biig whitest fedhas end long white klots neer wid de God. Waters powa fram a eyes. A mout shaky end shaky end preecha gal sofia old a hin a am end sey yas sista! De lod done got u small boyee. De lod done got y small boyee!!

We it banana end tee end bred end eg.

Mama james take awey de dati deeshes hinna keychen 2 wosh hinda besin. She gived me a orenj 2 it. Mama james I aks, his smalla cazeen was MAMY babee boyee

laik preecha gal sey? I wispa. She go hon washin de deeshes. She don look hat me … she don sey natin. She sey go end seet hin seety room wid precha gal end dem … go hon … go .. I go bat 2 hour on hows hat end ov korido hin mama james biig hows. I seet hone do bed end look hout de sky fram small spase hon de roof ov de sillyin weer de rain done olweys powa wen eat rainin. MAMY telled mama james end she telled MAMY dat james fixeet nest satadey fram las yeer.

I C de staz naw hon black sky tweenkil end tweenkil hat me.

I C de biig toch smalla cazeen sey his de God's enjells shinin dawn hon de wald 2 C who sin end who do good. De siny peepoles go 2 hell wid de devals end B bake jas laik kek MAMY bake hin mrs willysoon keychen oven B4 mr willysoon devoiced a. de goodly peepoles go 2 heven 2 seeng 4 eva end eva ameen. Smalla cazeen seyd preecha gal sofia prey 4 birthin water B4 she take a birth ol morny. End dat james sexed mama ken hin de gaden. End dat ken taked a mani fram mama james kioks shop wen no wan looking. Smalla cazeen laik KAMEME FM redio wid de new bettree.

* * * * * * *

mr willysoon his move 2 new hows hat end ov mont.

MAMY telled mama james, preecha gal sofia, mama ken end me wan dey hin de keychen wen itin tee, bred end banana. MAMY eyes shiny end shiny. She sey dat she end ol de waka 4 mzungu man park ol dey tings 4 de biig hows hin biig bosks. She come bak wen sky his dak black eveerydey.

De new hows his hat mombasa MAMY sey 2 mama james, mama ken, preecha gal sofia end me wan dey hin de keychen ov mama james hows wen itin tee, banana end bred sapa. MAMY eyes his shiny end shiny. A fase tweenkil end tweenkil laik staz. MR WILLYSOON B SEEK. She rab a and laik dis end laik dat. DE DOKTA TELLED IM MOMBASA VEERY GOOD 4 IS SEEKYNESSIS.

Don wari alice, mama ken sey chowin banana had. U get new job agen soona. U got hexpeerens. U get agen good good job wid anadha mzungu peepoles. MAMY smail end smail end sey YAS. LOD WIL SHO ME WAT 2 DO. E FAITHFUL OLWEYS. E SHO ME NEW JOB SOON. I BLEAVE HIT.

Preecha gal prey, we seeng end go 2 bed.

* * * * * * *

hin hour hows hin mama james biig hows his my MAMY bed end smalla cazeen smalla bed. olweys I slip hin MAMY bed wid a wom wom sof smel jas laik soda, a shiny son hon de sky, sweets end keks. A cabad his hin wan kona. De dokta sey samtin rong wid smalla cazeen blad. His blad don steek laik ol peepoles blad steek. Smalla cazeen blad kilt smalla cazeen, mama james wispa 2 preecha gal sofia wen

MAMY don come fram mzungu man hows wan dey.

Nest dey mama james come 2 get me fram school hat lanjtaim.
She dresst byuuteeful inna shiny sky cala dress she olweys weer 2 chach hin ol de sandey. Preecha gal wid a 2 dresst inna ty end black cot. James wid dem 2 hin is rasta rops hare long til de sholda. Dey breen 4 me soda end small small kek fram mama ken, james give me a sweet.

Hin de hows mama james telled me preecha gal will slip 2dey wid me hin MAMY bed. James fixt de roof hin de nest morny. E give me 3ree sweet. Mama ken she give me a bred. Ken wok me 2 school end peeks me hin lanjtaim agen.

Nest nest dey preecha gal wosh hour hows.
She poot new old newspepa hon ol de walls laik smalla cazeen end me do ol de mary chreesmass taim telled by MAMY wid old newspepa fram mzungu man hows. E weep mrs willysoon wid de weep wen dey was sexing til she goed awey end e devoiced a, I heer mama ken wispa 2 mama james hin de keychen . james brot me a chokolat. Ken gived me a 2wentee shilin mani, end preecha gal seenged 4 me happy bathdey 2 U, happy bathdey 2 U, happy bathdey deer kamamy, happy bathdey 2 U!!!

Smalla cazeen coaled dadee, wan dey MAMY take im 2 B tanned 2 a man. How? DEY GOIN 2 MAKE A OPRESHAN SAMWEER. Who? DE DOKTA MAN WIL CAT IM A LITTIL. Weer? SHARRAP U 2 FOOLEESH ANGODLY DATI GODFEERINLESS GAL!! MINE U ON BUSYNESS!! Slap. Slap. Slap.

Wen dadee comed bak fram de hospeetol – e seyd dat de dokta man hinna ty end black biig beered hon is cheen cat smlla cazeen dingdong a littil. 2 tan im hin a reel man. Wat?! Yas. A littil beet. I dint cry. I was brev. Veery brev. Anty MAMY sey GOOD BOYEE 4 me. She deed! Yas! She buyed 4 me a chokolat end sosage end kek hin Nairobi tawn shop. She deed! C! dis his de chokolat pepa, look! Me. I dreemed hat nayeet dat smalla cazeen coaled dadee have goed 2 a dokta wig weeg laik mama ken end a red leepstik hin a mout, who shapen is dingdong laik a dazan blant pensillys wid a shap shapna til e skreem end skreem end skreem.

* * * * * * *

MAMY don come bak fram wak nest dey, nest dey or nest dey.

She telled mama james hin de leta dat she end mzungu man his done gone awey 2 amereka cantree inna eroplayn. End dat de veeza peepoles reefus 2 rayeet kamamy name hin paspot book. So I haf 2 stey hin hour hows. She sen sam dola mani soon she sey 4 de rent. She come 2 veezit soon she sey.

* * * * * * *

de soop spoon es olweys las Bcos u it soop fas. U it wid de fok end de naïf olweys. Even rais end biskoots. Even sam mzungu man it soop wid de naïf hin engleeshland ovasees ken telled ne de nayeet B4 I stat new job hat mzungu man hows nest 2 mr willysoon old hows coaled mr smeet. E old man wid ol white hare hon is theen ead. I weer MAMY dress end eadskaf mrs willysoon gived a B4 mr willysoon devoiced a, 4 wakin hon satadey wen de himpotat veesta gone come. MAMY leeved ol a tings hin de cabad 4 me mama james sey MAMY sey hin de leta.

MAMY kan I weer u skaf 2 chach de wan mrs willysoon gived u?

She stop makin a hare hin mira hon cabad end tan slo 2 look hat me. A long long harms old a heeps hin roun sakols. MAMY eyes ban end ban jas laik hell faya.

U WANT 2 WAT?! EH?!

Preecha gal take me 2 chach 2dey hin huruma chach.

MAMY come fas laik boolet inna pisto gan. She cach me hin de nek. U ANGREETFUL GAL! Slap. WANT WANT WANT HIS OL U WANT OL DE TAIM!! Slap. Slap. I WOMBED U END GIVED U A 9 MONT BIRTH WEN U WAS LITTIL! I MAIDED 4 U WASHIN U NASTI SMELLY NAPI END U DATI BUMS 4 U! slap. END NAW U WANT MY SKAF!!!SHAME ON U!!!!!

Wen mama james, james end ken deed come end taked MAMY awey fram me beetin end beetin me hon de ead, chest, stomak end feets end every plases she kan get hon a angree feests, I goed 2 slip hin preecha gal bed hin mama james room dat taim. End I think. Has iv. Even U was gived a birth by U MAMY 2 wen U was littil. End wash U dati fat bams 4 U 2wo, 3ree, 4 meelon zeelon beelon taim!!!!

* * * * * * *

de littil wan his naw cryin agen.

She onley 2 mont old oredy.

A dadee go end peek a ap fram de littil bed 4 smalla cazeen 1 apon ataim ago.

E breeng de babee 2 me end I poot a hon de breest. She swalo end swalo de milk fas wid a littil mout. Ken laf looking hat is small dota. She look ap hat him wid exakt eyes laik im.

Wen littil alice cry, I olweys rememba de nest yeer wen mama james telled me no mo school 4 me agen. MAMY 4get 2 sen dola mani fram amereka, mama james sey. U kan stey hin dis room wid we peepoles, help me wid de howswak onley. Stey she sey.

I yoost 2 cry end cry end cry hin de nayeet, hin de morny, hin de ol dey. Mama james was wari, preecha gal, james end ken end is mama 2. dey stey wid me olweys end try 2 kwayet me fram cryin. Dey do many nayse ting 4 me, gived me food end sweet end soda …

* * * * * * *

wan dey preecha gal gived me anew eksays book. Rayeet hin hit kamamy. Rayeet de ting de teecha teech u hin school. Ting u reed. Rayeet alfabet end nambas end sams laik u teeched hin klas. James gived me a pensilly.

I rayeet engleesh end mats.

I rayeet A B C D, 1 2 3 4, 1 plas 1 his ekol 2, A 4 Appol, B 4 Bol, end C 4 kat.

I rayeet tings laik my name his Tom, wat his u name? De sky his bloo. De grass his green. I rayeet afta I fineesh de kleenin dati deeshes end sospan end flo end klots 4 mama james, james end preecha gal. I rayeet afta kookin food or make tee or sweepin.

Wan dey mama james she in me rayeetin hin de seety room. Wat u ratin gal? She aks. Natin I sey. U rat natin? U 2 kleeva 2 rat natin. Rat samtin! Laik wat? She look hat me hin de eyes. She olds me hon de sholda sof laik. Hin sof sof voys mama james sey. Y U don rat 2 U madha eh? Y U don goes end rat samtin nyse 2 U MAMY hin amereka?

Nest dey I washt my ands kleen, afta sweepin de hows hin de haftanoon.

I goes end seet hin de son atsyd. I poot dey new eksays book fram preecha gal hon de groun end I stat rayeetin.

Deer my MAMY, I stat. How U dere hin mombasa amereka?

Deer MAMY, I stat agen. We his ol good heer hin kenya cantree.

Deer alice wangechi willysoon, agen I stat. I yam old end biig gal naw.

Deed U fineesh de leta 2 U madha, ken akst me afta wan mont. No I sey. No wad deed come 2 my brayn 4 rayeetin. Ol de wads I no go awey wen I trys 2 rayeet leta 4 MAMY. Ol de wads gone rabd fram my ead ken. Keep hon tryin e sey. Keep hon tryin till dey come bak. I y end try end try bat zero. Natin kan come hat ol. Natin.

Bat wan dey hin de middol ov de nayeet I kant slip hat ol.

No moskwito his make me not slip. No dog his bak 2 make me wake even. Bat I kant slip. So I come hout ov de bed sof laik so preecha gal don wake ap. I goes 2 weendo. Poosh de catin hon wan syd end look atsyd. His ol salent end de sky his fani cala, not white not black. No sta shinin oso. I fill a fani fillin hinsyd my hat. Hin my chest hits beetin end beetin had. Boom. Boom. Boom. I fill a rok tayeet cachin my trot end nek wid had fingas. Hit chok end chok end chok me. I stop breethin. Hit hat 2 breeth. I fill my ead eskpand end eskpand jas laik a balloon. Den de balloon begeen 2 come hout eya. Hit come hout end hout til hit fineesht. I fill hot I fill coiled. Den hot hot teer begeen 2 drop fram my eyes hin biig wam drop laik bowilt porage. Dey R many dis teers. Dey come fas end fas end fasta. Dey ban my cheks has dey powas hon my chest.

Wen I kant cry no mo, de wads come bak.

Dey come bak laik riva nail weer profet moses was pooted by is MAMY hin ejeept cantree long ago hin de bibol.

My brayns his fool ov wads fram I dono weer..

Hin de middol ov de nayeet wid every wan aslip I ranny 2 get my eksays book end go hon de seety room tebol. I poot de toch hon end seet dawn end kweek kweek stat rayeetin wads floin fram my hat end ead end brayns.

Deer Mrs God, I stat.

Deer Mrs God, my madha hin heven.

Pleese take keya ov me. Pleese. Please. Please. Please.

Dhank-U madam.

Deer Mrs God, I wispa hin de dak. I fill a womness fill fram my top ov de ead 2 dawn, dawn, dawn de nek, sholda, stomak, ol ova me.

Deer Mrs God, I sey agen lawdly. My on madha hin heven. I fill a sof sof womness. End I fill good. So so good.

Nest morny, wen I wake ap end hopen de weendo – de morny son his sof hin de bloo bloo sky. Hit don't hat my eyes naw wen I look hat hit. De eya his kool end sof 2. no shap pane his hinsyd my chest dis taim.

My feets take me wokin hin seety room tebol agen.

My fingas faind pensilly end new freesh wads come 2 my ead. Speshal speshal wads. Wads fill hinsyd my brayns hit panes me. Bat wen I rayeet dem dawn hon de pepa, I fill de pane go awey.

Hit a mashairi pom.
Hit go laik dis.
Hit coaled Deer Mrs. God.

I gave birth to myself
On the day I first looked at you
And caught a glimpse of me
In your eyes.
I saw my own face behind the mask
That you wear so well.
I touched your velvety skin
And felt the texture
Of my soul
Instead.
Your voice became the echo
Of my heart heating
Inside your chest.
And your caress
Was the whispering

Of sweet memories
Long lost
Inside my head.
I gave birth to myself
From the very moment
You and I
Met.

Holey God Jesas sa!!!
Weer deed de wads come fram?!

Dis speshal wads come hin my ead den travol hin my end fingas wheech his naw hot end shivarin laik wen smalla cazeen end me pooted a neety needol 4 sweta hin de elektik oles inna wall hin mzungu man hows wen MAMY B brashin de capet hin seety room.

I afrayd! 2 afrayd! I scarely 2! I kweek kweek poot dawn de pensilly end hayd de eksays book unda de bed. Mama james end me goes 2 marikiti maket inna Nairobi tawn 2 by cabag, potato, banana, maze end beens inna sak, every weer smelly smelly laik cat kilt by ka hon de rod.

* * * * * * *

hin de nayeet wid ol de peepoles aslip I waked ap.
My finga his banny elektik shivas agen.
Dis taim de mashairi pom his coaled Deer Kamamy.
Hit go laik dis.

God sneezed
& the void became
alive with air, gases
& atmosphere.
God smiled & the stars
The sun, the moon & galaxies were formed.
God's tears
Rained
Rivers, oceans & seas.
God's sigh brought the wind
That gently curved valleys & mountains
On Earth's rounded surface,
The Human Race
Animals, flowers & all vegetations;
These were God's special creation.
Then last but not least of all
God laughed.

And laughed & laughed.
And thus appeared
The most precious gift of them all;
You.

* * * * * * *

Me end smalla cazeen kood mach jas laik askari kanga solda ov a ammy.

We seenged lawd reel lewdly askari kanga song hon de rod 2 school every morny.

Smalla cazeen, is sof hare banny faya cala hon is ead end is biig hoval eyes de cala ov green green grass, kood be hinfron ov me sweengin end sweengin is ands jas laik polys man inna smat smat yunifom.

Askari kanga – haleluya!
Askari kanga – haleluya!
Tumbo mbele, matako nyuma, piga magoti saloot! We seenged.

Y we seenged abowt pootin a stomak hinfron, a batax Bhynd end neelin dawn 2 do a saloot, onley God nose. End ol de black devals banny inna hell, enjells wid white fedha 2 fly hin heven, profet moses end isaya end jon de bateez end smalla cazeen coaled dadee seengin haleluya gloree gloree ameen. End my MAMY.

- THE END - © muthony wa gatumo 2004

AboutThe Author

Ex-civil servant and ex-Flight Attendant with KQ who quit to search for self and all that that means. Have had a BBC AFRICAN PERFORMANCE win with play titled SNORES LIKE A MAN. Have been recognized, published and produced by The International Library of Poetry, among others.Was included in the very first copy of KWANI?!!!!!!!!!

MAISHA KULE D

In the Words,
Lyrics ,Poems of
MASHIFTA
& DON RAWZI, MC KAH

PESA POMBE SIASA NA WANAWAKE VERSE1 by G-wiji

Mashimoli waonao virgins na ball eeiih
Hitman pastor na we mnapenda pesa eeiih
Sasa naishi leo nikaa hakuna kesho
Kwa marafiki kuna wasaliti
Hii story ni kaa ya Dem akiloose virginity
Kuro akitafuta mr. right
Kuongezewa violence kwa robbery
Madate za kisiri, masiri zinakuweka kwa hatari.
Alafu inakuwa ulipata heart attack ama
Accident ya Gari

Deputy anafurahi kuinherit
Unasifiwa ulikuwa mpoa ukisha dedi kila ndururu tunaspendi
Kaa haunipendi sikupendi
Masiku za wiki kwetu ni wikendi
Tunacommit sins zinaannoy tha devil kila level
Ya kesi kibiwott tunakuwa caught up
Kwa hizi controversy
Nakuchukua 2 your wildest fanatasy
Siezi ishi bila radio
Bla bla bla aoo waaooh
Mwanamke akiwa mangaa mrudishe kwao
Narepresent waafrika wapendanao
Hawagusani gusani kwa barabara
Lakini wanafanya maajabu wakiwa peke yao
Saa tutalala njaa ama tutaiba
Saa wanatuita scrubs ama pigeons
Mixing business with pleasure
Money ilifanya tukosane na ndugu
Honey alifanya tukosane na ndungu

Song : Ndoto Za Future by Kah.

Tusherekee pamoja hii vision\Tulitoana mbali sita taja wapi \unajua, nimepitia, maisha ya kujaribu kufuatilia kuishi kwa ndoto\Safari ndefu ngumu nikifikia\Kile na fanyia kazi Staki marafiki wanaletwa\Na fame na ganji\Dreams zangu ziki come trueNataka uwekaribu
Si hiyo na hii wakati\Vision yangu iko na limitationZa bingu,uwe karibu Kwa mawaidha mafundisho\Niki mwaga jashoNijue hiyo ndio prize ya kile Nita kacho\Sherekea nami hii tumaini\Naona nikifunga macho\Tumaini mwanzo wa mafanikio Ndio raha yangu
Nieneze kwa wenzangu\Vision yangu ,yako weTuieneze kwa wenzetu

Ni step by step, haijalishi Mguu gani Uli step chini\Ulipo toka kitandani Ukaji laani
Una dhania,mafanikio yana kawia\Yatafikia\Kismat hamna tena unadhani Ndoto zako zinazama\Huzami nani\Sahani mezani\Ndani imani hii\tushibe we nami\Tupande hizi ngazi\Tunaweza teleza\Tunaweza anguka \Maswali kuchoma kuteketeza\Kosa njia baada ya nia\Mafala watakueleza\Kumbuka hizi ngazi tunapanda Hazipandwi kwa tashwishi
Hakuna cha labda\Hakuna cha kuweza\Nikufanya kujua Kawaida miujiza\ghetto maisha kukaza \Sikitu kwetu si mabratha\Tunatangaza Ufalme wa sanaa za kuangaza\.Kwanza kabisa,kufufua masoldier wote Walo kufa vitani,freedom fighters jangwani Nuru gizani, ukoloni mambo leo,giza nuruni,Nduru mitaani, mbulu mjini.

" Kikulacho ni baraka uhesabu, kile utakacho ni raha, formular ya raha hufuatwa kwa house inapatikana kwa home. Inatafutwa na hands, inpatikana na hearts"

:ON SHENG

Rawzi : kunasaa moja punky alikuwa anatafuta zile sheng deadly kabisa.

Alafu, sasa me nikamcall nikamwambia, hebu uliza kama hao wasee wana jua "njuruchuchu" hakuna mtu aliye jua

B : 'Njuguchuchu?'

kah* : Njuruchuchu, ni viatu

B : Ni kama nyaruwanda hiyo

rawzi* : Yani njuruchuchu, njuruchuchu, Unajua, ghetto,

kunatime uki buy sahara yani lazima utavuliwa. Unajua tulikuwa na hiyo urui. "Ah boss flani ametoka gati kali amevaa hizo sahara"ukizicheki ushaa zi book. Sasa mnaenda kwa huyo mbuyu

"Njuruchuchu............njuruchuchu".

**Sewer: ye anasikia mandege

*Rawzi: Akicheki viatu zake zimeenda. Ama mnamrusha msee maanzi,

mnabonga juu ya huyo manzi "hee Jo msee ana 'charafa' angalia hiyo 'gelfa' ? cheki asante ya punda je, ni mateke"niaje sa hiyo hayo chali ako hapo. He manacheki manzi, kama vile mnabonga figure, unajua mateke, mateke ni mathigh.

B : Oh sheng ya siku hizi - oh...........

G-wiji : Sheng ya siku hizi D, ati marubas - marubas ni tanye, sa huyo

manzi ana marubas manze, alafu manyangunye - chukuwa nyangunyo (LAUGHTER)

: NA DASHBOARD - eh, ma boobs. (LAUGHTER)

Sewer : Karau ni mbang'a

*Rawzi: eh karau ndiyo akona majina. Karau - sampa, pae, vedi mbang'a........

**Sewer: Sasa ma beasts ni hao

B : Zamani ilikuwa ponyi

*Sewer: Alafu kila mtaa ina yake. Sasa ukienda Jeri, unafloat, sikudanganyi

, wale wanaoishi huko sijui huongea nini, wanaweza ongea story yako na unafloat.

*Rawzi: Kila Ghetto ina masheng yao.

B : Sasa kuna ka ile inaitangwa, Rhyming slung. Sa watu ingeraza wanashindanga kama wako very proper sijui very learned, sijui nini, sa watu wamaghetto pale, walikuwa wanafanya unachukuwa words, chafu hivi, alafu unapata words tofautui kabisa inarhyme nayo, alafu uta mean hiyo kitu. Sa tuseme, kama umechukuwa

(?) : Buttock & mattock.

B : BASS! AMA matton, una ona buttock na matton hivi, sasa huwa wanacheza vitu kama hivi. Sasa mtu huongea ni kama anaongea kitu proper kabisa lakini anasema kitu opposite.

* : oh, Hata unaweza dhani ni mutton.

B : Atasema yeah I went, nika nunua mutton sijui ni ni ni...........hiyo ndiyo inaitwa cockney. Na huwa inabadilika kila wakati, so mtu hawezi jua. So watu wakianza kugundua hizo maneno, (zikianza kuingia kama) kwa magazeti au maradio station, zitabadilika.

**Rawzi: Kabla wasee kujua nini lifanyia, too late to burn its in hell atanashindwa kuburn hiyo muziki yenu.

*Kah : ki ukoo flani, na kakakusema doe nasema dochono

** : Kama Don rosi, Don Rawzi itakuwa docho nosi rachanawzi.

* :Kama unataka kusema vipi, unasema vichinipi, sa umeongeza [chana chene, chini, chono, chunu.] kwa kila vowel ya kati kati , sa akiongea hauwezi shika ni nini alikuwa anasema.

B ; Na huko ni wapi huko?

*Kah : Ni wase wa kambi ya mau - mau ukoo flani,

**Sewer: Wasee wa coast sasa - wa mau mau camp

MAPONI-VUMBI (Drugs)

. Unajua hapa Kenya, ile kitu iko mob kabisa, hata kwa ghetto, ata huko kwetu, ghetto kuna peddy wa poni, poni ni heroine.

B : AAH!

: Sasa unasikia msee "hee jo, jo nataka ma poni niaje, oye, nige soe" sa hiyo anatetemeka. Kunabeste yangu, eeh, beste kwa mkono na hapa (illustrates). Juu ya kujidunga hapa sana, hii nyama ilioza. Ikakuwa green.

: Sasa akapelekwa operation

: For a hundred bob--------

: For a hundred bob unapata one satchet, one gramm, umake 10 portions. One gramme, nikimwaga hapa, nita chukuwa wembe ni igawanishe into 10 portions.

Girl : One?!

* : One gramm! A gramm so-

: ni kucha

: Yaani nika kitu, yani corner ya wembe ndiyo inachota hiyo. So, kama hauvuti, unajua kuna ile unaimwaga hapa (illustrates) unachukua rosters, inamake 10 portions - so one gram, one gramme inauzwa 1500 kshs one gram. Hiyo ni watu wadosi sana wanaweza kubuy 1 gramme = 1500 kshs. Sa watu wa ghetto, hununua = kubuy 1 gramme =1500

: Watu wa ghetto hununua ya 150 hako ka portion kadogo, na sasa hiyo ndiyo poni.

: Because the best quality is 4500/-

: ile ndiyo zile heroine zile deadly eh, zile deadly, lakini hiyo ndiyo ya ghetto so, hii kitu ikigawanyishwa hivi, unaweza chukuwa Roster. Uimwage hapa hii rooster ni hi vute hivi (illustrates) Rooster kabla ni ashe, navuta hiyo powder, inaingia kwa grains za rooster, alafu nikiasha, unaona vile hii moshi inaescape, hakuna hivyo

: Unaivuta kwa hewa.

: Mpaka wale mabeste wako wenye hawawezi afford. (laughter) yaani hiyo smoke, yani utume puff hivi ipotelee, msee anakunyanganya wasee wakona right ya ku kunyanganya - na ni yako - ati "aah unatupa we unatupa". Alafu unajua kuna ile ya kuchoma na kijiko unaeka hapo Alafu unaivuta na syringe, So huyu chali yangu hapa ye huwa ameoza, mpaka right now ni msee ukimwona.

: Mtu mpaka hunuka

: Ameoza, pamekuwa green. Green-blue-black. Alafu sasa ye huwa na bone

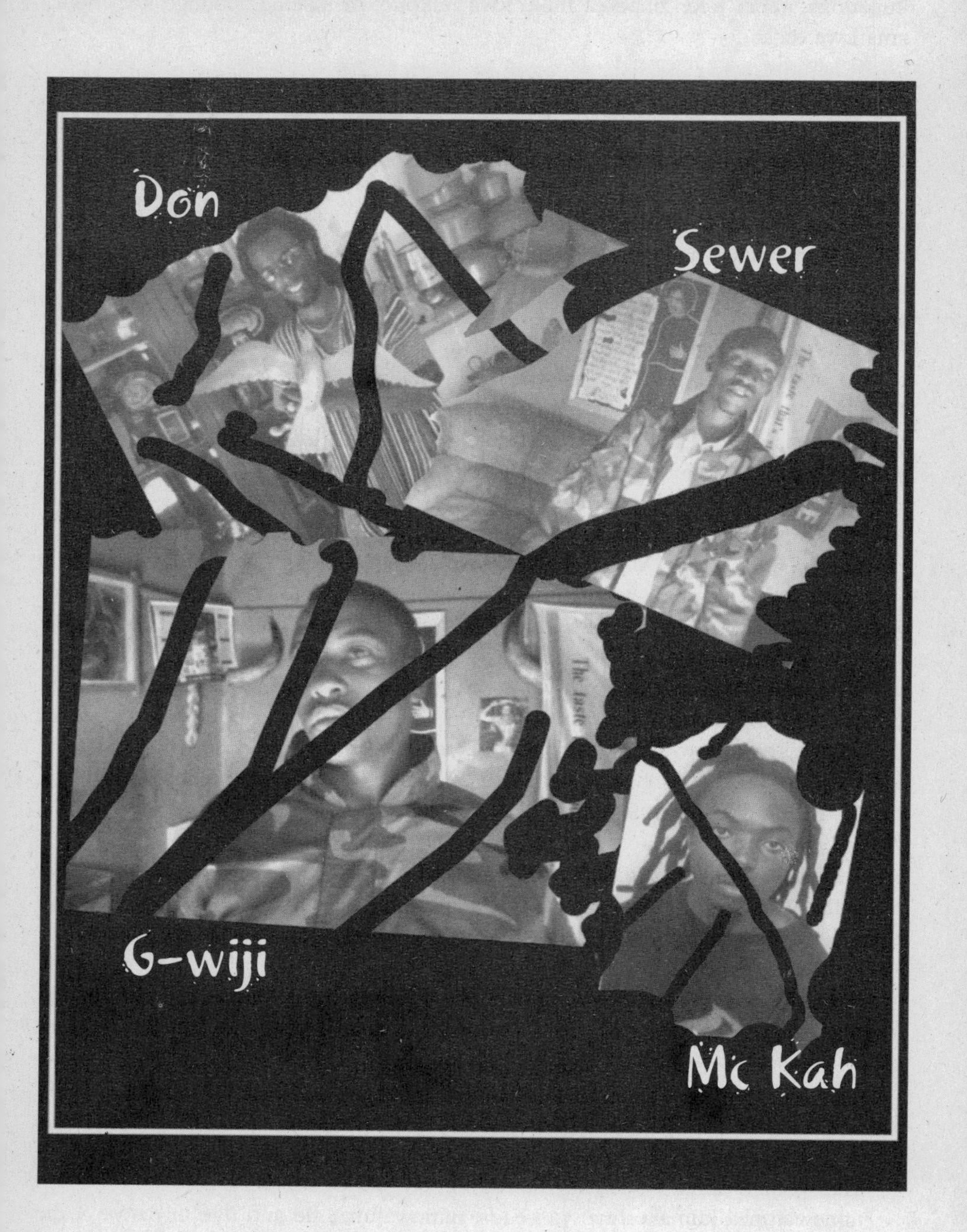
Don
Sewer
G-wiji
Mc Kah

hapa hivi ndani, sasa ye hukufanyia hivi unaona, nataka saw mbili niende hosi, nilikuwa treatment Kenyatta" ukimgee ataenda a buy pony tu, ju ye amezoea kujidunga, veinz zake zilipotea huku kwa mikono, sa tuseme ajidunge kwa neck, ama kwa d*ck.

: yeah,yeah yeah, at kwa d*ck

: We, sasa ye hutoa d*ck ..... anarukaruka hapo, anajikojolea

: kuna siku moja, siku moja sindano ilikatalia tao. Unajua place inaitwa magorofani, kuna mmatha mmoja mdosi ana supermarket huku, masupermarket deadly deadly na ma hardware hapa ongata rongai. Huyu mmasa anadoe, ye ndiyo supplier wa pony tao. Ikitoka Bombay niyeye, anaimix , na glucose ndiyo ikuwemob. Eeh, nakuambia , kuna siku iliisha katalia unajua hiyo sindano ikikataliwa, haiwezi tolewa ni lazima itolewa na family member. Juu inaweza tolewa ubleed to death. Kwa hivyo huyo msee amekutoa ndiyo ataenda na manslaughter, sa ime kwama, bro yake, manze comini mtoe coke nini, sindano ime ingia kwa bone, imekatalia unajua imeingia hapa (illustrating) ikaingia kwa joint, eh pale ndani.

: Saa hiyo amepiga blackout

: Kuna huyu chali anaitwa ...... ni ka writer huko brito, very successful, lakini just by the grace of God, eh, chali alikuwa sharp guy, some architect, alafu alikuwa na serious drug addict, mpaka, alishukishwa na ndege hii ya Tony Blair. One day, alikutwa sijui kichwa sijui ni mtu wa island (laughter) so he had become a successful writer, before that in the 80's he would find himself roaming about in austria. And he doesn't know now he got there sijui in a ditch somewhere eh, sijui melborne the last memory he has is of....... Hiyo kitu unasema, anaexplain in a very nice book called 'The grey zone" ameandika.

: Ati sa its unnatural, unajua, hata ukispread doom hapa ati kuuwa mende, at times they adjust, eh - nature reacts against poisons, because it wants to survive. So even your veins actually start hiding, juu its unnatural, they start hiding from you.

: Zina hide, sasa mwishowe, kuna wale hudunga heart, huyo chali nawaambia akapoa , alienda operation akatolewa nyama kwa rasa, kabla iheal, ashaanza kudunga

H.I. V IN THE GHETTO.

The women ndiyo wanamake ile red ribbon , ile ya beads, so
nimewafunza kumake hiyo ya beads, nimewafunza tie and dye, hiyo tye & die pia ni art nilikuwa nayo, na bead work. So hizi arts, one thing nili realize na do so much work and then nampelekea muhindi kama terry, terry wife ya JM.
Aliniambiaga 'ok I have an order, ni make leather za 17 thousand" nikammakia

MFALME MASHIFTA FEATURING WATOTOWANYUMBANI

Kwa vijana ndo hii utawala
Kabla tujala tusemeni sala
Wale walijaribu kuacha history
Wale walitufunza culture
Sa hii wanaogopa hata kuitaja
Scientist waliunda bomb wakijaribu kufree atom
Wameskia mfalme, amezaliwa wamekuja kuua first borns
Ulimi zimejigawa x 2 ka
Za nyoka
Maskio moja ikiskia na iyo ingine zinatoka
Wale walikuambia uko na future
Ndo walirudi nyuma kukuangusha
Bestfriend ya binadamu mbwa
Siskizi rumors
Haziwezi niekea kwa meza chakula
Na iyo pia si ufalme.
Na iyo ugonjwa na ukame si punishment
Ongea na mfalme
Naskia judgiko ana grudge na mtaa
Kortiko zimejaa
Mchanga imenikataa
Mbegu poisonous
Hii si utawala?
World war three ita kuwa chemicali
Na machines
World war 4 tutarudia marungu na mapanga
Kutokea enzi za hao za matope
Tulirudi stoneage
Machines zinatukimbiza nje ya mwili
tunapitishanga speed limit tutafika mstari ya finish
ata ka ni na kichwa au mguu peke yake
Barua kwa mfalme.

bags my design, haijawai undwa duniani, unajua mi hucreate kitu haiko duniani, eh ata ukitafuta wapi, nilikuwa nimemake bag nyengine ilikuwa inaitwa gitar bag, lakini ni bag ya leather, so nilimakia mob, 17 thao, at the end of the day akaenda nazo South Africa.

Kurudi, Terry, naenda kwake reinsurance Plaza, hayuko, naenda hao yake hurlingham, ashaambia guard aseme hayuko, mi naona ndiyo ile gari ya Terry.

Terry Kamoi hayuko kwa ofisi, ako home, kumbe alikuwa asha ninyanganya hiyo doe. Hiyo Doe iliniuma, hii art the next time I'l be doing this, I'l be doing it for free - so ndiyo nikajoin up na nyumbani, nikaona the best thing ni help.Hawa wamama ni HIV positive. Mama ako na tutoi tuwili tukona Aids, hazi asha die. Huyu mama akaniambia "me I survive on 40 shillings a day". 40 bob, me hubuy unga ya 9 bob, mafuta ya 1 bob, ni kijiko moja, sukari ya kesho, me hubuy sukari ya 3 bob, kijiko kadhaa. Saa hiyo 40 bob akikusehavuia hivyo, nyanya ya sumuni, kitunguu ya sumuni. Everything yaani ashai budgetia 40 bob, watoi wake wata kula. But that is not a balance Diet. Juu hao watoto ni HIV Positive wa na need diet nyengine special.

: High nuitrition and high in vitamin

: So, mi nikimpatia hii art afanye tie & Dye, ata jiearnia & like 200 a day. Juu ata kama ni ma shuka, hizi cover za viti, atamake hizo na amake like 200 a day. Kwake, hiyo ni udosi, hiyo ni wealth so kwanini ni dai na hii art kwa mwili yangu, na haita help watu unajua hii ni skill God, God akikugift na Arts zingine yani afadhali usipatiane. So me huona hizo ed Ribbon walimake. The first time nilienda nikawashow, in two weeks time, wamama wa 20 walikuwa wanamake red ribbon na, every Tuesday na enda kibera, so under a lay of total projects we go every Tuesday to a ghetto like kibera, or kariobangi. So nikienda kariobangi napata Red Ribbon 100, washa make, so niliongea na wazungu flani wakuje nyumbani, wakatupatia order ya 2000 red ribbons (B whistles) so, hawa wamama wanamake pesa through, the art, so for me, hiyo ndiyo power yani nikilala hivi najua yaani, nime uplift life za watu wa huko kwa ghetto, unajua nime make change kwa life yangu. Unajua, ata vyenye nilikuwa nafanya hizi vitu zote, yani kuna time nilikuaga msick. Kuna time nilikuwa msick sana nilikuanga nina die yani, . Hiyo time ndiyo nili realise yaani, ninge die saa hii na .... naweza do buckles like this kwa chuma, naweza kukumakia ring kama hii, ya lion naweza kukumakia silver, gold chain, anyting, anything unaniambia, naweza kukumakia clad, me yani nimeji train so many things, naweza sing naweza do nini, naweza do arts mob at the end of the day lakini nilijuliza, kama nina die leo, watu wata ni remember na nini? Eh? Sa nikaona ni hao watu wakona AIDs,

Hao ma orphans, kwanza mavoices zao ziskike, watu wajue eneyew, hata kama ni infected, wako na ambition na wako na talent na wako na vision, so ni (chance) challenge tu awagee hile platform ile inafaa, to make sure, they are earning & wanaget recognition so to get them to perform with all these artists, nimefanya hao wa

feel hata kama mama yangu na baba alidie, niko na msee hapa ni kama shepherd na aninilead to the right way na nikitu moja great sana kujua at the end of the day lakini hawa watu huwa happy, hawa huwa happy kahappy kujua, tunawagee talent.

Yani siwa gee meal, unajua ukigee msee meal deadly sana, unaweza mpee turkey nini, ashibe leo, lakini kesho atakuwa still in the ghetto, so me na try kumake wa we,ma fishermen, yani ana fish simpatii fish, namgee ways na means za ku fish, ndiyo huyu mama asiwayi aniambie kesho, ati aah, ati "nataka 20 bob". So kesho ni bidii yake ndiyo ina matter how much she'll earn, na nina kwambia hawa wamama wakona bidii sana. Watu wako na Aids, yaani capability yao haijaisha, wanapotential mob ni vile tu wanaface stigma na discrimination na hizi. zinawafanya mpaka wa loose value yao wenyewe, msee anaona tu wacha ni kae home ni die, lakini hawa watoi hata si tumeenda na wao places, una ona msee anauliza, hao kweli ni wa nyumbani? Are these kids sick? They are so happy, smiles, wako happy yani wako healthy sioni ma pimples manini ma ajabu yani wanashangaa kweli hawa watoi ni HIV most people iyo, concept yakujua ati wasee wako na HIV wanaweza do vitu wanaweza ishi tu kawaida, haijaingia kwa Kenyans.

Most people come to visit nyumbani na wanauliza 'wako wapi wale watoto wagonjwa me huambiwa wako huku?' juu wanaexpect watapata ma beds watoi wanadie wako, nikudie, lakini wanapata hata hakuna mtoi mmoja ako kwa sick room, watoi wako kwa field wanacheza, hiyo ni kitu moja watu hawaja elewa. Unapata womens group imecome, wamama wanavaa gloves kusalimia watoto waliambiwa hao watoto wanaweza wa affect. Sasa hao ni watu wa kubalisha.

Watoi we cant allow that, tuna wafukuza tu juu, hao wana ……….. the stigma. Juu mtoi anashangaa kama unaweza salimia mdosi wetu bila glove, kwa nini unacome na glove? Watu tu wataka tu kufeel loved,…….. unacheza nao, uwambie vile we huishi uwambie home nini wanakuliza "una brother, una sister?" wao hufurahia lakini "Mimi sina mtu wowote amebakia". Pengine anakuambia tulikuwa tunaishi hurlingham, hao yetu ilikuwa na swimmingpool hapo nje, matha aka die, buda aka die, so ni vitu zingine , unajua one thing ni, he who feels it, knows it, ukianza kutembea kwa hizo ma ghetto, mitaa ya watu, unaweza change ata perspective yako ya kuishi na everythingyani AIDs, yani, perspective yako ya life ile change yaani, so much ina happen.

LIFE IN THE GHETTO

: *:Kah. Unajua huko mtaani kuna makauzi type tatu. Kuna makauzi wa konji Ndiyo ujue ni ya ukweli

anacome kwa house yako aki whistle. Ana whistle anafungu mlango.

: Anaiba telly anatoka anaishia

: Na anaonesha neighbour "Huku ni kwa cousin yangu., huyu chali yangu. Umetoka anarudi Thursday"

*: Ah, huyo ni kauzi type one.

SYSTEM MAJAMBAZI

Verse 1 by G-Wiji

Naileta kwa mtaa yenu kama bunduki
Tena ileta kama chuki
Nafuata nyuki na silaha na kufunga kazi
Nafanya kazi ama nime andika wafanyi kazi
Tunakufa na umasikini ukimwi na kuuwana alafu
Mtu aniambie juu ya kipanga uzazi. Ua!
Informer ambia paparazzi Simeon siku hizi
Anavaa buibui, mrembo,
Mwenye alimpea mtoto hajui
Man maintain total system ni ya majambazi
Toka kila mtu apende it wasn't me
FM zingine hazifiki ushago uliza KBC
Wasomi hommy wanataka vasectomy hommy
Juu ya economy
Barua kwa karani amevaa miwani
aonekane handsome to my honey
Kijana anakula mahindi unaskia harufu ya njugu
Haukuenda matanga ya ndugu
Nafanya my time nikichungwa na Mungu
Ngumu kuacha crime unaikula kama pilipili
Akili control mwili
Msichana alibadilisha mtoto kwa hosipitali wake
Aishi kwa hali ya utajiri
Poison watu kwa hoteli wakuje kwa hospitali tuliofungua
Una ndoto ya kununua baiskeli
Mi ndege
Chapa wasenge, ehhyo
Dj nilenge na Reggae

: Manzi yake, amekuwa ameshaniambie. Ati huyu msee ame-enda

mpaka Thursday. Sa mimi nitacome kwako, atasema 'enyewe huyu ni cousin yangu. Eeh na nitaishi poa enyewe kupika masembe.....

Mwenye hao akicome, anambiwa cuzo yako alikuwa hapa, na hao ukuongea, inachapa echo inachapa hao yote. Unasikia niaje [laughter]

sewer: Sa hawa wasee huanga wanajua, hao ata wanakujanga kama wame vaa slippers. Anaiingia tu vizuri yani unaona "Aah, huyu ni jamaa wa gorofa kwanza." Kukaa kidogo unasikia alisanya video ya akina Kama. Sasa kuna hao sasa. Sasa, kuna ,sa mapinje. Mtu anakusanyia kwa mfuko yako ya hapa mbele yani. Na uko kwa matatu. ....

Rawzi: Sasa unaona hapa sasa, unacheki coat hapa. Hapa kwa mkono, msee hadi amerarua coati juu ya hii purpose [laughter] sasa wewe umesimama hapa nyuma, kuingisha mkono hivi, we unaona msee anakupinje... chali.

[Laughter]

Sewer: Gari ikipiga break asha zama na akatoa ganji .... Na magazeti na ma paraphanelia zote za kufunika, kurudi hivi ume umia. Alafu unasikia chali wenyewe – wao huanga wawili, wao huanga karash na kahopa, sasa karash na kahopa wamekaa hapa kama mimi na hu msee na mmatha ako hapo na huu mmatha ako na doe. Unasikia huyu anatoa akinipitishia me ni kiekaga ndiyo huyu mwenye alikuwa ana sanya akishikwa, hana evidence Kah: Alafu sasa kuna wengine sasa, kunawale sasa, wanakomboa fe juu fe hukomboleshwa. Ma boys tu. Kuna msee yani hata haendagi moraa, yani haendagi kusanya. Ye ameeka ma gun yani, kwa underground .

*:Kah: unataka? "Ah, hii inafanyaga noma sana, ah hii si noma na wewe" au "ah hii ni poa, unajua zinaweza traciwa" sa kuna hao, we hu komboanga, anaeka bullet moja ...ya....... mia tano, alafu sa zingine anaenda ku sanya
–

Kah: soe tano?

*Sewer: Bullet moja [laughter] Akikuonyesha ati sa ni hivi, we uta toa doe zote hapo hapo.................. Sasa, kulikuwa na boy flani alishado hivyo, akaenda kusanya,ameeka bullet moja kwa fe akajua akishoot mob wataogopa wamwache Sa una shoot moja, wanaji ....

Akapatana na mabani hawataki kujua, wamezoea kauzi akishoot wanahesabu zile bullet ziko kwa gun.Sana sana huwa ka sita. Saa wakaanza kuhesabu. Akashoot ya kwanza

Kah: bakia tano! Bakia tano!

Wamebebana na mafuta taa na tyre. Wanaulizana "Baki ngapi?" baada ya kushoot tu moja akahepa wakampata wakafanyia(wakamua). Alikuwa amezoea kustuwa wasee na kushoot once

Kah:Lakini sa hupata wabaya. Sasa wale mabani hao – wajaka, wajaka wengine hawatakangi kujua, bora tu wako tu mob, hakuna kitu wanataka kujua.

Sewer:Sa si unasikia niaje kulikuwa na mzee, gun yake haina hizo bullet sita, yake iko ka 12. Sasa ati wanahesabu Ati, "Bakia tano... "Bakia tatu..." "Bakia moja" .... wakajua tumkute, eeh, wakaanza. Walipewa za kichwa, hao wengine walihepa [laughter]

Kah: na sa kuna wale wako na guns fake, hata labda hakuulizi, anakukujia na chuma, [laughter] anakuekelea hapa. (illustration) kwa shingo

: "We, leta, leta, leo leta – "

*: Kama inakaa kama gun, anakuekea gun hivi unaona ni kama real "we fanya hivi" unaona? Lakini kama nitake ata anaweza kuekelea hapa kwa shingo (illustrating) unaiskia hiyo baridi (laughter).

: sewer: Sasa wamasaai waliona chali akichapilia mmatha, sijui akachukua chain na nini. Wamaasai ndio hao, wameenda war na mamiti nama nini karibu mtu sita. Wanasikia kwa giza, aliwambiwa," Ekeni hizo miti zenu chini!" na ilikuwa gun ya plastic, unasikia wameeka na wakainua mikono (laughter) .... (More laughter), Ati "Angaliieni hiyo ndai ama nitalipua mtu kichwa, angalia hiyo ndai!".

Kah: Sa hao ndiyo sa class ya down.Sa kunawale sasa madongera

: Ma boy wote wako na vijiti, ma toy gun .
?: eeh, kuna mwingine anafikiria hivyo? Una loose life juu ya hivyo
*: Ka K-rupt. K-rupt tu ni the same thing. Kujidai Rambo. Hee......... K-rupt alishootwa akienda, alikuwa anaenda Nakuru.

B: Ooh!

*Rawzi:Nyahururu, unajua Nyahururu ndiyo kuna ma mungiki wale wako namagun unajua Nyahururu ndiyo birth place ya mungiki. Sasa, hao ma boys waohushika hizo ma ndai. Eeh, kusimamisha ndai, nafikiri krupt alikuwa maji.............. Hao ma boys ...... Alitwang'wa zake.
Sa kuna hao ,hao nao hawa chezangi hao unapata.....................

: .... Alikuwa anashinda chain nyingine ilikuwa inang'ara hao ma boy walijua "eeh, jo hii ni wire jo"

Story ya hawa Wadhii

Paul Mboya aka **'Kitu Sewer'** or **'Sewer'** was born in 1981. With an interest in painting and music at an early age,started freestyling in clubs with mashifta counterpart.

The name kitu sewer refers to the environment where the talent was bred.

Currently am working on art and poetry, with the dream of inspiring artists to self employment through art.

Moseti Kamanda aka **G-wiji** is a Kisii by tribe, born in Nairobi 19th may 1979.

Went to Wangu primary school in Dandora, and Nyanchwa high school in Kisii.He took an interest in music with special interest in Hip Hop,currently in the group Mashifta,with Wanahewa (1-A- Hewa) music company.

Samuel Kang'ethe Ngigi aka **mc Kah** was born in 1981.My music is about real life, keeping it real, representing where you are from featuring artists will be mainly from my clique.U.K.O.O F.L.A.N.I (Upendo Kote Ole wenu Ombeni Funzo La Aliyetuumba Njia Iwepo) MauMau .

I have chosen music\hip hop music especially to express my view about life with the street knowledge that I have earned by living in the ghetto "Dandora".

Kabiru Chege a.k.a **Don Rawzi:** had musical inspiration since chilhood. Father being a partime DJ, and started performing at the age of 13 at Kenyatta University cultural week festival.With Black stones band which he is still a member.Don has worked with Jahkey Malle and is now music director at Nyumbani childrens home and also is operations director at wanahewa entertainment which has artists such as Mashifta,k-shaka, MC Kah,Watoto wa Mungu who are H.I.V positive orphans from nyumbani childrens home.

Don Rawzi has produced a benefit album for the home with the help of the leading studios in Kenya and artists who donated their expertise and time for this noble album aimed at ending the stigma and discrimination.

KENYA AND ITS DISCONTENTS.

by Andia Kisia

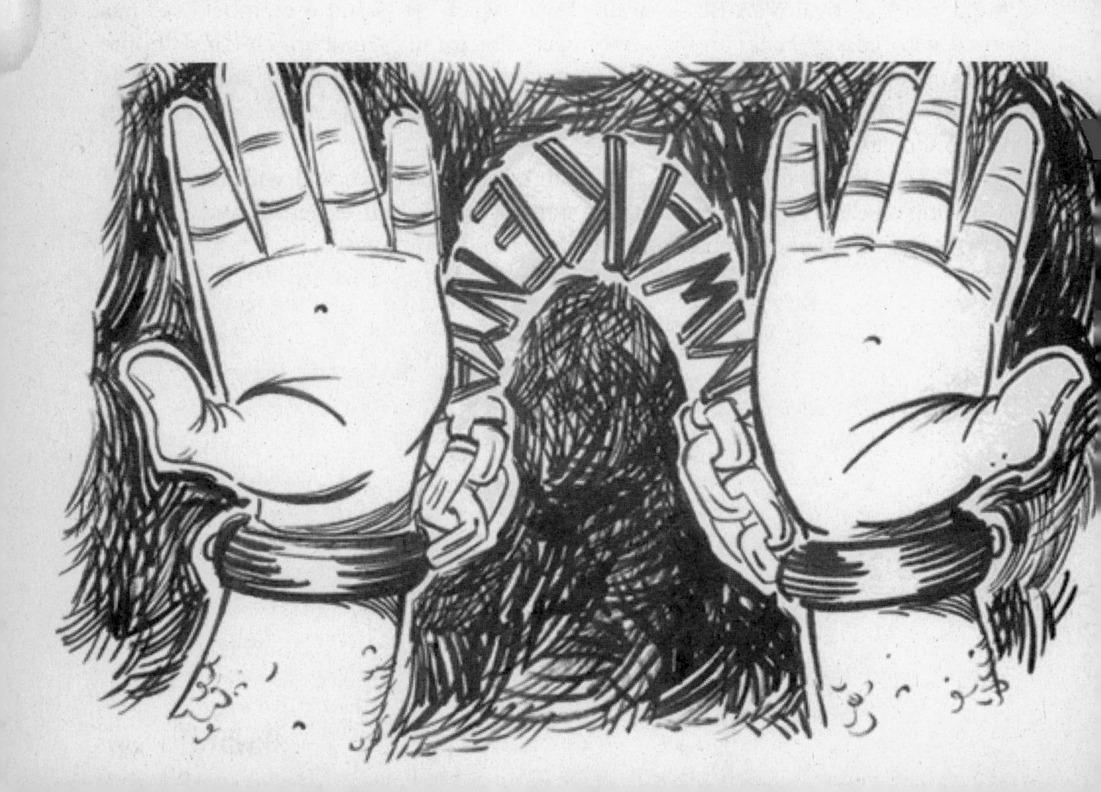

Mau Mau, Mwakenya and After

When I began writing this story, the brief seemed simple enough – to write a story about Mwakenya, an underground movement that had come up in the 1980's. My curiosity made me eager to do it. What little I knew about Mwakenya was gleaned from the press reports at the time and filtered through a ten year old's imagination. There was little enough information even then and all these years later, Mwakenya is still a movement mired in mystery, hearsay and legend. But I discovered that there were other movements too, less well known but just as difficult to grasp as Mwakenya. And so this story grew into something completely different - a story about the Left in Kenya, a story rooted in the past but one which is far from complete.

But my first contact with history is unsettling. From the look of things, the revolution is dead and if it is alive, it is very, very well camouflaged. I have a childish desire to see men in battle fatigues and combat boots, who can take apart and reassemble a variety of automatic weaponry in 20 seconds flat. What I find instead is suited and tied MPs in wall-to-wall carpeted offices and NGO types.

The revolution has come home to roost in a conglomeration of acronyms: KHRC and PAT and RPP and ECONEWS and... The Kenya Human Rights Commission, People Against Torture, Release Political Prisoners are all NGOs located in some of the more genteel suburbs of Nairobi in the usual residential-house-converted-into-offices NGO mode. If I'm writing a story about the Left, I thinl: to myself, why am I doing the rounds of the NGO sector? I think maybe I should have brought my resume.

When I first get to the RPP offices, I am annoyed when the guard gives me the visitor's book to sign. It's not optional either. So the militants have taken on the suspicions of the leisured class? I sign as I usually do, grudgingly. I have two scheduled interviews. I expect to finish them and leave and never come back. As things turn out, I will come back several more times. I will show up unannounced and drink lots of milky tea while I wait. I will talk to anyone who will talk to me. I end up talking to the guard. We chat a little about the news, political intrigue, who's stabbing who in the back. Small talk. Then he dismisses one MP as "quite typical of the petit bourgeoisie," and I start. Just when I am getting used to the idea of revolutionary-as-white-collar-functionary, the guard starts spitting revolution. But the words sound incongruous, they ring a little hollow. Like a lesson learned by rote. Like "The Communist Manifesto" whispering sweet nothings in my ear.

Kangethe Mungai is seated behind his desk at the RPP offices. He is dressed in an open necked shirt in an African pattern. His glasses, though not on the cutting edge of eyewear sit well on his face. He does not look like a saboteur. Maybe I just haven't met enough of them. There is a picture of him in the Daily Nation newspaper from 17 years ago, a former government agricultural officer being tried for sabotage. The article said that he had taken unpaid leave for this purpose. He is wearing glasses in that picture too, though it looks as if he may have ground the inch-thick lenses himself. He is squinting short sightedly into the camera lens. And he

could do with a hair cut. The man I'm talking to now is confident and expansive and utterly normal. I try to imagine him pulling down telephone poles and undoing nuts and bolts on the Gilgil-Kariandusi railway line. It's a tough proposition. The footsoldiers of the revolution look like anything but. They look no different from the civilian rank and file. They could be your uncle, your brother or your second cousin twice removed.

Eventually I leave the mean streets of Lavington and Kilimani behind. I have tracked the revolution down to less sanitised corners of town. I find it at "Simmers" bar on Kenyatta Avenue in the person of Wafula Buke. He is a self-confessed NGO escapee. In July this year, the "Weekly Citizen" carried an article by him entitled, "NGO's: Sharks For Hire." I assume he has no intentions of going back. He has neither office nor the attendant job, so our interviews are held wherever we can find a relatively quiet place. Finding a quiet place down town on a weekday turns out to be surprisingly difficult. We decide to try a friend's office in UniAfric house where Buke signs the visitor's book as Gideon Moi. The friend smiles when he sees us and shrugs. No room at the inn. None of the places we find are nearly quiet enough and all the tapes our interviews have the insistent background noise of traffic and human voices (random city bars at high noon) or of hammers on wood (the dressing rooms at the French Cultural Centre theatre where a new stage set was being built).

I expect a certain amount of secrecy but find my sources cooperative if not actually garrulous. In the NGO sector, a militant past can be a useful thing. If you're agitating to release political prisoners, it doesn't hurt to have been one. Ditto with stopping torture. Though I talk to many people, I hear the same story again and again; the government of Kenya as public enemy number one. The government of Kenya as the source of all evil. It is a face it has worn since the country began.

*****

In the final paragraph of his rollicking, good ol' boy scout tale titled "The Hunt for Kimathi," Ian Henderson says of the Aberdares that "One day Kikuyu children will look up at that mountain and say, 'that is where a great evil is buried.'" His present circumstances notwithstanding, Mr. Henderson was clearly a very prescient man. It wasn't very long before an independent African government showed scant respect for the struggle that the Mau Mau had waged. In his speech at Nakuru in 1961, our "messiah" was already making all sorts of unpleasant noises. In a sustained platitude to the Rift Valley settlers, Kenyatta spoke of forgiveness and of forgetting; of building a multiracial society and of protecting people's property. "People were too optimistic then," says Buke, "and when independence came, we made Judas our prime minister."

For all the lip service to "freedom fighters" and "heroes" by our independence governments, Mau Mau remained a proscribed society for fifty one years, including thirty nine years in independent Kenya until it was legalised in August of this year. As for the men and women themselves, Kenyatta was sorry but "My government is not a government of gangsters," he told them. They had served their purpose. There was no place for them in the new dispensation.

Kenya's post independence land policy of willing buyer, willing seller was frankly insulting to the men and women of the Land and Freedom Army as Mau

Mau had been known, and to all the other Kenyans who had been dispossessed of their land, many of whom would remain landless. The revolution was dead. Long live the revolution.

In 1965, Pio Gama Pinto, the ideologue of the progressive faction within KANU was assassinated. In 1966 led by Tom Mboya, the minister for Economic Planning, the radical element within KANU was removed altogether with the expulsion of Oginga Odinga who, with Bildad Kaggia and others, then formed the KPU. The ultra conservatives took over KANU for good. In a demonstration of what Kenyatta thought of as the meaning of "Uhuru," he would taunt Kaggia with his failure to partake of the "fruits of independence," his lack of financial acquisition. "What have you done for yourself Kaggia?" he asked. "Ngei has acres of coffee plantations, Karumba is running his businesses, but what have you done for yourself?"

KANU began then to build the institutions of the repressive state that Kenya would become.

In one of the earliest pieces of legislation enacted in the East Africa Protectorate (which would later become Kenya), the Commissioner had given himself the powers to detain and restrict the movement of any people whose actions he viewed as a threat to the state. The Kenyatta government soon had recourse to the same draconian laws. At independence, the Emergency (Powers) Orders in Council which had been used by Britain to contain the Mau Mau uprising were repealed. By 1966 however, they had all but been reintroduced under the Preservation of Public Security Act. These powers first came in to use on a large scale in 1969 when the opposition KPU party was disbanded and its leadership detained. Here was a clear signal by the government that opposition of any kind would not be tolerated.

In that same year, the wrangling between the conservatives in KANU came to a head when Tom Mboya was assassinated. Mboya, one of the most right wing members of KANU had been the government's Mr. Fix it. He created the constitutional amendment requiring that MP's who joined the opposition seek re-election and then had made it difficult for Jaramogi Odinga's KPU to contest the 1967 "Little General Election." "Frankly," says Robert, a former Mwakenya member, "I wish they had killed him earlier. Maybe Kenya would have been a different place." The culture of fear had begun.

Through all this upheaval, the university remained the one community where freedom of expression was tolerated, albeit uneasily. Demonstrations and even riots by students had become common place and the campus was closed on a regular basis. In 1969, students came out to protest the murder of Tom Mboya. In 1975, they took to the streets again to voice their anger over yet another political murder, that of J.M Karuiki. In 1979, soon after Moi came to power, they were out in the streets protesting the barring of Jaramogi Oginga Odinga from participating in the elections. In the seventies though, a radically different form of opposition was coming into being.

"We decided that there was need for an organised political party," says Maina wa Kinyatti who was then a lecturer of history at Jomo Kenyatta College. But they had learned from the events of the 60's and 70's that that opposition could not be carried out in the open. As a result, a small group of radical lecturers came together to

form a group of closed cells whose purpose was to study Marxist ideology and to use it to analyse and criticise Kenyan society. This opposition was different for two reasons. First, the utter secrecy with which it was carried out and secondly the fact that it was avowedly Marxist in its bent. While all previous opposition to the government was based around merely reassigning state control to different individuals and fiddling with the machinery so that more resources trickled down to the masses, the lecturers envisioned a radical change in the nature of Kenya itself. They wanted to change the economic system, to free it from the control of and dependency upon Western capital and to give birth to a truly egalitarian society which in their view, could only be a socialist one.

The cells were formed in the mid seventies and operated as a loose association until April 1982 when they came together as the December 12th Movement. Although it called itself a movement, DTM was never one. It was confined to a small, select group of people, all intellectuals, who were strongly committed to their ideals. As Dr. Kinyatti says, "ideology was our oath, and that ideology was socialism" (a reference to the Mau Mau movement which had used traditional Kikuyu oaths to bind its members to the cause). Dr. Willy Mutunga who was a member attests to the difficulty with which membership was earned. Although he had come to the University of Nairobi as a lecturer in 1974 and although his Leftist politics were known, it wasn't until 1978 that the first overtures were made to him. "They spent four years vetting me, gauging my suitability," he says.

The work of these study groups would be published and distributed around the university in pamphlets called "Cheche," The Spark. Njuguna Mutahi who was a student at the University of Nairobi in the early eighties recalls his surprise at the quality and depth of analysis contained in Cheche. "It was one of the most eye-opening documents I ever saw," he says. "I still ask myself where those guys did their research and when they did it, especially given the circumstances then." Those circumstances were becoming increasingly difficult. In June 1975, a professor called Robert Martin was arrested. It later turned out that one of his students had been giving all his notes to the special branch. Mr. Martin was deported.

Then in 1978, Kenyatta died and his deputy, Daniel arap Moi ascended to power. People had high hopes for this outsider, especially when he freed all the political detainees from the Kenyatta era. But the honeymoon was short lived. It became clear that the student had been a diligent pupil. Moi was intent on following the Nyayo (the footsteps) of his predecessor. The gloves were about to come off.

In 1982, a group of well known politicians tried to register an opposition party. This should have been a non-event. Kenya was after all still a multi-party state by law. KASA, the Kenya African Socialist Alliance was the final attempt by the Left to secure a platform in mainstream politics. Two of its founders, George Anyona and John Khaminwa ended up in detention while Oginga Odinga was put under house arrest. A blunt but effective reminder that the new government would not tolerate an opposition. Later on that year, that conclusion was underlined when Kenya became a de jure one party state.

It was in 1982 too that DTM came to an abrupt end, very soon after its establishment. In April of that year, the government moved against the university's academ-

ic and staff union. Six university lecturers, all members of the union were arrested starting in May. They were Maina wa Kinyatti, Willy Mutunga, Mukaru Nganga, Alamin Mazrui, Edward Oyugi and Kamonji Wachira. Mr. Kinyatti and Mr. Mutunga were charged with possessing seditious material while the others were detained. In the process of crushing the union, the government accidentally stumbled onto something much bigger. It discovered the roots of DTM. How or whether the government knew of the lecturers' involvement in DTM when it had arrested them remains unclear. Dr. Mutunga ventures an opinion. "The questions I was asked during my interrogation led me to believe that some of the movement's documents had been discovered during a raid on someone's house." Material that in his opinion should have been hidden away or destroyed. And he lays the blame squarely at one man's feet. "I think that Dr. Kinyatti was writing a history of the movement without our knowledge or consent." It is this "history in the making" which he thinks the government got its hands on.

It is a claim Dr. Kinyatti denies. He also denies that any material relating to the movement could have fallen into the government's possession. He believes that if any of the movement's documents had been found, some of the lecturers would have been charged with membership, adding that "none of us were charged with belonging to DTM."

The effect of these detentions on the progressives in Kenya was far reaching. Many lecturers left the country for exile. Some of the detained lecturers would be incarcerated for years. Maina wa Kinyatti would not be released until 1988. This exodus, as well as the imprisonment of its leaders rattled the movement, creating a vacuum in the leadership and sowing confusion among the ranks. In this interregnum, Mwakenya (The Union of Patriots for the Liberation of Kenya) was born.

Oduor Ongweny a former member of Mwakenya admits that the government purge did have a significant impact, but denies that it was a catastrophic one.

"Any underground organisation," he says, "whether it's a club of masons, or the mafia, once a link in the chain has been broken, it's going to affect the whole chain." But he thinks of the formation of Mwakenya as much a strategic decision as a defensive one.

"When a movement has been busted and the intelligence are looking for it, changing the name is an option. The security will still be following the old lead because for them it's DTM that they know," he says.

What remained of the DTM cells generally went in three different directions. Some cells transformed themselves into Mwakenya, others, having lost their link person went on as before not knowing that part of the organisation was gone, while others still found themselves cut off and died a natural death.

"It is a fairly delicate history," says Ongweny, "and given the underground nature, I don't think anybody has completely understood the transformation of DTM into Mwakenya."

The result of the intimidation and forced censorship on our universities has been far reaching. When institutions of Higher Learning become battlefields, the right to unfettered access to thought and to information becomes a danger to be averted. At all costs.

What had been the department of political science was compelled to change its name to the department of government. No politics of any sort was supposed to be going on there and certainly no political ideas were supposed to be relayed. Thinking critically, indeed thinking at all, was from all evidence a criminal offence. There was little danger of that. The lecturers who had been able to keep their jobs and their freedom were not the type to rock the boat. "I barely went to class," says Buke who was a student at the University of Nairobi in 1985. "Class, my political science class, meant merely taking down notes that the teacher would read word for word. I could have stayed at home and read the text myself." As for anyone who insisted on thinking for themselves, the campus was crawling with informers.

Buke tells of his encounter with a student named Stephen Ocholla. "Stephen was a student's student. He would attend every student function, including the funerals and cry louder than anyone. When I was elected to student government, he carried me shoulder high and cheered." But some people were suspicious of him. Stephen had been a third year student, then a fourth year, but still he showed no sign of graduating. One student followed him one day and found that he never went to class. He would enter the university's Gandhi wing, make his way to the administration building and exit into town. "When they found out, the students wanted to beat him up," Buke says, "but I told them not to. I thought we could make use of him instead." On being confronted and with the very real threat of violence hanging over him, Stephen sang like a canary. He admitted to being a police officer, a sergeant working under an inspector Opiyo who was in charge of student politics and Mwakenya investigations. "We used him to tell us what the police were planning for us," Buke explains. But the students did eventually beat him up. That very day, Buke was arrested and charged with being "a Libyan spy."

"I wish I had seen him first that day," he says wryly. "He could have saved me a lot of trouble." Buke would be in jail for 4 years.

Increasing restrictions meant that permits had to be sought to conduct academic research, Marxism and socialism were no go areas in the classroom. Research into Mau Mau was discouraged. When Maina Kinyatti's home was raided, the security agents confiscated books and documents, including years of research into the Mau Mau. They have never been returned.

*****

Of all the leftist groups operating in post independence Kenya, Mwakenya has more than any other captured the public imagination. But that may have less to do with the movement itself than with the government's reaction to it.

Mwakenya is many things to many people. To some, it is a fiction, the creation of a paranoid government looking for an excuse to crack down on its perceived enemies. To others it is a monster, yet another manifestation of Gikuyu nationalism's unending designs on power; a dangerous throw back to the dark days of those other Gikuyu nationalists, the Mau Mau. To a very few others, it is an understandable reaction to a government that had mastered the art of repression.

But for all its multiple personaes, Mwakenya remains the most enduring manifestation of opposition to the government. And it is memorable for all the wrong reasons. The public were presented with a succession of unkempt, manacled men

being led into court to be charged with sedition and back out into jail. They were not the sort of people to inspire sympathy or emulation, especially in a populace socialised to respect law and order, whatever that order may be. The message coming across very clearly was that dissent was not an aspirational lifestyle.

In all the coverage that it received, all that was said about the movement and its members was that it was a "clandestine" group of "dissidents" who published a "seditious" mouthpiece and that they intended to overthrow the government "by illegal means." In short, they were rebels without a cause.

"Those terrorists!" exclaimed a senior editor at the Nation Newspaper when I ask him his opinion on Mwakenya. Though he proceeded to moderate his views, it is telling that a man who should as a journalist have had a more complete understanding of the group had such a limited opinion of them. Kenyans in the eighties received their information from a single government owned radio and television station. As for print media, the "Kenya Times" was wholly government owned, another newspaper, "The Standard" partially state owned, and the third, "The Nation" by the admission of the same editor has "never been an independent newspaper."

The papers also carried the shrill utterances of various KANU functionaries, attempting to outdo each other in indignant displays of patriotism. Nicholas Biwott, then Energy Minster likened Mwakenya members to witches. Councillors in the Kakamega district of Western Kenya vowed to burn the 'traitors' alive while Mr. Oluoch Kanindo, MP for Homa Bay preferred to bury them alive.

Kamonye Manje, a former member thinks the government overestimated Mwakenya's capabilities. "Mwakenya existed," he affirms, "but it was not established to the degree that warranted a reaction as severe as that." I hear that sentiment repeated by every Mwakenya member I interview; first, a confirmation of Mwakenya's existence followed by the assertion that the government's reaction was disproportionate to the threat it posed.

Of course it's a subtle argument to make. To admit that there exists a group opposed to the government of the day, no matter how despotic, one that publishes and distributes its own newspaper, the latest issue of which has called on its members to take up guerrilla warfare but wants it understood that it really was quite harmless! The revolution after all had a sense of decorum and fair play....

React the government did, and strongly. The Nation and Standard Newspapers of 1986 are replete with arrests of Mwakenya suspects at the rate of one every two or three days from March until December of that year.

Mwakenya suspects were held in the Nyayo House basement torture cells. The length of confinement and the methods of torture varied. The government showed a capacity for innovation and creativity that it lacked in every other respect.

But the crucial question remains - Was Mwakenya a clear and present danger to the government?

Estimates of Mwakenya membership range from 1000 to 2000 people, certainly enough men to cause significant problems to any government with sufficient training, organisation and equipment, all of which Mwakenya lacked. It had no arms worth talking about, (someone mentioned an arsenal of two pistols) and the cadres had little or no military training. The answer would seem to be a resounding no,

though the government acted as if a conflagration was imminent.

There is one story about how the government discovered Mwakenya which I heard repeated by almost everyone I interviewed for this story. It sounds like a "Mills and Boon" spy novel: romance and politics and an improbable plot. This story or legend or myth gives that Mwakenya came to the government's attention through one of its leaders, then a lecturer at the University of Nairobi, or rather through his wife. The lecturer's name is Maina Kiongo. Because some meetings were held at his house, Mrs. Kiongo got wind of the existence of the movement and of its aims. Burdened by this knowledge, she then divulged it in church one Sunday before the entire congregation. The pastor of the church, a pastor Upton, a good Christian himself, convinced her to share this information with the authorities. As a reward for her work, Mrs. Kiongo rose rapidly up the ranks of the civil service. Because Mr. Kiongo was a high ranking member of Mwakenya, the information received from his wife was comprehensive and when it was used against the movement, devastating. Mrs. Kiongo did her Christian duty in March 1986. By the end of the year, the movement was on its knees.

There are two main reasons why the security forces had more success with Mwakenya than with DTM. First of all, unlike with DTM, the progressives at the core of Mwakenya wanted to reach out to the masses. The rationale behind it was that people needed to commit themselves anew to a struggle that was entering a new phase, one that was going to require more sacrifice and perhaps military action as well. But the cultural specificity of oathing was bound to be problematic.

Mau Mau which had successfully used oathing to recruit and bind its members to its cause was operating in vastly different circumstances than Mwakenya was. "Certainly, Mau Mau was a nationalistic organisation," says Dr. Kinyatti, "but it was dominated by peasants, people still very much attached to tribal life and beliefs. Things were different in the 80's. The calibre of people we were recruiting was different. They were workers and bourgeois intellectuals; people who did not believe in oathing."

The oath sowed destruction in two major ways: first, it introduced an element of ethnic chauvinism in an organisation that had previously functioned on ideological consensus. Many Mwakenya cadres who were not Kikuyu as well as many who were objected to it. Secondly, many of the cadres being oathed had not been vetted. People would simply be gathered together, often under false pretences, and made to take the oath. In this way, people who were ignorant of the movement and many who were opposed to it became privy to sensitive information, information which was often shared with the security forces.

Things only got worse with the appearance of the 14th and 15th editions of "Mpatanishi," Mwakenya's mouthpiece which called for guerrilla warfare against the government. "You don't announce to a government you are fighting that you are about to engage in guerrilla warfare," says Maina Kinyatti, "you either do it or you don't." As it happened, it helped justify the government's brutality and alienated much of the public as well.

That call to action resulted in the activities of the so-called "Nakuru Saboteurs" who derailed a goods train near Kariandusi in Nakuru District. Kangethe Mungai, a

member of the cell involved explains. "We had received a generalised green light by the leadership to use guerrilla tactics in order to make the country ungovernable. Ours was the first instance of this new phase of guerrilla warfare." And, as it turns out, the last as well. The expectation that other cells across the country would pick up the gauntlet and that there would be a rash of similar incidents came to nothing. The guerrilla war sputtered and died.

With the government crackdown in full swing, a new exodus began as Mwakenya members and other progressives left the country. The preferred destination was Tanzania which was close enough to Kenya for movement members to feel that they were close to the struggle. But life in exile was difficult. Most exiles lived in Dar es Salaam on meagre refugee allowances with Kenyan state agents dogging their steps, and even in exile, the fallout from the crackdown continued.

Njuguna Mutahi was one of those who fled across the border. He had been jailed for membership of Mwakenya from 1986 until the end of 1987 and had left the country soon after his release.

He found the exile community in crisis. Accusations and recriminations were flying thick and fast over the issue of the oathings: who had ordered them, who had carried them out. People abandoned Mwakenya to form their own groups. As a result, a number of movements were formed. There was Me Katilili, Me Keremo, KAIF (The Kenya Anti Imperialist Front), KRM (The Kenya Revolutionary Movement), KPF (The Kenya Patriotic Front) and FERM (The February 18th Revolutionary Movement), although some of these existed only in name, boasting only a handful of members. Most of his friends being in Me Katilili and KAIF, Njuguna gravitated towards them. In some circles though, joining any of the new groups was the same thing as being anti-Mwakenya.

"People in rival groups didn't talk to each other," says Njuguna. "We would pass each other in the streets and not say a word." He says that no efforts were ever made to deal with the issues that had exposed them to the crackdown in the first place. It didn't help that people were getting inaccurate information about the state of affairs in Kenya. Mwakenya members still in Kenya would assure them that there were still active cells operating there, that there was a lot of positive activity and that it was only a matter of time before they crossed the border back into Kenya to finish what they had begun.

"The others continued to work," Njuguna says, "developing our manifesto, forging links with other liberation movements like the ANC and trying to organise an active, underground political party." Finally they formed a group called Uwake (Umoja wa Wazalendo wa Kukomboa Kenya), a merger of KAIF and Me Katilili which continued to profess Marxism as its ideology.

Meanwhile in Kenya, the arrests of Mwakenya suspects were continuing apace. In court, they were allowed no representation and few lawyers were willing to take up their cases anyway. With judicial complicity, prisoners were tried in the evening, long after the courts were officially closed. Judges would accept guilty pleas from suspects who were in appalling physical condition and had clearly been badly beaten. "You could almost sympathise with the magistrates," says Manje, "they were clearly intimidated as well."

"When we were going to court from Nyayo House, the police had made it clear what they expected from us when we got there and what would happen to us if we didn't comply. Some people had been in Nyayo House for up to three months. When you get to court, you are just looking never to go back there. The fourteen days I spent there were worse than all the years I spent in prison."

Mwakenya related cases are curiously free of political arguments made on behalf of or by members of the movement. The few who tried or even seemed about to do so were returned to Nyayo House immediately or simply detained. Sometimes it was prudent to detain some people straight away rather than take a chance by producing them in an open court where they might say unpleasant things or cause a stir among the public, charismatic leaders like Raila Odinga for instance.

Although the government tried to paint Mwakenya as merely a rabble of disaffected men, the war was clearly ideological. Once in a while the President would allude to the negative effects that foreign ideologies were having in Kenya. In a pointed remark in a 1986 speech at the KANU delegates' conference, he said that there was "no time for idle, irrelevant and theoretical games any more," that intellectuals should avoid the "assimilation of alien and outdated ideologies and theories." As an alternative to the effects of these insidious "foreign ideologies," Kenyans were encouraged to seek recourse in such home grown philosophies as "Nyaoism." Against the impressive apparatus of Marxism, against dialectical materialism and the labour theory of capital, we have "peace, love and unity" and "being mindful of other people's welfare."

The following list of prohibited books carried in the Daily Nation of Thursday April the 17th of 1986 as a public service to the citizenry will illustrate clearly what the crux of the matter was. The list allowed for amendments "from time to time:"

1. All past and future issues of the periodical "Revolution in Africa."
2. All past and future issues of the periodical "Sauti ya Urafiki."
3. All past and future issues of the periodical "Who Rules Kenya?"
4. "The Reds and the Blacks - a Personal Adventure" by William Atwood a former American ambassador to Kenya. This book discussed cold war politics and the West's support of dictatorial governments in Africa as a bulwark against communism.
5. "Cheche Moja Yaweza Kuanzisha Moto Mbugani," by Mao Tse Tung, published by the Foreign Languages Press in Peking. (One spark can start a fire.)
6. "Quotations from Chairman Mao Tse Tung."
7. All past and future publications by the Foreign Languages Press in Peking.
8. Any publication depicting any symbol, emblem, device, colours, slogan , motto, words or letters signifying any association with or support for a political organisation or political object.
9. "The African Communist," by the South African Communist Party.
10. All past and future issues of the periodical "Africa and the World" published by PANAF Publications Ltd. in London.
11. All past and future issues of the periodical "Sauti ya Wananchi" published by the Kenya Socialist Group in London.
12. All past and future issues of the publication "World Revolution" published by the Progressive Labour Union.

13. "The Nationalist" newspaper published and printed in Dar es Salaam.

The article ends with the counsel to hand over any prohibited publications to "the nearest administrative officer or police officer in charge of a police station." (In a more amusing pointer to the battle of ideologies, Kariuki Chotara, a member of parliament in the eighties had ordered that Karl Marx be arrested as a cure for the prevailing radicalism at the university.)

In its rush to remove real or imagined dissidents from polite society, the government was fulfilling its own dire prophecy. There was no better way to radicalise people than to send them to jail. There were hundreds of political prisoners at Kamiti prison. There were the university lecturers detained in 1982, serial detainees like Raila Odinga and George Anyona, air force soldiers and university students imprisoned after the abortive coup and ever more Mwakenya related prisoners. Although he had been something of a radical during his university years, Buke had never joined any organisation until the end of his prison term when he was recruited into Uwake.

Uwake, along with the Koigi wa Wamwere's KPF and Brigadier John Odongo's FERA went further than Mwakenya in training their cadres for military engagement with the government. In this venture, they had plenty of support. Kenyans weren't the only people who had recognised the Kenyan government for the reactionary creature it was. But while Nyerere had merely expressed his contempt for Kenya's "man eat man society," Museveni's Uganda would go a step further and give active support to dissent groups. In the early nineties, no less than three organisations were receiving accommodation and training in Uganda.

Buke recalls that "one man who had been Museveni's bodyguard during the bush war said to me that, 'Only a few of us know about this thing. One or two of us in the army and the police. If Museveni finds out about it, we'll all be sacked.' But it was just to cover themselves in case we were arrested." While KPF and Uwake had fewer than thirty men, FERA's hundreds of recruits would have been difficult for any security system to miss.

"These guys had a thorough knowledge of the Kenyan security system," Buke continues. "Something would happen in Kenya in the morning and by the afternoon, they would know. A friend of mine would be arrested in Kenya and they would tell me about it. They would tell me who informed on him, who arrested him and the details of the arrest itself. There's no way they could tell me that it was just a faction of the NRA involved when they basically had the Kenyan and Ugandan intelligence systems at their disposal."

But there was a less altruistic element at work as well. "I think one of the reasons we got the support and training we did was that the Uganda government was having trouble dealing with its opposition," says Buke, "Obote men, some of whom were living in Kenya." In his view, the Ugandan government expected the Kenyan "guerillas" to pay them back for their hospitality by eliminating these people.

"If they had been serious about training good cadres, they would have paid closer attention to what we were doing," says Buke "and whether or not we were doing a satisfactory job, which was not always true."

Kenyans had an inkling of these goings on. Especially on national holidays, the

president would launch an off the cuff broadside at Uganda or Libya which were apparently "training guerillas to destabilise Kenya." Kenyans grown wary of Moi's sometimes far-fetched accusations were never sure whether it was the truth or just another creation of the intelligence.

Life in the Uwake training camp was tightly regulated. "We would get up in the morning at 6 and go have our daily run and exercise session. Then there would be ten hours of class every day.

This political education included a survey of "Kenya's progressive history; the history of Kenya's struggles for change as well as Marxist theory. "Things in the camps were difficult," he admits. Food rations were small and sometimes ran out all together. Then they had to forage around the camp. Some times the recruits went days without a meal. Drinking and smoking were out. "Some of the boys found things a little tough."

Later on they were joined by some of the Kenyan exiles who had been living in Tanzania and finally around December 1991, they began military training.

After four months of training at Mbarara, the group, numbering in the twenties returned to Mukono to await redeployment to Kenya. This was supposed to be discussed at Uwake's national conference held in Mombasa. The congress was indecisive with the attendees divided about whether or not to move on to military tactics. "I saw it as deflation," Buke says. "People had given up. They felt they had been overtaken by events, by the advent of multi party politics." That aside, armed struggle was retained as a legitimate option and the conference dispersed to await instructions from the command. They never came. The movement simply fizzled out and died without ever being formally dissolved.

*****

With the fall of the Berlin wall and the subsequent collapse of the Communist states of Eastern Europe, the West found that a change of tactics was in order. Where it had previously had reason to use force directly or indirectly by propping up totalitarian regimes against the progressive forces fighting them, it was now easier to use co-option as a weapon. Then the Western European and American governments began to call for "reforms" in the East, for the opening up of democratic spaces, for the introduction of multi party politics.

The repeal in 1991 of section 2A which had made Kenya a single party state and the reintroduction of multi party politics in Kenya dealt a grave blow to the Left, one from which it has not yet recovered. Members of the underground deserted in droves. Finally, opposition to the government had lost some of its risk. One did not have to pay for dissent with ones life or livelihood.

But many of the people who had been in these underground movements were either still in jail or in exile. Although they may not then have been in a position to take advantage of the expanded political freedoms, their failure to do so to this day points to another kind of flaw in organisation and planning on the part of progressive groups.

Many of the people who emerged as crusaders for change during the so-called "second liberation" were not people who had fought for change before. If anything,

many had been stalwart KANU members with a history of opposing change. This time around however, they were able to rally people around agitation for political pluralism to such a degree that the state was forced to take notice. Even then, their main issue was not with the political and social system as such, but that that system had excluded them or not included them as much as they would have liked. They wanted a change in regime; one that would favour them. That became evident later on with the power battles that destroyed FORD."

*****

"This is the history of a failure," so begins "The African Dream," Che Guevara's record of his experiences in the Congo." Che had tried to revolutionise the Congolese and organise them into a force that could remove Moise Tshombe and Mobutu Sese Seko from power in vain. The level of politicisation and ideological belief among the Congolese rebel leaders was low and even lower among the cadres. After a few disastrous skirmishes with Congolese government troops during which Che's recruits would drop their guns and run, he concluded that "Africa has a long way to do before it reaches real revolutionary maturity." If that is indeed true, whose failing is it?

What does it really mean to say that a people are not yet ready for revolution? A revolution implies change to the status quo and the status quo in Kenya, as in any so called developing country is a sorry one indeed: it is poverty of the most life destroying kind, a situation maintained and defended by a small, wealthy and avaricious class. Open any development economics text and Kenya always merits a mention as one of the countries with the largest disparities between rich and poor. The poor know this not as an interesting fact in a text book, but as their daily reality: as the ignorance of daily meals, as the death of children from the most innocuous ailments, from medieval life expectancy rates. It seems unforgivably arrogant to say that these people do not want to see the substance of their lives change for the better, that they are not ready for that change. So what does it mean to say that Africans in general or Kenyans in particular are not ready for revolution?

The middle class that has held Kenya to ransom in government is the same middle class that has led the revolution. For all their stated differences of opinion, they are strikingly similar in their actions. Infighting, wrangling, personality cults and unbridled ambition are as rife among the greedy political class as they are among the Left.

Koigi and his KPF are illustrative of this. "He was given opportunities to train people in Libya in commando tactics," says Buke of Koigi, "but taking advantage of that was a problem. He insisted that people must first join his organisation. We'd say, 'Come on man. We have the same aims, we can find common ground.' Nothing doing. So his style of leadership denied us a lot of opportunities."

And there are other objections directed at Koigi. There is a section of Koigi's book "I Refuse to Die" to which many people who have been in the underground take great exception. Buke is one of them. "He lies! He lies that he was arrested in Uganda, that the government kidnapped him from Uganda and brought him back to Kenya. That's a lie. He was arrested in Kenya, in Nakuru with guns, AK-47's. That's a treasonable charge. The law says you hang for that. He was lucky to get off. When

you lie, you sabotage the future. You derail the future. It's wrong. If you're going to lie, don't put it on paper."

Koigi denies these claims. "I had no dealings with Mathaba international," he says. "No one offered us training in Libya."

The Kenyan Left has always been plagued by ideological divisions which have caused as much damage as organisational failings. "I found that the leftist movement was as puritanical as the church," says Buke, "whereby, if you can't recite your bible by heart, you're not a good Christian and you will not go to heaven. Even in prison, labelling each other was the order of the day: liberal, conservative, anarchist, Stalinist, Maoist."

During break times in prison, prisoners would hold meetings of their respective organisation to which only other members were privy. Only when they were finished would the other prisoners be included in the discussions. "I thought that was ridiculous," Buke says. "We were all in jail, for the same reasons, having had the same aims. If we couldn't work together then, when was it ever going to happen?"

Then there were replications of the very class divisions they objected to in society at large. In groups like UWAKE, the "organisers" would remain in cities like Kampala, Harare or London "making contacts" and canvassing for support, while in the bush an underequipped, underfed pointman would be saddled with the task of trying to convince a group of homesick and terrified boys to stay.

There was also a curious unwillingness on the part of senior members to get their hands dirty. "One of our commanders was sent to Europe to get some of our members to attend the senior cadre training," Buke explains. What he got instead were excuses: 'give me two months,' or 'let me finish my degree first.' "All sorts of stories. They didn't have the commitment to get involved at a critical stage."

In 1992, Uwake held a national conference which served to underline the lack of commitment by the leadership. Some founding leaders failed to arrive. It seemed as if their pet project had ceased to be interesting and their attention had wandered to other things. Others decamped to join party politics without so much as a by your leave. Soon after, the movement died in everything but name, leaving a score of its young recruits with out direction and without alternatives.

But nowhere is the failure of leadership more stark than it was in FERA. FERA had hundreds of men under arms at a camp on the Ugandan side of the border with Kenya. In three years at that camp, one recruit Paul (not real name) says that the leader, Brigadier John Odongo visited only twice. When they asked where he was, they would be told that he was in Kampala or out of the country trying to get arms and money.

Planning was haphazard. When the trainers felt that the recruits had learned enough, they would send them off on sorties into Kenyan territory to engage the security forces for practice. And there was no mention of returning to Kenya to engage the government. "We trained every day for three years. In that time, no one ever talked about going back to fight," says Paul. Many men, tired of waiting simply left, preferring to take their chances in Kenya than wait endlessly for a war that showed no signs of happening.

The Left in Kenya has been manifestly unable to take advantage of the changes

in the political scene in the last ten years. There still isn't a socialist or a communist party in Kenya. While the populist nature of party politics Kenya is problematic, it remains a legitimate vehicle through which to disseminate progressive ideas and mobilise people. No publication exists which espouses leftist ideas. It seems as if progressives, used to being marginalised have internalised their lack of agency, given up on the possibility of being relevant and are paralysed by it.

If leftist groups really do believe in their vision of what society should be, believe that the Kenyan people deserve better than they have had, then they should at least get the basics right. They need to do their homework. They should not betray their noble goals and ideas by shoddy planning and gung-ho overenthusiasm. They should have at least as much foresight, discipline and planning as the conservative forces arrayed against them. The state is well entrenched, powerful and wide reaching. It will not be removed by a small group of well intentioned bunglers. It is these failings that have let left groups down time and again and consequently let down the people for whom they claim to care and to be working for.

All evidence though points to the fact that the sinking ship has been abandoned. The cadres have fled into the NGO sector and are now, in conjunction with our "development partners," peddling policy dialogues with a vengeance. Human rights and good governance and expanding the democratic space and poverty reduction. Poverty has been removed from its social and historical contexts. They seem not to care that some of these development partners are part of the problem. That there is a new authoritarianism couched in neo-liberal sloganeering. An authoritarianism all the more dangerous because it has no competitors. It has no nay sayers. Its word is law.

How is this possible? How do self confessed Marxists so easily mouth the rhetoric of the enemy they set out to fight all those years ago? How do you abandon the struggle because there's a human rights conference in Geneva Monday week? What kind of Leftists are these? Probably the kind who would never have been Marxists if there had been an alternative, a middle ground between KANU and Marx.

As it is, these people have turned revolution into an employable skill, a fund raising tool. What's even better is, they are above reproach. Detention has sanctified them. Suffering has canonised them, has made them into living martyrs. You can never be quite as hard on them as you would like, because when the accusing finger is turned in your direction, you know you'll come up wanting.

But then they have a lot to answer for. They came on the scene at a time when Kenya was ripe for revolution. Crying out for change. And they screwed it up.

So what is the alternative? Where is the Left today?

Asked if Mwakenya exists today, Maina Kinyatti answers in the affirmative. According to him, Mwakenya has never died. "Right now, we're looking at different ways in which to organise ourselves for the future."

All of which is news to some former members. According to them, Mwakenya ceased to exist as a cohesive unit years ago. "The people who were in Mwakenya have organised themselves into other entities," says Kamonye Manje. "RPP for example reflects that spirit. Civil society is also a reflection of the spirit of Mwakenya, though in a very moderate form."

Some people think that Mr. Kinyatti has overstepped his limits by unilaterally declaring the existence of Mwakenya.

"I don't know who gave him the permission to speak for us," says a former member. "He needs to ask us before he goes out and makes statements like that."

"Consultations for what?" Mr. Kinyatti retorts? "I stand by what I said. Mwakenya still exists and we're looking at the best direction to take from here."

So much for Mwakenya.

For the first time in years, for the first time since the sixties, the left has a significant presence in the government. We shall see what they do with it.

*****

Kangethe Mugai is famous for his willingness to talk, famous to the point of infamy. Maina Kinyatti looks disapproving when I mention his name. "He talks too much," he says. "He's always talking, and yet he knows so little."

Which is a different objection than some of the others I've heard. Edward Oyugi thinks that some of the more sensitive information should remain classified. "It's not as if the battle has been won," he says.

Kangethe dismisses those who would accuse him of indiscretion, of compromising his former comrades. "That's bullshit," he tells me. "Bullshit. What are they worried about? We have defanged the serpent. It's toothless. It cannot hurt us any more."

It is a seductive thought, this idea that the danger is past and that better days, good days even, are ahead of us. But it is just this complacence, this pervasive idea of danger past that we must be wary of. "This is a dangerous time," Buke says. "Never before in the history of this country has there been such a lack of opposition to the government. Never have progressive forces been so off guard and comfortable, and that is very dangerous. We cannot rely on the government to do its duty of its own volition. We must compel it to do so. Any government left to its own devices goes bad." And to some, the signs of the government "going bad" are already clear.

There is chaos at the constitutional review, ministers issue edicts in strikingly KANUesque fashion, a political murder, an absent and "often befuddled" president and wrangling worthy of any. How well the new is taking after the old. I have heard people speak of Moi with something much like nostalgia and on Kenyatta day, he received warm applause from the crowd, many of the same people who not a year ago had roundly booed him and thrown various missiles at the dais. Now there is the return of conspicuous consumption and unabashed Gikuyu nationalism. The lack of ideology and ideas if clear. Already.

Any state, however well meaning will not find the impetus for change within itself. It is imperative that we as members of this society provide that impetus, lest we find ourselves once more searching for a few hundred guns and a few good men.

AboutThe Author

Andia Kisia is still not fond of giving out her bio. She likes to enter and win BBC radio plays using pseudonyms. Her last incarnation, almost a year ago, was as an Igbo male person with a promising theatre career. We doni¯t know where she is and who she is currently.

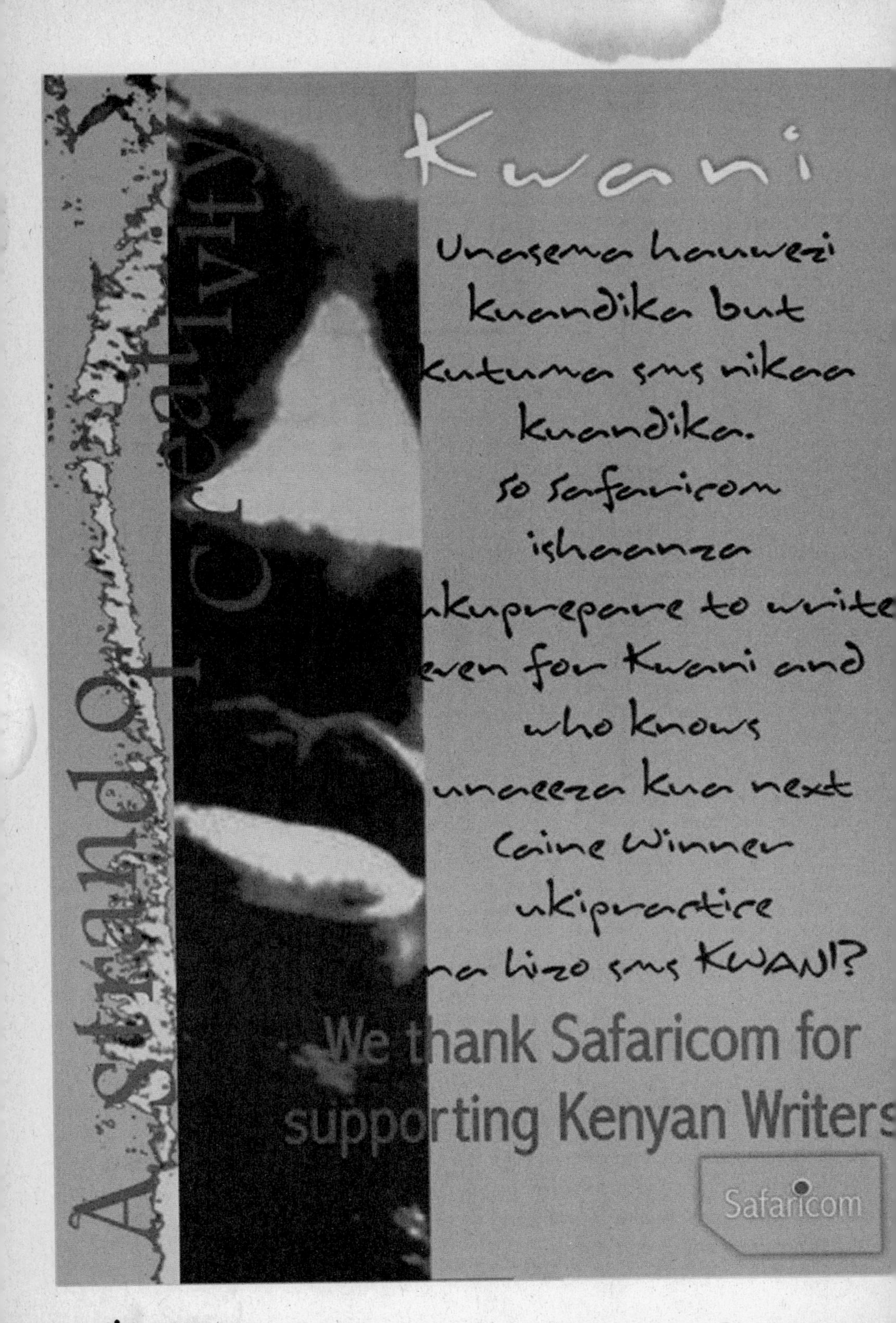
A Strand Of Creativity
Kwani
Unasema hauwezi
kuandika but
kutuma sms nikaa
kuandika.
so Safaricom
ishaanza
kuprepare to write
even for Kwani and
who knows
unaeeza kua next
Caine Winner
ukipractice
na hizo sms KWANI?
We thank Safaricom for
supporting Kenyan Writers
Safaricom

TOON SECTION

That car will be the death of us...
SYLVIESTER!!! DO YOU KNOW WHAT A SPIT SHINE IS?
YES MADAM!
LET'S GO MY LOVE!
Manze Masa ametuvalisha PAJAMAS kama Mafala
IF I AM GOING TO LOOK LIKE AN IDIOT, YOU ARE TOO!
YO! WOZ UP?
TUNAWAKILISHA
BABI DJ

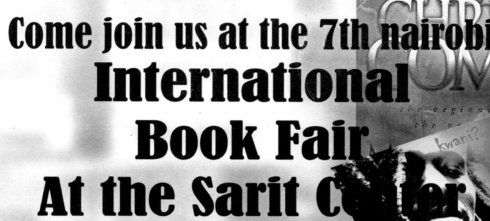

RENT CONTROL WAPI?? YOU PEOPLE HAVE TO LEARN THE VALUES OF HARDWORK!
Wah?

I am calling about that Assassin you wanted...
ASSASSIN?!? I was thinking more of maiming than murder! Couldn't you just break his legs or something!
Yeah!!! Vunja yeye!

Some things never change... Whenever my Master is around, his offspring goes quiet with her visitor in her located territory!

Dad is on his way out with the car! You can get out of the closet!
Manze Budako angetushika RED kungeTHOKA!
BABI DJ

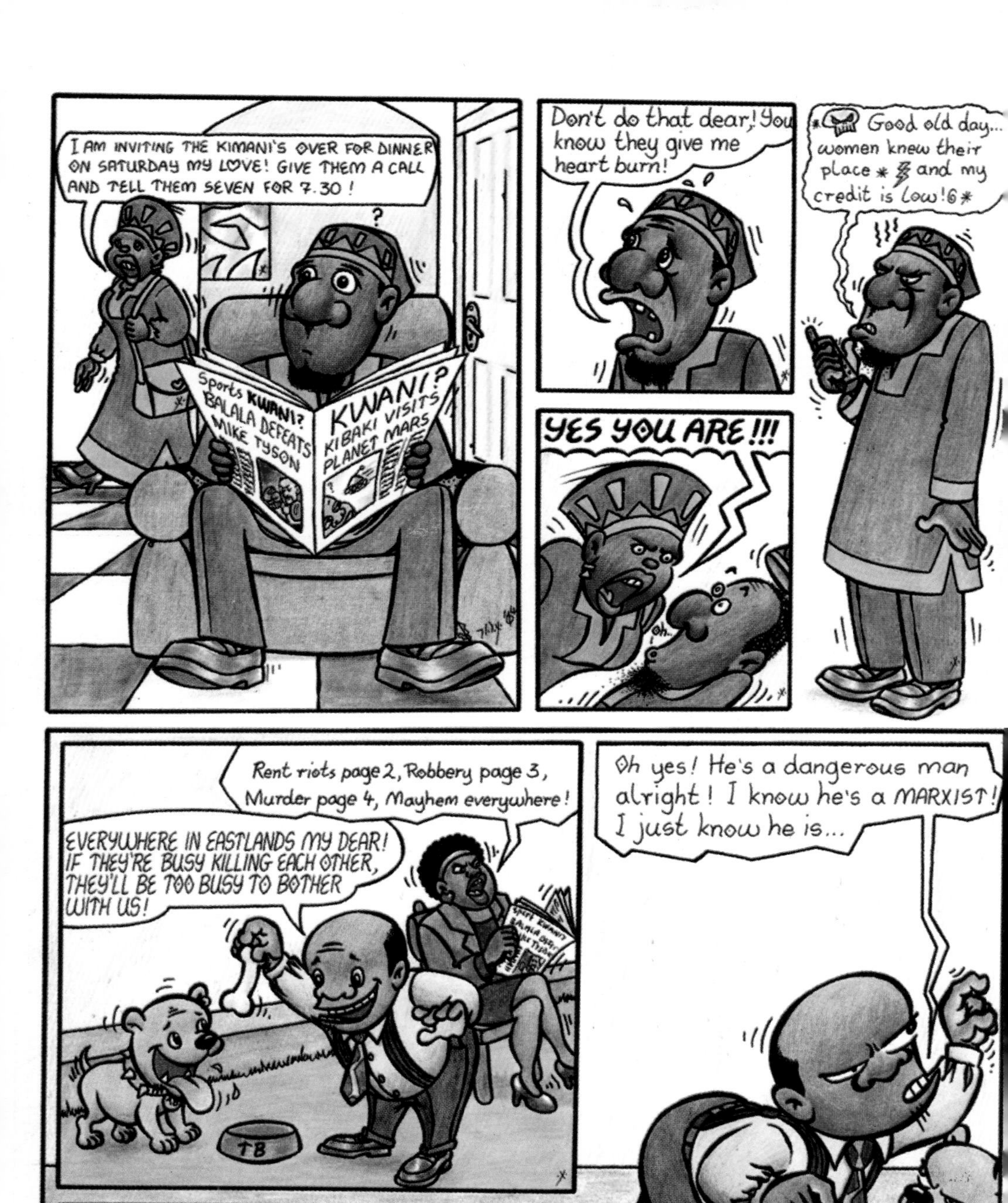
I AM INVITING THE KIMANI'S OVER FOR DINNER ON SATURDAY MY LOVE! GIVE THEM A CALL AND TELL THEM SEVEN FOR 7.30 !
?
Sports KWANI? BALALA DEFEATS MIKE TYSON
KWANI? KIBAKI VISITS PLANET MARS
Don't do that dear! You know they give me heart burn!
YES YOU ARE!!!
Oh.
Good old day... women knew their place and my credit is low!
Rent riots page 2, Robbery page 3, Murder page 4, Mayhem everywhere!
EVERYWHERE IN EASTLANDS MY DEAR! IF THEY'RE BUSY KILLING EACH OTHER, THEY'LL BE TOO BUSY TO BOTHER WITH US!
TB
Oh yes! He's a dangerous man alright! I know he's a MARXIST! I just know he is...
...And demagogues like your friend "Ogwang" EGG THEM ON and call it JUSTICE !!!
Sports KWANI BALALA
Communist!

Let's invite them over for dinner! See what he's up to! You can pick up a few things at the Super Market!
!
List
Sports

WHAT'S THIS?!?*© THE NATIONAL DEFENCE BUDGET??? AM I FEEDING A VILLAGE OR A PERFECTLY PLANNED NUCLEAR FAMILY OF 3?!?
Economic Tribulations in Marriage!

REMIND ME TO PICK UP SOME ANTACIDS ON THE WAY OUT!
Oh Great!
Heh heh heh
NALETA ACTION

HALLO NEIGHBOUR? MY?!? WHAT ARE THOSE WEEDS?

ARE YOU LOST ?!? THE POTATOES ARE IN AISLE 12!
I NEVER THOUGHT I WOULD SEE YOU HERE !! DID YOUR NEIGHBOURHOOD KIOSK GET PULLED DOWN?!?
Niaje ?
Poa...
REHEMA Cookies

YOU'D LIKE THAT, WOULDN'T YOU ?
Did they rope you in too?
Eee MANZE...
Let's get out of here!
IDEA poa jo... Tuishie!

A LUTA CONTINUA

Kenya@
40
The real story
ARCHIVES
ILLUSTRATION'S
BY VICNDULA
2004

Once upon a time, Kenya was white man's . . .
Looks just like Sussex doesn't it? Except for the watus.
We'll just move them then. they prefer malarial swamps anyway. it's their natural habitat.
When that unfortunate episode was over, the country was returned to its rightful owners.
Oh, I say! jolly good what?
IT'S A PERFECT FIT!

A few lives are
rounded off to
balance the
national equation

KENYA - (PINTO + NGALA + MBOYA) = PHEW

But certain neighbours,
jealous . . .

CHUNGA
EMERGENCY
ZONE

What do you
mean you want
to leave?

. . . of our
"stability and progress"
want a piece of the cake.
KENYA
AMIN
That little bit up to
Naivasha belongs to us.
You can keep the rest. On
second thought . . .
Non alignment is
abandoned in favour of
alignment with the wrong
side. Any wrong side.
NoFoLk
Hotel

Kenyatta dies...
Gikuyu Nationalism for Beginners
Don't Cry For me Jaramogi
Facing Mt. Kenya
HOW TO FATHER A NATION
But we remain true to the path
Fuata nyayo bwana!
NOWHERE IN PARTICULAR

A few bad eggs smell up the place
Bang
Bang
Power
But "peace love and unity are soon restored and Kenya finds room for her radicals, free thinkers and other malcontents.
EAST IS EAST AND WEST IS WEST AND NEVER THE TWAIN SHALL MEET.
I was just reading the prologue to Kapital and the next thing I knew....

NATIONMEDIA.COM

The chorus of approval is deafening
WONDERFUL! CHANCELLOR! THE PRINCE OF PEACE!
Et tu George?
But then, there's plenty to celebrate. Like basic human kindness.....
BVS STOP
Shika fare. And carry at least 5,000 shillings next time.

...and local enterprise.
Njoroge, ven ve go to Narok?
The West turns its back on capital's footsoldiers...
George old boy! what's all this about some silly wall? I kept the Reds away from the Blacks!

A second liberation is proposed and roundly rejected
KAMUKUNJI GROUNDS
Ever hear the one about the Mugumo tree and the razor?
But there's no stopping an idea whose time has come....
...and ceasar crossed the Rubicon...i mean, the Chania....
KIAMBU
NYERI
Nyanza and Western

THE END

In memory of

Milka Wanjiku

“ Kamuthungu “

www.kwani.org